Jodi Lynn Copeland
Anya Bast
Lauren Dane
Kit Tunstall

Spice

Spice

WHAT HAPPENS IN VEGAS...

ISBN-13: 978-0-373-60524-8
ISBN-10:   0-373-60524-2

www.Spice-Books.com

Printed in U.S.A.

CONTENTS

HOT FOR YOU
Jodi Lynn Copeland

ACKNOWLEDGMENTS

My thanks to:

P. G. Forte and Katie Bryan, who encouraged my muse on her first-person flight of fancy; Val Dorr, Denise Pattison, Jenn Wilkins, Devyn Quinn and, again, to P. G. Forte— dear friends who are always there and always care; and my family, without whom life would be tragically mundane.

Chapter One

Carinna

As much time as I spend at The Liege, between working in the casino's Taboo Tequila Bar as a cocktail waitress and visiting the progressive bingo room on Sundays with my grandmother, I'd never had the desire to play cards there until tonight. I can only guess that what propelled me through the door of the twenty-four-hour poker room and to the last available seat at a table filled with men and reeking of testosterone and cigar smoke was Hank's deception.

The bastard had lied.

We'd agreed the first time we hooked up that we were in it for two things: sex and more sex.

So what the hell was he doing proposing?

I liked Hank, but—Christ—proposing?

If he'd gotten to know me at all the past three months, he'd know I didn't do relationships, documented ones or otherwise. He clearly didn't know me. Not beyond the way I liked my martinis and men—both dirty as a girl could get 'em. Not beyond the fact that, unlike many women, I didn't have a problem sucking a cock bone-dry. In fact, I loved it.

The taste of hot, salty fluid sliding down my throat. The feel of a man's stiff shaft thrusting between my lips. The knowledge he was under my complete and total control. There was no better feeling in the world.

Or so I was telling myself when I eased my chair up to the poker table with a little hip-scoot shuffle, and discovered Jack Dempsey sitting three chairs away.

From the thick, wavy black hair that matched his mustache, to the graceful slide of his long fingers across the table's green felt as he pushed a stack of nickel chips into a fast growing pot, to the rasp in his voice as he confirmed the bet, Jack was de-fucking-licious. That I could say the same about the body beneath his clothes, and that being laid by him beat any mouth job I'd ever given, amounted to the biggest mistake of my life.

Four months ago, following the death of my father and one martini too many, I'd given in to the lust I'd felt for Jack since puberty and jumped his bones. He'd put up a marginal fight, saying it would ruin our friendship, and then jumped mine right back.

The way nearly every guy at the table stopped what he was doing to check me out said I could end tonight on a bone-jumping note, as well.

I'd changed out of the tit-popping top and barely crotch-covering miniskirt the tequila bar called a uniform, but— along with my Latina appearance—I'd inherited the body of a centerfold from my mother, and my snug black jeans and midriff-baring white tank top weren't hiding that fact. Having 34 Cs, a trim waistline and thirty-three-inch-long legs was a blessing when it came to pulling in tips at the bar. It was a bitch the rest of the time.

I couldn't make the trek from my apartment five blocks from the Vegas strip to The Liege without hearing speculation I was either a showgirl or a hooker. I gave total props to those who worked in either profession, but I didn't and I got sick to hell of the assumptions—and the lewd looks that were often accompanied by propositions of the open-legged variety.

The balding guy next to me—who was obviously going through a midlife crisis, from his orange rapper-style jacket and enough bling around his neck and on his fingers to get him taken out in the seedier sections of Vegas—pulled his gaze from the football game playing on the jumbo flat-screen television on the wall behind the dealer to send me one of those lewd looks. Since I wasn't about to make a scene in my place of employment by telling him I'd rather screw the seventy-year-old dealer than do his slimy ass, I feigned an oblivious smile, slid my bills to the dealer to cash in for chips and glanced down the table.

Jack's gaze met mine and I swear his blue-green eyes flashed a look as predatory as the one he'd given me four months ago, when he'd been buried cock-deep and screwing me to nirvana. Then again, since Jack and I had barely talked since that night, it was probably the cigar smoke messing with my head. That didn't stop moisture from gathering in my panties and my heartbeat from kicking up.

Hank had never been able to stir either reaction with a mere look. For all our deal had been based on sex alone, Hank had hardly known the right places to touch to make me climax. Chalk it up to over two decades of friendship and, up until four months ago, frankness on our sex lives, but Jack knew all the right spots. Knew I liked my loving fast and hard, then slow and easy. Knew I was greedy enough to expect to climax twice before my lover came. The lone night we'd been together, he'd doubled that rate by delivering four of the most stunning orgasms of my life.

Jack nodded at me. "Carinna."

Stacking my chips on the table in front of me, I shivered with the deep timbre of his voice. So cool. So classy. That was Jack. Till he got his hands on your body and then he was hotter than a four-alarm fire. Fitting, since he put out fires for a living.

Was there anything sexier than a man in a uniform? Given, a man out of a uniform, but other than that? Hank for damned sure wasn't as sexy as Jack, and he had a history of modeling. Mostly sock commercials, but even Jack's feet were hotter than Hank's.

For Jack, I might just walk down the aisle.

I bit my tongue over the thought as I slid the big blind chip into the center of the table. If I walked down the aisle with any man, it would be under the influence of something narcotic and illegal.

Ignoring the thunder of my hormones and the hungry pulsing of my pussy, I smiled. "Jack. Good to see you."

I might have imagined the predatory look, but there was no mistaking the surprise that flickered in his eyes. I'd been convinced he blamed me for propositioning him with sex that, just as he'd forewarned, had led to the decline of our friendship. Maybe I'd been wrong. Maybe he still thought I was pissed at him. So he'd ditched my bed in the middle of the night without so much as a goodbye note. I knew he had a job to do and he did it with pride. He'd waited three days to call and explain it was indeed a fire that had pulled him away, but so what? I'd never wanted anything more from him that night than a comforting shoulder and a good, long fuck. I'd gotten both.

Now, all I wanted was our friendship back.

After checking my hold cards, a deuce of spades and a seven of hearts, I folded with a silent snicker. I *did* want our friendship back, but with the addition of fringe benefits of the sexual kind.

Hank was history. Looking at Jack, registering the heart-slamming, panty-wetting way he got to me, I knew no other man would do for my next lover. Before this night was over, I was going to erase the biggest mistake of my life, by regaining my friendship with Jack and, in the meantime, getting laid by a guy who understood no-strings sex as completely as I did.

A half-dozen more junk hands came my way and I was seriously considering quitting the table, despite the mouth-watering view three seats away, when I checked my hold cards to discover pocket queens. I'd never had the desire to play cards at The Liege until tonight, but I'd played a shitload of poker in my time. Back before I'd gotten sloshed on martinis and given in to my Jack craving, I used to play Texas Hold 'Em with him and his younger brother, Ryan, every Wednesday night. Jack took almost as much pride in his poker skills as he did in his firefighting ones.

Not about to scare off the competition, I made a small bet, which half the table called, and I waited for the flop. The eight and nine of spades and the queen of hearts. Three lucky ladies in my favor.

Anticipation kindled as an idea formed. I put in a

moderate bet this time; the two players between me and Jack called it. Jack hesitated a few seconds, then raised my bet. Thankful he had a hand, or at least the urge to bullshit me, I eagerly called him, the balding slimeball to my left and the forty-something family man next to Jack following my lead. The turn showed a fourth queen for my hand, spades this time, and my pussy gushed with liquid excitement.

Only four hands could beat me and the odds of anyone having them were slim. I was going to have Jack back, as a friend and a lover.

Struggling to hold in my grin, I pushed my chips into the growing pot. "All in."

Slimeball and the guy next to Jack folded. Jack tapped a finger against his hold cards. My belly tightened. If he folded now, I was screwed. But no, I wasn't. In order to be screwed, he had to call me one last time, then agree to a side bet of the high-stakes sexual kind.

Five seconds passed. Ten seconds. Fifteen.

His voice deeper than ever, Jack uttered, "I'll call you."

My heart slammed against my ribs as he pushed in all but two ten-high stacks of red chips, matching my bet. Before I could speak the next words, the ones that would land him in my bed, he said them: "Interested in a side bet?"

The sudden, raw heat in his eyes said he wasn't talking about chips. He was on the same page as I was. I practically quivered with excitement. Outwardly, I didn't dare allow such an obvious tell. Inwardly, my pussy thrummed with anticipation for the long night of loving ahead.

Giving him a dirty-girl smile, I challenged him. "Name the stakes."

Jack

I couldn't believe my luck. First a nut flush draw that had become a straight flush on the turn, then Carinna's agreeing to my every fantasy. True, she hadn't agreed yet, but she would. With the cards showing on the table, she couldn't beat me, and that meant I was as good as fucked in all the best ways.

I'd been convinced she hated me after the way I'd walked out on her four months ago. The lame excuse I'd given about responding to a fire had obviously been enough to pacify her. But it had been an excuse. The only fire I'd gone up against that night had been the one burning in my gut with the realization I'd fallen hard for Carinna. I'd always known I loved her, but until that night I hadn't realized how far beyond friendship it went.

I'd lost my father to fast-burning flames and had seen too many others lose their loved ones the same way to consider a relationship while working full-time as a firefighter, so I'd bolted from her bed. And paid the price of knowing she'd been screwing some other guy for the past few months. A guy that my brother, Ryan, had informed me Carinna had kicked to the curbside just this morning.

I couldn't have asked for better timing.

A lucky run of cards had recently allowed me to turn my poker hobby into something more serious. Tonight I was playing for fun. Every day for the past week and a half, I'd gone up against some of the biggest names in the game. With four days left to go in the tournament, I was third in the chips lead. If I could hang on to a top-five position, I'd finish high enough in the money to turn my career focus onto starting up the classic car restoration garage I'd dreamed of for years and my personal focus on making Carinna mine permanently.

My cock had been hard since Carinna had joined the table and sent me her sultry smile. It gave an anxious twitch now, over the thought of having her again. And again and again. All that stood in the way of losing myself in her lush body tonight was a futile river card; all that stood in the way of making her mine in the long run was her cast-iron commitment issue.

Pulling my mind above my belt, I concentrated on the unfolding hand.

The aging dealer was looking at us like we were a couple of half-wits. He spoke slowly. "You can't make a side bet when you're the only two playing, or with a player who has all of their chips in play."

I glanced back at Carinna and gave her a quick perusal of her ample cleavage, hugged to testosterone-tormenting perfection in a navel-baring tank top. Lifting my attention to her face, I found she still held on to the remnants of the X-rated smile she'd flashed me moments ago. Out of respect for her job with The Liege, I relied on a naughty smile of my own to convey that we'd work out the finer points of the side bet later.

I nodded at the dealer. "Sorry. I was joking about the side bet."

The old guy continued as if I hadn't spoken. "Now, you both need to turn your cards over."

I almost snorted over the way he was babying us, probably two of the most skilled players in the room. Instead, I looked back down the table at Carinna. Her grin covered the lower half of her face, her full, sensual lips tinted with pink. She slipped her tongue out, moistening the soft flesh and my cock throbbed with the memory of my own tongue lapping at another area of her body that was just as soft and moist and pink.

The thought of her warm pussy sucking at my tongue had me returning to that fateful night four months ago. I wished it hadn't taken her father's passing to bring us together and show me our intertwined destiny, but, hell, her old man owed her for the way he'd messed with her head about relationships being the devil's handiwork, so maybe in a twisted way his death bringing us together was a latent form of justice.

With Carinna's husky laughter, I returned to the present to see she'd uncovered pocket queens. She flashed a cocky grin. "Sorry, Jack. But you can't win 'em all."

I let out a low whistle, almost feeling sorry for her. Almost. I couldn't feel too bad for a woman I planned to spend the night providing with ecstasy. "Four ladies. Nice. But you're right. You can't win them all." I turned my hold cards over, revealing the ten and jack of spades. "But you put up an admirable fight."

Her cocky grin faded to an appreciative smile, as the dealer turned the river card: the seven of diamonds. "Still got the touch, Dempsey."

While the rest of the players at the table congratulated me and shared their sympathies with her, I shot Carinna a wicked grin that said she would find out before the night was through just how good my touch still was. My hunger for her reflected in my voice as I said, "What can I say? Some things never die."

"They just get better with time." The sap who was sitting

next to her, weighted down by ten pounds of gold jewelry, intruded on our conversation.

Carinna gave the guy another of the fake-as-hell smiles I'd seen her aim his way earlier. Raking in my chips, I didn't bother with a smile but gave him a look of displeasure.

I played three more hands of cards, so as not to piss off the rest of the players by winning and running, then changed in my small chips for a short rack of fifties and hundreds. Carinna had stayed to watch the last few hands. I took that as a good sign. Grabbing the chip rack, I stood from my seat and moved behind hers.

Past the stench of cigar smoke, her scent hit me, a vanilla musk undercoated with something sweet and sexual that had my already stiff-as-stone cock ready to burst from behind the zipper of my jeans. "I'm taking off. Want to join me for a drink in the bar?"

"And spend time in my favorite place on my day off?" She pushed back her chair and stood. At five foot nine, she was a handful of inches shorter than me and right now her lips were so close it took almost more willpower than I had to resist their lure.

I lifted my gaze to her eyes to find their typically gray shade turned to smoke—a sure sign she was hot for me. Blowing out a breath, she pushed a tangle of wayward brown curls over her shoulder. She hated how thick and uncontrollable her hair was. I loved it, and my fingers itched with the need to get wrapped up in it. All it would take was a yes…

Finally, she said, "What the hell. I could use a drink after having my ladies dusted."

Resisting the urge to punch my fist into the air, I made

my way out of the poker room, cashed in my chips and followed Carinna as she headed toward the tequila bar.

Damn, the woman had an erotic sway to her hips. Each bounce of her curvy ass beneath her tight black jeans had my cock jumping against my zipper, ready to push between her supple butt cheeks and explode.

Unlike Carinna, I hadn't indulged in sex since we'd been together. If I was going to be the orgasm guru she remembered, I had to get my mind on something other than fucking her in the ass. "I was surprised to see you in the card room."

Without breaking stride, she lifted a slim, naturally golden-tan shoulder. "I've played poker on Wednesday nights since I was twelve. I wasn't going to stop just because we were too wrapped up in life to find time to play together."

"You've been coming here since I left…" I droned off with an inward groan. She'd boxed up the past four months of virtually no talk into a neat little "no time to play" package and I'd been about to unwrap that package to reveal a mess of shit.

Carinna stopped walking to turn back. Her astute look said she knew what I'd been going to say. The way her hip jutted out said she wasn't as fine with my leaving and not calling for three days as she'd led me to believe. "I've been playing with the girls. Tonight I wanted fresh competition."

"And instead you got me," I teased, hoping to lighten the conversation.

Her gaze lost the shrewd edge. The heat I'd witnessed in her eyes at the poker table returned as she swiveled back and started walking. She might not be as fine with my departure as she'd let on, but she was glad I'd been in that card room tonight. Damned glad she was going to get me time and again before the night was through.

I resumed walking as a fresh wave of sexual adrenaline cruised through my bloodstream. Ten steps before she would have opened the frosted glass doors of the tequila bar to release the steamy beat of Latin music, I quickened my pace and walked past both her and the bar's entrance. Almost instantly, her fingers curled around my upper arm, sending shards of heat dancing up to my shoulder. She tugged and, ignoring the curious looks of the passersby, I let her pull me around.

Her lips pushed into a sexy little mew. "I thought we agreed to a drink?"

Carinna never pouted. That she was doing so now, coupled with her potential ongoing anger over my actions four months ago, gave me hope it was more than sex she wanted from me. Of course, sex was the starting point. That being the case, I gave her a smug smile and went for it. "We can have a drink. Or you can get started on paying off that side bet the way I know your juicy-wet pussy is aching for you to do."

A hot puff of air shot from between her lips. Her eyes narrowed. For a second, I thought I'd read her wrong, that she didn't want me. Then she grabbed my other arm and pushed me hard up against the wall, her breasts rubbing my chest while her thigh moved between my legs to press none too gently against the swollen bulge of my cock.

"I have four words for you, you arrogant bastard." A feline smile of elation took over her mouth. "Your bed or mine?"

♣ ♠ ♥ ♦ ♣ ♠ ♥ ♦ ♣ ♠ ♥ ♦

Chapter Two

Carinna

Your bed or mine?

I couldn't believe I'd asked Jack that question. My pussy was dripping so badly with the need to feel him inside me I'd never be able to make it to my apartment. The rental house he shared with his brother, when one or both of them wasn't on the clock and sleeping at the firehouse, was even farther away.

"Something the matter with the family bathroom down the hall?"

Hearing the desperation in his voice, I laughed. "I don't trust the locks, and I'd never forgive you if some kid walked in and caught us." I darted a glance around. We were already getting enough looks—both disapproving and lustful (only in Vegas would a stranger hope for a sex show in the hallway)—standing the way we were. Getting it on anywhere nearby was out of the question. That didn't rule out upstairs.

Sweet relief jetted through me, coming to rest as liquid warmth between my tingling thighs. As much as I wanted to kiss him, I remembered how thoroughly and incredibly he wrecked me with that masterful tongue and I knew it would only tempt me to take more here and now. "Give me two minutes."

Having connections with the front desk crew had its advantages. I was back in one-and-a-half minutes with two key cards for a suite on the seventeenth floor. Even with my employee discount, the suite was pricey, but tonight was about indulging, while getting back my friendship with Jack. I'd gladly dip into my "Dream B and B" piggy bank for that.

"Race you to the elevators," I teased.

For the twenty seconds it took us to get to them, we were the bosom buddies of our youth, totally oblivious to raging hormones and the pleasure to be found in horizontal mambos. Then we reached the elevators and one of the cars pinged open. An older couple dressed to the nines in head-to-toe black stepped out, leaving the car empty. Jack yanked me inside, jabbing the "close door" button, followed by the "17" button.

He was on me the instant the doors slid shut. His mouth slammed over mine, his tongue pushing past my lips, devouring me with hungry little suckles I felt all the way to my throbbing core. His hands went to my waist, popping the button on my jeans and jerking the zipper down. I feverishly met each lap of his tongue, whimpering into the moist cavern of his mouth as the cool air of the overhead AC hit my hot, wet folds.

One big, rough finger parted my pubic curls to pet my slit from clit to perineum.

One stroke.

Two strokes.

My pulse spiked as warmth coiled low in my belly and chased its way up my torso. My pussy flooded with cream.

Three strokes.

Four strokes.

His tongue left mine to start a wicked dart and thrust game, and my toes curled expectantly in my heeled sandals. His finger pushed past my slit, lightly entering my sheath. The change in action pulled me from the hedonistic haze I'd sunken under the moment his lips touched mine, forcing me to acknowledge we were in a Liege elevator. And I was naked from midway up my thigh to nearly my belly button.

Wondering when Jack had inched my jeans and panties down, I lifted my lips from the sinner's heaven of his mouth and managed in a throaty voice, "Jack! I work here."

"Want me to stop?"

His finger sank into my creamy pussy, finding and fondling just the right spot—a spot whose existence Hank had been oblivious to—and I screeched out my bliss. "Fuck, no!"

His mouth returned to mine, consuming me with his lips and tongue and teeth as if going four months without me had left him starved. Another finger joined the first, thrusting into my sheath with hard, sure strokes meant to deliver me to happy land good and fast. Just the way he'd known I needed it the first time.

My mind spun as liquid fire licked through my body, pulsing a river of wet need deep in my pussy. My sex contracted around his skilled fingers. My hips bucked wildly, without any set rhythm. Tension barreled the length of my spine, shaking my legs. Orgasm was about to take me over.

He pulled his fingers out before it could.

"Jesus, Jack!" I wanted to slug him.

He laughed loudly, his eyes shining with arousal and amusement, then cut the sound off sharp to turn me around and push me up against the rich mahogany wood of the elevator's side. The soft jingle of a belt buckle and the whisper of material against flesh registered seconds before he plowed into me from behind, his big cock finding its mark and delivering me to climax in a rush of dizzying sensation. I cried out, unable to keep my mouth shut no matter the risk of being caught.

He started thrusting then, driving his cock deep inside my pussy, igniting the sort of exquisitely intense pleasure only rear entry could accomplish.

"When you say 'all in,' you aren't kidding," I moaned, as sensation after heady sensation tore through me.

Rich male laughter reverberated inside the elevator car, while one of his hands cupped my breast through my shirt, finding and pinching my nipple. Hot need shot from the straining crown to my quivering sex. I curled my hands into fists against the side of the elevator as orgasm built anew.

Jack pulled free of me before I could erupt a second time.

I was ready to slug him for real, when he said in a voice thick as lava and twice as liable to burn me for the way it destroyed my ability to think straight, "We're here."

I looked over to discover the elevator doors open to reveal the pale gold shot with red and orange wallpaper of the casino's seventeenth floor. Thankfully no one was standing there watching us. Not that I had a problem with exhibitionism, but I wasn't ready to lose my job, not even over mind-blowing sex with Jack.

"Race you to the room."

He made the suggestion this time, not in a teasing voice as I had but in a rough, strained one that said how fast he'd be inside me once we reached the suite. My clit fluttered with the thought and I tossed back, "Last one there owes me oral sex."

"Can't wait to see you go down on yourself," he commented wryly, then started screwing around with tucking his cock back into his jeans.

I checked the hall and surmised no one was around. Pulling my jeans back up without bothering to shut them, or straighten my panties, I dashed to our suite and slid the key card through the lock mechanism. By the time the door was open, Jack was at my back. His hands came around my waist, lifting me an inch or two off the floor, and hurried me inside, kicking the door closed before setting me back against the wall next to it.

Eyes flashing with dark arousal, he shoved my jeans back down my hips, taking my panties with them. Pulling the lips of my pussy apart, he thumbed my clit. "You cheated."

Trembling with his errant stroke and the way his sexy, raspy voice increased the hedonistic sensation, I buried my hands under his navy polo shirt. I pushed the shirt up and over his head to reveal mouthwatering, hard-packed muscle owed to ten years as a firefighter. Hoping I didn't look too much like the proverbial Pavlovian dog, I splayed my fingers over his killer torso and laved my tongue across his small nipple, making it go erect. "You can't wait to eat me out."

Shivering with the damp swipe, he went down on his knees and blew on my parted pussy. Beneath his mustache, wicked intent curved his lips. "Then why bother waiting?"

My heart skipped a beat as his warm, rough hands cupped the sensitized flesh of my ass. In the next instant, his mouth covered my sex. He licked down the length of my slit, then back up again to circle my bloodred clit. My heart stampeded and I bit my fingernails into his shoulders, dying just a little with the raw way he made me feel, both physically and emotionally.

Christ, he could get to me.

Tears of ecstasy filled my eyes as he tormented me with the rough scrape of his mustache and then pushed his tongue deep inside me, fucking me fast again, hard again, knowing I'd want it that way, just one more time before the slow sweetness started.

Shudders of erotic pleasure built within my belly and worked their way to my pussy. I pinched my nails harder into his flesh, loving the idea of marking him as my lover, hating it all the same.

What the hell was I doing here with Jack?

Or maybe the better question was, "How could I have forgotten the way he'd made me feel the last time we'd been together?"

The emotions he'd surfaced in me that night were the real reason I'd stayed away from him for so long. Because I truly could see myself shacked up and tied down with Jack. After all the two-timing sleazebags I encountered on a daily basis at the bar, and hearing my father's firsthand accounts of the way commitment ruined every one of his relationships and ultimately made my mother leave us, that scared the hell out of me.

Clearly that reality also scared the logic out of me because the next words out of my mouth were, "I missed you, Jack."

Jack

You would have thought I'd won the World Series of Poker championship tournament for the frenzied way my heart thumped against my ribs. Along with a title and the respect of most of your peers, winning the championship came with a six million-plus cash prize. I'd have paid that and more to hear Carinna admit she'd missed me.

My mind spinning with hope and expectation, I pushed my tongue inside her pussy a last time, loving the musky scent of her arousal and the way her hot, soft sex hugged my tongue tight, like it hated to let it go, and then spread her swollen labia wider and closed my lips over her clit.

I tugged at the bundle of nerves mercilessly. She bit her nails into my skin so hard I could feel it as pleasure pain all the way to my balls. Surrendering my grip on her butt cheeks, I coated a finger in the juices at the rear of her sex. With a second tug on her clit, I sank my damp finger into her crack, finding and fingering her ass bud.

"Holy shit, Jack!" she cried out with the rapid entry.

Climax rippled through her in the next instant, making my abdominal muscles tighten and my cock ache for its own much-needed release. My cock would have to wait. I'd spent the past four months fantasizing over this moment, and I'd be damned if I was coming until I was buried inside her sweet body.

She panted out hasty breaths as her limbs shook and cream leaked from her spasming pussy. I wasn't coming yet, but I could sure as hell savor.

Releasing the pearl of her clit, I lapped at her silky essence, relishing the hot, sexy taste of Carinna until every last drop of cum was cleaned from her pretty pink folds.

To the sound of her rasping breaths and the thundering of my own wild pulse, I slowly rose, coasting my hands up her lush curves until I stood at my full height. Her eyes were back to the color of smoke and her lips swollen with passion. I'd more than enjoyed feasting on her cream, but it was nothing compared to consuming her full lips.

Sinking my tongue inside her mouth, I shared her cum in a tangle of lips and tongue and slow, unhurried sucking that fogged my mind with raw desire.

Placing a hand on the wall on either side of her head, I pulled back to give her a smile of pure conviction. "I missed you more."

Something indefinable flashed through her eyes. "Show me."

If not for the words, I would have wondered over the fleeting look. The words stopped me from doing so, in that they were one-hundred-percent Carinna. She wasn't a greedy lover by definition but merely one who knew what she wanted, as did I. After the hard, fast tongue fucking she would want it slow and sweet. Since I also knew she'd make sure I was generously rewarded, I was only too happy to see to her every demand.

Nipping at her earlobe, I skimmed my hands beneath her tank top. Slowly, I pushed up the shirt, dropping my mouth to the soft flesh of her flat belly, peppering it with moist kisses. Meeting with the front clasp of her bra, I used my teeth to gently unsnap it. Her breasts sprang free, full and firm and tipped with large, dusky nipples that had filled my dreams more than a couple nights these past months. Hell, more than a few *thousand* nights since I'd hit puberty and realized what a knockout I had in a best friend.

Praying that we'd be best friends again, as well as a whole lot more, I loved each supple mound, suckled at each nipple. Carinna fisted her hands in my hair and sighed loudly.

The throaty sound pulsed through me as desperate need straight to my groin. Straightening, I lifted her in my arms and carried her into the bedroom. With each brush of my tongue and lips over her sweaty flesh, my cock felt ready to explode. Still, I lay her on the plush gold-and-red blanket and undressed her with care, making sure no part of her remained uncaressed. I wanted every nerve in her body on end with anticipation. To see her as wild with her need as I was with mine.

Her hands gripped my bare shoulders and the muscles beneath my tongue tightened as I teased the sensitive flesh just above her pubic curls with damp circles.

"Enough, Jack!" She sounded as desperate as I felt. "I can't get any hotter. I need you to fuck me now."

Make love. She needed me to make love to her. The time for corrections would come later; now I stood from the bed and hastily stripped off my clothes.

Carinna leaned up on an elbow, sending her long, dark curls to play a tempting game of peekaboo with her hard nipples. My attention automatically moved to her pussy. She purposefully bent her right leg, exposing every one of her feminine secrets. My mouth went dry and pre-cum leaked from the head of my cock as I savored the site of her labia splayed wide, her center dripping fresh cream. And then she moved a hand down her body, past her navel and between her thighs.

She rubbed two fingers back and forth, up and down her glimmering pussy lips with torturous slowness and then thrust her first finger into her opening so hard the breath lodged in my throat. Her labored breathing and the slurp of her building juices sounded like a roar between my ears as she finger-fucked herself with an abandon I'd never before seen in a woman.

She added a second finger and rode them together all the way to the edge, to the point her juices ran in rivulets down along her thighs, and I could see her pussy muscles pulsing around her fingers, gripping with a hungriness that said orgasm was seconds away. And then she stopped, pulled her fingers out and brought them to her nipples, wetting the straining tips with her essence while I did all I could to stop from coming on the spot.

With supreme effort, I pulled my gaze back to Carinna's flushed face, found her eyes dark as night with commanding lust. Sliding her tongue along her puffy lower lip, she ravenously eyed my cock. "I want to suck you, Jack."

I knew she wasn't going to go through on her want. Still, a fresh spurt of pre-cum seeped from the head of my shaft and my cock bobbed like a broken pendulum, only capable of moving in her direction. "But you're too far gone to do the job as good as you'd want to do it."

Some of the lust left her eyes. She stopped fingering her nipples to frown and lay back on the bed. "You know me too damned well."

I didn't like the frown any more than her tone. She sounded annoyed with my ability to read her. And that made me think I was up against a virtual impossibility when it came to winning her over to the relationship side.

Climbing onto the bed, I stretched over her, until my throbbing cock pressed against the welcoming wetness of her pussy. I forced a carefree smile. "That goes both ways."

"Trust me, knowing that's my only salvation."

She was never cryptic with me. Despite the overheated state of my body, I considered gambling on ending the night without her in my arms by pushing her for clarity. Before I could make a decision, she tilted her hips and thrust upward, driving my cock halfway into her pussy.

Slow and sweet was how she would want it now, but four months of nothing but jerking off in a solo shower while fantasizing it was Carinna's moist, pink lips wrapped around my shaft made that impossible.

Twining her fingers in mine, I reclined back, raised her hands above her head and pushed the remainder of the way inside her hot body. She gasped with the speed of my entry and all trace of annoyance left her expression, returning to the look of commanding lust I knew was reflected on my face.

One lone thrust inside her slick sex and my balls snugged tight against my body and I could feel the tension of orgasm gathering at the base of my spine.

Shit, I was going to be the worst lay of her life.

Hopefully not, but I definitely wasn't about to be the best. I'd make it up to her. "I'm sorry, but I can't go slow this time. It's been too damned long."

I slanted my mouth over hers and pushed my tongue inside as I set a frantic pace. She didn't speak denial but curled her fingers tighter in mine and met me, with both tongue and body, thrust for hasty thrust. The only sound was that of our harried breathing and the slap of flesh against sweaty flesh, for all of thirty seconds, and then I cursed aloud my lack of staying power as climax rippled through me.

The coupling was fast, hard and nothing like she'd wanted. Yet I heard her cry out and felt her clamping down around my cock with her orgasm as my own shook through me as a tumultuous wave of sensation stronger than anything I'd ever experienced.

For long seconds I lay there gasping for breath, listening to the erratic play of my pulse, feeling the remnants of her release milking my deflating shaft. Then I realized I was probably squashing the shit out of her.

Since we'd entered the suite, I hadn't been acting like my usual, admittedly cocky self. In many ways, Carinna was acting off, as well. From our last time together, and the many times we'd shared details of our sex lives, I knew she was a loud, vocal lover. It was probably a bad sign she was being so quiet. I should've said something to make her talk, but my gut told me pretty much anything I said right now would have her going on the defensive. I wasn't ready for her to pull from my arms or my body, so I rolled us onto our sides and stayed limp but embedded inside her.

She yawned, in a way that was obviously feigned. I took it as legitimate, anyway, pulling the portion of the covers we weren't lying on over us and switching off the light on the nightstand next to the bed.

Inhaling her sexy vanilla scent, now mingled with the smell of our lovemaking, I brushed my lips across her forehead. "G'night, Carinna. For the record, I'm not working this week and I plan to be here in the morning."

"That makes one of us."

Her tone was light, teasing. I wrapped my arms a little tighter around her all the same. From her mind to her body to her suddenly unpredictable behavior, Carinna was the hottest flame I'd ever encountered and I'd yet to go up against her high-burning commitment issues.

Carinna

There was a reason I'd never worked first shift until two months ago. Before ten in the morning and a pot of black coffee, I was a total bitch. Bitchiness was not the mood to be in when dealing with men who'd lost their asses at gambling and now hoped to pick up a cocktail waitress to help lick their wounds, along with their cocks.

If I was going to lick anyone's cock this time of the day, it would be Jack's. Since I'd left Jack in the suite upstairs over three hours ago, that wasn't on the agenda.

"Hey, baby." The drunken idiot at the table I currently served punctuated the words by grabbing my right butt cheek.

I growled under my breath, resisting the urge to upend the tray of partially empty glasses balanced on the fingers of my left hand over his lap. Sometimes it really blew working for tips. Sure, I could have the guy tossed out for sexual harassment, but it would cost me the twenty I'd seen him slide under his empty rocks glass for me to find when I bussed. If I was going to forgo making money, I might as well have stayed in bed with Jack. Let him use those dynamite hands on me a little longer. Not to mention that tongue that could get me climaxing in seconds, or his impatient cock that had strayed from my choice routine and still had me coming for a third time.

I shifted, realizing my pussy was moist from just thinking about the way he'd gotten me off last night. Spotting Jack at a table across the bar didn't help matters.

I gave the drunk a sympathetic smile. "Sorry," I said loudly, to be heard over the salsa music blasting over the speaker system, "but my boyfriend's watching and he doesn't take kindly to my sleeping with other guys." I sent a pointed look Jack's way, who in return shot my ass-grabber a glare.

Ass-Grabber squinted, as if he was having trouble making Jack out—given his state of inebriation, he likely was. "Don't look too big from here. Bet I could take 'em."

"Probably." In his dreams. Jack was twice the man this schmuck was, in both size and character. "But since I happen to love him, I'd appreciate it if you didn't try."

I loved him?

I nearly dropped my tray when the words left my mouth. I loved Jack, sure, but in the sort of way that had to do with being friends since we were old enough to pee standing up. I snickered to myself as I made my way to Jack's table. At nine, he'd bet me I couldn't master the fine art of vertical urination. I have no clue what the stakes were, but I'd won and without a stray trickle.

Jack's words cut through my reflections the moment I reached his table. "You're still ticked about the way I took off without saying goodbye last time."

Apparently he'd taken my flippant good-night words to heart and believed I'd ditched the suite early this morning as a form of payback. After the sappy-ass way I'd confessed to missing him last night, and the even sappier way my heart had warmed with his response he'd missed me more, the thought had crossed my mind, but that wasn't the reason I'd left.

I rolled my eyes. "Flatter yourself much? I had to work the morning shift. I didn't bother leaving a note because I was running late and I knew this would be the first place you'd look."

"Since when you do work mornings? You're not even nice to yourself before noon."

"Since Tammy went on maternity leave two months ago. They needed someone to pick up a few extra shifts every week, and it just so happens I'm saving up for something special. You'd be surprised how that kinda thing motivates a person."

He smiled knowingly. "Still holding out for the Sudsbury property?"

My heart gave a funny little kick. I would have liked to have passed it off as arousal, but I could never lie to myself that effectively. Others knew about my dream of buying the Sudsbury property—a three-acre parcel located on a private lake ten miles outside of town—and turning it into a B and B. Not one of those others had inquired on my progress in months. I liked it too damned much that Jack had been back in my life less than twenty-four hours and was already asking over my dream.

I tried to dismiss it with a shrug. "Sooner or later it'll happen."

"How close are you?"

"The dip in the economy helps, but I'm not buying a welcome mat anytime soon." So he wasn't ready to let the conversation go; not a problem. After all, I wasn't the only one with a dream. As much pride as Jack took in fighting fires, his true career goal was to own a successful classic car restoration garage. "What about you?"

"Someday." He looked like he wanted to say more but then glanced over at the table I'd just left behind and frowned. "Do you always let guys grab your ass at work?"

A warning sounded in my head louder than the dinging of the slot machines coming in from the casino's main gaming floor.

Why the hell was Jack acting possessive?

He understood no-strings sex as much as I did. At twenty-eight, he'd yet to have a real relationship and had no desire to do so as long as he was a firefighter. Those were the reasons I'd known it was safe to try for sexual fringe benefits while renewing our friendship. If he'd changed course on me, was even now thinking of ways to get into my heart beyond friendship, I was going to have to kick his ass.

I gave another shrug. "He brushed my butt and I gave him a dirty look for it. What's it to you?"

"Nothing. I just don't like the thought of you being taken advantage of."

My insides tightened. I believed he didn't want to see me taken advantage of, but the "nothing" part of the equation was a bold-faced lie. Survival instincts had me jutting my hip out. "Are we okay?"

Jack's gaze narrowed—yet another testament to how well he knew me, that with just a little hip action he could tell I wasn't happy. "We're fine."

"Then it won't hurt your feelings when I tell you I don't want you here."

He smirked as he stood. "You *are* still ticked."

"No. I'm on the clock. Standing around shooting the shit with you isn't exactly raking in the dough." I uncocked my hip and grabbed the nearly empty glass from the table in front of him—obviously he'd been drinking soda because he never touched alcohol before dinner. "See you later, Jack."

His fingers settled on my arm, staying me when I would have turned and run away like the chickenshit his uncharacteristic behavior had me feeling like. His smirk was gone, replaced with a sensual tilt to his mouth that gave a glimpse of his tongue and immediately had my thong damp all over again. "When later?"

I'd meant the words as a figure of speech, and I should have told him so. But I couldn't stop thinking about those three incredible orgasms he'd given me last night or how amazingly good it had felt to fall asleep in his arms, and so I proved I was one card shy of a full deck by saying, "I'm working doubles the next two days—"

"In other words, you'll be too tired for sex."

"In other words, you'd best plan a full-body massage into your foreplay. I get off at seven."

His mouth curved fully, into the cockiest grin I'd ever seen him wear. "And eight, nine, ten and eleven."

I liked my bad boys, and I liked his arrogance so much that if it wasn't for the tray of drinks and the glass shower that would ensue if I dropped it, I probably would have said to hell with my job and slid onto his cock there and then.

Since I did have that tray and I really needed this job, I somehow managed to stand my ground. "If you plan to use me that much, you'd best add a bottle of gin and an extra-large jar of olives to the schedule."

♣ ♠ ♥ ♦ ♣ ♠ ♥ ♦ ♣ ♠ ♥ ♦

Chapter Three

Jack

Though I knew my brother had today and tomorrow off work, I held out hope Ryan would be gone when I arrived at the rental house we shared. No such luck. His Jeep was in the garage and when I opened the door that led from the garage into the kitchen, Ryan was less than a foot away, looking ready to kill.

Green eyes narrowed in a death glare, he stuffed his hands into the front pockets of his sweatpants. "I didn't hear any emergency backup calls come over the fire scanner last night, so I'm guessing a piece of ass would be the reason you never made it home."

I almost laughed at his tone: a mix of concern and anger. I'd experienced the same feelings too damned many times when we'd been teenagers and Ryan had failed to come home by curfew. Back then, Mom had been working nights on a stamping production line and, with Dad gone, I'd taken it upon myself to see that Ryan didn't end up in a jail cell. As fate and his miscreant ways would have it, he had ended up in the slammer a handful of times, but never for anything more than misdemeanor offenses.

Although he still had his narrow-minded days, my brother had come a long way since then, was a valuable member of the Ladder 19 fire crew and a guy in whose hands I'd put my life more than a few times while on the job. That didn't mean I wanted him tracking my every move. I sure as hell didn't want him referring to Carinna as a piece of ass.

Since he knew about Carinna's relationship phobia, and I could guess he would think I was a hopeless fool to still be making a long-term play for her, I didn't want him knowing I'd hooked up with her again.

I dismissed his words with a shrug. "You're the one who's always saying shit happens. Besides, how was I to know you'd be spending the night home playing curfew cop?"

Dressed as he was, in baggy gray sweats and a faded black T-shirt with a picture of a bunned hot dog and the words Bite Me beneath it, Ryan didn't look like a ladies' man. The endless string of females that crossed our threshold on his arm and proceeded straight to his bedroom proved he not only cleaned up well but knew how to work his year-round tan, dark good looks and muscles honed on the job to their best advantage.

"That wasn't the plan," he said dryly. "I had a blind date that five minutes in had me wishing I really was blind so I could trip over a rock and fake my death. I got in around ten, watched a couple movies, then headed to bed around three, wondering where the fuck you were." He gave me the death glare a few more seconds, which was pointless since I was the one who'd taught him the look fifteen years ago in an effort to get a schoolyard bully off his back. Finally, he let the glare go and gave me a conspiratorial smile. "So, how was she?"

The best of my life.

I might not have liked the way our talk had gone in the bar that morning, but memories of loving Carinna and holding her well into the night had a euphoric smile tugging at my lips. I knew Ryan would see it and know damned well who was behind it, so I pushed him out of my way and headed for the coffeepot.

Thankful to see the light was still on, which meant it hadn't been brewed too long ago, I poured a cup before turning back. I was shitty at lying, but attempted it anyway. "*She* was a poker table down at The Liege. I was hot as hell last night."

Ryan settled at the kitchen table, reclining back in one wooden chair and propping his bare feet up on the seat of another. "Did you see Carinna?"

"Should I have?" I groaned inwardly as I slid onto a chair across the table from him. Shit, I'd sounded defensive.

The amusement that passed through Ryan's eyes said he hadn't missed my reaction. "Like I said yesterday, she dumped the foot-fetish dude, model, whatever the hell he is. I checked in on her last night to see how she was handling things and she was about to head out for The Liege. She wasn't dressed in that itty-bitty-titty costume, either."

In the midst of sipping my coffee, I winced at the mention of Carinna's uniform. I hated the way the black sarong-style top spangled with gold sequins was cut so low her cleavage risked spilling out. The matching miniskirt was a waste of about three inches of material, given every time she moved it threatened to expose her entire ass. In the twenty minutes

I'd been in the tequila bar that morning, I'd caught a glimpse of the black thong sheathed between her firm butt cheeks three different times. I'd been hard with the first glimpse, aching with the second and ready to throw her over my table and fuck her in front of every patron in the place with the last. The knowledge most every other guy in the bar was experiencing the same reaction killed that urge.

"I didn't see her." My disapproval of her uniform came through in both my voice and the way I slammed my mug onto the table, sloshing coffee over the rim. I mentally calmed myself before adding, "Like I said, I was in the card room all night."

Ryan snorted out a laugh. "Nice try, bro. But you can't lie any better than I can. You saw her. You were probably just too much of a pansy to talk to her."

There were times I hated living and working beside my brother 24/7. It made it impossible for him not to know exactly what buttons to push. Calling me a pansy was a pretty damned big one. "Fine. She was in the card room. I talked to her. Happy?"

He smirked. "Was that before or after you bent her over her bed and tapped her ass?"

Damn, I should have known I'd never be able to get last night with Carinna past him. At least he wasn't mocking me for wanting her. Yet. "You're pushing it, Ry."

"You deserve it for not calling. So what's the status quo? Friends again, or just fuck buddies?"

"I don't know. We don't fuck." We had tidy, missionary-style sex. Okay, so that wasn't true, but I hated the way the word *fuck* made sleeping with Carinna sound so detached from emotions.

"Maybe you don't, but I've heard too many of Carinna's tell-all sex stories to believe she doesn't. Hell, that time I stopped by her house last summer to see about borrowing her Crock-Pot, I could have heard her shouting about what an amazingly big dick the guy with her had even if the windows hadn't been open."

I knew Carinna's track record, as well as she knew mine. It shouldn't bother me to hear about her past lovers, but my gut roiled in a way that made it seem my one sip of coffee had been toxic. "Are you trying to get your ass kicked?"

Ryan narrowed his eyes astutely. "What I'm trying to do is get your ass in gear. You know how Carinna works. She'll have a new fuck buddy by the end of the month and I'd just as soon see it be you. Why don't you invite her over for poker tomorrow night? It's been too long since we played together."

"She's working a double."

"That never stopped her before. Make it a late game, and I'll make it a point to be home."

"Planning on a threesome or chaperoning?" Or why the hell was my brother pushing the idea so much?

"Neither. I just know you well enough to suspect you didn't walk away from Carinna with a simple goodbye this morning. You probably did or said something to freak her out and the odds of her seeing you again so soon will be that much better if she knows I'm part of the equation."

He was mistaken about her seeing me again. She would see me tonight, and in her own apartment, no less. At the same time, since I was liable to do exactly as he'd guessed, and do or say something to concern Carinna come tomorrow morning, I kept my mouth shut and accepted that the reason Ryan was pushing the idea so much was simply because he was my brother and, as such, he wanted to see me happily laid. It was simply chance the woman doing the laying would be Carinna.

Jack

Carinna and I had exchanged keys years ago, when we'd first moved into our respective places. I took advantage of that tonight, slipping into her apartment ten minutes before I expected her home from work, in order to prep her bedroom.

She'd suggested I add olives to tonight's schedule and while I was reasonably sure she'd meant for her martinis, I'd spent the four hours since today's tournament play had ended imagining a hundred-and-one olive-enhanced scenarios that had nothing to do with drinking alcohol and everything to do with dirtying her pristine-white silk sheets.

Hearing her enter the apartment, I popped the lid on the olives and tucked the jar between her dresser and bed. She appeared in the doorway of the bedroom seconds later. Any fear I might have had about looking guilty faded the instant I saw she hadn't changed out of her cocktailing outfit.

I hated the scanty getup as a uniform. But I loved it as a vice to get me hard on sighting

Tonight, the uniform looked naughtier than ever. At some point during her double shift, she'd added black stockings to the ensemble. Seductively sheer nylon hugged her shapely legs, ending in a lace band a few inches shy of the miniskirt's hem.

My cock pressed rigidly against my jeans as I rushed to

the door and tugged Carinna into my arms. If I was in the mood for tact, I would have taken the time for a long, hot welcome-home kiss. Between having a bad run of luck in the tournament today, dropping me to eighth place, the way Ryan's warning Carinna would have a new fuck buddy by the end of the month kept eating at me, and now those damned sexy nylons, I wasn't in the mood for tact. I was in the mood to fuck the beauty in my arms, show her exactly how much we belonged together, so I turned her around, grabbed her around the waist and hurried her to the bed.

With a touch of my hand at the small of her back, she bent over the side of the mattress, splayed her fingers on the baby-blue blanket and wiggled her round ass in my face.

Little tease. She knew good and well the throbbing effect that wiggle had on my cock.

I gave in to my fingers' restless urges for a moment, caressing the backs of her smooth legs, from thigh to calf, then journeyed my hands up to her inner thighs, teasing the soft, naked flesh for seconds before her body ignited with shivers and my need became too great to bear.

Tossing up the tiny hem of her skirt, I fisted the rear of her thong, until my fingers and thumb met at the hot divide of her buttocks. Then I jerked the thin cotton from her body with a twist of my wrist.

My shaft jumped with the primal sound of shredding cotton. Carinna jerked on the bed, her breath catching. "So much for the massage and martini."

Her appreciation for my feral behavior rose from between her thighs to color the air with the hot, musky scent of her arousal. Cream dripped from her sex, seeping down her toned inner legs to catch in the lace band of her stockings. My fingers were restless again, and I couldn't resist coating one with her juices and sucking it between my lips.

Fuck, she tasted so sweet. I could barely stand the thought of pushing an olive into her plump pussy and eating it back out dripping in her cum. "I didn't forget the olives."

If she thought the comment odd, she didn't say so. Then again, it could be she was too busy gasping as I yanked my zipper down and rammed into her from behind.

Carinna dug her nails into the blanket, her knuckles going white in stark contrast to her naturally golden-tan skin. "You could warn a girl," she panted out, already rearing back to meet the second thrust of my glistening cock.

I laughed thickly as I lifted her hips higher and stroked into her deep. My eyes all but rolled back into my head with the feel of her hot pussy pulling me deeper yet. "Like you want the warning. You like the surprise. You like it dirty."

"You don't know me that well, Jack."

If she'd meant to sound convincing, she'd failed. She was holding out hope I didn't know her as well as I did, and that meant she was beginning to understand what I wanted from us was more than a sexual friendship. That also meant she didn't want anything to do with that particular want of mine.

She would.

There would be no new fuck buddies for Carinna. We were it, meant to go the distance. If she couldn't see that truth in how suited our bodies were, then somehow I would convince her of it in words, prove to her we were worth risking a relationship. That somehow eluded me right now, so I concentrated on the moment, on pumping into her delectable pussy and losing myself in each moist, hungry grip until I could feel her orgasm clenching tightly around me, drenching my cock in her juices, and finally I gave in to my own climax.

Carinna

Jack didn't forget the olives. He'd told me as much twenty minutes ago, before he'd given me one of the fastest, hardest, most incredible fucks I'd had since our first time together.

I'd been too caught up in pleasure, as well as concern over his continued need to point out how well he knew me and what exactly that said about his state of mind where our friendship was concerned, to get his meaning until two seconds ago—when he'd pushed my thighs wide and buried a pimento-free, green olive in my slit.

The ends of his carnal grin disappeared into his mustache as he bent his dark head, used his thumbs to pull my slick pussy lips so wide they burned with wicked pleasure and skewered the center of the olive with his tongue.

My fingers pushed savagely into his hair. Sizzling heat pooled in my blood and shot from my center to my freed, bouncing breasts. Keeping my hips from thrusting against his face was an impossible feat. I could feel the push of the olive inside me, mini-fucking me with each of his forceful strokes, but even more arousing, I could see it.

The closet at the foot of my bed was finished with mirrored doors and Jack had been careful to position me at an angle where I could view his every sinful move.

My hips bucked on the bed and my blood pumped wildly

as I watched his expert tongue work in and out of my hot, wet body, licking at the slippery folds of my pussy and the cream-coated olive, then go racing toward my clit.

The bastard never touched my clit.

He just kept teasing, both with his tongue and the slow circling of his fingertips along my swollen labia. Always coming so close. Making me ache so badly I hurt with my need.

It was the sweetest of slow, sensual treats and, given he'd already supplied me one fast orgasm, it should be the last thing I wanted. But I did want it, wanted it to go on all night long. Only, the increased tempo of his tongue and the way he turned his teeth on the olive, attacking its tender, tart meat in seconds to expose my dripping sex, told me it was about to turn into a fast orgasm, after all.

Hell, at this rate, I would be lucky to last a minute.

Keeping the exquisite pressure of his thumbs on my spread lips, he cupped my ass with his fingertips, lifted my center more fully to his mouth and twisted his tongue, French-kissing my pussy. My nipples stabbed with throbbing sensation. My toes curled. Sweat gathered between my breasts.

"Is it nine already?" I sang out as orgasm approached in a dizzying rush that had me forgetting the erotic sight in the mirror to release Jack's hair, fall back on the bed and dig my nails into the blanket.

His tongue kept up its tender assault, licking, twisting, lapping at the walls of my sex until climax took me over, and then he pulled from my body to devour my juices.

I came back down from a happy little orgasm cloud to find him sitting at my feet, his lips glistening and his grin huge. "Eight-thirty," he finally responded to my question. "And I didn't forget the gin either." He winked one of those devilish blue-green eyes. "Just wait till nine. We're going to play a round of The Disappearing Bottleneck."

I laughed hard and long, while my pussy gave an eager flutter and exploded with a fresh burst of arousal.

Despite my claim to the contrary, Jack had been right. I did love my dirty sex and he knew exactly how to provide it. It was just one of the many reasons I loved him.

I loved him.

My laughter stopped short. I dragged in a steadying breath. Why did I keep coming back to those damned words? Could I actually love Jack beyond friendship the way I was coming to think he might love me? And what did it matter if I did? I didn't do relationships. I knew too well how they ended in ruins and heartache.

No, I couldn't love Jack that way. And even if I did, I wasn't about to admit it to him.

Carinna

We were back to being bosom buddies. When Jack had left my apartment that morning—after giving me an open-mouthed kiss that had left me wet and horny and an adoring look that had left me fearful that I could end up breaking his heart if I kept letting him sleep with me—I had never thought that possible.

But here we were, sitting around Jack and Ryan's kitchen table, dressed in our oldies but goodies, tossing chips into a poker pot and shooting the shit like the three of us had done every Wednesday night for nearly fifteen years. It was Friday, but the scenario still felt more like a homecoming than anything I'd ever experienced. These guys were my family as much as, and probably more than, my parents had ever been, and I belonged here with them, as a friend and the sister they'd never had. And that meant I needed to stop sleeping with Jack. Forgetting how quickly and thoroughly he got to me wouldn't be easy, but for our friendship's sake, I could do it.

Or so I was trying to convince myself when Ryan grabbed a bag of salt-and-vinegar chips and another of pretzel rods from on top of the fridge and tossed them on the table. The pretzel rods were my favorite, the salt-and-vinegar chips Jack's favorite. I knew even before Jack pulled the bag open and popped a chip into his mouth I was in deep trouble.

It wasn't the way Jack ate his chips that bothered me. It was how he licked the residue from his fingers, so as not to get grease on the cards or poker chips. One at a time, starting with his index finger, he trailed his damp tongue from knuckle to knuckle, onto the next finger, the next knuckle. Lick. Lick. Lick.

His gaze flicked to mine without warning, far too fast for me to stop my ogling or close my slightly open mouth. A cocky grin curved his lips. Wicked intent sizzled in his eyes. His licks turned to a fervent suckling of the sensitive web of flesh connecting his thumb and first finger.

My heart raced. My pussy pulsed. I stifled my moan, just barely.

I could feel that suckle straight to my core, like he was slurping the juices from my sex, eating the cum clean from my body the way he'd done that morning, after delivering me to ecstasy by way of the vibrator he'd found stashed under my bed. Feeling the flesh-colored dildo quivering inside me had always felt good. Knowing Jack had controlled its every move had tripled the sensation, until I hadn't been able to stop from writhing on the bed and grinding my pussy against his hand while I'd screamed out my pleasure.

"What's up, Carinna?"

My breathing coming too fast, I glanced over at Ryan, aware he'd spoken but not sure about what. "Huh?"

"You calling or what?"

I grappled for the pretzel bag and yanked it open. Stuffing a salty rod in my mouth, I sucked on it hard in an attempt to dislodge the totally arousing and completely unwanted thoughts from my head. "Yeah. Sure."

Ryan laughed so obnoxiously I looked back at him. Humor curved his lips and gleamed in his sea-green eyes. "I oughta hold you to your word and make you give me all your chips, but something tells me your mind isn't on the game."

And something told me he was right as rain. Speaking of rain, I felt like a major downpour had let loose in my sweatpants.

Pushing aside the urge to shift in my seat, I glanced at the table in front of Ryan and then at the pot and realized he'd gone all in. A look at my hold cards had me inwardly cringing. Nice. I'd called him on an off-suit two and nine.

Not about to admit I had a one-track mind that revolved entirely around getting Jack naked, I stuck out my chin and narrowed my eyes. "I have cards."

Ryan's smirk said he wasn't buying it. "Then put your chips in the pot and prove it, sweetheart."

"Do I look like an idiot? You already made it clear you have a winning hand." I folded my hold cards into the deck, giving it an absent shuffle just in case Ryan decided to look. Too much of a chickenshit to meet Jack's eyes or look at his mouth again, I stood. "I need a beer. Anyone else?"

"Please," Jack said as I made my way to the refrigerator.

"Okay." *Just stop licking your damned fingers.* Not that the deep timbre of his voice was any less lethal. "Ry?"

"You know it. There're longnecks in the crisper bin."

Longnecks.

Without thinking, I slanted a look at Jack. His eyes had been teasingly wicked, now they smoldered with a sensual heat so forceful it guaranteed he shared my thoughts. Those of how he'd lived out his promise and used the bottle of gin on me last night, fucking me with its neck. Not to orgasm, just long enough to have me trembling on the edge. And then Jack had been there, his big cock filling me up while his tongue delivered my mouth to an erotic palate paradise.

Did Ryan know we were sleeping together? Did he know how Jack had used that bottle on me? Is that why he'd brought up the longnecks? Why he'd gotten out those damned torturous potato chips?

One thing was certain, I wasn't up to handling a longneck. Hell, I was barely up to playing Texas Hold 'Em.

I opened the fridge door and basked in the coolness that greeted my hot body. Several long seconds was all I could risk without raising questions. Then I grabbed two bottles of Bud from the crisper and a can of Bud Light for myself from the top shelf and returned to the table.

Ryan had the dealer chip, which meant Jack's hands were

free to roam. Any relief I'd gotten from the cold air of the fridge was forgotten the instant his hand went into the chip bag. The damned chips went in his mouth. He started chewing. Any moment now he would be licking. Sucking. Slurping.

Popping the tab of my beer with one hand, I stuffed a fresh pretzel rod in my mouth with the other and attempted to suck my stimulation away. That proved as ineffective as trying to steal my gaze from Jack's mouth to look at my hold cards.

Right on cue he started in on the licking. Right on cue my pussy let loose with juice. Right on cue a husky moan barreled up the back of my throat and attempted to push free of my lips.

Jack's mouth opened. I waited for his tongue to escape, to start in on the next round of silent but sensuously deadly torture. Instead, he said, "Carinna?"

"What?" Christ, could I sound any more breathless?

"You're bleeding all over the freaking table, that's what," Ryan answered.

"What?" I looked down to find blood oozing from the tip of my index finger to pool on the table's wood surface. "Shit."

"You probably cut it on the rim of your can," Jack supplied. "There are Band-Aids in the medicine cabinet in the upstairs bathroom."

Squeezing my finger with my good hand to staunch the blood flow, I stood and then realized where he'd instructed me to go. The master bath, which was hooked to his bedroom. Feet away from his bed. Where he slept naked. The same way he'd slept the past two nights. Naked and with a monster hard-on prodding against my ass crack. A monster hard-on I wasn't supposed to be thinking of. But, Jesus, how could I not?

"I'll help you," he said, as if he honestly thought following me up to his room was a good idea.

"And I'll see you two in the morning," Ryan put in smugly as we exited the kitchen and headed straight to what I was sure would be more carnal temptation than I could possibly resist.

♣ ♠ ♥ ♦ ♣ ♠ ♥ ♦ ♣ ♠ ♥ ♦

Chapter Four

Jack

"He knows," Carinna said the instant we stepped inside the master bath directly off from my bedroom.

After taking a Band-Aid out of the medicine cabinet and handing it to her, I shrugged, surprised she cared. "You know how shitty I am at lying. Besides, Ryan's thrilled for us."

Downstairs, she'd looked pretty damned thrilled herself, in a way that had to do with being wet between the thighs. Now, she appeared to be walking the thin line between worried and pissed.

She ran her finger under the faucet until the water ran clear, then put the Band-Aid on and turned to face me. Her hip shot out. "Let me guess. He thinks we should have been sleeping together years ago?"

I ignored her irritated tone to consider the question. Did Ryan feel that way? I'd always presumed he'd laugh in my face if I admitted I had plans for Carinna of the commitment kind. Maybe I'd been mistaken. Maybe the reason he'd pushed for tonight to happen wasn't because he wanted to see me happily laid but, rather, just plain happy. "Pretty much."

"What do you think?" The temper left her stance and her lips pushed together in a thoughtful pucker.

"That fourteen hours is way in the hell too long to go without seeing you naked."

Poker-night attire consisted of sweats, T-shirt and an optional ball cap. Apparently, Carinna considered underwear optional, as well. The warm, supple skin of her backside filled my palms when I pulled her up against me and shoved my hands down the back of her sweatpants.

"Jack…" Warning rang in her voice.

Ignoring that warning, I cupped an ass cheek in each hand and ground against her pussy. I thought I'd caught a whiff of her arousal earlier in the night. Now, there was no thinking required. Her excitement rose up, rich, musky and tinged with vanilla, to play a number on my senses. "Don't tell me you weren't hot for me downstairs. Hot, and teasing the hell out of me with every one of those pretzel rods."

Surprise passed through her eyes. But, no, it couldn't have been. A woman with Carinna's knowledge of the male anatomy and how to torment the shit out of it would know exactly what she'd done to me.

As if to prove me right, she slid her hands beneath my shirt and ran her nails over my chest with teasing light pressure. "Fuck, yes, I was hot for you! But like you have room to talk."

"I wasn't eating pretzels."

"No, but you were certainly having a good time licking the salt-and-vinegar residue off your fingers."

That hadn't been purposeful seduction. I hadn't even

realized she was paying attention, until she'd taken too long responding to Ryan's play. The moment our gazes had met and I'd registered the smoke color of her eyes, I'd known what I was doing to her. I had thought to make tonight about friendship, at least until the poker game was over. Seeing her raw desire, knowing she was as hungry for me as I was for her, the idea of unsettling her even further had been too tempting to pass up.

Speaking of tempting…

"Licking?" I slid my hands from Carinna's sweatpants and hers from beneath my shirt. "Like this?" Taking one of her hands in mine, I brought it to my mouth and dabbed at the end of her first finger with the tip of my tongue.

A tiny sigh escaped her and I ran my tongue the length of her finger. Down. Back up again. Her pupils dilated and my own internal fire kicked up several notches. Slowly, I pulled her finger into my mouth, let my tongue circle for several long, teasing seconds and then sucked hard.

"Oh, God, Jack," she moaned. "That's more than a lick."

And her moan was more than a sound to echo off my bathroom walls. It coasted down my spine and past my ass crack to come to rest between my legs, making my cock throb and my balls tighten.

I could stick with Carinna's choice routine and take her fast and hard, relieving myself quickly in the process. Or I could show her just how incredible it felt to step outside the norm into uncharted terrain and give her a dose of slow, sensual loving both the first and last time around. I wasn't much for metaphors, but I couldn't help note how the second option metaphorically fit with my quest to get

her to give uncharted terrain a try by entering a relationship with me.

I glanced at the Jacuzzi tub that dominated the right side
of the bathroom. "Ever do it in a hot tub?"

"You already know that answer."

My gut tightened because I did and I wasn't pleased about
it. I let go of my jealousy of the men who'd come before me
to concentrate on the present, on driving Carinna so crazy
with passion she'd forget she'd had past lovers. "But never
with me. I promise it's an experience you won't forget."

She looked to the tub, to me, back to the tub. She wasn't
a woman I associated with hesitancy where sex was concerned, but when she again met my eyes it was with lust and
uncertainty warring in her own. "What about Ryan? We
can't just leave him downstairs."

"Trust me, he was serious about seeing us in the morning.
By now, he's long gone to find a piece of ass. Too bad for
Ry he doesn't stand a chance at finding one as fine as you."

Shit. Thanks to Ryan's observation yesterday and planting
the crude phrase in my head, I'd made it sound like Carinna
was nothing more to me than a piece of ass. I would have
clarified my meaning if she hadn't chosen that moment to
give in by reaching for the hem of her T-shirt and yanking
it over her head. Her bra matched her panties, in that it
didn't exist. Her lush breasts were bare, and my mouth
watered with the desire to latch on to a dusky erect nipple
and suck. Knowing that route would deliver us to a fast
finish, I stood my ground.

Teasing flashed in her eyes. She glanced toward the hot
tub. "Race you into the water."

I'd never been able to resist her teasing or her challenges. I sure as hell wasn't starting tonight. "You're on."

I stripped in seconds and, without a hint of finesse, jumped into the tub like the sex-crazed man she made me.

Carinna

Jack thought of me as a piece of ass.

Relief cruised me even as my heart gave a nasty little bump I hated to acknowledge was disappointment. I didn't want a relationship with any man, but I loved waking up in Jack's strong arms.

Too much.

It was good that I'd been mistaken about his feeling more for me than friendship. And not just because it meant I could safely give in to my lust and sleep with him tonight. Though, I will admit that was the biggest reason on my mind at the moment. How could it not be when all that beautifully defined sinew and sun-bronzed skin was winking my way?

Jack stretched across to the far side of the tub, muscles rippling in his back as he turned on the jets. Bubbles churned to life within seconds. He pushed a second button that released soap into the water, which foamed the surface and stole my view of everything from his waist down. I almost pouted. He'd concealed some of my most favorite parts.

The scent of the soap hit me then. Something light, floral. Possibly lilac. Not even close to Jack's style. Had one of his previous lovers given the soap to him?

My belly ached a little with the thought. I mentally eased the sensation aside, aware it had more to do with the idea of some other woman giving him better sex than me than the thought of his actually being with someone else. Maybe he'd had better lovers up to this point, but that was about to change. I knew Jack in a way some random woman paying his body a night or two of homage never could.

I knew about his fetish.

It wasn't just the sleek, hot body styles and the growling thunder of the engines that fueled his love for classic cars—he had a serious chrome fetish. A fetish that extended to the moldings and fixtures of his Jacuzzi tub. A fetish that was about to grab him by the balls.

Flashing an X-rated smile, I stepped free of my sweatpants and climbed over the side of the tub. Jack's eyes were dark with carnal anticipation. He expected me to sink into the tub, or plop in, the way he'd so inelegantly done—and knowing I destroyed his grace gave me no small pleasure.

And it was no small pleasure on his face when I bypassed his expectation and lowered myself onto the arm of the tub's faucet. My pussy lips opened around the glistening shaft. Cold chrome kissed my hot folds, splintering ache deep in my core.

I'd never honed my contortionist skills, so I couldn't take the shaft inside me, but the drooping of his eyelids and the gradual parting of his lips said it didn't matter.

Well able to imagine the throbbing of his cock, I closed my eyes, tossed back my head and ground my pussy up and down the length of the shaft. My clit hit hard with each pass. I didn't bother to hold in my throaty sighs. Jack's moan punctuated the third one, the hot, husky sound bringing to standing attention every sexual neuron in my body.

My belly warmed, tightened. Heat spread up my torso,

making my breasts feel heavy and achy. I blinked open my eyes with the intensely fast-building orgasm.

Jack's lips were pressed in a firm line, his eyes riveted on my crotch and his right hand working beneath the water. I couldn't see past the damned bubbles, but I easily imagined his long, strong fingers petting his cock, fingering the plump head, squeezing when he was about to blow it because he wanted to save his orgasm for when he was buried inside me.

My legs shuddered, a cross between fatigue from the way I was squatting over the shaft and thrill to know Jack would soon impale me with his own much bigger, longer, thicker shaft.

"How's that chrome fetish working for you now, Jack?" I taunted, as I brought a hand to my sex and spread my folds wider, wanting to ensure nothing blocked the show of my pussy exploding with cream.

"Never better."

He sounded strung out, pushed to the edge and ready to snap. I took mercy on him and increased the pumping of my hips, applying my full weight as I ground the sensitized pearl of my clit hard against the chrome shaft.

Once.

Twice.

My clit throbbed. My pussy spasmed. Pleasure pain erupted deep within my core. I worked the fingers that separated my folds in a quick and carnal up-and-down rhythm. Orgasm raced through me so intensely it threatened to topple me into the water. Jack stopped that from happening.

His hands holding my thighs in place, he bent his head and feasted on the juices seeping from my body. The lash of his tongue up my center and against my clit started a second wave of tremors, even stronger than the first. These ones I couldn't stop from crying out over.

I screamed my ecstasy. "Jesus, Jack! I *love* your tongue! Never stop licking me! Never *ever* stop!"

Jack

I should have felt languid and highly sated after first watching Carinna masturbate and then feeling her ride my cock until we both climaxed with the sensual friction of the hot tub's many jets surrounding us. But all I could think about was giving her the slow, sensual loving I'd intended to provide before she'd rubbed her pussy along the tub's chrome shaft and destroyed any chance I'd had at maintaining control.

I quickly finished drying off with a large green bath towel, then spread the towel over the shower curtain rod to dry. Carinna stood naked in front of the bathroom sink, finger-combing her wet hair. I met her reflected gaze in the mirrored medicine cabinet. "Come downstairs with me."

She stopped brushing to glance down at her body, still warm and flushed from our lovemaking. "Now?"

"Now. I have something to show you."

She looked indecisive for a few seconds, but then crossed to the hot tub. With her back to me, she reached to the tiled floor for her sweatpants.

I groaned with the sight of her curvy ass right there in front of me, the rosy hole all but begging me to sink inside and take her hard. Tonight I wouldn't be having her that way, but soon. "Don't get dressed. I'm not."

She straightened and turned back, frowning. "What if Ry—"

"I told you he's gone out."

I still wanted to set her straight on my earlier slipup, but the more I thought about it, the more I realized doing so would reveal the depth of my feelings and she wasn't yet ready to accept them. My gut tightened with the knowledge she might never be.

How concerned she seemed over my brother catching her in the buff registered then. That had to be a good sign.

I tested the waters with a cocky smile. "Right. As if you'd care if Ryan saw you naked. C'mon, Carinna. I know you too well not to think you'd be turned on by the idea of him watching us fuck. Or joining us."

Lifting a slim shoulder in a shrug, she smiled a little too brightly. "Hey, I'm all for threesomes and Ryan's definitely doable. I just didn't think you'd feel comfortable if the third party was your brother."

Despite the fact her smile looked artificial and I probably deserved her remark for laying the words out there, jealousy grabbed hold of me. The truth of it was there had been a time when I was as open to a threesome as Carinna claimed to be, but that time had long since passed. Now, it wasn't just the thought of my brother sleeping with her that made me feel uncomfortable, but the idea of anyone but me touching her in such an intimate way.

Because I didn't trust my voice, I left the bathroom. Not giving her much choice but to follow or be left alone, I made my way downstairs and through the kitchen to the garage. My jealousy eased up when I discovered Ryan's Jeep missing.

Even if she didn't want him, I could see Carinna fucking my brother, just to show me that being tied down in a relationship with one man could never work for her.

I was inhaling the much-appreciated cooler air of the garage when Carinna padded barefoot and equally bare-assed through the kitchen door less than a minute later. Admiration flashed in her eyes and she parted her lips in an O the instant she caught sight of the 1950 Mercury Coupe Lead Sled dominating the right side of the garage. Without a word or glance in my direction, she went to the car, stroking her palm along the red-and-black flames that licked across the hood. "Pretty."

I felt like a prime stallion, for the way her what-should-have-been innocent stroking had my recently deflated cock back to rock solid. It was my chrome fetish back at play. She wasn't touching anything chrome at the moment, but she was close to the trim and wheel rims and apparently, in this case, close counted.

Moving up beside her, I ran my hand along the hood next to hers. "Pretty damned incredible is more like it. It wasn't in great condition when I bought it. While you were too wrapped up in life to talk the past few months, I needed a distraction to fill the time we used to spend together. This was it. And it felt great. I haven't solely restored a classic since the '67 Cougar I gave Mom for her fiftieth birthday."

Carinna looked like she wanted to comment about these past months. Instead, she gave me one of those luminous smiles that covered the majority of her face. "You did great, Jack. Whenever you get your garage going, it's gonna be a huge success."

I basked in the glow of her compliment. I'd brought her down here to drive her wild with ecstasy, but, just as much, I'd wanted her praise. Now that I'd gotten the latter, it was time to get down to business on the former.

"I have something else to show you." I reached into the coupe's open passenger-side window to the bench seat. My cock throbbed when my fingers came into contact with the red fur-lined handcuffs I'd found in a floor compartment when I'd done the initial detailing. I'd nearly thrown them out. And what a waste that would have been.

Pulling the handcuffs through the window, I lifted them in front of her and gave in to a wolfish grin. "Look what came along for the ride."

Carinna's smile went from luminous to naughty in a heartbeat. She took in the rigid state of my cock and then nodded at the handcuffs. "Hoping to break those in, were you?"

"Maybe I've already used them a few times." Shit, I didn't know why I'd said that. But, yeah, I did. Just once I wanted her to be the jealous one. To think that between when we'd slept together four months ago and again this week I'd been with at least one other woman, if not a couple dozen.

"Maybe you'd better get to putting them on me, if that's your plan. Otherwise, I can always use my beauty sleep." Her smile went just a little brittle at the edges, her tone not even coming close to sounding nice.

My grin turned arrogant, my hope for us fueled by her response in a way I'd never seen coming. It was no longer enough to drive Carinna crazy while making slow, sweet love to her. Now that I knew she might feel jealousy over me, I had to show her she didn't need another man or two men in her life or bed because no other man knew her as well as I did. No other man knew what her dirty-girl side craved.

Truthfully, Carinna had never even hinted at the idea she would enjoy playing the part of the submissive. After all, where would it fit into her usual routine? Nowhere, since surrendering her control so completely meant both giving her absolute trust, and opening herself up emotionally. Just as I knew she would bask in the pleasure pain I was about to inflict, I held on to faith she would let her emotions free.

Grasping the handcuffs in my left hand, I moved behind her and palmed her breast with my right hand. I tugged her back against me, until my cock nudged between her thighs to rub along her pussy lips from behind. All the blood left in my head threatened to shoot to my groin with the sensual slide. I fought the sensation off and took my body's anxiously aroused state out on Carinna by pinching her nipple and rearing back to rub along her slit a second time. A shallow cry slipped from her lips. I rubbed some more, playing with her nipples, pinching, rolling, pulling, letting her arousal build slowly.

Her breasts rose and fell heavily beneath my touch, her breathing heightened. My own breath drew in on unsteady rushes as silky cream seeped from between her folds to coat my cock and tinge the air with her hot, musky scent.

With the next thrust, I angled my shaft to brush against her clit but not come close to piercing her opening. I didn't dare enter her, not if I wanted this to continue. Carinna didn't seem to care about it lasting. One of her hands moved to her pussy, her fingers spreading her labia, shamelessly exposing her clit to rub against my cock as thoroughly as possible, while she moaned and reared back, pumping her ass into my groin.

She was already so close to climaxing. Already so close to making me come, as well. Too close for either of our sakes.

I let go of the straining nipple I currently toyed with and pushed her toward the front of the coupe. "Lean against the hood," I ordered in a dark voice, "with your forehead touching the metal and your ass in the air."

She didn't turn back, or comply, just flung a haughty, "Feeling dominant, Jack?" over her shoulder.

Her disobedience fit my intentions perfectly, made me feel just a little high with the control she was about to submit to me. I pushed my knees into the backs of hers, forcing her to go weak-kneed. A subtle shove had her legs plastered up against the chrome grille. "Get on the hood, Carinna. Now!"

"Yes, sir. Right away, sir," she said in an amused voice that suggested she thought I was teasing, that I would let up any minute now and sink inside her slick pussy.

Eventually I would do that. But not until her emotions had a chance to fully rise to the surface. Not until she wanted me so badly she begged.

She planted her hands on the hood and reclined against it slowly. Too slowly. I pressed my hand against the small of her back and pushed her down. Her breasts plumped against the decades-old metal in a totally erotic display that would be forever engrained in my mind. Her supple ass pushed up in the air, her puckered hole inches from my mouth.

My tongue ran over my teeth with the raw urge to sink inside and tongue-fuck her asshole.

Had any man ever done that to her? Probably. I couldn't remember her sharing the experience and didn't want to.

My need to command her grew with the thought.

"Having fun yet, Jack?" Carinna tossed over her shoulder.

Her voice was still light, airy. And that just pissed me off. This was no game. This was a voyage into uncharted terrain for her. A place where she came to terms with the depths of her feelings for me and shouted them aloud.

"Don't say another word unless I tell you to speak."

As I knew she would, she said another word. "Just remember what comes around goes around, Dempsey."

I gave in to a hard laugh. She was out of her mind if she thought I'd take the words as a threat. I'd play the submissive for her any day. Just not today. Today I was the dominant one. And I'd never felt more like I fit the part.

"I warned you, Carinna," I allowed, and then slid my hand over her bare bottom, which only made her push it out farther.

She wiggled her rear end, just daring me to give her more. I gave that more gladly, pulling my hand back and letting it fall hard across her buttocks. Her startled gasp echoed through the garage, along with the sharp sound of my hand spanking her soft flesh a second time. Then a third.

My cock throbbed a little more with each whack. My blood warmed as red flared across her backside to rival the red of the flames licking beneath her prone body.

Her ass had to sting, but Carinna didn't say a word because, as I'd instinctively known, she basked in the sinfully carnal sensation rioting through her with each slap.

I struck her ass four more times, the fourth whack finally

earning a small throaty gasp. It was enough to egg me on. "Put your hands behind your back and spread your legs wide."

Her breath came faster with the order, heavier. Still, she didn't say a word, just moved her hands behind her back and bridged her fingers together like a good little submissive. And that was so unlike the Carinna I usually knew, I almost ruined the whole thing by giving in to amused laughter.

I didn't laugh, but took her wrists and locked the cuffs around them, making her as vulnerable as I hoped she'd ever been to a man. Squatting behind her, I ran my fingers up her legs slowly, from ankles to inner thighs, barely skimming the outer edges of her pussy lips before retracing the path back downward. I made the journey again and again, only relenting when her juices streaked down her legs and she quivered with her need.

Still, I didn't give in to her want and the mad thrashing of my own heart. Just stopped the torture of my fingertips, so my hands were free to grip her thighs and push her legs wider.

I crawled between her legs and blew upon her wet, parted folds. Her clit trembled and a squeak broke from her lips to do a number on my overly hardened body. I went with the raw need gripping me to the core, let it dominate my voice. "Your pussy is so sexy this way. Spread wide open and dripping cream down your thighs. I'd like to keep you this way the rest of the night. Would that bother you? If I kept stroking your legs and thighs, kept blowing on your hot pussy? You may speak, Carinna."

"Fuck you, yes!" she bit out.

I tsked. "Not a very nice way to talk to your master. And here I was about to be kind and give you my cock. Don't worry, I'll still give you my cock, just not in your aching pussy." Grabbing her by the manacled wrists, I pulled her off the coupe's hood and pushed her to the garage floor, careful to see she landed on her knees on the slide of carpet I'd used while working under the car and not on the hard cement.

"You're an asshole, Jack," she vented. "I never knew that about you."

I laughed again, deep and dark and wickedly. "I find it hard to buy you believe that when your voice is so thick with lust I can barely understand you." I rounded to her front, enjoying the way her shackled arms thrust her breasts right up into my face. I wanted to go down on my knees and lick first one generous globe and then the other. Instead I stood my ground and forced a hard edge into my voice. "Shut up, Carinna, and put your mouth to good use."

Fisting the back of her hair, I guided her lips to my jutting, pulsing cock. She kept her full pink lips sealed for an instant and then devoured my shaft nearly to the hilt. I closed my eyes with the intensity of her warm, moist mouth surrounding me. Her lips closed tightly around my cock then, her tongue stroking with a divine technique that showed just how many men she'd blown through the years.

The reality she'd been with so many others should have been enough to quell the tension gathering too fast at the base of my spine and the heat building in my groin, but apparently not even that was enough to thwart Carinna's stunning mouth performance.

My hips thrust toward her lips of their volition. My heart beat madly. I curled my fingers tighter in her long, thick curls. It was damned tempting to let her finish the job, to fill up her lovely mouth and throat with my seed, but that wasn't the point of our being in this garage.

I used my hold on her hair to tug her mouth free of my cock. "Enough!"

Passion and trust glazed her smoky eyes as they met mine. Earning her unconditional trust was one half of the reason she was in the position she was in, but not the whole reason. I had to see the rest of that reason through, so I pushed her head back down again, unable to meet her eyes without driving into her pussy immediately. "Don't look at me unless I tell you to."

This time she gave in to my order without comment. I rewarded her gladly. Moving back behind her, I placed a hand at her belly to brace her, and bent her forward, so that her ass was raised high in the air and her face hovering centimeters from the carpet slide.

I brought my fingers back to her ankles, started the slow, sensual upward journey once more. This time when I reached her junction, I didn't move back down to her ankles. This time I bent my head, gripped one thigh and demanded, "Fuck my tongue, Carinna! I want to feel your tight asshole contracting around it. I want you to love it as much as you love feeling my tongue eating at your pussy."

As much as you love me.

Before I could give voice to the dangerous thought, I licked up and around her puckered hole and then shoved my tongue just inside. Her asshole opened and closed around me, waiting, wanting. She whimpered as if to ask for more. I pushed my tongue farther inside. She reared back without hesitation, gliding the length of my tongue, slowly at first and then faster and faster as her lubrication grew. Like everything else I'd done so far, tonguing her asshole was clearly a major turn-on for Carinna. Her breathing came in fits and starts and her abdominal muscles tensed beneath my hand, a foreshadowing of her impending orgasm.

Too bad for her it wasn't time to come. Not just yet.

I pulled my tongue from her ass and sank it into her pussy, licking at her rich cream with slow strokes meant to keep her on the edge. Strokes that had me on the edge, as well.

Realizing how likely it was I would come before she either gave in and begged for relief or let her emotions free, I layered my words with conceit. "I love the taste of your pussy so much, I could go on eating you for days. And you'd let me, Carinna, because I'm a master with my tongue."

She heaved out a huge sigh. "What you are is an arrogant bastard and if you don't stick your cock in me soon, I promise I'll never forgive you. Fuck me already, Jack. Please!"

I stilled my licking with a massive sigh of my own. Thank God. Finally words. Finally begging.

Grabbing her around the waist, I lifted her off the carpet, hauled her back over to the coupe and reclined her once more on the hood, sunny-side up.

"You wouldn't want me any other way," I vowed and finally gave her what she'd been wanting for so long now.

What we'd both been wanting for too damned long, I knew with the first push of my cock inside her dripping sex. All it took was that one shove to have her pussy muscles clamping down around me. To have her crying out, "Holy Jesus, Jack! I *love* it when you're a bastard. *Love* it!"

And all it took was hearing her confession to have orgasm

seizing me hard, making me come in the throes of carnal sensation so acute my vision swam and I nearly gave in to my own words of love. Only not just about her attitude, but the whole entire packaged deal.

♣ ♠ ♥ ◆ ♣ ♠ ♥ ◆ ♣ ♠ ♥ ◆

Chapter Five

Jack

Carinna hadn't confessed to loving me as I'd hoped by pushing her to the edge last night, but she had used the *L* word several times. For that reason, I wasn't surprised when she rolled from my arms to the side of the bed and started soundlessly across my room.

I rose up on an elbow, enjoying the erotic sway of her ass and the memory of the appealing red left behind from my spankings, before asking, "Sneaking out?"

She stiffened on a gasp. Then went soft again to toss over her shoulder, "Going to the bathroom."

Maybe she had been. Maybe she hadn't. Unfortunately I didn't have time to lie around and find out. The tournament play started early today and, since my and Carinna's future was riding on it, I wasn't about to show up late.

I was pulling on my pants when she came out of the bathroom, wearing the T-shirt I'd had on last night. I'd never seen Carinna in my clothes. It was endearing in a way that had me wanting to shout my love for her even more than I had wanted to do so last night, after granting us both the right to come.

Thank God for the stricken look on her face or I would have probably done so and ruined any chance I had with her.

She frowned as I pulled on a shirt. "What are you doing?"

"Getting dressed. I have to be somewhere by nine, and it's already half past eight."

"Oh. I should check in on my grandma, anyway. Make sure we're still on for bingo tomorrow."

From her deflated tone, she really had been on her way to take a leak when I'd woken up. Probably had planned to crawl back into bed and make good on last night's threat, by turning those handcuffs and God only knew what else on me.

Damn, how I wanted to let that happen. Tomorrow, if I was lucky. And many, many days after that, if I was even luckier.

I went to my dresser and pulled out a pair of socks. "I'm planning on taking the guys lunch at the firehouse today. Just pizza, but there'll be plenty to go around. You should stop by. I know they'd love to see you." I crossed to the bed and sat on the end of it. "Vernelli keeps asking when I'm going to bring the hot chick with the big tits back around," I added jokingly.

"He's cute. Any idea what kind of hose he's packing?"

I was thankful to be looking down, tugging on a sock. If I hadn't been, Carinna would have seen the rage on my face.

Had my attempts at surfacing her emotions last night been completely lost on her? Or how the fuck could she still be thinking about screwing some other guy, and seconds after she'd been thinking about screwing me, no less?

"I don't make it a point to check out other men's *hoses*," I said as calmly as possible. "Besides, he's half your age."

She snorted out a laugh and whacked me on the shoulder. "Thanks for the compliment, dickhead. Always nice to know when my tits and ass have sagged so much I could pass for a fifty-year-old."

I shouldn't have touched her when I was about to head out the door, but the idea she might be serious about wanting Vernelli had me anxious to stake a claim. This time, one that went beyond the emotional. One that was right there out in the open for all to see and recognize Carinna as mine.

I slid my hands up her sides as I stood, dragging the T-shirt along for the ride, until her breasts were bared and her pussy peeking out from its curly brown hiding place.

The age crack was pure irony. Her ass and breasts were both as tight as could be and her skin flawless. That latter made me feel a little guilty over what I was about to do. Assuring myself the mark wouldn't be permanent, I pushed aside her hair to expose her neck to my mouth. I brushed my mustache across her skin until I heard her laugh, and then I sucked her skin into my mouth and applied enough pressure to bruise.

I stuck my finger in her mouth with her sharp inhale, moments later replacing it with my tongue. Morning breath didn't appear to be an ailment that plagued Carinna. She tasted as hot and heavenly as ever.

By the time I was done kissing her, my hands had found their way to her breasts, pinching and fondling the nipples, and my cock was so hard I could only hope it would be flaccid by the time I reached the tournament casino.

"So, what do you say?" I asked, wondering if I should rescind my offer, knowing Vernelli would be at the station.

The hickey already surfacing on her neck eased my tension enough to continue. "Lunch at eleven-thirty?"

She looked uncertain for just a moment, but then gave me an amused smile. "Better make it twelve. I'm gonna need at least an extra half hour to fix this aging disaster of a body."

Carinna

I'd considered covering the hickey on my neck—silk scarves were fashionable enough these days. In the end, I'd chosen not to cover it, since I didn't want Jack to think it bothered me.

It did bother me because I knew he'd done it on purpose. It concerned me a hell of a lot more to think what he'd been after last night, with his little dominance show, was more than my admission over how much I loved it when he acted like a bastard. Despite his referring to me as a piece of ass, his behavior resurfaced my concern he had feelings for me that went beyond friendship and, by pushing me to the emotional edge, he'd hoped I would own up to feeling the same way about him.

My concern—both over how he felt about me and that for a while there last night I'd considered once again that there was a very real chance I *could* feel the same for him—was great enough to have me tossing the cabbie a twenty and jumping out of the taxi the moment it reached the firehouse to run inside in search of Vernelli.

Landen Vernelli *was* younger than me, but only by two years. While he was good-looking in a cute blond sort of way, he was no Jack. But then, no man would be Jack but Jack himself. I had to accept that and move on.

Vernelli was the perfect guy to move on with. Jack couldn't

possibly hang on to romantic feelings for me when he heard about my sexual exploits with another guy on a regular basis. And Vernelli would talk—of that I had no doubt.

My heart squeezed painfully when I spotted Vernelli alone in the apparatus bay just off from the truck garage. It was a pain I could easily guess was guilt.

Fuck, I hated hurting Jack. But it just wasn't avoidable.

Having planned this before I left my apartment, I'd worn my Liege uniform. If Jack asked, I planned to use the excuse I had to work at two and figured that lunch might last till then. The reality was the uniform made me look and feel like a piece of meat and I was counting on Vernelli not being able to resist so much temptation.

I took a few seconds to plump up my breasts so they risked the confines of the tank top even more than usual—the miniskirt was already as sinfully short as it could go—then I sashayed my way toward Vernelli, a naughty smile in place.

He spun around fast when I slapped his ass through his tan canvas shorts. His blue eyes warmed with sensual invitation and a grin slid into place as he gave my barely clothed body a lingering once-over that didn't do a damned thing for me.

His eyes met mine. "Hey, beautiful. Where've you been all my life?"

Accepting my hormones would kick in when the time was right, or at least once Vernelli was pumping away inside me, I flattened my hands on his chest and practically purred, "Waiting for you to come along and sweep me off my feet."

"I'm here."

I wet my lips tauntingly. "Then start sweeping."

"You got it."

With more finesse than I would've thought he possessed, he bent and lifted me into his arms. For a moment, I considered he might think this was all a joke. Then I noted the very real hard-on pressing against my hip.

"Where to? My bunk, or do you wanna see what it's like to go crazy on the top of a fire truck?"

"Definitely the truck." I'd never screwed that high up in the air. Once we got started, the possibility—slim though it was—of getting a little too wild and rolling off the truck would have to appeal to my kink factor and get my pussy wet.

With an eager grin, Vernelli exited the apparatus bay and started for the trucks.

"Put her down!"

Jack's growl echoed through the firehouse so loudly, I jumped in Vernelli's arms.

Vernelli didn't seem as fazed. He kept walking, tossing over his shoulder as he went, "She seems to like it where she's at just fine."

Jack appeared past Vernelli's shoulder in an instant, his forehead creased with small lines and his face red with fury. He grabbed hold of the sleeve of Vernelli's T-shirt, whipping him around so fast I let out a screech and clung to his neck for dear life.

Jack fixed him with the death glare he'd perfected as a twelve-year-old, thanks to my help. In hindsight, that probably wasn't something to be so proud of. "I said, put her the fuck down!"

Vernelli looked to me for answers. As much as I thought this had been the right approach to convincing Jack I didn't want a place in his heart beyond friendship, seeing the very real threat in his eyes, I started to second-guess myself.

I nodded at Vernelli. "Better put me down."

He set me down. Spreading his hands out in front of him, he eyed Jack regretfully. "Sorry, man, I didn't realize you had a claim on her."

Where I didn't want Vernelli getting his ass kicked, I didn't have any qualms about personally taking on Jack. "He doesn't. We're friends." I moved into Jack's personal space, got right up into his face the way I knew he hated, unless it was for sexual reasons. "Got that, Jack? Just *friends*."

Nostrils flaring, Jack sent Vernelli another hard glare. He looked back at me, his blue-green eyes iced over, and then stalked across the garage to the end of the row of fire trucks.

I should have left him alone to work out whatever the hell it was in his head that said he had a right to try to put a claim on me. Only, I couldn't. Because up until last night, when he'd temporarily made me believe he didn't have intimate feelings for me, I'd seen this coming all along. If there was a chance of our friendship continuing after this, I had to set things straight immediately.

I followed Jack's path to the last fire truck in the row. He leaned back against its side, cursing a blue streak in between hauling in deep breaths.

I cocked out my hip and landed into him. "What the fuck is your deal?"

He glared at me, speaking none too gently. "I don't like seeing you get taken advantage of."

"That's what you said two days ago. I thought you were full of shit that time, too. News flash, Jack. Vernelli's not half my age and he wasn't taking advantage of me. I *wanted* to fuck him."

He smirked and pushed away from the fire truck, took a menacing step toward me. "Now, who's full of shit? You want to fuck *me*. Not Vernelli. Not Ryan. Not any other goddamned man or a set of men. *Only* me."

I gasped at his arrogance. I liked my men cocky but, Christ, he was seriously pushing it. "I don't want to fuck *only* you, you arrogant bastard. If I wanted to be with just one man, I'd be engaged to Hank."

He laughed uproariously. "Liar. Even if you weren't scared shitless of relationships, you would never have agreed to marry Hank. He was wrong for you in every way possible."

And what? Jack was right for me in every way possible?

Even if I wanted to ask the question, which I didn't, I wouldn't have had a chance to get it out. He covered the few feet between us in an instant, then spun me around and pushed me face forward toward the fire truck.

As it had when he'd pushed me against the car hood last night, the breath whooshed out of me. Only this time I had farther to go and the landing was that much harder because of it. My hands hit first, bracing for impact, so I didn't do a complete face-plant. Then I made the mistake of taking the time to steady myself. It was all the time Jack needed to get his hands back on me and show me exactly how kind he'd been in his handling of me last night.

One hand coiled around my forearm, fingers biting into my flesh, while the other moved beneath my skirt. The warmth of his fingers brushed my rear end, and then he was yanking aside my panties, exposing my ass to the kiss of the air.

My eyes widened with the hiss of his zipper. Fear and— Christ, there was obviously something wrong with my head— uncontainable excitement coiled in my belly as the plump head of his hard cock pushed against my crack. He jammed two fingers inside my pussy, which had been ridiculously and shamelessly wet from the moment I'd witnessed his possessive rage. He fingered me just long enough to get his fingers coated in my juices and then shoved them in my asshole. I sighed with the forceful entry. Sighed louder as he started pumping.

Once.

Twice.

He pulled free and shoved inside again. Only this time not with his fingers. His cock filled me in a violent thrust.

Tears spilled from my eyes as pleasure pain so exquisite I could barely breathe rippled through my body. I curled my fingers tight, gripping on to the truck's side rails as he pounded into my ass like some feral beast.

"Jesus Christ, Jack!" It was all I could say. It was all too much. Too forceful. Too raw. Too damned good.

Past the rage of a blossoming orgasm that promised to be one of the best of my life, I became conscious of voices. Men talking. Men laughing. Every guy in the firehouse was probably watching Jack take me in the ass.

Like the dirty girl I was, I'd never been more excited in my life. Or shouted so loudly, as my pussy contracted with spasms and I came in time with Jack's cum spilling into my ass.

He pulled out of me seconds later, spinning me instantly in his arms. Regret over his behavior filled his eyes and I had no doubt the same would come out of his mouth if I gave him the opportunity. I wasn't about to do that. I didn't want apologies from Jack. The naughty part of me wanted a repeat of the violent coupling. Fortunately, the girl that knew when to walk was back to calling the shots.

I pushed my palms against Jack's chest and sent him stumbling backward a few steps. Without another look his way, I started for the front door, settling my drenched panties back into place and managing to strum my still aroused clit in the process. I wasn't quite able to stop the moan that slipped from between my lips, so I simply went with it.

I gave the dozen or so guys—thankfully Ryan wasn't among them, though I knew he'd hear all about it soon enough, along with every other person on the crew not present—who stood ogling and more than likely sporting some major wood, my dirtiest smile. "So, what do you say, boys? Was it as good for you as it was for me?"

Leaving them to stare and grin and give childishly inane wolf whistles, I walked through the firehouse door in search of the nearest cab and then a bottle or two of Bombay Sapphire, hold the vermouth.

Jack

As days from hell went, this one topped the charts.

I'd thought my possessive explosion over Carinna and subsequently taking her in the ass in front of the bulk of my coworkers had been bad enough. But that had been only the beginning. Shortly after arriving home from the tournament play that night, I'd gotten an emergency backup call.

I watched in abject horror as the members of the Ladder 19 crew still inside the blazing chemical plant raced out as it exploded for what had to be the eighth time since we'd made the bad call of going inside. A sick sense of foreboding had been with me since the first explosion, when I, along with several other members of the crew, had been lucky enough to get out. That foreboding threatened to overtake me as I counted heads through the billow of wind-caught black smoke turning the early-evening sky dark as night.

I came up one short and my stomach went queasy.

Ryan.

No, I couldn't make that assumption. Dressed in the heavy, yellow protective fire gear the way they were, it was nearly impossible to distinguish one person from the next.

I yanked off my helmet and face mask. Others followed suit. Ryan's face came into view and, though I hadn't realized I'd held it, my breath came whizzing out.

It sucked back in on a painful note when I realized who was missing. "Where the fuck's Axe?"

A few guys shook their heads, their faces revealing a mix of loathing and unshed tears, but no one offered words.

Finally, Ryan approached, sorrow filling his eyes. He laid a hand on my arm, speaking quietly. "He didn't make it out, Jack. The roof gave away when he was on the middle of it."

Bile rose up in the back of my throat. I gulped it down and drew in a hard breath.

Didn't. Make. It. Out.

They were the words every firefighter feared and the ones no one would voice. Until the time came when you had no other choice. Even now, only Ryan had been able to get them out.

I shook my head, not wanting to accept that possibility,

refusing to believe it. The undeniable grief in my brother's eyes told me it was a stark reality.

My throat burned in a way smoke inhalation could never replicate.

Jesus, Axe. Tony Lorent to his family.

His family.

He had a wife. Kids. He was fucking thirty-two years old.

My tears came fast and hard. I swiped at them with the back of my hand, wiping soot into my eyes that had them stinging like a bitch.

"Goddammit!"

I loved these guys, they were my family, but that didn't change the facts. I had to get the hell out of this job. My father had been a fireman, as had his father and so on. My father had been killed in the line of duty when I was four and Ryan one. I wouldn't let that happen to my kids. And I would have kids. With Carinna.

Maybe I hadn't been successful in surfacing her emotions last night, but what happened at the firehouse today, how she'd been able to find pleasure in a moment that should have been humiliating for her, proved how thoroughly we were involved. It proved, despite everything she did and said, she loved me.

One more day in the poker tournament and I could put this life behind me. Unlike every other facet of the day, my luck in the tournament had been better, brought me back up to fifth place. All it would take was a few good hands to come out the winner, or at least close to it. I would get those hands and get the fuck off of a fire truck.

Right now I had to get to Carinna. Had to lose myself in

her kiss, feel the welcoming warmth of her sweet body. And she would welcome me inside, of that I held no doubt.

Because she was mine. Even if she wasn't ready to admit it.

Carinna

With the jiggle of a key in my apartment door lock, I looked up from the couch, where I sat watching a Bermuda Triangle special on the Discovery Channel. Jack stormed in seconds later. The acrid smell of smoke clung to him and his face and clothes were dusted with soot. Some women might have been turned off by his appearance. I was hotter than the blaze he'd clearly just put out.

I'd forgone the gin and gone to work at two as scheduled. I'd spent the afternoon being bitchy to my customers and pissed at Jack, nearly as pissed at myself. I'd planned to ream his ass the next time I saw him. Catching the glint of raw need in his eyes, I knew I wouldn't do it. Couldn't do it.

When he opened his arms to me and silently begged with his eyes, all I could do was stand from the couch and go to him. Yelling, accusations, my need to move on—they could all wait. Right now it was clearly physical warmth he needed.

I pushed my hands beneath his dirty white undershirt and attacked his mouth with my kiss. He buried his hands in my hair and kissed me back with a hunger I felt from the rock-hard points of my nipples all the way to my toes.

Even as my pussy swelled with moisture, my heart squeezed tight for whatever demons filled Jack's head. It made me want to speak words I had no right saying. The kind of affection-laced words I knew would give him hope.

He'd spent years making me believe he was on the same page relationship-wise as I was. In the end, he'd turned out to be just as big of a liar as Hank. The difference was Hank had never been my best friend. And with Hank it had never been anything more than fucking.

With Jack, no matter how rough or wild or kinky it got, it was lovemaking. I tried to deny that truth, but I couldn't do it any longer. At least, not to myself.

Before we could become victims of our emotions and say words one or both of us would regret, I pulled free of the kiss and went down on my knees. I made quick work of freeing his shaft. Then I took his cock between my lips and savored his salty male hardness with my tongue, in a way he hadn't allowed me to do last night.

His fingers had eased from my hair as I moved. With the stroke of my mouth around the velvety flesh of his rigid staff, they returned, holding on so firmly to my unruly brown curls, it was as if the caress of my mouth was his life source.

Using my hands on his balls, cupping and massaging their heavy weight, I licked the underside of his cock, trailing the swollen blue vein that ran the length of it.

Jack moaned and his fingers curled tighter in my hair. "Yes. I need this."

His words were soulful, as if he felt he owed me an explanation for giving in to my silent offer. I knew why he would feel that way and it went beyond what had happened at the firehouse today. It was because I was a greedy bitch about my orgasms. I'd always thought that okay. Why shouldn't I expect to come a couple times as advance payment for all my hard work getting a guy off?

Only it had never felt like work bringing Jack to climax. And, right now, I didn't care about coming myself. I didn't care about anything but making him feel good and, in doing so, chasing away the demons that haunted him.

I pulled my mouth free of his cock to look at his face. His eyes were as soulful as his voice, revealing—what before I could only guess at—his love for me so keenly it stilled the breath in my throat. My heart went from squeezing to a chaotic beat of desire for things that went well beyond the flesh and the pleasures to be found in it.

I pushed my storming emotions aside and gave him a re-assuring smile. "I want to give you this, Jack. And I don't expect anything in return."

The gratitude in his eyes said more than words could. Before my own eyes gave me away, I returned to my goal of making him feel good.

Sucking the meaty pink head of his cock between my lips, I circled his length with my tongue while I continued to play with his balls, alternately gripping the sensitive sacs and teasing them with little taps. His shaft pulsed in my mouth. His groin pistoned against my face. The deliciously masculine scent of his arousal lifted on the air, filling my senses and making my inner thighs tingle with sensual ache.

I increased the pace of my mouth, loving him quickly, with firm, solid strokes. Stopping when I could feel his sex quivering beneath my tongue, telling me he was on the verge of climax.

Because I knew this had to be our last time together, I wanted to give him the orgasm of his life, push his control to the brink again and again before it finally wore thin. I did so with little licks of the pre-cum oozing from the tip of his cock. Teasing touches of the sensitized skin and the black hair that surrounded his proud member. By drawing his balls into my mouth one at a time and loving them with my tongue and the gentle scrape of my teeth.

Jack's full-bodied groan and the shaking of his thighs told me when he'd reached the limits of his control. Eagerly, I returned my mouth to his succulent cock, slid my lips down his length and fucked him in earnest.

His hips joined the lightning-fast pace, his shaft thrusting between my lips with exquisite pressure that had the head of his cock tickling the back of my throat and my panties growing unbearably wet despite this moment not being about my pleasure.

He lost control on the fifth thrust. I nearly came as his cream filled my mouth with the hot, salty, delectable taste of Jack.

Gripping my hair with tightly clenched fists, he cried out my name, something I'd always thought of as cliché, but with Jack I loved hearing my name in his deep, rough voice.

I loved.

There were those forbidden words again.

I tried my damnedest to forget them as he slipped his cock from my mouth and sank to his knees on the carpet in front of me. He pulled me into his arms and buried his face in the crook of my neck.

I forgot about my fear of those nasty, niggling words to concentrate on Jack. His emotions had been all over the map today. I'd never seen him as angry as he'd been at firehouse and I'd never seen him act as needy as he was acting now. His cocky side appealed to my inner dirty girl, but this needy side spoke to an even bigger part. He was giving me a trust I hadn't realized he'd previously held back. My face burned with the want to accept that trust, along with everything else he had to offer.

"I love you, Carinna."

Everything but *that*.

My stomach pitched. "Jesus, Jack." I'd guessed how he felt. Still, hearing it aloud made it feel like he'd poured a gallon of liquid smoke down my throat.

I pulled from his arms as gently as possible, which wasn't all that gentle, given I wanted to hail a cab to some little Podunk town he wasn't liable to ever find me in.

I came to my feet and, clinging to survival instincts, jutted my hip out. "You don't love me. You're just strung out on emotions. What happened tonight? I thought you weren't working this week."

Jack stood. He focused on righting his clothes; still, I could hear the catch in his breath. He looked at me, eyes that were soulful a moment ago now filled with unshed tears. "I wasn't supposed to be, but an emergency backup call came in." His tone softened. "There was a chemical explosion. Tony fell through a four-story roof. The crew couldn't get to him. He's dead."

I blinked with the force of the words. My heart gave a painful squeeze. Not over the loss of Tony—although I felt terrible about that—but the idea it could have been Jack who'd been killed.

I couldn't risk giving in to the bitter ache the thought triggered, or pulling Jack into my arms to comfort him. If I did, the odds were slim I'd be able to release him without confessing my belly-cramping concern that I just might have fallen for him, too. "I'm so sorry. That's awful, horrid. I know he was a good friend of yours."

"I'm through with fighting fires, Carinna."

Thank God. But no, not thank God. It was selfishness that made me think that way, fear of losing him forever. "That's crazy talk, Jack. Firefighting has been in your family for five generations. You love it. It's your emotions making you think otherwise."

The sheen of tears left his eyes. "Damn it, it isn't my emotions!" he barked out, then gentled his voice. "I've wanted to quit for a long time. It's a good job, an honorable one, but it's not where my future's at. You know how long I've wanted to open a restoration garage. All I needed was the money to make it happen. I'm one day away from having that money."

"How?"

A small smile curved his lips. "Poker. I'm in a tournament at the Rio with some of the best in the industry. Tomorrow's the last day and there's a good chance I'll win."

I should have been happy to know he wouldn't be risking his life anymore, yet still doing a job he loved. And truthfully I was, but I was also jealous as hell to think he would be living his dream while I'd probably spend the rest of my life having my ass grabbed at the Taboo Tequila Bar while I saved for mine.

I forced a smile. "That's killer, Jack. You're going to realize your dream."

The subtle twitching of his lips told me he hadn't bought my bogus smile. He stepped toward me, lifting his hand to my face and caressing my cheek before I could stop him.

"That garage isn't my only dream, Carinna. Not even close to my biggest one."

My heart missed a beat, only to start back up as a wild tattoo. "Don't say it."

"I love you. And I want to marry—"

He'd fucking said it!

I covered my ears and jerked from his touch, uttering a na-na-na chant to make any seven-year-old proud.

Jack had come here in his moment of need, much the way I'd relied on him after my father's death. I wanted to be his comforting shoulder, as he'd been mine. But I couldn't do it at the cost of what he was asking. I couldn't even allow him to finish his proposal, for fear I'd listen to my heart and respond in the affirmative.

"Get out!" I screeched. His crumpled look wouldn't allow me to stick with the harpy tone. I uncovered my ears and softened my voice. "I'm sorry, Jack. I know you're a great catch, but I don't want to be the one who catches you. I don't do relationships and not even you can change that. Just go. Please."

I thought he would try to change my mind—he'd never been one to give up easily—but Tony's death had obviously taken all the fight out of him. He didn't say another word, just turned and walked out my door.

Chapter Six

Jack

I'd spent the past three days trying to talk myself into believing Carinna and I were better off as friends. It was what she wanted and if I loved her as much as I said I did, I should want to make her happy. The only problem was I didn't believe deep down that being my friend alone was what she wanted. Deep down, she wanted the same happily-ever-after I craved.

The kind of happily-ever-after Tony Lorent and his family never got the chance to realize.

Fresh emotions threatened as my gaze automatically moved to the closed casket at the front of the viewing room. Closed casket because there was nothing left to Tony but ashes. Sarah, Tony's wife, had refused to use an urn. When they were older the kids would understand the horror of their father's final moments, but for now she wanted to make it as easy on them as possible.

Which wasn't goddamned easy at all.

Nothing in life was easy. Every dream worth chasing came with the potential for failure. For hurt. For pain that would never be forgotten. But in the end that pain was worth enduring for all the good times that came before it.

Sarah Lorent knew it, and soon Carinna would know it. I was through playing games, doing everything I could think of to get her to realize her feelings for me and admit them aloud. The next time I saw her, she would admit that we belonged together. She would eagerly confess her love for me.

First, I had to break the news of my retiring from Ladder 19 to Ryan.

I caught up with my brother a few minutes later, sharing memories of the pranks Tony used to pull around the firehouse. Vernelli was among the group. As I'd done all week, I mostly ignored him while I listened to a couple stories, needing to laugh almost more than I needed my next breath.

I nodded at Ryan then. "We need to talk."

He frowned. "Now? In the middle of the viewing?"

I would be the first to admit the timing wasn't the best, but I couldn't put this off a second longer. "Now."

Ryan exchanged a few more words with the guys, then walked with me to a vacated room on the other side of the funeral parlor.

He sat down in a folding chair that headed up a long row of them. He took his time getting comfortable, before asking, "What's so important it can't wait a few hours?"

"I'm quitting the ladder."

I'd expected shock, maybe denial that I was serious, rather acting on emotions the way Carinna had surmised. Instead, he nodded soberly. "I saw this coming. Hell, I'm surprised you lasted as many years as you did."

"You aren't upset?" I honestly hadn't known what to

expect of Ryan. A side effect of reaching his mid-twenties, I guess, but lately his mind seemed to be running outside the narrow-minded circles it used to follow.

"Why would I be?"

"It's the family business."

Smirking, he nodded. "Right, and every firstborn son for the past five generations has gone into it. You did your time. Now, it's time to do what you really want." His smirk became a lopsided smile. "Or should I say who?"

"You honestly think I stand a chance with Carinna in the long run?"

"She'd be a fool not to want you. Really, how many guys do you know who'd play to her dirty-girl side by doing her in front of a crowd of horn-dog firefighters?"

It was the last thing we should be talking about here and now, and I laughed so hard my gut hurt. I gave my brother a noogie—a holdover from our childhood days. He groaned and swatted at me now, just as he'd done back then.

I smiled. "You turned out okay, considering what a cocky little prick you were in your teens."

"Little hint, bro. Cockiness is just another of those family biz deals. The difference is, unlike firefighting, you can't leave it behind."

Carinna

He loved me. He wanted to marry me.

What the fuck was wrong with men today?

All I wanted was to give them a piece of ass and all they wanted was to put a ring on my finger and a bun in my oven.

And then what would become of that bun when either Jack or I decided to bail on the relationship?

Jack wouldn't bail. Not knowing what he'd gone through, growing up a kid without a father and feeling endlessly responsible for his younger brother. And I couldn't bail. I'd known spending those four months without Jack had been hard, but I hadn't realized how hard until he'd returned to my life.

I loved him. I loved him so much it sucked—and went well beyond friendship.

It wouldn't even take anything illegal or narcotic to get me down the aisle with him. And that's exactly why I couldn't go. Neither of us would bail and so in the end we'd spend decades together in misery.

All relationships eventually led to misery. It was what brought cheating spouses to Sin City every year. It was the reason my mother had walked out on my father and me, and left us both hurting in a way neither time nor another's love could fix.

No, I couldn't marry Jack. I loved him too much to hurt him that way.

Only that couldn't be true. If I really cared so much, I would have been there for him this past week. I would have accompanied him to Tony's showing and funeral, held him close when he'd shed tears over the loss of his friend and colleague. But I hadn't been there for him. Hadn't even called to share my sympathies.

Jesus, when had I become such a coldhearted bitch?

I spent the next minutes pondering the question, or maybe it was hours I sat balled up on the couch, I honestly didn't know. The doorbell pulled me from my haze and had me walking by rote to the door.

Jack had left my apartment over a week ago. With each day, I feared I would never see him again a little more, both because he didn't think I wanted him in my life and because I was too much of a chickenshit to go to him and say otherwise. But my peephole revealed he stood outside the door, looking more delicious than ever.

That he was ringing the door, instead of using his key, told me how accurate I was in thinking he believed I didn't want him in my life. Damn, how that made my heart hurt.

Jack's neutral expression turned to a frown when I opened the door. Concern filled his eyes. "What's the matter? You're crying."

"I am?" I lifted my hand to my cheek, pulling it back to find my fingers damp. "I didn't realize."

His look said he wasn't buying it. "People normally know when they're crying. There's usually a reason for it."

"I just woke up from a nap," I lied. "Bad dream."

"I don't believe you."

I went on the defensive automatically, opening my mouth to tell him I didn't give a rat's ass what he believed. He used his fingers to gently close my mouth before I could say a word.

"I didn't come here to argue, Carinna. I came here to tell you I didn't win the poker tournament."

I didn't think I could feel any worse. But I was wrong. I felt horrid for my jealousy over the idea of his realizing his dream. "I'm sorry."

He smiled. "Don't be. I came in second. In my case, that's just as good as first."

The jealousy didn't return. Possibly because I was too

struck by his sexy smile and my unbearable need to kiss him until we were both breathless. "That's great, Jack."

"It is." He offered his hand to me. "Take a ride with me."

Sit in his truck, inhaling his scent, feeling his warmth so near, knowing I didn't dare touch him? I shook my head. "Sorry, but I need to get to work."

"Nice try, but it's your day off. I stopped by The Liege first."

Fine, he wanted to play hardball. I could go that route. "I meant to work on cleaning the place up. The girls are coming over for poker tonight."

He glanced around my apartment, which I'd cleaned top to bottom several times over the past days in an attempt to fill my mind with something other than Jack. "It's neater than my house has ever been. Yours, too, for that matter. Take a ride with me, Carinna. Please."

Not the *please*. Anything but that damned *please* and the accompanying pleading look in his eyes. There was no way I could say no. I heaved out a breath. "Fine. I'll go. Just quit making yourself look like a schmuck by begging."

Jack

I shut off my truck across the road from the home Carinna had reasoned would one day fit in her budget and make a charming bed-and-breakfast.

She looked across the center console at me, eyes narrowed. "Why are we here?" She glanced at the two-story bungalow that sat an acre off the road and was surrounded by lush green grass that probably cost a bundle to keep up in the midst of a desert, then back at me. "Christ, you didn't buy it for me. You can't buy my love, Jack. Not even with this place."

The last thing I should be feeling was cocky, and yet I couldn't stop my sardonic laughter. I didn't need to buy something I already had. Carinna's actions told me she loved me as much as I loved her. What I was after here was her trust in the one area I knew no man had ever had it. I wanted her to forget her father's many rants and the faithless assholes she saw every day at the casino and accept that entering into a relationship with me would be the best decision of both of our lives.

"I didn't buy it." The front door of the home opened, emitting a preschool-aged boy followed by a brunette in her late twenties. They ran to the side yard where the woman lifted the boy onto a swing and gave him a push. My heart clenched with the thought of watching Carinna doing the same with our child. "It was already sold."

"Oh. That's a relief."

I almost laughed again, her deflated tone contrasted so sharply with her words. But I loved her too much to laugh over her sorrow or allow her to think her dreams were dead. The bungalow was the place she'd reasoned she could afford, but not the one she'd truly wanted. "I bought you the one you really want across the lake."

Shock must have settled at first because it was a good twenty seconds before Carinna gave me a look that skirted the fine line of wanting to kill me and wanting to kiss me. "Good God, Jack! Why? I just told you that you can't buy my *love*. And since when is that place on the market?"

"Since the previous owner lost his wife. He said it doesn't

feel right living there without her. When I told him I wanted it to share with the woman I love, he was eager to cut a deal."

She cringed a little with my use of the word love. "Even cutting a deal, it had to cost you a bundle."

"I told you I was playing poker with some of the best."

Carinna looked across the lake, to the rambling, three-story Victorian estate house that would make the perfect B and B, and double as the ideal place to raise a family.

I heard her wistful sigh before she jerkily waved a hand toward the place. "Second paid that much?"

"Most of it. I had the rest saved."

"For your garage."

I shrugged. There was a sizeable pole barn on the estate that could easily be converted into a garage. Not the multi-story, glass-walled garage of my dreams, but some dreams were better slightly altered. "There's a place for my garage. Until it's ready to open, I'm sure your B and B can use a handyman."

She whipped her head around to frown at me. "You wouldn't stay on with the firehouse?"

"I told you I don't want that life. I don't want to have to fear the reality I might head out to some fire and not make it back alive. I don't want my wife living with that same fear. It's bad enough just worrying over Ry."

Her eyes misted, but she stayed true to Carinna form and jutted out her chin. "I don't care if you were charbroiled and still smoking, I'd kick your ass if that ever happened."

I chuckled. "I don't doubt it for a second, not even if you had to chase me all the way to hell to do it."

"You're not going to hell, Jack," she said softly. "I might, but never you."

I eyed her soberly, surprised by the words. "What could you have possibly done to justify being sent to hell?"

"I lied to you, about wanting Vernelli and your brother. I didn't want them, Jack. I've never wanted any man the way I want you." She gave in to another sigh before relaxing in her seat and closing her eyes. Several seconds passed before she spoke again, so quietly I had to strain to hear her. "I wish you wouldn't have bought me that place."

"And I wish you'd stop living in fear of failing and give in to what you want. Give us a chance. Your father put ideas in your head. Ideas I know you think are true because of the cheating bastards you encounter at the bar. But those ideas don't apply to us." I reached across the seat and grabbed her hand, settling it on the bulge of my cock through my jeans. I didn't want to turn this moment into just another sex-capade, but I knew the move would be enough to open her eyes, literally if not figuratively. "C'mon, Carinna, if there was ever a time to put all your chips in the pot, it's now."

Another few seconds passed. I held my breath. Her hand moved, petting my cock into instant hardness. She opened her eyes and straightened in her seat. Lust, love and something that looked a whole lot like acceptance turned her eyes the color of smoke. "I wasn't done. I was going to say, I wish you wouldn't have done this because you've made it damned hard to turn you down."

She unhooked her seat belt and crawled across the center console onto my lap. Twin bolts of elation and desire filled me as she feathered her fingers through my hair. "Fuck, you don't play fair." Her eyes misted anew, this time the tears fell, trickling slowly down her cheeks. "No one has ever done anything so selfless for me, Jack. It makes me want to be a total hypocrite and gamble on us."

Carinna slanted her mouth over mine, kissing me long and hard and with an emotion she'd never before allowed. It told me that while she might still fear relationships, she was in for one with me with all her heart.

"Then do it," I said, brushing the tears from her cheeks when she lifted her lips from mine. "Say the magic words. I dare you."

Amusement flashed in her eyes as she reclined back against the steering wheel and tugged my shirt from my jeans. "You know I can't back down from a challenge any more than you can. I'm scared," she surprised me again by admitting, "but I love you and I'm all in."

I sucked in a breath with the damp swipe of her warm tongue across my nipple, even as my heart swelled with euphoria.

Decades of making love with this woman while we lived out our dreams…I didn't know how I'd come upon such an incredible run of luck—to attain all those things I wanted most in one week—but I wasn't about to complain. What I *was* about to do was finally give her the slow, sweet lovemaking she deserved.

"I'll call you." I took advantage of her midriff top and moved my hands beneath to cup her breasts. I twisted an erect nipple through the silk of her bra, grinning with her husky cry for more. "It's a pointless play, though. This is one hand we're both going to win."

★ ★ ★ ★ ★

STRIPPED
Lauren Dane

To Ray—forever and ever and a day more than that.

ACKNOWLEDGMENTS

Special thanks to Laura Bradford because she always believes in me. That means more than I can say. It's kind of mushy and all, but it's pretty cool to have your agent be your friend, as well. I'm fortunate to be able to say so quite honestly.

Susan Swinwood—who has a fabulous sense of style and made me laugh a lot at the *RT* conference. Thank you for buying this story, for your editing suggestions and for dealing with all my pestering with patience.

No list of thanks would be complete without Megan Hart and Anya Bast—both such lovely friends and great sources of advice and information. A more fabulous set of crit partners a girl could not ask for. Dahlia and Nash's story is far better for your critical eye (or rather, eyes). You read so many incarnations of this story and you never complained. Thank you also for petting me when I got low and kicking my butt when I got whiny.

Mom and Dad—who never censored what I read, who cheered every success, who raised me to believe anything I wanted to do was possible if I worked for it. You raised me to love words and to believe in myself. Those things come in pretty handy. I love you both.

My beta readers: Tracy and Renee—you both rock my socks. Thank you for dropping everything to read for me. Your advice and feedback are invaluable, as is your friendship.

My readers, because without you reading my books, well, I'd be writing this note to myself pretending I had a book deal.

There's a scene in *The Matrix* where Trinity is being chased by agents. She's at the bottom of a set of stairs, pointing her weapons, frozen in fear. She says, "Get up, Trinity. Get up," because she knows to be frozen by fear is to never make it to where she needs to be. There have been times when I was there, frozen by fear, and an old friend reminded me of that scene. Thank you, Luahiwa.

Chapter One

The low, sensual beat brought her onto the stage like a siren. One gloved arm wove through the slit in the curtain, parting the fabric as she stood, framing her for a long moment. Her dark hair was piled up on her head artfully. Long, fake lashes framed big brown eyes. A deep blue satin dress hugged every curve lovingly. Her breasts pushed up and out of the scooped neckline and as she walked, the slit on each side of the dress showed glimpses of her legs to the upper thigh.

She let the music grab her senses and her rhythm as she slowly sauntered out onto the narrow stage. Dancer's heels, still very high, led her through the beginning of her routine as she carefully maneuvered the long feather boa to keep from tripping.

Caught in the music, Dahlia's muscles burned as she did a high kick leading into a round kick, swiveling her body away from the audience—all in a seamless set of movements.

A feather from the boa stuck to the sweat on her neck as she slowly rotated her hips in time with the horns in the jazz band. Her hands rose, slowly winding the boa around her body. Down it went until she finally stepped over it, kicking it to the side.

Giving her back to the audience, she raised one hand into the air as she turned her head, winking over her shoulder.

Rocking her hips from side to side to the smoky jazz beat, she brought the tips of her gloved fingers to her mouth to bite the material and pull it off slowly.

The first glove went over her shoulder, into the bar pit the stage encircled. As she stood in front of the trumpet player, she peeled off the second glove, winding it playfully.

With a bump and grind she circled the band and lay down on the side of the stage near where the bottle service tables were. Kicking a foot into the air, she gave the audience a lot of leg to look at as the folds of her dress slid open. Rolling up onto her knees, she unzipped the front of the dress and shimmied out of it. Then she turned, coyly giving them her back and a view of her boy-short bottoms with a winking kitty on the ass.

The dress dropped as her forearms came up to cover her breasts and she bent, looking at them all upside down through the V of her legs.

The cheers and applause bolstered her confidence. Onstage she was beautiful and desired and that was okay. More than okay. It felt marvelous.

Still facing the band she reached out quickly, grabbing the hat off Timmy's head. The trumpet player widened his eyes in a choreographed move and she spun, clutching the prop hat just so to cover herself.

Sensual smoke and mirrors. Dahlia didn't show the audience any more than she'd show at the beach. They wouldn't see her nipples, and her panties would stay right on her booty with the fishnets below that.

Still playing coy, she waved with one hand, pretending to almost drop the hat as she took the first step back up to the dressing room. And another step and two more. Once her body was in the doorway she turned and tossed the hat back to Timmy. With a hand over her mouth stifling a pretend giggle, she kicked up her leg and was gone behind the curtain.

Her robe hung just inside the doorway and she grabbed it, putting it on as she made her way back to her dressing area. She smiled as the music started for Roseanne, the dancer who shared the 10:00 p.m. time slot.

Tapping her foot to the notes of "Viva Las Vegas," Dahlia took off her makeup and got changed. She usually tried to hang out at the club twice a week or so to watch her friends dance and also have a few drinks. She'd met a lot of interesting people and oddly enough, gained a following of sorts.

The Dollhouse was a burlesque lounge. The dancers did not strip totally nude, and Dahlia thought of the show as an elaborate celebration of women's sensuality. The women there always reminded Dahlia of the Elvgren pinup-girl art her grandpa used to have in his garage. Dahlia loved the coy sex kitten she embodied onstage. She often felt as though Dahlia was her other half, the part of her she could release only up there for those minutes she was performing. The half she put away when she turned back into a pumpkin. Or, more precisely, a graduate student.

The club had only been open for six months and already had a hip, young following with lines outside every night. The lounge itself was small and intimate; it didn't hold more than seventy-five people. The interior was subtly sexy with lush fabrics and deep-colored leather. A nice place to hang out and have a drink with her friends, a place she'd never have been able to afford were it not for the fact she worked there.

Emerging from the back of the club and walking into the lounge area, she searched for her friends. Catching sight of them, she also noticed her boss at his usual table. William Emery was a very sexy man. High-powered, charismatic and extraordinarily successful. He'd broken ground on the first retro-style burlesque club in Vegas, and now others copied him. He seemed to constantly be in motion, working twelve- to fifteen-hour days. She admired that, even if he did come off like a cold asshole sometimes.

He certainly liked a wide variety of women. Although she'd give it to him that he seemed to keep a professional wall between himself and his dancers. He flirted, but he didn't prey on them. He paid her well and didn't hit on her and she was down with that. Smiling, she sent him a wave and a wink as she made her way past.

Nash Emery sat with his brother William, the owner of The Dollhouse, and a bevy of beautiful women at one of the VIP tables. He'd been sipping a very fine Scotch when he caught sight of the statuesque dancer who'd just been onstage.

The smoky taste smoldered on his tongue as his heart sped at her saucy, sexy wink. He drank in every detail of her face and body—as much as he could anyway, in the low light of the club. Her black hair was drawn up into a chic, fifties-style ponytail, and bright red lipstick painted her carnal lips.

The captivating sway of her walk and the jiggle of her breasts in that dress mesmerized him. Her legs were miles long and she was all curves and valleys—the kind of woman a man wanted to sink himself into for days without coming up for air.

The kind of woman they didn't make anymore. Coy and smoking hot all at once. Suddenly, he felt a little less jaded and a lot more interested.

He leaned into his brother. "Who is that?"

William's eyes quickly raked over the woman before turning back to Nash. "That's Dahlia. No shit, that's her real name. From some hick town, grad student. She's one of the favorites here. Not too often you see a package like that, even here in Vegas. Hot, isn't she?"

"*Hot* isn't a word that does her justice," Nash murmured as he extricated himself from the knot of people at the table and moved to intercept her.

She hadn't been paying attention and ended up bumping into him, her hand moving to his chest to keep from falling. That small touch sent electric warmth through him.

"Oh, I'm sorry! I didn't see you there." Big brown eyes met his, and damned if his cock didn't jump. Her voice, like smoke and whiskey, low and sexy, stroked over his skin.

The scent of her perfume just beneath the smell of cigarettes, alcohol and sweat in the club tickled his senses. Reaching out, he put his hand at her waist. The abundance of her body and the incredible beauty of her face knocked him out. Damn, he couldn't recall being so excited by and interested in a woman in a very long time.

"No need to apologize, honey. I'm Nash. Why don't you come and join us?"

One perfectly shaped eyebrow rose slowly. Imperiously. She took a step back, out of his grasp. "That's all right. I have friends waiting."

He reached and took her forearm, caught sight of the cherries on her dress, the red fingernails and toenails through the open toes of her very high heels. The woman was a fucking sex bomb, and he wanted to detonate her right then and there.

"Wait. Can I give you a call? I've got a very nice penthouse here on the Strip. What do you say we go there? Drink some champagne while I scrub your back in the bathtub. You can show me what was under the hat. You know, be my private dancer." He laughed, teasing her.

Her lip curled in a sneer as she pulled out of his grip. "Private dancer? Like a whore? Oh, sure. Give me your number and I'll just show up, blow you and be on my merry way. Because that's what all showgirls do, right?"

He put his hands up in defense. "I…uh, I didn't mean to offend you."

Her fisted hands rested on her hips like an angry Amazon. "What the hell else would I be? You don't know me from Adam and you're propositioning me thirty seconds after you bump into me? Didn't your mother raise you with any manners?"

Holy shit, was this going badly. He'd really fucked this one up. It'd been a long damned time since a woman had turned him down, about as long as it'd been since he'd misjudged one so severely.

"You're right. I apologize. It was rude of me. In my defense, you're so beautiful I sort of lost my mind. I do hope you won't hold my terrible behavior against me in the future." He bowed. "Can we start over? I'm Nash Emery and I really was raised with manners, I swear to you."

"You're going to have to do better than that. That was the fakest apology I've heard since, well, since the last rich asshole hit on me."

Nash might have been offended but he couldn't help but like her fire. And he *had* been an asshole. Cocky was a fallback position for him. Women usually dug it. Not this one. A smile crept back onto his face.

"You're a hard woman. I'm sorry. I was a jerk. But I meant it when I said you were beautiful. And you do knock me out. Can we start over?"

He held out a hand. Cocking her head and hesitating a moment, she took it. "Emery, huh? I suppose you're the playboy brother I've heard all about. Although frankly, I'd expect some more original lines from someone with your reputation. 'Private dancer,' gee, I've never heard that one before. I'm Dahlia Baker and I am not a round-heeled tart. I'm getting my MBA at UNLV."

He laughed, chagrined. Okay, okay, so he'd made some snap judgments. He'd taken one look at the eye-popping body and face, added it to the fact that she danced in a bur-lesque show and made some assumptions.

"I don't know if I'd say I was a playboy, and I'd love to know what you've heard about me. Can I buy you a drink, Dahlia? I promise to be on my best behavior." He sent her his most charming smile.

"I bet you would." One dimple at the right corner of her mouth showed as she fought a smile. Nash wanted to lean in and lick it. Until she continued speaking. "No, thank you, Nash. I don't have drinks with patrons, and my friends are waiting for me."

"Oh. Well, all right. Have a nice night, Dahlia. Again, I apologize for offending you." He wanted to argue he wasn't a patron but he'd done enough damage for one night. Dahlia Baker tickled his fancy, and Nash Emery wasn't a quitter. He'd be back to wear her down until she went out with him. He just needed to come at it better.

She shrugged and turned on her heel. "Just behave yourself."

"What the hell was that all about?" Roseanne demanded, looking over her shoulder at the table where William and Nash sat.

Dahlia had been heading to her friends' table, knowing Roseanne was in the back changing and would be out to join them soon. Then she'd run into a very hard, hot and fragrant wall of man.

And oh, my, what a man! She'd looked up into a pair of sexy, half-lidded green eyes and melted a little bit. His face was handsome with an edge of pretty. High cheekbones and a strong chin covered in one of those beards that would look disheveled on most men but it just made her think about spending the weekend in bed. All his features had a bit of sloppy about them—mussed-up, tumbled-out-of-bed sexy—but it worked. He looked elegant, but the hint of rakish good looks only made him more attractive. The kind of man that set off her bad-boy alarm and made her simultaneously want to wrap herself around him and run for the hills.

His cologne was just right. Not the kind that strangled you and held you down as you gasped for air, but the sexy hint of masculine with a bit of spice. Nicely dressed. The feel of the fabric under the palm she'd laid on his chest when she'd bumped into him said money. Even with her stilettos on he stood a good three inches taller than she was. All in all, a very winning package.

She'd been close to just leaning in and taking a whiff of him when he'd thrown cold water all over her naughty, naked fantasies. Teach her to get all gooey over a man before he opened up his damn mouth and proved himself to be the ass he truly was. It wasn't a novel experience, getting hit on by the moneyed jerks who hung out at the club. But Nash Emery had hit buttons she usually ruthlessly ignored when others made their play.

Dahlia avoided the question until she could take a swig or two of her drink. That little interlude had left her off balance. Ass or not, there'd been no small amount of sparks between them. It'd been a while since a man had lit her fuse that way.

"Is that who I think it is? The lady-killer brother?" Rose-anne went in for another pass, and Dahlia knew she'd never stop until she had an answer.

"Yes, that's Nash Emery."

"Ah! He's usually here on Friday nights. But I haven't seen him up close until now. I saw your head whip around and your hands were on your hips so you must have been giving him what-for. What did he do wrong?"

Dahlia had Friday nights off because it was her heaviest class day, so she'd been spared the arrogant hotness of the younger Emery brother.

"He's certainly not hard to look at, even if he is an arrogant asshole." Taking another drink for good measure, Dahlia related the story and they all looked surreptitiously toward Nash's table.

"Well, a man like that makes a girl *want* to be slutty," Rose-anne said matter-of-factly.

And while Dahlia could agree that Nash Emery and his honey-blond hair, two-day beard and piercing green eyes made her nipples hard and her pussy ache, she also knew that no man was worth being slutty over. She wasn't allergic to a good time in bed, but it wasn't going to be with a man who took one look at her and thought big boobs equaled Good-Time Sally.

When she was up on the stage with the lights so bright she couldn't see the audience, it was okay to be sexy and sensual. Dahlia Baker from Liberty, Washington, was a distant memory when she embraced the thing that had made her an outcast simply because she had a wicked body and a beautiful face.

She hadn't gotten the hell out of Liberty to come to Las Vegas and lose her head over a man. Especially a man like Nash Emery. He might be the most attractive man she'd ever laid eyes on, but her legs weren't going to fall open at the flash of perfect teeth and a Rolex, either.

Oops, open legs and that mouth… Heat flashed through her at the thought of looking down her body as his head bent over her pussy, licking and nibbling. She'd sift her fingers through his hair as she held him in place. Dahlia fanned herself with her napkin and pressed the icy glass to her forehead, trying to cool off.

Nash had sent over a round of drinks, which she wanted to refuse, but her friends grabbed the glasses off the tray and told her to shut up about it.

Throughout the rest of the evening, she snuck looks in his direction and found him looking back with unabashed interest. There was something exciting and discomfiting about it all at once. A man like Nash had powerful charisma and presence; as guarded as she was, it still appealed to her.

Of course, when she left after one o'clock, she didn't fail to notice Nash wasn't hurting over her rejection. Three women stuck to him, and each one of them looked as if she'd feel at home on a high-fashion runway. He'd get his champagne bath with someone tonight.

Even so, he sent her a courtly bow and raised his drink at her as she passed.

Chapter Two

She thought she'd be able to put Nash out of her mind but he showed up a week later.

"Hey, Dahlia. Nice job tonight. You're really good at those high kicks." He sat down at the table with her and her friends, and all conversation stopped as the women stared at him.

"Uh, thanks."

He looked around the table. "Hello, ladies. I'm Nash."

Grudgingly, Dahlia introduced him to her friends and wasn't surprised when he bantered and flirted with them. However, he kept the bulk of his attention on her.

Being the center of his interest was flattering and totally overwhelming. Yes, she'd seen his type a few hundred times, but there was something *more* about Nash Emery. He was charming, witty and really smart, yet there was something indefinable about him, too. More alluring than she wanted to admit to herself. He was dangerous to her peace of mind.

Still, the parade of beautiful women constantly inserting themselves into his face served as a powerful reminder of his reputation. It helped her turn him down when he asked her out again. Even so, when he gave her a sexy pout, it took a lot of willpower not to lean in and grab that bottom lip between her teeth.

The next week, he didn't come to the club, but he sent flowers—dahlias in vibrant colors.

"Why can't the man send roses like every other schmuck?" she mumbled, annoyed at herself for being touched he'd sent something unusual and special but not extravagant. If he'd thrown money at her on some typical thing like roses, he'd be easier to blow off.

Two weeks later, he'd caught up with her as she exited the side door after her set.

"Dahlia!"

She spun and smiled as she saw him approach. "Hi there. I wasn't expecting to see you tonight."

They walked to her car. "I can't seem to stay away when I know you'll be here."

She wished it sounded like a line, but the more she was with him, the less clichéd he sounded.

After tossing her things in the backseat she turned and they began to chitchat. Until politics came into the discussion. Dahlia's politics were decidedly more liberal than Nash's and once they got started, the heat built as they debated hammer and tongs for an hour.

"Damn it, you're sexy when you argue," he said, a grin breaking over his features.

She groaned. "You'd be a lot easier to resist if you were a Neanderthal or an asshole. Not that your political and economic ideas aren't totally wrong, mind you."

He leaned in so close she smelled his skin and saw the pulse beat at the base of his throat. "Why resist?"

Her heart stuttered a moment and she swallowed hard. "You and I are not in the same league, Nash. I have to go. Have a good night." Quickly, before she lost her resolve, she got into her car and drove away.

Nash placed Dahlia's usual drink on the table in front of her and sat down. "I'm liking this new act. You look gorgeous in red."

Dahlia had given up asking herself why a man as scorchingly hot as Nash Emery would hang out at the club on her nights. She'd also given up fighting her pleasure at seeing him as she walked out into the lounge from backstage.

He'd asked her out several more times and she'd turned him down, however reluctantly. What they had was the beginning of a great friendship.

Not that he didn't sneak looks at her tits when he thought she didn't notice. But he seemed to actually care about what she said. It was irresistible, and her resolve to resist his romantic and sexual charms weakened a bit more every time she saw him.

Part of that, she knew, was how she'd been treated in the past. All her life she'd been judged after one look and written off as a bimbo. Even when she'd been working her way through college the office jobs she got were nightmarish. Either the men hit on her mercilessly or the women hated her. She'd taken to wearing jeans and hoodies to keep people from focusing on her body, and even at work she often chose muted colors to try to blend.

It was odd, but dancing at The Dollhouse was the first job she'd felt comfortable going to every day. Strange but true—in a lot of ways, it had changed her life. Being seen as something more than her body and face meant something to Dahlia. It meant something that the friends she'd made had gotten past stereotypes and looked deeper, getting to know the real Dahlia.

She knew her looks were her Achilles' heel. Her lack of money and the way people had reacted to her outward appearance throughout her life made her jumpy and distrustful. It took a long time for people to earn her trust. It drove her nuts that she was so confident in other ways but she found it hard to believe in people's good faith.

She shook off her mental dialogue and smiled. "Thanks. I thought something with a Latin feel would be a good change of pace." Her new routine was a sexy-hot number with hip rolls and some slinky moves on her hands and knees. The crowd especially loved the hair flipping as she artfully covered her bare breasts with the fan she used as a prop.

"You're a really good dancer. Have you had formal training?"

"Fifteen years' worth. My mother thought it was important for every girl to have dance lessons so I had tap, ballet and jazz."

His eyes glazed over a bit. "Were you a cheerleader?"

Unable to resist, she leaned in a little closer to him. "Why? Do you have cheerleading fantasies, Nash?"

His eyes slid down to her breasts and then back up to her face. "Where you're concerned, Dahlia, I have a lot of fantasies."

God, three months of this and she was past frustrated and well on her way to insane. She knew she shouldn't flirt but she couldn't help herself around him. She'd spent most of her life downplaying her sexy side except for those minutes onstage. But something in Nash called to her, made her feel playful.

That and she hadn't had sex in six months, and this man's regular presence in her life had caused her battery bill to go through the roof. There was only so much that handheld silicone and the showerhead could do.

"Nash, darling, how are you?" One of the usual random beauties pushed her way between them at the table and stuck her rack in his face.

Dahlia suddenly remembered why a showerhead was preferable to a swelled head. She hated that she couldn't get in a normal conversation with him! It was disappointing it happened so damned much, but she just wouldn't be able to live with herself if she turned into one of those women who threw herself at him. And Dahlia refused to get into the game-show-for-men business. She would never compete for a man's attention like that, and she wished these other women had some self-respect.

Tipping her head back, she drank the last of her club soda and stood. "Good night, Nash. See you around."

Nash got up and unsuccessfully tried to extricate himself from the octopus in stilettos who had wrapped herself around him. Frustration on his face, he reached in Dahlia's direction.

"Wait, we barely even got to talk."

"It's late and you're busy. I'll see you the next time you're in town."

Helpless, Nash watched the tantalizing sway of her hips as she walked out of the place. Sitting back down, the woman who'd perched in his lap—*Darla? Kendra?* Whoever—made breathy sounds, and her hand found its way down his pants and around his cock.

A year ago, Nash would have been fucking her in a bathroom stall by now. Not only would he have thought it was great, he most likely wouldn't have given Dahlia a second look. If one woman wasn't interested, there were three more who were, sometimes at the same time.

But in the past few months, even before he'd met Dahlia, he'd begun to realize how empty his life really was.

He had his job. Essentially, he introduced people to make deals—songwriters to musicians, actors to directors, screenwriters to producers, CEOs to other CEOs—he had all sorts of connections and people hired him to facilitate whatever it was they were looking for. It was a career that took him all over the world.

But he came home to nothing at the end of the day. Sure, he had women in his bed all the time, but they weren't there when he came back to Vegas a week or a month later.

He had very few true friends because he couldn't always trust people's motives. People had agendas. He didn't even share all of himself with William. They were close, but after his older brother's engagement had broken off several years before, William had closed himself off from everyone with his work and a parade of women that boggled even Nash's mind. Nash's one true confidante was his personal assistant, whom he trusted with his fears and ambitions.

But Dahlia Baker was real. She was a genuine person who cared about everyday things and lived a normal life. Or as normal as you can get living in a city like Vegas.

When he was with her, he was more than the rich playboy. She saw beyond that, beneath that, and made him feel special. Conversations with her weren't skillful mind games where the only real goal was to get the most out of the other person. He wanted to know Dahlia and to be known beyond the surface.

Not that he didn't ache to touch her. There was no denying she was the hottest damn woman he'd ever met. God, he wanted her so much that he walked around hard every moment. The woman on his lap could easily be on the cover of a magazine, and he couldn't have been less interested in fucking her.

Making his excuses, he finally freed himself from his admirer and headed home. Once there, he stood at the windows and looked out over the Strip.

Living in a hotel had appealed to him because it was easy. He could order room service if he wanted. Housekeeping looked after the maintenance. If a button was missing on one of his shirts, the concierge took care of it. But it wasn't warm. Nash bet Dahlia's apartment was warm.

The Dollhouse was dark on Tuesdays, and that's when Dahlia did the majority of her schoolwork for the week. Sitting in the library, she was supposed to be working on a paper, but she could not get her mind off Nash. The man was a damned distraction.

The thing was, she was pretty sure she could have sex with him and it wouldn't be slutty. At least, she'd talked herself that far. She knew him well enough to understand he liked her. He saw her as a person, respected her, even if he was a terrible flirt.

She'd run the benefit cost analysis on sleeping with Nash, and so far, fucking him was outweighing masturbating herself into frustrated blindness.

But she'd be ten other kinds of frustrated if she didn't finish the paper in front of her! She was graduating in one more semester and did not have the luxury of fantasizing about getting on her knees and unzipping his pants.

She knew he'd have a nice cock; she'd seen it pressed against the front of his pants after she danced often enough over the past three months. When she licked around the crown, would he groan or hiss? What would his skin taste of? She could imagine the weight of his balls in her palm as she slowly wrapped her lips around his cock and slid him as far back as she could. She'd hum in satisfaction and his hands would tighten on her shoulders. Or would he grab her hair? A thrill at the thought slithered through her.

Her head fell back and whacked the wood of the chair, knocking sense back into her. Okay, paper first! *Come on, Dahlia, focus and then fantasize.*

The next afternoon she and Roseanne worked on a new routine at the club during daylight hours when it was closed. It was a happy surprise to see Nash in William's office talking with his brother, when she and Roseanne were on their way out.

"Hey." He smiled warmly. "Fancy seeing you here."

"We were working on some new stuff. What are you doing here?" God, he made her feel like a giddy teenager. She only barely resisted the urge to twirl her hair around a finger.

"I just got back into town and came by to say hello to

William, who is of course always working. I thought *I* was bad." William barely looked up from his work and Roseanne found something fascinating to go look at across the room.

Man-oh-man, did she wonder just how bad he was.

"How was New York?"

"You remembered." His smile widened. "It was good. I had dinner with Bob De Niro at his place in Tribeca."

"Of course I remembered. You just told me a week ago."

"Can you come to dinner at my place?"

Dahlia started at the sudden nature of his request. He was usually so much smoother when he asked her out. That crack in his suave veneer was utterly charming. She decided to take that as a sign.

"I don't think so." She watched his face fall and felt bad for teasing him. Quickly, she added, "How about you come to my place? I'll make you dinner."

The change in his expression made the girly giddiness she always felt around him even worse. He went from crestfallen to surprised, and once he realized she'd said yes, he put the smooth face back on. Lord help her, she thought it was cute.

"I can't believe you finally accepted. Three months, Dahlia. I've asked you out seven times and you've said no every time."

"Not that you're keeping track or anything."

He laughed. "Nah. Just of the total amount of scars on my ego."

"I'm sure your ego will survive." Even as hers was given a boost by the way this man reacted to her. How could she resist?

Nash stifled the urge to pump his fist in the air victoriously. He'd vowed to himself not to ask her out again for at least another month but impulse had taken over. She'd looked so beautiful, her face clean of makeup, simply fresh and natural in jeans and a plain blue T-shirt. He hadn't been able to help it.

He wanted to pin her down before she changed her mind or backed out. "Okay, so when can we do this? I'm going to be in town for the next four days."

"I'm off Friday night."

He seized opportunity with both hands. "You got it. Friday night at eight. I'll bring the wine."

Reaching into her bag, she pulled out a pad and wrote out the directions to her house. "Are you allergic to anything? Have a food you hate?"

As if. He'd finally gotten her to agree to a date—even if she made something utterly inedible he'd gulp it down and ask for seconds just to spend time with her. "No green peppers. Everything else I'm good with."

"Okay, I'll see you the day after tomorrow then." She walked off with Roseanne and waved as they exited through the back doors.

He came to watch her set on Thursday. Just as she turned to walk offstage, she caught a glimpse of him. She liked him there, liked the feel of his gaze on her. Made her feel even sexier.

When she emerged from the back she caught sight of him waiting for her. She couldn't leave right away, not once he smiled at her.

"I can't stay very long. I have four classes tomorrow." She had to stand close to be heard over the music. Not that she minded the excuse.

He motioned to the doors leading to the area just outside the club and she followed.

"That's better," he said once they'd gotten out of the smoky, loud space.

"I don't even notice it anymore." She shrugged, laughing.

"I didn't expect to see you tonight." He didn't often come on Thursdays.

"I know. I have a meeting at nine in the morning, but I thought of you here and I wanted to be here, too."

He looked so handsome, leaning casually against the wall. His hair sat in tousled disarray around his shoulders, but it looked artful and sexy instead of messy. She suddenly felt distinctly frumpy in her sweatshirt and jeans and fought the urge to smooth down her hair.

"You say the best stuff. I don't know how to react when you say things like that."

Reaching out, he tucked a stray curl behind her ear and then drew a fingertip lightly down the line of her jaw. "What can I say? You inspire me. I suppose I'd be pushing it if I tried to get you to grab a drink with me in the piano bar? Just one?"

His perfect teeth flashed with that boyish grin and she shivered. Dahlia knew she couldn't spend just twenty minutes with him. She lost all sense of time when he was near.

"I'd like to, I really would, but it's already midnight and I have to be up early. You're still coming to dinner, right?"

"I wouldn't miss it. Should I bring dessert?"

"I'm making lasagna, salad, flash-fried spinach with red pepper and garlic bread. Hmm, ice cream maybe?"

"Oh, man. You're making all that?"

"Is that a problem?" He placed a finger over her lips.

"I'm impressed, not appalled. I can't tell you the last time someone made me dinner like this."

Without meaning to, she opened her lips and took his finger inside. Sucking gently, she grazed his fingertip with her bottom teeth before releasing him.

He stood still for long moments, pupils wide, breath quick. "Um. Okay then. Shit. I'd walk you to your car, but I seem to be a bit indisposed."

She looked down and saw the bulge at the front of his pants. "Oops. Well, it's okay, I don't need you to walk me. I'm just right out the door anyway."

He grabbed her as she walked away and hauled her back to him. "Of course I'll walk you. It's not like I've made it a big secret that I'm attracted to you. Besides, you're the one who sucked my finger and made me this way to begin with."

Liking the way he felt there against her, she didn't pull away and they walked out to her car, his arm around her waist.

He stopped her as she moved to get into the car, his body caging her against her door. The heat rolled off him in waves, making her slightly dizzy.

"Good night, Dahlia. I'll see you tomorrow."

His lips brushed over hers gently once, twice, and he started to pull away only to return, crushing his mouth over hers. She could do little more than reach up and hold on as he plundered her mouth with his own. Lips, teeth and tongue worked in concert to completely devastate her defenses against him. If there'd been any at all to begin with.

Body to body, she pressed into him, wanting more contact, needing more from him. The ragged moan she swallowed from his lips excited her senses as much as the heat of his hand that lay on her hip, just beneath the sweatshirt against her bare skin. His thumb stroked back and forth over her hip bone, sending bursts of electric sensation through her.

It took all her will not to throw her leg up over his hip and grind into him. God, she wanted him desperately. Wanted to rub all over him like a cat.

His tongue stroked sinuously and seductively over her own, making her weak in the knees. He tasted like good gin and cigars. Like sex and sin and trouble.

When he pulled back and broke the kiss she put her hand to her lips, still tasting him there.

"Sweet dreams." He looked deliciously tousled as he took a step back, one hand in his pocket, the other raised in a wave.

Mechanically, she got into the car and pulled away.

Whew! That was the hottest kiss she'd ever experienced. The man was a freaking genius with his lips. It made her wonder what his oral technique was. She snorted—it wasn't like she hadn't been wondering that since the first time she'd met him. Now that his tongue had been in her mouth, she could imagine far better how it would feel against her clit.

She was so totally going to jump him tomorrow night. She just hoped she could contain herself until after dinner.

Once home, Nash hit the shower. God knew he couldn't just go to bed after that damned kiss. Stripping off, he turned on the showerheads and let the water heat as he laid out towels and turned on the stereo. He'd been on a Tito Puente kick lately—he didn't have to guess why.

He scrubbed his scalp and soaped up his body, a shock of pleasure echoing through him as he ran a hand over his cock. He wasn't going to lie to himself; he'd known he'd have to get himself off when he got home. The same way he had just about every time he'd seen or even thought of her.

Leaning back against the marble wall of the enclosure, the four showerheads pelted him with water as he closed his eyes and thought of Dahlia. Imagining her wet there with him, rivulets of water sluicing down those magnificent breasts, drops beaded like diamonds on her eyelashes. He'd taken close enough notice of her body when she'd danced; he knew her legs were strong and muscled, knew her belly was flat just before the generous curves of her hips and thighs.

He'd slide his hands over her, slick with soap, as he kissed her.

Slowly, he pumped his fist around his cock, imagining it to be her hand holding him. Absently, his thumb flicked over a nipple. Would her tongue feel that way?

From their kiss, he knew she'd be responsive in bed. Dahlia was a woman who would embrace all the pleasure she could bear. They'd be well matched that way.

His breath caught as he felt his climax approach. His thumb rubbed circles over the head of his cock each time he pulled his fist nearly all the way off. Moving his other hand down, he alternated—one hand grabbing at the base, pulling all the way off, replaced by the other hand. Over and over. Faster and faster as he imagined her mouth around him, her tongue where his hands were, imagined plunging deep into her pussy as it fluttered around him, tight and hot.

First he'd take her hard and fast, her legs wrapped around his waist. He'd have access to her breasts and her luscious, carnal mouth. He'd watch as she came, watch her eyes go passion-blind. Would she beg him? Was she a moaner? Imagining the sound of her voice as she came sent a wave of pleasure straight from his brain to his cock.

Then he'd wait until they caught their breath before going down on her. Oh, he couldn't wait to taste her pussy. He'd take his time, drive her up slowly, feast on her body as well as the sounds she'd make and while her pussy still fluttered with climax. And then he'd roll over and have her ride his cock, going hard and deep and letting her set the pace.

A moan ripped from low in his gut as he came, hands still stroking over his cock until he was spent and began to soften.

And he was hard again ten minutes later, wanting her for real.

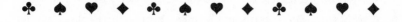

Chapter Three

Dabbing a tiny bit of frangipani essential oil behind her knees, Dahlia took a last look in the mirror. It had taken four clothing changes to find the right mix of casual and sexy. She'd never felt so much anxiety about setting the right balance of pretty and alluring.

To that end she'd decided on a white haltered sundress with red roses silk-screened on it. The skirt was full and hit just below her knees. She'd grown up in a house with a mother who sewed, knitted, baked and canned. Dahlia couldn't knit, bake or can to save her life, but she could sew. Which was a good thing because she loved clothes but didn't have the money to buy much. And it was also a nice way to share that connection with her mother.

Her hair stayed loose around her shoulders, held back by a wide red band, and pretty silver hoops in her ears finished the simple look.

The scents of garlic bread and fresh basil painted her senses. If they both ate garlic it wouldn't matter. And she loved garlic.

Hearing the doorbell, she smoothed down her skirt and padded, barefoot, across the small living room to the door.

When she opened it she nearly fell over. He stood there in sand-colored jeans and suede loafers. A deep green button-down shirt set off his eyes. Hot damn, he looked good enough to grab hold of and lick.

"Hi. You're right on time. Come in." She stood back and waved him inside, watching his trim, high, hard ass as he went.

He handed her a bag and she peeked inside. "Café Gelato! How did you know?"

He grinned. "I didn't, but it seemed more appropriate to have gelato with what you were making than mere ice cream. I got pistachio and chocolate. I hope you like at least one of them."

She smiled and leaned in quickly to kiss him. "Pistachio gelato is like the best thing on earth to eat. Thank you."

Pride warmed Nash at her appreciation of his silly gift. He'd had to drop off some papers at the Bellagio for a client who was staying there, and so he'd seen the gelato on the way out and thought of her. Well, he'd thought of her when he'd seen the giant chocolate fountain at the entrance to the small shop. Stunned by the vision of her naked, drenched in warm chocolate, his heart had nearly burst from his chest. It was then he realized that gelato would be better than ice cream and stopped in for some.

It was a novel experience to be with a woman who got excited by fifteen dollars' worth of gelato instead of an expensive bracelet. Refreshing.

As she led him toward the kitchen, he took the place in. He liked her apartment. It wasn't the luxurious penthouse he lived in, but it was warm. He'd been right about that.

Deep oranges and reds filled the place with hints of turquoise blues and white. An odd explosion of color, but it worked. It was vibrant and earthy like she was. She'd made it into a home.

She poked her head around the freezer, where she'd just put the gelato. "Can I get you something to drink?"

"Oh!" He handed her the bottle of red wine he'd brought. He'd restrained himself from bringing the really expensive bottle he'd picked up first, not knowing if she'd be offended or not and settled on a nice mid-priced bottle instead.

"Perfect. Will you do the honors? I need to pull the lasagne out of the oven, get it on the table and toss the salad." She pointed to the opener and the glasses on the counter and he obliged, taking them to the table.

"Sit," she ordered absently as she brought the rest of the food to the table and finally sat down.

Taking a sip of the wine, she sighed happily. "This is quite lovely."

"Just like you. This looks amazing, Dahlia." The table was filled with beautiful food, and something in him warmed, knowing she'd made it for him. People didn't do that for him, and he realized how much he was missing now that it was there.

"Flatterer. My mom taught us all how to cook. My brother is better at it than me or my sister. But knowing how to cook helps make macaroni and cheese and ramen a bit more palatable night after night." She laughed and waved at the food. "Help yourself."

They filled their plates and ate for a few minutes, silent until they'd gotten a bit full.

"So how did you end up with a name like Dahlia? It's not one I hear often."

"My great-grandmother was named Dahlia. My grand-mother and great-aunts were named after flowers. My gran was Violet, her sisters were Rose and Daisy. You get the picture. But they didn't name their daughters that way, and my mom thought it was a nice tip of the hat to that older generation."

"Ah. Interesting. Are you close? With your family, I mean."

She sighed. "I love my family very much. They're good people and they work hard. They want what's best for me."

"But?"

With a rueful smile she took another sip of wine. "They don't think being in Las Vegas is what's best for me. They *really* don't think my job at The Dollhouse is what's best for me. This was supposed to be four years and it's been nearly six. While getting my economics degree I discovered just how much I loved business so I decided to get my master's degree in business administration." She shrugged.

"But my full-ride money was for undergrad and not for grad school. I've had to pay for pretty much all of it since I've been in the MBA program. I've gotten a few grants but mainly it's loans and lots of ramen noodles." Pausing, she took a bite of her spinach before continuing.

"They wanted me to come back home and go to school there for my master's degree. But the MBA program here is exactly what I needed, and they admitted me, which isn't such an easy feat straight from undergrad. And now they're pretending like I'm coming back when I graduate."

"And you aren't?" His esteem for her rose even higher, knowing that she worked hard to get ahead and finish school. He and William had been damned lucky to grow up with the affluence they had. Still, their parents expected them to work for a living instead of turning into the trust-fund trash he saw so often in the gossip sheets.

"I could never go back there. I'm not the same person anymore. I'm not cut out for Liberty. Don't get me wrong, it's a nice place to grow up, for the most part, but it's not for me. I may not stay in Vegas, depending on my job options, but I won't be going back."

"What do you want to do with your degree?" The idea of Dahlia not being around after she graduated made him sort of nervous.

"Run or manage a business. I want to be a CFO someday. It's why I like Las Vegas so much. So many opportunities with all the hotel management groups and corporations based here. But…well, it hasn't been as easy as I thought it would be."

"But what?"

"Nothing. Anyway, it's not like shaking my ass on a stage is helping, but I did an internship the last semester of last year and through the summer and that was really helpful."

"Why do you shake your ass onstage? Not like I'm complaining. I like your ass. I especially like it when you shake it."

"Money. Internships don't make you much money, if any at all, and I can't afford that. So I did the internship and then I did both when I started working at The Dollhouse. I have a job interview in two weeks with the corporation I interned at. They liked me and my ideas."

They finished dinner as she told him about the internship she'd completed with the Tate Group and the job she hoped to get. He knew the CEO of the group that ran that particular hotel and several others in Las Vegas as well as New Orleans. He resolved to put in a good word on her behalf. He got the feeling there was more than she was saying about her reasons for working at The Dollhouse.

After dinner, they cleaned the kitchen as a team and retired to her couch, which, thankfully, was cozy enough to keep her close.

"I talked an awful lot about myself tonight. I want to know more about you and your family. Your brother. What you were like growing up. I know you grew up in Boston, but you also said you spent a lot of time here in Las Vegas. What was that like? You've told me some but I'd like to know more."

He took her wineglass and put it on the end table and turned her chin so that she faced him. "That's for our next date. Right now, I need to kiss you. I've thought about little else since last night about five seconds after I kissed you last."

Not for the first time, Dahlia wondered at his ability to render her speechless and giddy. It made her wary—she wasn't sure she liked anyone having that much of an effect on her. At the same time, it felt wonderful to drop her guard and let someone get close. The intensity and depth of the feelings he inspired brought everything to do with him into vivid focus. She'd locked herself away for years after the experience at Warner Industries. Since then she'd just stayed focused on school.

Her gaze locked with his for long moments as his thumb brushed along the space on her neck just below her ear.

Leaning in, he took her lips.

He started slowly, his mouth brushing lightly over hers,

his lips warm and soft. The edge of his beard tickled her, but it wasn't scratchy. A shiver went through her as she imagined how it would feel against the soft skin of her inner thighs.

Without meaning to, a soft moan escaped her and he pulled her closer as his tongue slipped into her mouth. The kiss was sure without being overly aggressive. His taste marked her, filled her.

"God, more," he gasped, bringing her astride him.

Her skirt rose up to her thighs and pleasure arced up her spine as her pussy settled over the hard line of his cock. He rolled his hips, grinding himself into her as his tongue lazily stroked into her mouth.

The cool silk of his hair tickled her hands as she held him. With a last tug of her bottom lip between his teeth, he moved to her chin and across her jawline to her ear. His palms slid down her back to her waist, holding her to him as he rolled himself into her.

Heat began to build as his movements brought him over her clit through her panties. She was so damned turned on she wondered if she'd come just from that contact. That brief concern melted as he moved his mouth down her neck and her head fell back.

Humming with aroused satisfaction, Nash moved his hands to her breasts, fingers playing softly around the nipples through her dress.

Hands gripping his shoulders, she held on as he bent her farther, and the heat of his mouth found the upper swell of her breast.

Then cool air hit her skin as he pulled the bodice back, exposing her to his hands and lips. All rational thought shut down when the tip of his tongue traced around her nipple and she gave in to the pleasure of the moment.

Triumph roared through him as Nash felt the last bit of her hesitation melt. She was fire in his arms. The heat of her pussy against his cock seared him, made him want her with desperate intensity.

Her nipple hard against his lips and tongue indicated she wanted him as much as he wanted her. And what a beautiful nipple it was. Her body was amazing! He'd seen a lot of it while she danced, but the dusky color of her nipples, the shape and size of them, had been a question he'd been pondering in detail for months.

The hand that had rested on her bare thigh slowly moved upward. Giving her time to refuse and getting no indications in that direction, he continued up under her dress until he reached the edge of her panties with his fingertips.

A pretty gasp came from her and then she moaned softly. Unable to resist any longer, he brought the edge of his teeth against her nipple and she arched, pressing herself into his mouth.

His fingertips traced the line of her pussy through the lacy material of her panties. She was wet and hot and the swollen bundle of her clit greeted him.

Groaning, he moved the panties to the side and slid his fingers into her, moving them along the slicked furls of her sex.

"Yes," she whispered.

"Yes, indeed, Dahlia. You're almost there already, aren't you?" He spoke against the flesh of her nipple and she writhed against him, rocking herself over his fingers.

"More, baby? Like this?" He pressed one finger and then two into her gate and they both gasped. Tight and inferno-hot. Her inner muscles fluttered around him. Shifting his wrist, he pressed the heel of his hand over her clit and fucked into her pussy with his fingers.

Her breath came in pants as her honey rained hot onto his hand. Her nipples glistened from his mouth, still hard and darkening. The line of her body gleamed with a light sheen of sweat against the warm light from the lamp across the room.

"I want you to come for me, Dahlia. I need to hear it, feel it. Give it to me," he murmured as he kissed from one breast to the other.

"Ohhh, yes," she hissed. He felt the clench and flutter of her pussy around him as she thrust herself onto him, grinding into his hand.

He kept loving her with his mouth and hands as her orgasm engulfed her, the heat of it rolling off her in waves, catching him. Just watching and feeling her had been enough to drive him right to the edge, but he didn't want to come right then. He wanted the moment to be all about Dahlia.

Finally, she slumped forward, laying her head on his shoulder as she caught her breath. Gently, he slipped her panties back into place and felt the exact moment she really realized what had happened between them was deeper than just an orgasm.

Her back stiffened and she sat up. "Oh, my. Well. I…"

Shaking his head, he pressed fingers over her lips. "Thank you will suffice. Now come here and tell me about Liberty."

He pulled her from his lap up against his side, snuggling her to his body.

Reaching out toward him, she looked up into his face, but he stopped her from touching his cock. God knew if she did he'd come right then and there, and he wanted that first time to be slow and hours long.

"What about you?" Her eyes moved to the hummock of his cock pressed against his jeans.

Leaning down, he kissed her and then once more because he couldn't get enough. "I want tonight to be about you. Next time there'll be naked and sweaty and lots of coming. You're so beautiful when you come, Dahlia. Let me keep that in my head for a while."

Confusion marked her face and he shook his head, understanding. "No, I want you tonight, Dahlia. I really do. But I'm in no shape to do this right. I'm on the edge just with watching you come. A guy's gotta have a little dignity about these things and coming two seconds after you touch me would get me tossed out of the cool-guys club."

Rolling her eyes, she laughed. "I owe you one, then. And thank you."

"I'm not lying when I tell you it was my pleasure."

They talked and broke into the gelato. Nash was sure he'd never get the memory of how she looked licking her spoon with relish out of his brain. Hell, she did everything with relish, another thing he loved about her. She was just herself, as if trying to be something else wasn't worth it. So few people he came into contact with were like that.

His cell phone rang. He'd ignored most of the calls, but that particular tone belonged to his assistant. "I'm sorry, Dahlia, I have to take this one."

Ten minutes later he hung up and sighed. "I won't be able

to come to the show tomorrow, or rather tonight. I just got called to Paris a day early. I'm sorry."

She shrugged. "It's your job, Nash. Don't apologize for having to do it."

"I'll be back in a week. I'll see you then, all right? I have your e-mail now, so I'll keep in touch while I'm gone."

"I'd like that. Take some pictures and send them to me, please. I've never been to Paris."

He'd have to remedy that. He wanted to shower her with presents, but he knew she'd be uncomfortable and with the way he'd acted when they first met, he understood why. So he'd have to wait and bide his time and figure out ways to do things for her that wouldn't make her feel bought.

She walked him to the balcony just outside her door. "Which one is your car?" Looking out over the parking lot she laughed. "Never mind. I'm guessing it's the dark blue GTO?"

"Yeah. Isn't she lovely?"

"She's hot. I love the new design."

He looked surprised.

"What? Oh, I see. Women aren't supposed to have opinions about cars? Or is it that Bambi and Kitten just liked to look pretty in them?"

"You're a smart-ass. I've liked that from day one. I'll have you know I've never dated anyone named Bambi."

"But Kitten?"

Surprised laughter burst from his lips. "Busted. I don't think her given name was Kitten though. So, changing the subject now." He raised an eyebrow at her, and she smirked. "You like cars then, I take it?"

"I do. My dad runs a mechanic shop back in Liberty. My

older brother and brother-in-law work there, too. Dad restores cars on the side. The first one I helped with was a 1967 Mustang Fastback. The last time I was home he was working on a '53 Chevy."

Nash practically salivated. "Really? Beauty. I bet that '53 is sexy."

"Oh, yeah. Big and hard and makes a nice throaty sound."

"Suddenly, I'm even harder. Dahlia, each new thing I find out about you pleases me more. I have a '54 'Vette."

Her eyes widened. "Get out! You do not!"

Pulling her flush against his body, he spoke, lips just barely touching hers. "I do. What'll you give me to drive it?"

"Well, my goodness." The tip of her tongue darted out and traced the line of his lips. "I wouldn't want you to crash or anything, but a car like that just calls out for a blow job with the top down."

He shivered at the thought of watching the midnight fall of her hair over his lap as he drove. Those lush lips wrapped around his cock. "God, you're perfect."

She laughed, tipping her head back. "There's no way I'd actually really drive it, by the way. I'd be terrified of even scratching it. But I'll still make good on my offer. And, just as a related piece of information? I've always wanted to be fucked on the hood of a muscle car."

"Damn it, Dahlia, how am I supposed to wait a week to see you again?"

"Hunger is the best sauce, Nash."

Reluctantly, he walked back down to his car and turned to wave goodbye. She waved back and didn't go inside until he'd driven off.

♣ ♠ ♥ ♦ ♣ ♠ ♥ ♦ ♣ ♠ ♥ ♦

Chapter Four

Dahlia filled her days with school, class work, job hunting, and at night she worked at The Dollhouse. If she stopped for one minute she'd think of Nash and she couldn't afford to. Hell, he already consumed her thoughts twenty-three hours a day as it was. Nash made her want things she shouldn't want. A man like Nash wasn't for her. Her mind knew that but the rest of her wasn't so damned convinced.

Her body won out at least in part. The day after he'd left, she'd thought all day long and had come to the decision that an affair with a man like Nash would be fun. She'd have a great time in bed and most certainly learn a few things, and she liked him. He seemed to like her, too, although she wasn't quite sure if a hundred percent of his niceness was real or practiced seduction.

The fact was, they both knew sex was going to happen. As long as she went into the fling knowing it had an expiration date, she'd be all right. No harm, no foul and a lot of heat between the sheets for a while.

True to his promise, he did e-mail. As ridiculous as it was, when she opened each one, a thrill went through her. Undeniably, she was touched by the pictures he sent, sharing Paris with her through his camera phone. How could she not be bowled over by the gesture? It seemed so unlike a man of Nash's reputation.

Feeling better for making her decision about the fling with Nash, as well as creating some emotional boundaries for herself, she'd been rustling through her bag for her keys as she walked up to her apartment. She failed to notice him standing at her door until she was nearly on him, jumping when he said her name.

"Shit! I didn't see you."

He looked sexy in jeans and a dress shirt, open at the collar. His smile warmed her. "Sorry, I didn't mean to startle you. I got home early. You got some time for me?"

Without another word, she unlocked the door, motioning him inside with her chin. Closing it with her foot, she bolted it, dropped her backpack on the chair and toed off her sneakers.

"I have lots of time for you. Question is, are you going to have enough strength for what I have in mind?" She moved toward him and he grinned.

"I'm all yours, babe. I slept on the plane. You look good."

He took a step to her and suddenly their bodies were wrapped together from lips to toes.

"Bedroom?" he gasped, breaking the kiss.

Tugging his hand, she led him to her bedroom and he slammed the door behind himself. "You. Naked. Now."

"Oh. My." Her hands went to the hem of her shirt, pulling it up and over her head, tossing it aside. She shimmied out of her jeans and got rid of her socks, standing before him in nothing more than some lip gloss and a matching panty-and-bra set with cherries on them.

He managed to make a mental note to buy her some lingerie with the cherry motif. She seemed to like it, and God knew he did.

"You have an amazing body, Dahlia. So pretty. Let me see it all."

Reaching around, she unhooked her bra and let it slide to the floor just before she stepped out of her panties. She was a goddess. Absolutely gorgeous.

"The first time I saw you I thought, now there's a woman a man can sink himself into for days. Only, I had no idea just how alluring you were. Lay back."

Moving to lie down on her bed, she looked up at him, eyes filled with sex and trouble. "That's really nice. You're good with the words there, maestro. So, now, when do you get naked?"

He chuckled. "Good things come to those who wait, Dahlia."

Lightning quick, he grabbed her ankle and pulled her toward him, bringing her ass right to the edge of the mattress. She stared up at him, pupils huge, lips parted, and when he dropped to his knees she gasped.

Openmouthed, he kissed and licked up the inside of her leg, from ankle to knee, stopping to lave the hollow at the back. The skin of her inner thigh was velvet-soft and he could smell just how much she wanted him. Her scent did something to him, tightened things low in his gut. His cock throbbed in time with the frantic beat of his heart, and he fought to control this rampant desire she brought out in him.

Spreading her thighs wide with his shoulders, he parted her labia with his thumbs and looked his fill at the pretty pink furls of her pussy.

"Damn, this has be the prettiest pussy I've ever seen. And all swollen and wet just for me. I like that part the best." Looking up, he met her eyes as she stared down at him.

Moving his thumbs, he used the flesh of her labia and clitoral hood to stroke against her clit, slow and sure. He alternated between watching her pussy swell and darken and looking into her face as she fell deeper and deeper toward orgasm.

"Please!" she finally burst out, sounding desperate.

"Please what, Dahlia? I want you to tell me what you want."

Her eyes narrowed and she swallowed. "Make me come, Nash."

"With my fingers like this?" He slid two fingers deep and squeezed her clit gently between slippery thumb and forefinger of the other hand. A ragged groan tore from her lips as she rolled her hips into his hand.

"No! Or yes. Sure. Whatever!"

He chuckled and took his hands away. "You don't sound so sure. How about with my mouth like this." Leaning in, he took a swirling lick from her gate up around her clit, tickling the underside of it with the tip of his tongue.

"Yes! Oh, yes, like that," she whispered urgently.

"Now that sounds sure. It also sounds like you like to be told what to do. I'll have to keep that in mind for later," he murmured just as he got back to work.

His mouth on her was sure and aggressive, much like he was. Dahlia gave in to the sensations that rode her spine from clit to nipples to brain. Every inch of her skin felt alive and electric.

There wasn't an inch of her pussy his mouth missed. As her hands gripped the bedspread, his tongue surveyed every fold, every dip and bump. Lapping, licking, grazing with the edge of his teeth, rolling his lip against her clit, his erotic assault on her was relentless.

Dahlia was sure nothing had ever felt so damned good. Her head whipped from side to side as she begged for more, writhed and clutched the blankets. He was as good with his mouth when it was eating pussy as he was with those damned compliments. The man was a menace.

And then he pressed two fingers into her and turned his wrist, curling the fingers until he found a spot so sweet inside her she was sure she'd never experienced such sharp and intense pleasure before.

It was all over when he slowly sucked her clit between his lips, grazing it ever so gently with his teeth. Her back bowed as a hoarse cry came from her. Orgasm rose up and sucked her under. There was nothing else but his mouth on her, his hands holding her, touching her.

He continued to push her right into another smaller but still intense aftershock climax. He would have continued for another but she couldn't take the intensity any further and scrambled up the bed, away from that wicked, wicked mouth.

She felt him move next to her and cracked open an eye. "That mouth of yours ought to be registered as a lethal weapon."

"Just wait till you see what I can do with my cock."

She moaned, rolling to look at him. "Let's go. Show me. But you're not naked. This perturbs me."

He grinned and sat up, quickly divesting himself of the

shirt before scrambling off the bed to deal with his pants, socks and underwear. His upper body was delicious. A chest that wasn't too hairy, nicely defined pecs, wide shoulders leading to a tapered, narrow waist. Muscled biceps and forearms made her wonder just how many surfaces he could fuck her against as he held her up.

She rolled off the bed, following him. "Let me do that." Falling to her knees, she unbuttoned the jeans and slid them and the boxer briefs down muscled thighs, helping him out of them and his socks.

"I've had this recurring fantasy," she said, looking her fill at his gorgeous body.

"What a coincidence. I've had this one before, too," he said drily.

Her hands slid up his calves and thighs. Nice and hard. "You work out." Palms smoothing over the hard lines of his abdomen, she trailed a fingertip around his navel and then down the arrow of brown-blond hair leading to his cock.

Without any further preamble, she wrapped a fist around the base and angled his cock to take him into her mouth. Round and round her tongue slid over the head and crown, tasting the salty tang of pre-cum that beaded at the slit.

He sighed her name and she smiled momentarily before moving to take more of him between her lips. Rocking back and forth, she moved on him, taking him into her over and over, learning him, loving his taste.

Hands sliding through her hair, he held her in a sure grip, guiding her, and a thrill moved through her at the control he exerted. Cupping his balls in her palm, she pressed two fingertips to the spot just behind them and he jumped and then groaned.

★ ★ ★

Nash looked down to see her kneeling there before him, all lush curves and carnal beauty. Those big brown eyes were closed, the lashes swept down against her cheeks. As she moved forward on him, her hair slid and covered a nipple just partially, playing a game of peekaboo hotter than anything she did onstage.

That this woman, a woman he'd been fantasizing about and pursuing for months, was on her knees, her mouth wrapped around his cock, blew his mind. Her taste still painted his lips, her scent on his hands and face. Here in her room, surrounded by her, she marked him and it only really occurred to him at that very moment just how deeply.

He waited, watching her as his orgasm approached, weighing coming with wanting to fuck her right at that very moment. It was the idea of seeing her, watching as he slid into her that made his choice, but Dahlia was having none of that.

"Baby, wait." He tried to step back but she shook her head and continued. "I want to be inside you when I come. I've been dreaming of fucking you for three-and-a-half months. And after you came apart on my lap, coming so pretty the last time I was here, I've wanted you even more."

She pulled off and looked up at him. "Oh, you'll be fucking me. But now you're going to let me finish this. I don't plan on letting you leave for many hours."

Before he could argue she took him deep and hard, swirling her tongue around as she did.

"Fuck!" Damn it, that felt good. The woman had some skill, that was for sure. It only took another minute or two until he locked his knees and his head fell back as he came on a hoarse cry.

Giving the head of his cock a parting kiss, she stood and pushed him back onto the bed. "Rest up. I'm going to order a pizza. I haven't eaten all day and I think I'm going to need my strength. I know *you* will." She grinned. "You do like pizza?"

He smiled. The whole thing was novel to him. The student apartment, take-out pizza and making love to a woman he…well, he really liked. "Anything but anchovies. Do you have beer?"

"Do I have beer? What kind of silly question is that?" She leaned over the bed, her luscious ass in the air as she riffled through some papers. He saw the glistening lips of her pussy and his heart skipped a beat.

Sitting up on the bed she called for pizza with expertise that told him she'd done it many times and then turned back to him. "Beer now? I'm going into the kitchen."

"Sounds great. Thanks."

Lying there, hands behind his head, he watched the captivating sway of her ass as she left the room. From his spot he could see her go into the kitchen and grab two beers, pull the bottle opener off the fridge and crack them both open one-handed and come back toward him.

"It's Friday night. Pizza won't be here for an hour or so. Whatever shall we do in the meantime?"

He grabbed the beer out of her hand, took several long pulls and put it on the nightstand. "I'm ready to fuck you now."

Without another word she put three condoms on the nightstand next to his beer. "Let's go."

Reaching out, he took her wrist and pulled her down to the bed with him. "Open those thighs, Dahlia." He slid a fingertip along her labia, grinning. "Still wet, I see. Good."

One-handed, he rolled a condom on and pushed her knees up and apart, holding her wide open for him. She reached around and guided the blunt head of him true just as he thrust into her body with one long, hard movement.

Her eyes widened as a gasp tore from her lips and then closed momentarily as she sighed softly.

He held her open to him, with his grip on her legs. The weight of his body spread and positioned her just the way he wanted her, her skin soft and warm under his palms, her breasts swaying with each press he made deep into her pussy. The clasp and clutch of her body welcomed him with each roll of her hips.

Her hair spread about her head, eyes looking up into his face, lips parted just so, glossy and still swollen from sucking his cock—so fucking beautiful and desirable his chest hurt just looking at her.

"Arms above your head, grab the headboard." Smiling, he took in her reaction as she did it. Her breasts hitched up, her back arched and her eyelids dropped to half-mast. Ah, she liked being dominated. Good, he liked dominating her.

The room was quiet but for the wet sounds of cock meeting pussy and her soft sighs and whimpers. Oranges and purples colored the walls and her skin as the sun began to set.

Each piston of his hips sent his cock deeper into her body, building, building his orgasm from the top of his head to the soles of his feet.

Her bottom lip caught between her teeth and a pretty flush began to pinken her skin.

"Dahlia, make yourself come. I want to feel your pussy come around my cock."

Oh, how she loved a man who knew what he was about in the bedroom! Even more, a confident, dirty-talking man with an edge of dominance. Yum.

"Can I move my hand?"

Leaning down, he nipped her bottom lip. "Yes."

Bringing her hand to her lips, she wet her fingers and he groaned. The deep sound echoed through her body. Her hand slid, slowly, down her body to her pussy. Knowing he was watching her thrilled her right to her toes.

Her clit was a hard knot beneath her fingers. Reaching down to where they were joined, she brought more lube upward, slowly circling it, a soft sigh coming from her lips.

"Does that feel good, Dahlia?"

His gaze didn't give her any room to deny or ignore the question.

"Yes."

"It does indeed. Your pussy is hot and greedy, Dahlia. Every time I pull out, it grabs me and sucks me back in. It feels so good. Tastes good, too, soft and wet. I can't wait to taste you again."

Words failed so she just nodded enthusiastically. Hell, yes, she wanted that, too.

A razor-thin space held her back from climax. It threatened just behind a wall of time, and, with a moan of pleasure, it burst through her, blinding her to anything but the two of them—his hands holding her open to his thrusts, her fingers playing against her clit, the smell of sex hanging in the air and the weight of his body over her own. Coming always felt so immense when a cock filled her pussy, made her feel just slightly out of control. And as a woman who put a high premium on control, such moments meant all the more.

"Damn, that feels good," he whispered just as she felt the first jerk of his cock, climax bowing his back as he made one last, deep press into her pussy and held himself there for long moments.

Watching him above her, a slow bead of sweat rolled down his neck. Utterly unable to resist, she leaned up and licked from shoulder to earlobe, tasting the salt of his skin.

He sighed, rolling to the side and dealing with the condom. Moments later he was back, pulling her against him while they caught their breath.

The doorbell rang and she got out of bed, grabbing a robe near the door. Snorting, he pulled his jeans on quicker and moved past her. "You think I'm gonna let some punk of a pizza guy see you nearly naked? Uh-uh, that's my special treat."

"There's a twenty near the door!" she called out as he left the room and she headed to the bathroom.

She emerged to find him laying out plates at her table. The smell of a fully loaded pizza wafted through the air, mixing in a very wonderful way with sex. Pizza, Nash and hot sex? A very nice combo. If there'd been chocolate involved it would have officially been Nirvana.

"What are you thinking about? That's one wicked grin you've got there." He laid two pieces of the pie on her plate and then on his own. "And I quite like that you're a super combination pizza sort of woman."

"Why is that?" Taking a bite, she closed her eyes, savoring the taste.

"You're a woman of voracious appetites. I like that. Lush, carnal, intellectual, funny and not afraid to eat. That's really rare these days."

Opening her eyes, she cocked her head, watching him. "You give wonderful compliments, Nash."

Pausing, he smiled. "Thank you. I meant it. I love unique things—you're one of a kind."

His words felt cuttingly familiar. "Like a '54 'Vette? Where do I fit in your collection?"

She'd been there before, and there was no way she'd go back again.

Putting down his pizza, he took her wrist, pulling her against his body. "Is that what you think? That's pretty unfair, Dahlia. I meant it as a compliment. You're not something I collect, nor have I given you reason to think so."

Looking into his eyes, she believed the hurt in his voice and realized he was right. He had been good to her. Nothing like Warner. "You're right. I'm sorry. It's just an old wound, I suppose."

Nodding, he kissed the tip of her nose and let her go. "Apology accepted. But someday I'd like to hear that story. The one my comments brought back for you."

Waving it away, she shook her head. "Some things are best left in the past. But for tonight, I have some movies I rented. Do you have the time?"

"Absolutely, and I'd love to spend it with you."

Grinning, she walked into the living room and put her plate down. Moving to the TV she saw the money still on the table near the door. Picking it up, she turned to him. "You forgot this."

He rolled his eyes. "No, I didn't. You made dinner last time. I got the pizza. It's only fair."

Narrowing her eyes at him a moment, she shrugged, putting the twenty into a little container on the shelf near the door. "Thank you."

Settling on the couch, they watched the first hour of a sci-fi movie before the kissing got too hot and heavy and they'd fallen to the carpet in a mess of writhing, tangled limbs.

♣ ♠ ♥ ◆ ♣ ♠ ♥ ◆ ♣ ♠ ♥ ◆

Chapter Five

Nash was sure he'd never had a better time than the night he spent with Dahlia at her tiny apartment drinking beer, eating pizza and having the best sex of his life.

Damn, the woman was a firecracker. Sexy as all get-out, smart, passionate, talented in the kitchen and onstage. But wounded. There was a hesitation in her when it came to his intentions. It stung, he had to admit to himself. He wanted her to trust him. At the same time, that vulnerability did something to him, made her all the more appealing, and he wanted to prove himself to her. Let her know she could trust his motives.

Tenderness came over him when he remembered the shy hesitation in her voice as she'd asked him to sleep over. They'd made love the third time and lay in an exhausted heap on her living room floor, and she'd whispered it so sweetly.

Did he want to wake up next to her sleep-warm body and slowly slide his cock into her pussy? Was that a rhetorical question?

And he had woken up with her ass snuggled up into the cradle of his hips, her head pillowed on his shoulder. Slowly, he traced circles around her nipple while the other hand slid between her thighs.

She awoke on a gasp as climax unleashed within her and he'd kicked off the best Saturday morning he'd ever had.

That'd been two weeks before and they'd now officially been dating a month. He'd seen her every chance he got, working around both their busy schedules to spend as much time as possible together.

Naturally, the first thing he did when he returned to town from a trip was head to see her. Which was why he sat there at The Dollhouse, watching Dahlia's last set of the evening.

She currently had hold of the strands of pearls lining the wall behind the stage, her ass thrust out, swaying from side to side. Fishnet stockings adorned her legs, giving a flash of skin between upper thigh and the sweet cheeks of her ass peeking from the ruffled boy-short bottoms she wore.

Leaning out, she twisted her body and turned, inserting herself between the wall and the pearls, covering her breasts.

A smile curved his lips at the coy, kittenish look she wore while she slowly slid to the stage into the splits. Quickly, she snatched up the tie she'd worn with the dress shirt and tuxedo pants already discarded and slid it over her breasts, arching into the silk material.

Goddamn, the woman was hot. Looking around, Nash saw the same mesmerized look on every male and many a female face he could see.

Turning back to her, he caught the *look*. The look that made his cock hard as granite. Lowered lashes and the bottom lip caught between her teeth. Only he'd seen it directed at him with genuine heat behind it. If she ever really figured out how much erotic power she had, she'd take over the world in a week.

Step, click, step, click, she headed up the stairs to the dressing rooms in very tall heels for a woman who'd just danced her ass off with athleticism and grace.

A look back over her shoulder as she put the tie on over her head, her bare back to the audience. A blown kiss and she was gone.

With a satisfied sigh he leaned back in his chair and closed his eyes. Hell, he needed to smoke a cigarette, she was so good.

"How is she in bed?"

Cold water thrown over his very hot Dahlia fantasy, Nash opened his eyes to see Lara Warner, a woman he'd had a brief relationship with at the beginning of the year, standing over him. The elegance of her impeccable designer ensemble stood in direct contrast to the sneer she wore on her face.

"That's none of your business, Lara. It's also vulgar of you to ask."

"Vulgar? Like fucking a stripper? For God's sake, Nash, have some class. We all bring clients here for some entertainment, but these women aren't for *relationships*. It's all over town that you're having a fling with this stripper. Don't think she's something special, Nash. And don't forget what your place is. Or hers. She's nothing special. Don't let some cheap slut cloud your mind."

He sighed. "I don't owe you an explanation. My place, or, for that matter, anyone else's, is none of your business." Standing, he moved past her. "Have a nice night, Lara."

He didn't want Dahlia to hear any of Lara's jealous

bullshit. He knew it would hurt her. She was sensitive enough about that kind of thing. Not for the first time, Nash wondered what the story was. He knew Lara's—ex-husband, a former business associate of Nash's, was a philandering asshole. Clearly, Lara's view of relationships had been skewed by that.

Frustrated, he walked back into the hallway where William's office was.

The entrance to the dressing rooms was also at the end of the hall. He knew which one he preferred, but there were other women back there in various stages of undress, so he waited for her, sipping his drink, trying to let go of that nasty scene with Lara.

Ten minutes later she walked out, smiling as she caught sight of him. He'd been in L.A. for a few days and knowing she was happy to see him affected him.

Without a word, he opened the door to the back hallway of the club leading to the extra liquor and the other supplies. Catching the look in his eye, she opened her mouth to object but he shook his head and grabbed her around the waist, pulling her inside. Darkness fell upon them, cool and quiet as he shut the door.

His lips met hers as he swung her body to the wall behind them, his arm around her waist taking the impact. A soft sound of arousal left her lips and he swallowed it greedily.

His tongue hunted hers, possessing her mouth as his hands found the hem of her skirt, reversing and pulling it up, baring her thighs and the tiny G-string panties she wore. Pulling the material to the side, his fingers found her already slick.

Her hands tore at his belt, getting it undone along with

the button and zipper of his trousers, freeing his cock as it spilled hot and ready into her grasp.

He let go of her long enough to roll on the condom he'd readied while he waited for her outside.

"Lift your leg over my hip and put my cock into your pussy," he whispered into her ear and she whimpered with barely leashed desire.

An athletic thigh wrapped around his waist as she braced her back and guided him to her gate. Easing her body down, she took him into herself, slowly, so slowly.

Too slowly—he needed her right then.

Moving his hands to her waist, he flexed his hips upward and thrust into her to the hilt, filling her completely.

Fucking into her body, he found her ear again. "Anyone could walk in at any moment, Dahlia. Don't make a sound. Or…would you like that, baby? If the bartender saw us, saw your pretty pussy bared with my cock deep inside it? Do you think he'd be hard afterward? Would he imagine you as he slid a fist around his cock later tonight? I bet he does anyway, after watching you onstage. I know I do."

A strangled moan muffled in her throat as he smiled against her earlobe. His woman had an exhibitionistic streak—that much he knew from watching her onstage— but the idea of being caught really did it for her, too. He felt the heated silk of her honey as it nearly scalded his balls.

It made him want to push her boundaries to see just what else she liked. God knew he liked that the idea of being walked in on made her pussy cream. Loved the thrill of turning her on. He'd just done it because he could not last another moment without fucking her after seeing that last set. But now that he knew another thing that flipped her switch, he planned to keep it up.

"Finger your pussy for me, Dahlia. You know how much I love to feel you come around my cock." He loved to watch her, to feel her make herself come for him. The contractions of her inner muscles usually pushed him right over the edge after her.

A soft sigh came from her as she moved her hand between them. He ground himself into her, adding to the friction she gave herself. Her breath gasped in his ear. He knew it wouldn't be much longer for her and within moments her breathing hitched and a soft cry came from her as she began to come. With mindless pleasure buffeting him, he continued to hammer her body with his own.

In the darkness of the hallway he found his own pleasure as stars lit his eyelids and her name whispered from his lips. He set her down gently and kissed her. "You're so amazing," he murmured into her ear, loving the way his compliment made her lean into him a moment.

When she let him in that little bit, opening her heart as well as her body, it touched him deeply. True, they had amazing sexual chemistry and she was scorching hot in bed, but in some ways, she hesitated to fully embrace the whole of her sexuality.

As he'd gotten to know her over the past months, watched her react to things, learned her triggers and some of her vulnerabilities, Nash believed a big part of it was other people's perceptions of her because of how she looked.

She seemed to struggle with her own power as an amazingly sensual and beautiful woman. That vulnerability was what enabled him to stay with her, push her to let him in. He didn't walk away from her when she was prickly and difficult because she was worth staying for. The woman beneath her armor appealed to him on every level.

It should have frightened him, freaked him out. He'd always run from feeling deeply, kept himself with women he supposed he felt weren't worthy of him. And he guessed that didn't say much of what he thought he was worth, either. Instead, Dahlia Baker made him put in the time and effort because she was worth it and so was he.

Smiling, he turned back to her after he checked to make sure the outer hallway was clear.

Dahlia set herself to rights, smoothing her dress back down and finger-combing her hair as he gave a quick look to be sure no one was outside.

Her hands shook, her knees were rubbery. Nash Emery had just given her what was undoubtedly the hottest five minutes of her life. That bit about being caught had taken her by surprise, but his naughty words in her ear painting that vision had seared straight to her core.

He had a way of exposing her deepest desires and fantasies that was terribly alluring. But also frightening. Letting someone know her that well made her feel stripped. Stripped of pretense. Stripped of defenses. Naked and open. She'd have to let go of the way she'd believed things were, and that was a risk.

Blowing out her anxiety, she exited the room quickly when he gave her the all clear and they headed out the side door of the club and they walked through the casino.

Halfway out, Nash turned to her, pulling her body tightly against his own. She didn't fail to notice the woman who'd just come out of The Dollhouse giving them a dirty look. Or Nash's response, a raised eyebrow before giving his attention back to Dahlia.

Lara Warner. Dahlia tried to push the memories back, the memories of those six months she had worked for Bill Warner back when she'd been an undergrad. First, he'd been so helpful, mentoring her. But then he'd started to come on to her. It had been subtle at first, and because Dahlia had trusted him, she'd let it go further than it should have. She hadn't done anything with him but she ignored it too long. The last straw was when he'd backed her into a corner in his office and stuck his hand up her skirt.

The ugly things he'd said to her after she'd shoved him away and told him off still rang in her ears from time to time. Those things had made it difficult to get another office job after that. Lara Warner had been only too gleeful to blame her husband's behavior on Dahlia.

And since The Dollhouse was a magnet for the rich and fabulous, women like Lara Warner haunted it and Dahlia had been unable to avoid her.

No matter how smart, no matter how professional she was, people always took one look at her tits and decided she was a whore. But she wouldn't let assholes like Warner and his ex-wife stop her from achieving her dreams.

Shoving those thoughts away, she turned her attention back to Nash, tracing a finger over his bottom lip. Her pussy flooded when he sucked her fingertip into his mouth, closing his eyes a moment.

"Mmm. Tastes like your pussy," he murmured, and she shivered.

He kissed her hard and fast before asking if she minded him playing a few hands of blackjack. Shaking her head, they walked hand in hand to the door that led to the high-roller tables.

Standing behind him at the blackjack table, she looked on as he won five thousand dollars in the first two hands. Not even blinking as he won more than she made in two months. The anxiety at their differences clawed at her gut.

She also didn't miss the looks the other women sent Nash's way. It didn't bother her so much when the waitresses did it but when it was the other patrons, women from his social circle, she felt uncomfortable, out of her element. Reminded that hers was a short-term position, she felt alternately invisible and like a pretty accessory.

Dahlia hated the sick dread in her gut at the thought of it being over between them. Of perhaps being his sexy showgirl to slum with for a while. Of her feelings for him being stronger than his for her. Could she be that carefree woman who laughed and kissed both his cheeks as he moved on? Dahlia wasn't sure she had the strength.

He turned and spoke to the woman beside him, both of them laughing. The diamonds in her ears cost two years' tuition. Dahlia stood, utterly unable to move. She was so out of her element it wasn't funny. What the hell had she been thinking? This man wasn't for her. Years' worth of derision and being perceived as nothing more than a pretty opportunist came to rest in her head, hanging heavy in her stomach.

Turning, she waved a waitress down and wrote a quick note. "Give this to him in five minutes, please."

With tears blurring her eyes, she headed quickly to her car and went home. Hoping like hell she'd made the right decision.

At home an hour later, Dahlia heard a pounding on her door. She knew who it was and sat in the dark, hoping he'd go away and praying he wouldn't all at once. He pounded again, said her name and then once more, louder.

It was after two and if he continued, he'd wake up her neighbors. She went to the door and opened it a crack, but he wasn't having it.

He gently but firmly reached in and moved her back, came inside and locked up behind himself.

Before he said a word, he grabbed her and kissed her hard. No tongue, just a crush of his mouth against hers. Enough that his taste rushed through her system, bringing her body to life, her desire for him cutting sharp.

"Now. Sit." He motioned to the couch and she narrowed her eyes, crossing her arms over her chest.

"Who do you think you are coming in here and ordering me around this way?"

"Fine. Stand, but I'm talking here. You showed atrocious manners tonight, Dahlia."

"*I* showed atrocious manners?" Her voice rose along with her back. "You know, where I come from, bringing one girl to the party and coming on to another is bad manners. But maybe manners are different on your side of the tracks."

"You know, your attitude about my money is really tiresome! I work hard, Dahlia, and it's insulting that you assume otherwise!"

"Don't you yell at me in my house! I know you work hard, Nash. But that doesn't erase the fact that you took me to the high-roller room and five minutes later you're hitting on another woman."

"In the first place, I wasn't hitting on anyone. I was there with you and I don't want that to change. I was talking to a friend. In the second place, you didn't explain why it's okay for you to make the tracks comment."

"Oh, my God!" She threw her hands into the air. "You run in a totally different crowd, Nash. The moneyed crowd. You and William work for your money, but a whole lot of your circle just plays. All the time. Everything and everyone is a game to them. I've dealt with them quite a bit since I arrived in Vegas. Men who think a D cup is license to fondle my tits when I just want to learn how to run a business! Or that I'll fall down with my thighs wide for a few sips of expensive champagne at the club. You thought so, too, that first night, don't lie!"

He tossed himself onto her couch. On the way he reached out to grab her waist and bring her down with him, not letting her go.

"I don't deny I was a stupid asshole that first night. But I'd like to think I'm a better person now. Yes, we come from different backgrounds, but I don't understand why you'd want to break up over it." His voice was gentle as he traced over the curve of her bottom lip.

"Tonight I saw a glimpse of my future, Nash, and it hurt," she said softly, emotion in her voice. "I'm not that sophisticated. This is…more for me. I just can't be an accessory. It hurts too much."

"You're not an accessory. Dahlia, I'm *with* you. You. I don't want anyone else. I've thought about nothing else but you for months. I admit I've not been as sensitive as I could have been in the past when I've broken it off with women, but I'm a better person now. Because of you. Won't you please tell me the story? I saw the way you looked tonight when Lara came out of The Dollhouse and glared at you. And I heard the anger and pain in your voice when you talked about wanting to learn how to run a business but being groped. Tell me. Please. How can I understand you if you won't share with me?"

Dahlia told him about Bill Warner and his nasty ex-wife. She didn't tell him about high school or any of the other experiences she'd weathered; it wasn't necessary. She wanted to underline their class differences and also give him the story he seemed to want so damned bad. She'd see just how special he thought she was now.

"Dahlia, my God. I'm sorry. For what it's worth, Bill Warner is known as a philandering asshole and I'm sure you weren't the only intern he abused that way. Lara is bitter." Leaning in, he brushed his lips over her forehead. "I understand more now. I'm going to pop Bill in the face if I ever see that bastard again.

"I wouldn't humiliate you like that. I may not be the most sensitive guy around but I'm not Bill. You deserve better and I want to give it to you. But I can't if you're always assuming the worst of me. I'm trying. I admitted I saw you as a stereotype and I stopped. Won't you do the same?"

It was going to hurt like a bastard when he finally moved on; she knew it, but she didn't have the strength in her to let him go. Not yet. And he'd touched her with his reaction after she'd unloaded her story about Bill. It felt so good to be able to tell someone about it.

"Oh, all right. I suppose I can keep you around awhile yet. You're awfully good in bed."

"Let's just make sure of that, shall we?"

Nash awoke to an empty bed. For a moment he lay there, breathing her in from the sheets. The scent of their lovemaking sent warmth through his system.

Stretching, he got up and followed the aroma of coffee, stopping to appreciate the sight of her standing in her kitchen, looking cool and elegant in a gray pinstripe suit.

"Wow. You clean up nice."

She blushed. "Thank you. I look okay, then? You'd hire me if you weren't fucking me?"

He heard the note of uncertainty in her voice and his heart constricted for a moment. "You look very professional," he reassured her as he poured himself a cup of coffee. "I take it you're interviewing with Joseph today?"

One of her eyebrows went up. "Joseph? Joseph Tate? How did you know it was him?"

Chagrined, he sighed. "Okay, so I do a lot of business with the Tate Group International people, and Joseph is a friend. You mentioned the upcoming interview and I happened to see him last week. He likes you, thinks you're a hard worker and smart. I didn't tell him anything he didn't already know."

"I like to do things on my own, Nash."

"You have. You are. Look, Dahlia, you're an MBA. You *know* the world of business isn't just about how hard you work but who you know. Joseph isn't an idiot. He wouldn't hire you just because I talked you up. He already thinks you're a good candidate and if my speaking to him adds to the reasons why he should hire you, that's not a bad thing, is it?"

Swallowing down the last of her coffee, she stopped fighting her smile. "Okay. I appreciate that, Nash. But this kind of thing is really important to me. I want to make this on my own merits, you know?"

He put his hands at her waist and drew her closer. "I do know. When you grow up with money, people assume you got ahead because of that and not your own work. I would never sabotage you or try and make an end run around you like that. I'm really good at talking to people, you know. It's what I do."

"I can see you're very good at it."

Nash couldn't hide his pleasure, leaning in to kiss her neck, not wanting to mess up her lipstick. "He was impressed with the work you did for them."

Joseph had also said that once the women in the office had gotten to know Dahlia, the hostility level had dropped and her work had improved even more.

She blushed, clearly pleased. "God. Okay, I can't think about that right now. I need to go. There's food in the fridge. Just lock up when you leave."

Something inside him quailed a moment and then eased. "Will you call me later on to let me know how it went?"

She kissed him quickly and pulled on her suit jacket. The deep gray complemented her coloring, but she appeared very professional.

And, still, her sensuality smoldered. It wasn't overt. She

wasn't trying, she just *was* sexy. He loved that about her and hoped she'd find it within herself to accept that as a part of who she was. Anger at Warner boiled up for a moment, but he shoved it away—she didn't need it.

"I'll call you this afternoon when I come home to eat before work."

"Why don't you come to my place for a change? We can eat there and I'll go to the club with you. Spend the night, Dahlia."

She eyed him suspiciously. "You sure?"

"Why do you ask like that? Of course I'm sure or I wouldn't have asked. I want to see you later. I like having you within reach when I wake up. That's very handy."

She rolled her eyes. "Okay, then. What time should I be there?"

He told her where to park and that he'd be home after three, and she kissed him once more and left.

Chapter Six

Dahlia looked out the window as she used the StairMaster. StairMaster time was what she imagined hell to be. Every second felt like a year as her thighs burned.

Still, she didn't lack for things to think about. Her interview had gone really well, and this job could totally change her life.

She'd miss The Dollhouse, but she'd have a regular schedule and be doing something exciting and challenging. And she certainly had no complaints about the salary and benefits. Not living like a student had a lot of appeal after six years.

Still, if she did get the job it wouldn't start full-time until toward the end of next semester. It was all theoretical at that point, so Dahlia didn't want to get her heart set on anything until she knew more.

The winter break was approaching and she had to decide what to do. Her mother wanted her to come back home to visit for Christmas, and she did miss everyone.

But that led into the other big thing she'd been thinking about. Nash. She'd been seeing him for a month. If he was in town, they were together. He kept in regular contact if he was gone. He'd become a part of her life before she'd realized it. Maybe she needed the time away to figure it out.

Or maybe not. *Gah!* She thought too much, she knew that. If she overthought the thing between them, she'd ruin it.

"So how are things with Dahlia?"

Nash looked up into his personal assistant Amy's face and shrugged.

"Don't tell me you're dumping the poor woman! Nash, you shouldn't have pursued her if you didn't mean it. From your stories, she seems too sensitive for you to toy with."

"Does everyone think I'm a total cad or what?" He stood up, scrubbing his face with his hands. "It's been a month. I've never been with a woman this long before, not on an exclusive level. And I like it. I like having her in my life. I like waking up with her. If I'm not here I like knowing I'm going back to my hotel room and calling or e-mailing her. It's a completely new thing for me."

"I don't think you're a cad. But I do think you go through women like potato chips. But in your case, most of them seem to be okay with that. I have to say it cheers me to hear this one is different."

Sitting next to her, he squeezed her shoulders briefly. "She's smart and funny and sarcastic as hell, and, well, I've told you what she's like onstage. But she's also shy and so scared of herself. Of all her power. She doesn't trust me like I wish she would." He told her briefly about the situation with Warner.

Amy sneered. "Bill Warner is an ass. But, Nash, honey, you have a reputation. And it's well deserved. I know you're a good person beneath the trail of discarded women, but she sees those women and imagines herself as one of them. It hurts to be tossed aside. And she has this history of being misjudged. You can't avoid that."

"I don't want to toss her aside, Amy. I think I'm falling in love with Dahlia. I had this moment this morning when she told me to lock up behind myself at her place. It was so normal. My body started to freak, but then my heart realized how good it felt to belong to someone like that.

"She's got class issues and I don't know how to handle it. She's concerned that she's not in my circle. But I couldn't care less about that! I want her, not her bank account or the tag in her clothes."

"Which is easy for you to say."

"Why does everyone say that?" Nash moved off the couch and began to pace. "I'm not a snob."

"No, you're not. But you *are* a man who vacations in Italy. You think nothing of the class issue because why should you? You've never struggled. I know you work hard. You've built this business up from nothing and made Emery Incorporated into something your father would be very proud of. But she's working from nothing. She's on the outside, Nash. You're inside wearing Gucci loafers and lounging on a leather couch. Cut the girl some slack. And it's about time you fell in love. It sounds to me like she's worthy of you. And I know you're worthy of her. When do I get to meet her?" Amy stood up and began to gather her paperwork.

"Stay for another few minutes. She's coming over for dinner before work."

Amy smiled. "Oh, good! And how does William feel about it?"

Nash sighed. "He likes her well enough. She's one of the big draws at the club. But he's a product of our household and while I may not be a snob, my mother is and so is William. He sort of thinks it's just a fling and as long as he thinks I'm just having a fling, he's fine. I need to talk to him more seriously about her and soon."

"Are you going to your mother's for Christmas and New Year's?"

"Yeah. Since Dad's been gone, it's become really important to her. She may be totally demanding and manipulative but I believe how lonely she looks. I don't want to leave Dahlia for that long, and I don't think she could handle my mother for a week. God knows I barely can."

"She'll never be ready for Leticia. Who would be? But you're wise to hold off until next Christmas. Let the girl get to know you better. Build a track record with her first so you have ammunition with your mother. Because she won't be pleased you're with a woman with no pedigree."

When the valet called to say Dahlia was on her way up, Nash met her at the elevators.

Stepping into the foyer she stopped and gaped. "Holy shit, Nash. This is a palace. My place must seem like a dark little closet by comparison."

Kissing her quickly, he took her bag and then her hand. "Don't be stupid. I love your apartment. It's vivid and colorful, just like you. Now come on in and meet Amy."

A look of panic flashed across Dahlia's face and he

caressed her cheek. "She's a very nice person and so are you." He tugged her into the living room where Amy was straightening up.

Dahlia's mind couldn't quite let go of the fact that Nash lived in what had to be the most luxurious place she'd ever seen in person. And then he sprung the personal assistant on her.

She knew Amy was important to Nash. He spoke of her with great affection and respect, and hers was one of the few rings Nash always answered on his cell phone. If Amy didn't like her it might well be the kiss of death in her relationship with Nash.

A tiny woman with silver hair pulled up into a ponytail grinned at Dahlia as she came toward her. "Finally! I've been nagging Nash for weeks to introduce us. I've heard so much about you. It's nice to meet you at last. I'm Amy Freeman."

Dahlia smiled, responding to the other woman's warmth. Dahlia took her hand but Amy tiptoed up and kissed her cheek instead.

"It's nice to meet you, too. Nash speaks of you often. I'm glad to know he's got someone to keep him in line when he's out and about."

"Oh, I just remind him where to be and mail things for him. It's not that hard. Nash is a pussycat." Amy put her bag on her shoulder. "I'm off. My husband is taking me to dinner. You two have a nice evening and I'll see you again soon, Dahlia."

Nash excused himself to walk her to the door. Dahlia moved

to the windows, amazed at the view. The mountains stood in the distance, but most of the Strip lay below and to the east.

She felt him approach and leaned into his body when he wrapped his arms around her, melting at his touch. "Dinner will arrive in a few minutes. Is Indian all right?"

"Yes, wonderful. This is some view."

"It is, isn't it? Wait until it's fully dark. The lights are so beautiful." His hands slid up under the hem of her shirt, palms smoothing over her bare skin. "You're so warm."

"Mmm."

"Sweatshirt off. Hands on the window. Spread your feet."

Her eyes slid closed for a moment as she obeyed, the glass cool against her palms.

One-handed, he peeled the cups of her bra back, baring her breasts to his touch, rolling and tugging her nipples. Dahlia opened her eyes to catch the mirrored view in the window of his hand moving down her stomach and beneath the waistband of her yoga pants. She'd considered changing into something fancier, but she was glad she hadn't as clever fingers burrowed into her panties and delved into her pussy.

"You're so beautiful reflected there, Dahlia."

Her eyes flicked up, catching his gaze in the window.

What a picture she made! Leaned back into him, one of his hands doing naughty things to her nipple, the other in her pants. No one had ever made her look or feel the way he did. She wasn't afraid of her sexuality with him. He made her love that side of herself.

"I'm going to make you come. Just a quick one before dinner. And then we'll take our time. Give it to me, Dahlia."

"Work for it, Nash," she gasped as his rhythm against her clit sped up.

A dark chuckle was her reward, hot against her ear and neck. "Tough talk for a woman standing in front of my living room windows with my hand down her pants. Your pussy is hot and juicy in my palm. Do you wonder who can see you?"

Her eyes moved from his to the city below. As her orgasm built, she did indeed wonder. Was there a man in his hotel room with binoculars? Did he see how wanton she was, writhing, rolling her hips against Nash's hand?

"Dahlia Baker has a kink in her laces." His voice was teasing and she wanted to laugh but instead gasped as she began to come, fingers pressing against the glass, eyes locked with his again.

Some moments later he put her bra back in place and pulled his hand out of her pants. Reaching up, he drew a fingertip over her bottom lip and spun her, kissing her mouth.

Her taste mixed with his, dizzying her. As always, the dark edge of his sexuality turned her on. Her entire being sparked with electricity. Nash Emery made her feel so alive.

The doorbell sounded and he pulled back with a sigh. "Dinner is here."

Over dinner he asked her about the interview, and she gave him some details.

"I hope it doesn't scare you when I tell you I love the idea of you getting a job here in Vegas. I like you here."

She wasn't necessarily scared, but she was touched and thrilled because she liked being there with him, too. Damn, when had she fallen from attracted to him to really heavily into him? Trying to push that from her mind, she also told him she thought she'd be heading to Liberty for a few days at Christmas.

"I'll be going home, too. William and I leave here on Christmas Eve. I'll be back on the tenth. I'm going to New York right after New Year's and then to London.

"I hate being gone so long. Hell, I wish you could come with me to London. It's really pretty in the winter. I get the feeling I'm going to have trouble sleeping. I like you in my bed. Or me in yours."

Two weeks would be the longest they'd been apart since they'd started dating. Dahlia realized just thinking in those terms meant Nash had begun to mean a lot to her. She also didn't miss that he omitted wishing he could take her home for Christmas and wondered what that was all about.

"I like waking up with you, too. And I'll miss you. But it's important to be with family at the holidays. I'm sure your mother misses you during the year. It's not much to ask that you give the woman who birthed you a week of your life once a year." There, she said it. Told him she'd miss him— and she would.

He laughed. "You should be her press person. She has no problem saying any of that herself, though. My mother isn't afraid to use guilt. You know William is closing the club. He could have left it for his manager to run, but he's a control freak that way." He put his fork down and leaned over to kiss her temple. "I'll miss you, too."

They finished eating and then moved to his couch to watch the purpled sky fade into darkness, snuggled up together.

"I want to muss you up. But I'll want to even more when you get offstage, so I'll save it until tonight."

Turning, she moved to straddle his lap. "Are you on a mussing-Dahlia-up diet or something? Is there an only-one-mussing-up-per-day rule? If so, you totally broke it about fourteen times so far."

His eyes darkened and she found herself on her back on the carpet looking up into his face.

"You're playing with fire, Dahlia. I want you every moment of the day. It's an entirely new experience for me."

"Is there something you haven't told me about yourself, Nash? I just assumed that with two women attached to you like remora at all times, you liked girls."

He laughed and ground his cock into her. "Remora." He rolled his eyes. "It wasn't that bad. But I much prefer this one sultry dancer on my arm."

"Lest you think I'm fishing for compliments, I want to say I'm at a loss for words when you say that stuff. I don't know what you mean."

He kissed her softly and pulled back enough to look into her eyes. "I've never been one for exclusivity. But I assume we have that and I'd like it to stay that way."

"And this counts when you're in London or L.A. or wherever else?"

"You have plans for a new man while I'm away?"

She socked him in the arm playfully. "I mean you. I'm too busy when you're away to get caught up in an intense affair. I save it all for you."

Knowing how she was, knowing her fears and weaknesses about her place in his life, this admission from her knocked him out.

"God, you're amazing, Dahlia." He rained dozens of tiny

kisses all over her face, needing to be sweet and gentle with her for the moment. He ached to spread her out and love every inch of her body, slowly and surely. But she had to be onstage in three hours and he wanted more time than that.

"I am?" Her voice was breathless. "Because I don't have a few other dudes stashed away when you leave town?"

He stood quickly and pulled her up with him. "Come on. Let's go for a drive. You've got three hours. Remember that comment about muscle cars and their hoods? Shall we take the 'Vette?"

She nodded eagerly and stood.

But when they got to the car, she gasped. "I want to fall to my knees in reverence," she whispered, approaching the '54. Candy-apple red, whitewall tires, gleaming chrome. "This is just hot, Nash."

His face lit up as he grinned at her response. "I feel like I'm in church every time I see it. You ready to take that ride, Dahlia?"

"Lots of room to get to your cock as you're driving."

"God, the perfect woman." He sighed happily and pulled keys from his pocket.

He pulled the top off and let her in, liking the way she looked there in the passenger seat a whole hell of a lot.

Once off the Strip they headed out of town toward the lake. The roads weren't too crowded and the evening air was nice and warm, even for early December.

"Now, I think I've got a debt to pay."

Nash heard her seat belt unbuckle and groaned as her hands moved to his pants, opening the button and zipper, reaching in to grab his cock. The flutter of brightly colored silk caught in his peripheral vision as she took off her scarf, freeing her hair to the breeze. She turned sideways and leaned over, swirling her tongue around the head of his cock.

At once the shock of her mouth sent him into erotic overdrive. One of her hands slid into his boxers and grabbed his balls while the other gripped the base of his cock to hold him steady as she went down on him.

Speech left him as he took a side road and pulled into a near-deserted area. He loved the idea of a trucker seeing this gorgeous woman sucking his cock, but she wasn't wearing a seat belt and he didn't want to crash and hurt her, either. Precisely when she'd become so precious to him, he wasn't sure, but the bare fact was there, nonetheless.

The moon hung full and heavy overhead as he leaned back into the seat, watching down the line of his body as that ebony spill of hair rose and fell over him. Each flick and swirl of her tongue, every stroke told him how she felt in words he knew she couldn't part with just yet. Despite the fact that he was in a completely new place, too, he felt only tenderness for her. After a long time being the playboy bachelor, he was hanging up his old gig and grabbing this woman with both hands.

And as it had been with every single time she'd touched him, climax threatened very quickly. He sifted his hands through her hair, letting the wet heat of her mouth continue to bring him pleasure. She was so beautiful he ached knowing she had trouble accepting that beauty. Ached even more at the reasons why.

"Dahlia, baby, wait."

When she looked up at him, there was nothing he could

do but kiss her on those lips so delightfully swollen from sucking his cock.

"You and I have a date with the hood."

"I don't want to scratch it. Your GTO is one thing, but this 'Vette is a work of art."

He got out of the car and pulled her along with him. "Dahlia Baker, I want to fuck you on the hood of this shiny red car under the full moon. Would you deny me that? I'm just a hardworking man who loves the little pleasures life offers him." He pouted and she snickered.

"How do you want me?"

"Well, now. Acquiescent is a nice start. Hands on the hood, baby. I want to take you from behind. But first, take the shirt and bra off."

She moved to the front of the car and pulled off her shirt and bra, tossing them both into the passenger's seat. And with a look back over her shoulder at him, bent forward, her palms resting on the hood.

"Man you're beautiful with moonlight on your skin." Leaning in, he licked the curve of her spine from the waistband of her pants to her neck before reaching down to pull off her pants and toss them with her shirt.

Thank goodness he'd remembered to tuck a condom into his pocket before he'd left the penthouse! He rolled it on quickly and tested her readiness. "So wet. Always ready for me. Do you know how that makes me feel? Knowing your body responds to me this way?"

She sighed softly and it touched him deeply. He caressed the bare skin of her back and thighs as he slowly pressed his cock into her pussy.

Over and over he thrust all the way into her, as deeply as possible and then slowly pulled out. The rhythm he built was hypnotic, the scent of her body mingled with the crisp smells of the warm earth and the bark of some nearby trees.

Something in him shifted at that moment and he wanted to just hold her in his arms for hours. Nothing mattered but the two of them and how they were joined, his hands on her, the way her body took him in, sheltered and received him.

Dahlia only barely held back the tears that threatened to fall on the hood. Never in her life had she been touched with such tenderness. Nash made her feel treasured and truly beautiful. With him she could imagine being a whole woman. He knew what she was and accepted it. There was no judgment; he appreciated her mind and spirit as well as her body. She knew a man of his reputation wasn't after marriage but there was something between them. Something important, and that was enough.

When he reached around to circle her clit with a finger-tip it took only moments until she was coming. Her growing emotional attachment to him and the way he made her feel and see herself had ramped up her readiness. There in the moonlight—stripped naked, stripped of fear and her de-fenses—Dahlia gave herself to him utterly and completely.

♣ ♠ ♥ ♦ ♣ ♠ ♥ ♦ ♣ ♠ ♥ ♦

Chapter Seven

What a difference being a thousand miles north made. Bundled up in her heavy coat, Dahlia sat out on the porch sipping coffee and avoiding her father.

His words to her played around in her brain, edging at her heart. That he didn't see her for anything more than a pretty face hurt more than when strangers thought so.

"Hey."

Dahlia's sister, Iris, joined her on the glider swing.

"You're different, Dahlia. In a good way," Iris added quickly. "Confident. Tell me."

Dahlia told her sister about the job with Tate and how excited she was at the possible opportunity.

"You're the only one who seems to have trouble believing you're worthy."

"And Dad."

Iris sighed. "Back to that in a minute. Tell me about the guy. There's got to be one. I can tell."

Dahlia laughed. "His name is Nash and he's… God, Iris, he's amazing. Runs the family business with his brother. It's hard to explain what he does, but essentially he takes people who need things and introduces them to the people who can provide them and gets a commission for it. Only it's people like Robert De Niro and Sheryl Crow and stuff. He's cultured and rich. I don't know how to deal with it. I'm afraid that it means more to me than to him."

Dahlia paused and her sister waited.

"I think I'm in love with him and it's not quite been two months. I'm worried I'm going to end up dumped with my heart in a thousand pieces. I'm in way over my head, but I can't help it. I feel so alive when I'm with him."

"What are you worried about, then? Do you think he's just using you?"

"I want to trust what he says. He's the one who pushed for us to be exclusive. But he travels a lot and everywhere we go women fall over themselves for him. It's… I don't know how to handle that."

"Dahlia, why can't you see how truly special you are? I know you see how gorgeous you are. And life hasn't always been easy because of that. But you have such a problem understanding that a man would want *all* of you. Why?" Iris shook her head. "Okay, so I do know part of why. But so some guy from the hill dumped you in your senior year because his parents thought you were trash. You aren't, Dahlia. You were always better than Chris Foster and his stuck-up family. It's time to rise above all that. Some people will judge you no matter what. You can't do anything about it other than be a person of worth. And you are.

"If this guy knows what's good for him, he's in love with you, too. Give him a chance. Don't judge him the way you hate to be judged. But if he hurts you, I'll come down there and kick his ass."

Dahlia laughed. "I love you."

"And as for Dad, Dahlia, you're just going to have to accept that he doesn't get why you'd want to leave Liberty, and he won't—ever. He's a good man, he loves his family, but he doesn't have big dreams, and part of him feels inadequate because you do. Like the life he worked so hard for wasn't enough."

Damn, her sister was right. Dahlia felt ashamed she'd never thought of it that way.

Iris put her head on Dahlia's shoulder briefly.

"Let it go. Be happy."

Relief poured through Nash as the plane took off for Heathrow. A week with his mother shoving women at him was more than he could take. Even after he'd told her he was seeing someone.

More than anything, this time apart confirmed that he was developing some seriously deep feelings for Dahlia. All he thought of was her scent, the way she laughed. That hip thing she did onstage and in bed. The way she felt first thing in the morning, sleep-warm and always willing to open her arms and legs to him.

With other women, he got bored at a few weeks. But it had been five months since they'd first met and his fascination with her had begun. Two since they'd been officially seeing each other. He'd tried to talk with William about it, but his brother had blown him off, assuring Nash it was just a phase. And Nash, wanting to avoid a scene, had let it go, promising to revisit the subject soon. William seemed to like Dahlia well enough, but Nash noted how suspicious he seemed of her motives.

His brother was where Nash had been six months before. Married to his job and enjoying the favors of every woman he could.

For Nash it was like he'd been living half a life. He hadn't noticed how much he'd been missing until Dahlia filled in all the corners, making him whole.

Rushing back to Vegas from London, Nash headed straight to Dahlia's place. He knocked on her door and it swung open. Concerned, he peeked inside and saw her there, sitting in a chair and staring off into space.

"Dahlia? Baby, are you all right?" She never left her door open, and her usually animated features were slack. Alarmed, he rushed into her apartment and she turned, jumping up and into his arms laughing.

Relief nearly stopped his heart when he realized she was all right.

"Joseph Tate just called. I got the job, Nash. And you're back. Oh, my God, you're back and I missed you so much. What are you doing back so early? I thought you weren't due back for three days."

He put her down and kissed her quickly. "Congratulations! That's great news. I'm so proud of you. I finished up as fast as I could because I wanted to see you. I missed you, too. You look good."

She looked down at her hoodie and jeans. "Yeah, the

height of fashion." He'd just said he was proud of her. More than any other compliment, that meant something to her.

"Come to my place. It's your night off so we can get dressed up, grab some dinner and hit a club to celebrate. Afterward, we can go back to my place, take a hot bath and I'll lick you dry."

"I don't know. Where do you want to go?"

"Lupo? Chinois? Fleur de Lys?"

Good Lord, the man had expensive taste. Still, it'd be nice to celebrate.

"I see hesitation and I wager it's about how much things cost. Stop. You just got offered a great job. You're my girlfriend, let me do this. And you don't let me shower you with expensive presents the way I want to all the time. So this is for me, too."

She blushed and smiled at his saying she was his girlfriend. "Oh, all right. The pains a girl has to endure when her boyfriend is rich."

He grabbed her and pulled her close. "You just admitted I was your boyfriend."

"Is it a secret?" she teased.

"Sometimes it feels like you think so." He raised an eyebrow at her. She watched as he whipped out his cell phone and procured an impossible Friday-night, last-minute reservation at Le Cirque.

When he did stuff like that she was impressed and also felt like a hick. "Well, that was something. I've never been to Le Cirque."

He laughed. "You're in for a treat, then. And we can get gelato afterward. I like to watch you lick the spoon."

"I told my family about you," she blurted out.

Looking ridiculously pleased, he took her hand and kissed it. "You did? Wow. Thank you, Dahlia. That means a lot to me."

She shrugged and noticed he didn't say he had told his mother. A pang of doubt rode her again. Was he ashamed of her?

Back at his penthouse she nearly ran back out the door when she saw the literal heap of presents. She had something for him in her bag, but it paled in comparison.

"Go on. Open up!"

She sat, and he handed her a large, flat box. When she opened it, a beautiful red dress slid toward her. She picked it up and the material made her want to weep. "You bought me a dress from Chanel?" She couldn't even act outraged— the dress in her hands was a work of art.

"Yes. It's beautiful and I saw it and knew you had to have it. Please, Dahlia. I know you're uncomfortable with my spending money on you, but I have it and I wanted to buy it for you. Won't you let me? I promise to restrain myself but for birthdays and major holidays."

How could she refuse the dress in her hands? The look on his face? "Thank you."

There were other lavish gifts, things she'd never have been able to afford. Still, each one was clearly something he'd thought about carefully.

"I'm just overwhelmed. Thank you, Nash. You're so generous. I have something for you, too, but it's, well, it's not a Fendi bag."

He touched her chin with a fingertip. "It's from you. That's what matters."

Reaching into her bag, she pulled out the package.

Gleefully, he tore it open and looked at the shirt inside. "Dahlia." He picked it up and looked at it.

"Do you like it?" Suddenly she felt eight years old. God, what made her think making him a shirt was a good idea? A man like him? She wanted to crawl into a hole.

"Do I like it? Did you make this?"

She nodded. "My mom helped. This was over my head, but she rocks with a needle and thread. I stole one of your dress shirts for your measurements."

He pulled off his shirt and put hers on and she had to admit it fit perfectly. "This is brilliant, Dahlia. I love it. Thank you."

Good God, she'd made him a shirt. Made it with her own hands and creativity. Crap, his presents didn't even compare to her thought and effort. He was a fortunate man.

"I'm wearing this tonight."

The smile he got in return made him want to toss her over his shoulder and stay in instead. He loved it when she was exposed like that. Not trying to hide herself from him.

But what he got was nearly as good as a sweaty romp. He got the intimacy of her standing next to him in his dressing area as she applied makeup and did her hair. It was a normal moment, but it meant so much. And the woman was made for expensive clothing. She looked so fucking gorgeous in the dress and shoes he wasn't sure he wanted to take her out in public.

Her hair cascaded down her back in fat curls. Red lips matched the dress. Her body, generous, voluptuous, was framed by the deep scarlet of the dress, her breasts hugged lovingly. All of this accentuated by the height of the strappy heels.

Yep. Sex bomb—and she was all his.

It was so deceptively simple then for him. This life with her. He wanted it, and he wanted it for good.

♣ ♠ ♥ ♦ ♣ ♠ ♥ ♦ ♣ ♠ ♥ ♦

Chapter Eight

Six months after that first dinner at her apartment, Dahlia could admit without hesitation that she loved Nash Emery. She was pretty sure he loved her, too. He certainly treated her that way.

But the doubts remained. Every time they were out and one of his friends would approach, she saw how they looked at her. They spoke of things she didn't know, of people and places she was unfamiliar with. Many of the men looked her over in ways that made her feel cheap, and the women, if they addressed her at all, were patronizing, and it was clear they didn't think much of her.

She hated that. Worse, she hated her hesitation in bringing it to Nash, who seemed totally clueless. She was a confident woman! She wanted to believe what her heart told her and she loathed the weakness she felt over it. Still, things were going better than they ever had, personally and professionally. Her job was amazing, and she was nearing the time when she'd be leaving The Dollhouse for good.

She headed into The Dollhouse a little early to stretch before opening.

Even better, she heard Nash's voice coming from William's office and she moved toward it, happy that he'd returned a few days early.

"I know what Lara says, William. She's got a point…"

"Don't be stupid. Dahlia's got no family name. I can see the appeal, she's a hot number. You fuck a girl like that. You buy her some expensive gifts, enjoy the hell out of her body for a while and you move on.

"You've been seen all over town with this girl for months now. It's time to remember who and what you come from. Dahlia isn't one of us. She can't fit into our life. And you shouldn't want her to. She's not made for it. Can you imagine what Mother would do if you brought her home? You can't. You bring home a woman like Lara Warner."

Dahlia held her stomach, nausea holding her hostage as her world crashed around her head.

"Hey, Dahlia! Nice to see you tonight," one of the bouncers called to her as he walked in the front doors.

The discussion in William's office halted and she pushed the door open to see both brothers looking toward her guiltily.

Nash started to speak but she held up her hand as she stalked to William's desk.

Rage warred with shame as she took a long look at her former boss. "You can go fuck yourself, you goddamn snob. I quit." With that she turned on her heel and ran past Nash, shoving at him as he tried to grab her.

She heard him shouting her name moments later, but she ran to her car and drove the hell away from The Liege and the man she thought loved her.

Smacking the steering wheel with her hand she gnashed

her teeth. Who the hell did Nash think he was, anyway? *Lara had a point?* She'd fallen prey to his charms and forgotten herself. That she'd actually thought he loved her made her feel like an utter fool, but, damn it, what made him and that prick brother of his better than her? She worked hard! Made her own way in the world.

Her phone rang. She tossed it down when she saw it was him.

Finally arriving home, she'd started to pull into the lot but saw Nash's GTO. Reversing her car, she headed to Roseanne's.

Roseanne took one look at her face and pulled her into the apartment and gave her a hug. "Honey, what is it?"

Her phone rang so many times she turned it off and told Roseanne the whole story.

Roseanne made a face. "What the fuck? I don't understand. Look, Dahlia, I don't know a lot of things but I do know Nash Emery is in love with you. William is an asshole, yes. But Nash? Honey, his face lights up every time you walk into a room. I don't buy the idea of some secret hate about your lack of a pedigree."

The tears came then, and Roseanne held her tight until they passed. "Oh, God, I'm in love with him. He always avoided talking about taking me to meet his mother. He's ashamed of me. He'd say he wished I could come with him to London or Milan but never, ever that he wished his mother could meet me. I should have listened to my inner voice about it."

"Sweetie, I think you should let him explain. If it's not what you want to hear, what have you lost? But what if you misunderstood? You said you only heard William talking. Are you going to write this off so easily?"

"I don't know what to do!" True, it had been just William. But what about that comment about Lara's being right? And what about his being ashamed of her? The possibilities struck her frozen, unable to think about anything.

"What do you have to lose?"

"My heart. My dignity."

"Girl, you already lost your heart and what the fuck is dignity when you're sleeping on a garage-sale couch in my living room when a man like Nash just might truly love you?" Roseanne rolled her eyes. "I'm going to work. If you want to stay, the bed in my spare room is made up. I love you no matter what."

Roseanne walked out and Dahlia put her head in her hands.

Nash had thought of nothing but Dahlia the whole plane trip back from New York. It was high time his family accepted that he was in love and with this woman for good. He also wanted to push through the last of Dahlia's emotional walls and tell her he loved her straight out. He'd shown her, he'd said it in a hundred other ways but he wanted to tell her.

Knowing his mother would be the biggest battle, he decided to go to William first. He'd dropped his bags off at home and gone to The Dollhouse.

When he'd confessed the depth of his feelings for Dahlia, William's attitude had gone from amusement to concern that Nash may have been the target of a gold digger. He hadn't had any real idea of just who Dahlia was. Part of that was Nash's fault for not having her around William more socially so he could get to know her better.

Worse, Lara Warner had been talking shit around town. Though she did have a point. Nash did have a responsibility to his station in life—a responsibility to make it one-hundred-percent clear that he was with Dahlia Baker. Not as a fling. Not as a pretty bit on the side. But for good.

He'd been on the verge of interrupting his brother to re-iterate just how deeply he felt for Dahlia, to tell William why he trusted her, when they'd heard Dahlia's name being called. Time had slowed as he'd turned to see her standing there in the hallway.

Nash would never in a million years forget the look on her face as she'd stood there, obviously hurt and humiliated. He'd jumped up to explain, but her hand had flown up, cutting him off, and she'd stalked in, told William off and stormed out.

He'd been so stunned by the whole thing, that lapse of time had given her a head start. He stood there, watching her taillights, his stomach sinking. Grabbing his phone, he called hers and got voice mail as he got into his car and raced toward her place. Arriving first, he thanked his forethought to take the back way.

Using his charm and a hundred-dollar bill, he managed to convince the manager to let him inside her apartment. Nash had been there often enough that the guy knew him by sight.

And then he waited.

After her mailbox filled up he called William and chewed him a new one.

"I didn't know she was standing there!" At least his brother sounded guilty.

"William, how can you work with these women and

think about them the way you do? She's a good person. Do you know I have to talk her into taking presents from me? She could have worked me for tens of thousands of dollars by now, but she goes out of her way to pay every bit she can. I love her. I mean to be with her and if I can get her to take me back after this mess, I'm asking her to move in with me and marry me by the end of the year."

"I think she's out of your comfort zone, Nash. I think being with a woman like Dahlia is going to be a big test for you."

"A test? What the hell are you talking about? We've been together for six months. It's not like I'm nineteen years old and I met her yesterday."

"You're going to bring her to social functions and she'll be uncomfortable. Your friends and family will be uncomfortable because she's not one of us. It'll eat away at both of you."

"This isn't about you and Leah, William. Or is it? Is that why the two of you broke it off?" Leah had been William's fiancée of two years. They'd broken off the engagement suddenly, and William had refused to talk about it. Nash began to wonder just how much of William's feelings about Dahlia, about women in general, had to do with Leah.

"Not your business at all. When it comes down to it, Nash, you can't trust this woman because you have something she doesn't. Money."

"This *is* about Leah, isn't it? Was Leah a gold digger?"

"We're done with this subject. If you love Dahlia, fine. That's enough for me, but I want you to remember this is not going to be a bed of roses. It's easy for you to downplay the class thing, but she's the one who has to suffer for it."

"I'm not asking you to name a hospital wing after her,

William! What I'm asking is simple—accept her because I love her. It's not a hard choice for me and it's a bullshit ultimatum."

William sighed and Nash wished like hell he'd known more about the breakup between his brother and his ex.

"You're right. I'm sorry. I'll do whatever I can to make her feel welcome. I'll even call her and offer her her job back." William chuckled. "She sure told me, though."

Nash laughed. "Yeah, she's everything, William."

"Well, then, go get her back."

After hanging up, he picked up a book and settled in to wait.

For want of something to do to make the wait easier, he called her cell again and was able to leave a message. At least her mailbox was empty. She'd listened to her messages. Or he hoped she had without just deleting them all.

After she stared at her phone for an hour, she decided to listen to her messages. The first ones were just demands that she talk to him, call him back, meet him and let him explain.

But the last one he'd talked until he'd gotten cut off. He told her he loved her and was in the process of explaining that to his brother. He said he'd been about to interrupt William to defend her when she'd overheard.

He loved her. Or so he said.

Curling up on the couch, she watched reality television and fell asleep.

Nash hadn't been sleeping when his phone rang. He'd been lying in her bed, breathing her in, seeing her every-where and wanting to hold her so badly he ached.

Surprisingly, it was Roseanne from The Dollhouse. "Yo,

Emery, I hear you tossed Dahlia to the curb. You lookin' for some action? I can help you move on really easily."

Indignant, Nash sat up. "Hey! I thought she was your friend. I didn't toss Dahlia to the curb. I love her! What the hell is wrong with you?"

Roseanne laughed. "Okay, you pass, Nash. Of course I'm Dahlia's friend. I was testing you. She's here in my guest room and she's strung out and you've made her cry so much her face is a mess. And you know how much it takes to make a face like that look a mess? I am very displeased with you."

"That was a test? You were yanking my chain for fun? Is she all right? Can I come and see her?"

"You had a reputation for a reason—I wanted to be sure you really loved her. She doesn't know what to do. She loves you and she feels betrayed and humiliated. No, you can't come over. She'd kill me if she knew I told you this much. Plus, I want her to rest. She has classes tomorrow. She'll go home after that. If you're lurking, don't be stupid and park in the lot where she can see you." With that, Roseanne hung up.

♣ ♠ ♥ ♦ ♣ ♠ ♥ ♦ ♣ ♠ ♥ ♦

Chapter Nine

Dahlia got up and out of Roseanne's first thing the next morning. She moved through her day in a daze, not really hearing anything anyone said. Finally, at four, she drove home on autopilot, relieved and saddened that Nash's GTO wasn't in her lot anymore.

Slumping up the stairs, she let herself into her apartment and tossed her bag to the side only to jump three feet in the air when Nash spoke from where he was sitting on her couch.

"Are you all right?"

He looked tired. Sad. A tiny bit lost. And, damn the man, he still looked handsome and sexy.

"Your car is gone! What the hell are you doing here?" she demanded, arms crossed over her chest.

"Dahlia, please listen to me. I'm sorry you heard William say that. I know you must feel hurt being spoken of like you were just a cheap lay but…"

"I was so stupid. I should have known better. I knew what you were and I fell for it, anyway. It's my fault, really, for thinking that a playboy who fucked everything willing would have real feelings for me other than wanting to bang me."

He stopped like he'd been slapped. Storming over to her, he grabbed her up and tossed her gently on the couch. "You're going to sit there and listen to me. Yes, you *are* stupid, Dahlia. You're so fond of talking about how everyone judges you and how you're so hurt by stereotypes, but you continue to hold on to this stereotype about me that isn't true anymore. I have never, ever, given you any reason to doubt my feelings and commitment to you." He began to pace and she watched him warily.

"I want you to name one instance, other than the first time I hit on you, that I've treated you badly. Made you feel anything less than like the woman I love. Yes, that's right, Dahlia Baker, I love you. Even though you're difficult and prickly and you have a major stick up your ass about my money. So go on. Tell me and if you can come up with one time I've acted like a playboy out to fuck anything willing—other than you—I'll walk out that door and never bother you again."

He sat on the chair across the room, staring at her with his arms crossed.

Standing up, she went to the kitchen and got herself a bottled water and went back to sit down, tossing him one as well.

He was right. Aside from that crap in William's office and the first time he hit on her, he'd been genuine and caring with her. Made her feel beautiful and respected and, yes, loved. He'd cheered her on with her new job and had appreciated how much she loved the creative outlet of dancing at The Doll-house. As it turned out, not very playboy-on-the-make at all.

Putting her head in her hands, she leaned forward. "You're right. I'm sorry. I judged you the same way people have judged me all my life."

She looked up at him and saw the unshed tears in his eyes.

"But it still doesn't excuse you talking about me like I was a whore."

Staying in the chair, he stared at her. "Even after all of the stuff you said, you still don't trust me. *William* was the one who said all that shit. Who did you hear talking, Dahlia?"

"Both of you! William said most of it, but I heard you say Lara had a point!"

"She did! About me having a responsibility, about us being from different backgrounds. My responsibility was to make sure everyone knew what you mean to me. But you didn't even let me explain. You just jumped to some kind of conclusion that I was an asshole just using you. I haven't done anything to make you feel that way, and I'm sick and goddamned tired of you being so defensive and distrusting when I've gone out of my way to show you how much I treasure you!"

She blinked in the face of his anger. He'd never been that way with her before. He'd always just accepted her defensiveness and her moodiness with his laid-back calm.

"What have I done to deserve to be treated like shit, Dahlia? Haven't I shown you how much I love you?"

"Why haven't I met your mother, then? Every time you bring her up, you avoid the subject of us meeting. You talk about your responsibility but doesn't that prove my point about you hiding me?"

"Damn you, Dahlia!" He stood up and began to pace. "Why are you trying to push me away? I'm not going to let you do it, but I'm not going to let you continue to punish me for the sins of other men in your past, either. It's insulting and I deserve more. I've given you time. I've given you space. I've done everything I could to show you how much I care for you. I tell you I want to be sure everyone knows what you mean to me and you turn it around and make it a negative. It's time for you to give something, too."

Shaking, she watched him as he moved. Terror gripped her. The idea of losing him made her sick to her stomach. He was right; he had been good to her. She hadn't given as much as he had and, yes, she'd held on to her fears that he was nothing but a playboy. She supposed it was a way to protect herself if he did turn out to be an ass. It just made her one. But that didn't explain the mother thing.

"Is this an ultimatum?"

"So she speaks." One of his eyebrows rose. "Yes, I suppose it is. I won't let you chase me away totally, but if you can't trust me, I have to back off. It hurts too much to be with you like this. It's not right for you to expect me to stay if things are one-sided. But I love you. And, damn it, I am pretty much begging you to be with me."

She took a deep breath and thought hard.

He sighed. "I'm going to run home and clean up. I need to make some calls. Why don't you think about it and if you can be with me and give me your trust, come to me. You know the code to my penthouse. I love you, Dahlia. With everything I am. I want us to be together. I want *you* to want that, too."

He looked at her one last time and left.

She sat, staring at the door for what seemed like an hour as she replayed their entire relationship from his first insulting pickup line to that moment where he walked out her door.

The laughter, the fear and the pain all flowed over her. She'd been in love with him for months. Her anger at him dissolved because he was right. She was the one who was wrong.

Her lack of trust in him crashed through her. Her doubts, her stupid fucking past, had hobbled her and she'd allowed it. Thought she was so damned strong, but she'd held on to stereotypes to keep herself from truly being happy with this man.

She'd been so wrong. He'd given her his heart, saw her stripped of everything and loved her, flaws and all. And she'd thrown it in his face. She'd run out on him, not even letting him explain, and when he'd tried, she'd yelled at him. She'd been a total coward.

She would not lose him. Nash Emery was hers. Her arrogant, very hot, very sweet man and she meant to make things right. Even if she had to deal with his idiot of a brother and get to the bottom of this crap about his mother.

Standing up, she went into her bathroom and showered, changing into the dress he'd given her for Christmas. Pulling a coat on over it, she headed to him.

Still shaking, she took a deep breath, pressed the entry code into the elevator and rode it to his penthouse.

It had been the hardest thing Nash had ever done, walking out on Dahlia. He'd watched her shake and tremble. Had known how upset and shaken she was, but his outrage and hurt had trumped his concern for her. He deserved respect and trust and he had to demand it. They had a future together, he knew she knew that. But they wouldn't last if she didn't let go of the last bit of her fear and trust him to love her.

An hour passed with no word from her, and he began to

worry. What if he'd pushed her away completely? He did need to explain about his mother—he should have done so at her place. What if she used that to hold him back?

Well, fuck that! He'd go back over there and make her listen. Damned stubborn female!

His heart skipped a beat when the concierge called him to let him know Dahlia had arrived and was on her way up. Taking a deep breath, he went to the doors to let her inside.

When the elevator opened, she stepped out and he saw she was wearing the red stilettos he'd given her for Christmas. That was promising, wasn't it?

Her smile was hesitant and he saw the emotion on her face. He held out his hand and she reached out, taking it, and he knew they had a fighting chance. But also knew he'd have to hold strong.

"Hi."

She smiled and he led her into his place. When she took off the coat, he saw she was wearing the Chanel dress.

"I know, I'm overdressed. But I thought—" She shook her head and exhaled sharply. "I don't know what I thought. It seems stupid now."

"Tell me. You're not stupid. I'm glad you're here."

She reached out, touching his face gently and he leaned into her hand.

"I thought that if I wore this, you'd see that I accepted it. Accepted the part of you, one of the parts, that scared me before."

"And it doesn't scare you now?"

"I'm going to try very hard not to let it. I'm sorry, Nash. You were right. I blamed you for what William said. I let my fears grab any little straw to push you away, and that was stupid and wrong. You've been so good to me. I do trust you, Nash. I know I haven't acted like it. But I do, and I'm sorry."

Letting out the breath he'd been holding, he pulled her into an embrace for long moments, letting the feel of her against him calm him.

He moved to look into her face. "I'm sorry, too. Sorry you had to hear that and sorry that you had enough history to make you wonder about me. I'm not ashamed of you. But I won't lie. It'll be difficult when you meet my mother. I didn't want you to meet her because she's a hard woman. But that's about her, not you. I've called her and told her about you and how serious things were. I'm giving her time to digest it but made it clear there's no other option but to accept it.

"You haven't commented on my telling you I loved you. How…do…aw, hell, do you love me, too, or am I just an idiot?"

Reaching out to touch his cheek, she nodded. "You're totally an idiot but I do love you. And since I'm an idiot, too, I suppose we'll be okay. Although the mother thing makes me nervous. I want her to like me."

Nodding, he kissed her forehead and the tip of her nose. "Thank you for loving me. And let's just take it one day at a time with my mother, okay? Now, before I ravish you, I need to get a few things settled."

She pouted. "Oh, all right. Speed it up, then. I want to get to the ravishing."

He sat on the couch and pulled her onto his lap, facing

him, pushing up her skirt. "This dress is pretty figure-hugging. Not a lot of room to ravish in this thing."

"This is what you wanted to get straight?" Standing up, she pulled it off and laid it on the chair behind her.

"Holy crap. How am I supposed to concentrate with those tits staring me in the face?"

"Get to it already!"

"I think you should move in with me. We can get a place together. The penthouse isn't a home and your apartment is too small for me to have an office."

Dahlia's heart pounded erratically. "I don't know what to say!"

"Yes, you do. You want to say yes, but you're afraid."

She rolled her eyes. "Okay, so I want to say yes but I'm afraid."

"See? How hard was that? I'm afraid, too. So there. I made an appointment with a Realtor for Sunday afternoon. Don't argue, we've already agreed you want to say yes and we'll get through the fear stuff together. My plan is lots and lots of sex."

"You're really pushy. But since I quit my job at the Doll-house, I'll have Sundays free. Of course I won't have a lot of money. Certainly not enough to buy a house in your price range."

"The second thing is that you'll stop freaking about my money. I have it and you don't. Yet. But you will when you start working full-time at Tate. Not as much as me because, well, I have a shitload of cash, but stop being so damned sensitive about it. Anyway, the house can be your wedding present."

She gaped and he laughed. "Still scarring my ego, Dahlia.

Give a guy a break. I love you and you love me. We're moving in together. We've been together for six months. Let's just say we're getting married New Year's. If you find out something terrible about me that's a deal breaker like you hate my laundry soap or something, you can back out. If not, marry me on New Year's."

"You know, Nash, subtlety is utterly lost on you. Yesterday I was just your girlfriend, but now you want to set up house and marry me?"

"We've already established my greed. But I'm charming, good in bed, a good provider. And I love you. I want you to be happy and I want to be the one who makes that happen."

"I hate when you're charming and I'm utterly helpless against it."

"You're so romantic, Dahlia. Is that a yes?"

Sighing dramatically, she nodded. "If I say yes, will the ravishment take place sooner?"

He kissed the tip of her nose. "Dahlia, this is serious. I love you. I want to be with you. I want to plan this wedding and have our house and build a life together. I want you to agree because you want it, too."

Her heart softened. "I love you so much it scares me. There's nothing to hide behind with you. I feel naked. Vulnerable. This is all so wonderful, I'm afraid it'll go away tomorrow."

"I'm not going anywhere. We'll work out the rough spots. There will be rough spots, I know that. I choose you. I told William that yesterday and I told my mother that this morning. I want you to always know you're first with me. *We're* first. Make a pledge to stand with me and do the same and we will make this work."

"Oh, God, I'm causing trouble with your family already!"

"If there's trouble, it's not your choice or your problem. But I have faith because you're impossible not to like. If she doesn't, you'll hold your own because I'll be there right beside you. Where a husband should be. Come on, Dahlia. I'm calling, let's see those cards."

She threw her arms around him. "You're stuck with me. I'll sign a prenup but I'm keeping my last name."

"Hyphenate and no prenup."

"Okay, let's not negotiate this right now. I've been promised ravishment and you've provided exactly none. We can't seal the deal without a meeting of the pink parts so let's get ravishing."

"You're a very bossy woman."

"Yeah? But you can put a stripper pole in our bedroom and you'll get a great show. I'm totally worth it."

Leaning forward, he pressed his face into the softness of her breasts briefly before laying his head on the back of the couch.

"Take the rest of your clothes off, Dahlia."

"At last. I was beginning to think you were all hat and no cattle if you know what I mean." She stood, taking her panties off, shimmying out of her bra. Reaching up, she pulled the clip from her hair and it fell around her shoulders.

Looking up at her, he took it all in. The long lines of her body, the lush thighs and breasts, the curves, the inky blue-black curls that tumbled around her face—she was the total package. But more than that, her brains, her sense of humor and her strength of character along with her love of cars made her perfect for him. He didn't lie to himself; her looks and innate sensuality had drawn his attention from day one, but it was the inside of Dahlia Baker that kept it and made him yearn to know more.

One-handed, he unbuttoned and unzipped his jeans, pulling his already-hard cock out and lazily stroking it.

"That's nice. There's something really hot about watching the way you hold your cock." Her eyes greedily watched his every move.

He grinned. "Something else we have in common. I like watching the way you hold my cock, too. See, it's meant to be. Go into the bedroom and lay down on the bed. I'll be right behind you."

With an extra sway to her hips, she sashayed past him and into the bedroom. He heard her settle onto the bed and when he walked into the room he was naked, too. And ready for some serious ravishment.

Pulling up a chair, he spun it and sat on it backwards, arms draped over the back, watching her avidly.

"All that talk of watching made me hungry for it. You've made yourself come when I've been inside you but I haven't watched you do it. And I think that's what I'd like to do now. Show me, Dahlia. Show me what you do when I'm away."

She blushed, chewing on her bottom lip for a moment. "All right." Reaching out, she slid open the drawer to his bedside table and rustled through it until she pulled out a vibrator. "I can't believe I'm doing this," she mumbled, rolling a condom over it.

"I'm so glad you are. Even more glad I had that genius idea to keep a vibrator here to use on you. You have no idea how sexy you are, do you? You wreck me, Dahlia. I can't stop thinking about you. I can't stop wanting to touch you. Each time I find out something new about you it just adds to your allure. You like to be watched, we both know it. Give me a show, baby."

She shivered at being known so well and settled onto her back, her head on the pillows so she could look at him.

Slowly, her fingertips played over her nipples. Just a feather-light touch at first before beginning to roll and tug them. Her eyelids slid shut as bursts of heat began to spark and spread through her body.

Reaching out, she grabbed the vibe and turned it on, the low hum filling the room. Dahlia heard Nash moan softly when she lubed the tip of it and drew it over her nipples.

"Warming lube," she gasped and he swore under his breath. Her body smoldered and her limbs grew heavy as her pussy bloomed and slicked with desire. Knowing he watched her added to the excitement.

She drew two fingers around her nipple and put them into her mouth, smiling when she saw his reaction, his knuckles white as he gripped the chair back. "Tastes like cinnamon."

"I remember."

She got to her knees and then on all fours, drawing the vibrator slowly toward her pussy.

"Wait, I can't see it all." Standing, he moved to her, sitting on the bed behind her so he had an unobstructed view of her pussy and of her face in the mirror over the dresser across from the bed. "Much better." Her eyes met his and watched his face change as she slid the vibrator into herself.

Her nipples brushed the blankets as she moved, ass up, head down to angle the vibrator better and to reach her clit.

She wouldn't last long; his eyes on her and this position would bring her off quickly.

The lube warmed her pussy, made her clit slick and tingly as she flicked it with the tip of her middle finger. Her breath came quick and short.

She caught the blanket between her teeth as she cried out when climax slammed into her body. She rode it, vibe still deep inside her until she felt Nash behind her, slowly pulling it out and replacing it with his cock.

"That is the sexiest thing I've ever seen. Holy shit, Dahlia. Do you really masturbate that way?" His voice was strained as he settled himself behind her and began to thrust in short, hard digs.

"Yes. Oh, God, yes. It's almost like getting fucked. I love coming with a cock buried inside my pussy."

He swore again. "Do you fantasize about me when you do it?"

"Yes. Even before we went out I had to come home and masturbate every damned time I saw you at the club. But fantasy has nothing on the real thing."

Hands gripping her hips tightly, he began to fuck into her body with a rhythm that told her he'd be there a while. She closed her eyes and fell into herself, letting it just be about that moment. She'd deal with the enormity of what had happened over the past twenty-four hours afterward. But for then, it was about Nash and Dahlia.

Her body parted around his, making room for the inexorable invasion of his cock. She was made for him, for this. And the admission of that point didn't scare her as much as it had before. With his hands holding her, anchoring her, she felt safe. Safe to feel everything he made her feel. Without guilt and without shame.

Nash looked down at each bump in the curve of her spine, at the creamy curves of her waist and hips. He couldn't see her face but he suspected she was as near overwhelmed as him by what had passed between them. In a way he was glad to be able to close his eyes and remember how she'd looked as she'd brought herself off just for him. What a turn-on and what a gift she'd given him of such intimacy!

Her pussy clutched at him, hugging his cock in a heated embrace. The cool, soft skin of the back of her thighs brushed against the hair on his thighs as she squirmed back against him, meeting his thrusts.

If he hadn't been gripping her hips so tightly, he was sure his hands would be trembling. This was his woman. No longer just the woman he was with, he was hers and she was his and that made it different somehow.

A long, low groan came from her and he leaned down and kissed the back of her neck. "You okay, baby?"

"The heat," she gasped. "The lube has warmed me up. Each time you push into me it feels amazing."

"I want to fuck you without a condom. Very soon." He yearned to feel her pussy, naked against his cock.

"Soon. Oh, God, please come. Please," she cried out.

Reaching around her body, he found her clit slippery and begging to be touched and he obliged. Within moments he felt the change in her pussy as her inner muscles clenched and fluttered with climax. He continued to stroke into her deep and hard as he tried to resist the siren call of those damned inner muscles, but it was a losing battle. The memories of how she'd looked and sounded as she'd fingered herself and the way she felt then rushed through him.

Pushing one last time as deeply into her as he could, pleasure exploded around him as he came.

After long moments, they fell to the mattress and he moved away for a few seconds, coming right back to pull her body against his.

"I love you, Dahlia."

She moved to face him. "I love you, too, Nash."

★ ★ ★ ★ ★

RED-HANDED
Kit Tunstall

♣ ♠ ♥ ♦ ♣ ♠ ♥ ♦ ♣ ♠ ♥ ♦

Chapter One

Amy watched with wide-eyed horror as Kevin went all-in. Pretending to check her watch, she brought her wrist to her mouth to speak into the microphone that transmitted to his earpiece. "What are you doing? That bet will get security's attention."

Kevin ignored her. Her gaze remained glued to the PDA she had tucked discreetly under her arm. She had designed the electronic system that allowed her cousin to control where the roulette wheel stopped. He had possession of the device, so all she could do was watch on the tiny screen as he once again made his number come up, this time collecting several hundred thousand in the process. He hadn't listened to a thing she'd told him about gambling. He was supposed to stagger his winning numbers and never bet more than a few thousand at a time. Yet he had amassed so much money so quickly that it seemed impossible security hadn't taken him aside already.

She breathed a sigh of relief when he collected a ticket for his winnings and walked to the cashier. Surely, he had made enough with tonight's bets so that they wouldn't have to do this again. Amy followed her cousin's progress as he sauntered from the casino, looking like he didn't have a care in the world. Once he had cleared the doors, she tucked the PDA into the sleeve of her oversized hoodie and stood up, prepared to slip out behind him.

Amy ran straight into two men who looked like they could bend her into a pretzel. They wore identical black suits, white shirts and black ties, along with matching frowns. The only contrast between them was the shade of their hair. Her stomach clenched with fear, and she suddenly had the urge to urinate.

Somehow, she managed a small smile. "Excuse me." Even as she tried to brush past them, she knew they were there for her. It didn't surprise her when the blond put his hand on her arm.

"Mr. Cavello would like to see you."

Amy tried for a blank look, but she knew exactly who he was. Roan Cavello owned The Liege casino, where Kevin had just screwed up her careful system and attracted unwanted attention. "I'm sorry, but I really must go. I'm meeting a friend...he's a cop," she added with a hint of desperation.

"Mr. Cavello insists."

Amy thought about struggling but quickly discarded the notion. She would only make a fool of herself, and her protests wouldn't garner help, anyway. The other gamblers might look up from their various tables and machines if she yelled, but they certainly wouldn't step away from their games to intercede on her behalf with Security.

She shrugged, affecting a nonchalance she didn't feel, and trudged between the two men, noting they kept her within touching distance at all times. They didn't make contact, but she knew they would grab her in a second if she tried to run.

As they led her from the gaming floor to a door marked Private, her stomach clenched again, and she had to suppress a wave of nausea. If her research was correct, they would be taking her to an area that resembled an interrogation room in a police department. It was a way to hold her until they were ready to turn her over to officials with the Nevada Gaming Commission.

Depending on how the casino operated, there might be cameras in the room but maybe not. Without witnesses or recording devices, they could do anything to her. In the old days, the NGC wouldn't have even been called in. Amy never thought she would be relieved at the thought of being turned over to legal officials.

The hallway was nondescript, with pale yellow walls and a white tile floor that squeaked under the soles of her Kmart sneakers. Amy cringed each time her shoes squealed, having the irrational notion it called more attention to her.

Amy quickly lost all expression when the men steered her through an unmarked door into a room with thick concrete walls, a scarred metal table and a bare bulb hanging from the ceiling. She sat without protest when the brunette steered her to a chair in the corner. The table and the two goons' presence blocked her in, making it that much more difficult to reach the door.

She scanned the room with nervous eyes. Her heart skipped a beat when she saw a camera high on the wall, angled in her direction. At least there would be a record of the interview.

Hands clenched tightly in her lap, Amy didn't try to speak. These men couldn't and wouldn't help her, and they certainly weren't the ones who wanted to speak with her. They simply did Roan Cavello's bidding, just like every other employee in the building.

She wondered if Kevin had made it out without being caught. Concern for his fate tempered her anger that he had messed up everything and landed her in this predicament. Amy had to admit it was difficult to worry overmuch about her cousin when her own future was in doubt at the moment. What would Roan Cavello do to her?

As if thinking of him had conjured the man, he entered the room. His walk was silent and stealthy, like a hunter stalking prey. Amy gulped audibly when she saw the predatory gleam in his dark blue eyes. Then she gasped when the full force of Roan's presence hit her. If she weren't so frightened of him and her circumstances, she would have found him attractive.

He was tall and solid, even without the bulk of the two security men. Roan's physique suggested he worked out for maintenance rather than hulking muscles. The expert cut of his suit revealed the perfection of his body in a classy way. The dark color was a perfect foil for his blond hair, slightly tinged with red. Smooth planes and sharp angles made up a striking set of features. A shiver went up her spine when she met his gaze. He knew she had been cheating, and he definitely didn't plan to overlook her dishonesty.

He took a seat across the table, and his two goons backed away, framing either side of the door he had shut behind him upon entering. When Roan placed his hands on the table to lean toward her, she couldn't help admiring the strength in them, undiminished by the manicured fingernails.

"You've stolen from me, boy."

His voice was smooth, with just a hint of a rasp. She didn't bother to deny his accusation, knowing she would lack conviction. She hadn't directly stolen the money, but had engineered the process that allowed her cousin to do so. "I…" She cleared her throat. "I really need to go."

"Her friend, the cop, is waiting on her," said the blond, with a smirk.

"Maybe he'll be the one to arrest you." Roan leaned even closer. "Electronic surveillance tracked a signal from your PDA to a location inside the casino. They isolated the algorithm and determined you were monitoring one of the games. We didn't find the device emitting the signal, but it's just a matter of time before we catch your partner. Giving us a name and location will make this easier on you."

Amy dug her fingernails into her palms and refused to speak. She couldn't betray Kevin. Too much rode on his getting away with the money. Instead, she leveled a look of outrage at Roan. "I don't appreciate being accused of cheating. Either let me go or call the police, but don't talk me to death."

Roan stood up, kicking away the chair with a thud as it hit the floor. He strode over to a utilitarian metal cabinet sitting in the far corner of the otherwise bare room to open a drawer. The blond guard went to the security camera and unplugged it from the back. Amy's need to pee returned with increased urgency.

When Roan returned to the table, he carried a small metal case. She couldn't tear her gaze from his long fingers as he opened the container to reveal a set of knives. She couldn't look at them for long, but they appeared to be show-quality, as one might use in a performance. A lead weight settled into her stomach as she pictured herself strapped to a wheel while the enraged man across from her carelessly threw knives, not caring if he hit or missed her.

Roan removed a slim knife. Amy made herself look at it, judging the silver blade to be a mere four inches, with an ivory handle about the same length. It didn't look like much of a knife, save for the wicked glint of light reflecting from the blade. She swallowed the lump in her throat. "Is that supposed to frighten me? If you try anything, you'll be the one in jail, not me."

Roan touched the blade lightly. "Will it matter to you where I am if you're in a shallow grave? Las Vegas is surrounded by desert, son."

Her eyes narrowed when she finally realized he thought she was a boy. The flash of anger was out of proportion to the offense, and pride made her want to correct the assumption. Yes, she wore a ball cap, tinted glasses and the black hoodie, but did it really obscure her femininity that much? A deep breath helped her quell the urge to rip open the zipper and show him her breasts.

It was insane to worry about his mistaking her gender when he was threatening to kill her. She made herself focus. "People saw me come in. You have cameras recording everything."

"Not in here."

She lifted her chin a notch. "It doesn't matter what happens in here, recorded or not. There are still witnesses and video."

"For whom do the witnesses work?" A nasty smile flashed

across his face, startling her. Not the expression, but her reaction to it. The look made her want to do all sorts of naughty things a Washington farm girl shouldn't know about. The spark of desire was unexpected and unwelcome in the circumstances. "Who pays the salaries of those monitoring the recordings?" He laid the knife back into its spot in the case and picked up another one. His methodical actions served to obliterate any reaction save fear. "Do you really think you're the first one to cheat in my casino, boy?"

She watched the knife as he stood up, walking toward her. Some part of her brain insisted it was all for dramatic effect, but terror was drowning that out. As eight inches of steel neared her, she couldn't resist the flight impulse. Amy slid from her chair and scrambled across the table, desperate to flee.

Roan grabbed her around the waist, arresting her escape. She wasn't thinking any longer, was only reacting, and instinct propelled her hand. Her palm collided with his cheek, and he drew in a breath through clenched teeth. She didn't know if her daring had stunned him, or if she had actually inflicted harm, and she had no chance to find out. The last thing she saw was his fist flying at her face, seemingly in slow motion. She tried to duck but wasn't successful. It connected with her jaw with a meaty thud. Amy heard a cry escape her as she blacked out.

Roan cursed when the boy slammed into the table with a thud that echoed around the room. He shook his hand absently to dissipate the sting and dropped the knife so he could check the kid's pulse.

"Holy hell." He hesitated, hand poised at her throat, when he saw the long fall of hair spilling from the baseball cap. A sinking sensation filled him and he peeled away the Mets cap, tossing it aside. The sunglasses joined the hat, and he groaned. It wasn't the most beautiful face he had ever seen, but there was no denying it was a woman lying on the table, not a young man as he'd initially thought. "Dammit," he said under his breath as he scooped her into his arms.

"Sir?" asked Tim Duffy. "Is something wrong?"

"Nothing, except he is a she." A corner of his mouth quirked when he thought of how angry his father would be with him if he found out he had hit a woman. It wouldn't matter to Robert Cavello that Roan hadn't known the cheater was female. He would still be ready to whip his son for breaking one of his most deeply ingrained rules. A real man had no need to hit a woman.

She was light as a feather, and he carried her without effort to the elevator. When his guards made to accompany him, Roan shook his head. "Have Security buzz me through to my suite." He pushed the *P* button with his elbow to take them to the penthouse floor, and the doors slid closed. The elevator conveyed them smoothly to his private quarters, and he watched the girl the entire time.

She had an interesting face, with a narrow nose, high cheekbones and a broad forehead. Her full lips softened the face, adding delicate femininity. Her pale skin was an unexpected contrast to the honey-brown shade of her hair.

As he walked out of the elevator, Roan ignored the security guard posted in the foyer, barring access to those not authorized to enter his private quarters. As instructed, Security had unlocked his suite, sparing him the need to use his key card, and he crossed the threshold.

He caught his breath when the girl curled closer to him, pressing her breasts into his chest. They were small for his tastes but felt firm. His fingers itched to remove the hoodie and whatever he found beneath, to explore the mounds pressed against him. Roan shook his head, caught off guard by the thought. He wasn't accustomed to being attracted to women instantly, especially cheaters.

He laid her on a sofa and used the phone to summon the casino's doctor. He doubted he had done any permanent damage to the young woman, but a pink splotch on her jaw had formed, and he expected it would become a nasty bruise.

She stirred, and he held his breath, wondering if she would awaken. When she simply changed positions, he gave in to the urge to examine her more closely. Roan walked over to her, perching on the couch as he unzipped her sweatshirt and peeled it off her front, leaving it bunched up at her sides. Underneath, she wore a tank bra that did nothing to hide the dusky pink of her areolas, or the buds of her nipples pressing against the white cotton.

Feeling like a pervert for noticing them, no matter how blatant they were, he moved his gaze lower, over her flat stomach, to the curve of her waist. She had slight hips, but a womanly derriere that would fit perfectly into his palms. Roan licked his dry lips as he imagined cupping her ass in his hands while his cock drove into the heat of her slick pussy. His cock swelled at the thought, and he closed his eyes, taking a deep breath to regain control. What the hell was he thinking, lusting after this woman? It was creepy to be watching her without her knowledge, to be thinking of sex when he'd never want to get involved with someone who'd stolen from him. He preferred a woman to be up-front about her avarice, without being an outright thief.

Torn between guilt and curiosity, he continued his perusal, deciding she had nice legs from what he could see under the baggy denim. In her current state, she was a six, but, with right tools, she could definitely be an eight.

When she had been a man to him, his plan had been straightforward. He would scare the cheater into revealing the name and whereabouts of the person with his money, along with just how much they had stolen, and then turn the kid over to NGC and the police for arrest. The knife business had worked many times in the past, and he had yet to use the antique collection for anything but scare tactics.

Everything had changed when her cap had fallen off and he had realized she was a woman. It wasn't just the guilt of having hit her that made him reluctant to turn her over to authorities. She wasn't the first woman he had caught cheating, so it had nothing to do with a gentlemanly instinct to protect the fairer sex. No, there was something about the woman that made Roan want to protect her from prosecution but not punishment.

He quashed the impulse and rose to his feet to answer the knock on the door. Regardless of his bewildering attraction to the girl, she was still a thief and he would treat her accordingly. People did not rob The Liege and walk away scot-free.

Chapter Two

Amy awoke with a splitting headache. For a moment, she thought it had all been a dream. Kevin had never shown up at her door at two in the morning four days ago, desperate for her help. She had never agreed to give it, had never built an electronic device for him and had never been caught cheating.

As soon as she opened her eyes, she knew it wasn't a dream. She had never been in this room before. Its opulence was way beyond anything she was familiar with. Sheets of the finest Egyptian cotton cradled her body, and a pillow softer than a dream padded her head. Silver-threaded wallpaper decorated the walls, providing a perfect backdrop for the smoky-gray carpet and charcoal-shaded furniture. The only prints on the walls were monochromatic abstracts in shades of gray, probably done by an artist who had become insanely rich with the simple concept.

She scanned the room, noting its distinct masculinity. Amy was definitely in a man's room. A rich man's room. Roan Cavello's room?

"I see you're awake."

She bit back a gasp when she heard Roan walking over

to her. A glance in his direction revealed a wingback chair where he must have waited for her to rouse. Amy wanted to pretend she was asleep, to buy time to think, but it would be futile. Her initial movements upon waking, slight as they had been, must have given her away.

She decided to confront him instead. Amy sat up higher and turned her head in his direction, forcing herself to meet his gaze as he loomed over her. His eyes seemed to be eating her up, and she shivered under his stare. "Where am I?"

"My room." He brushed his finger lightly against her jaw. "This will be an ugly bruise. I'm sorry."

His touch made it difficult to breathe, but she would have been hard-pressed to identify why—fear or a spark of desire? Amy turned her head away. "It's fine. Let me go, and we'll call it even."

Roan's laugh contained the same rough edge as his voice. "Sweetheart, we aren't nearly close to even."

Amy swallowed the lump of fear in her throat. "Don't call me names."

She gasped when he cradled her chin his hand, forcing her to look up at him. "I'll call you what I want, my little cheater." His voice changed abruptly, becoming brusque, and he released her. "You're a thief."

Amy remained silent, unable to refute his accusations. She couldn't pretend as though she hadn't cheated, not with him having proof and her at his mercy.

"Do you know what they're going to do to you in prison?" He was unemotional, which made his words even scarier. "You can't be as young as you look, but that innocent air is going to have them eating you alive."

She tried to hide her reaction but knew the shudder that racked her body betrayed her fear.

He arched an eyebrow. "I should call the police right this instant."

With brazenness she didn't feel, Amy asked, "Why don't you, instead of holding me captive in your bedroom?"

Roan shrugged. "I wanted to make sure you weren't injured." He shrugged again. "Old-fashioned ideals my father instilled in me, I guess."

"I'm fine, so call them." She bit her tongue to hide how afraid she was of facing the police. Other than a speeding ticket, she'd never been in trouble with the law and had naively assumed it would remain that way all her life. The pit of her stomach twisted when she realized she would lose her teaching credentials once she had a criminal record. That, even more than going to prison, brought tears to the backs of her eyes.

Roan stood up, walking a bit closer to the bed to loom over her. "You're eager for me to involve the cops. You have a lot to lose, sweetheart." He pressed on before she could reply. "I'm willing to work out a deal with you."

Her eyes widened, and she looked down to make sure she was still clothed. Why he brought her to his room was no longer a mystery. He expected her to sleep with him! "You're disgusting."

He blinked, looking puzzled. "I'm trying to be generous, and you're calling me names? You really are a…" With a twist of his lips, he trailed off. A deep chuckle broke his half second of silence. "Oh, I see. You think I'm trying to get you into bed." He laughed harder.

Amy glared at him. "What's so funny?"

It took Roan a moment to compose himself, but when he did, it was as if he had never laughed. His voice was emotionless again. "I was going to let you repay me in cash within twenty-four hours. You aren't worth that kind of money. No woman is. I wouldn't trade hundreds of thousands of dollars for a night with any woman."

"It doesn't have to be just one night." Amy didn't know who was more shocked by her utterance. The words had jumped out of her mouth, catching them both off guard.

"What are you suggesting?" He seemed reluctantly intrigued.

She floundered. Just what *was* she suggesting? Was she seriously contemplating offering herself to this man to repay the debt she owed? When it had been his idea, or so she'd thought, it had repulsed her. But now that she thought about it, the solution would be ideal. Wouldn't it? Being his mistress for a short amount of time had to be better than losing the career she had worked so hard to attain, not to mention going to prison. Right?

"Well?"

Amy licked her dry lips. "I could be your…companion…for a time. Until the debt is paid." She couldn't help jumping when he sat on the bed. "Just for a while."

Roan regarded her with an intensity that had been absent in his gaze before. When his eyes examined her from head to toe, she could feel him undressing her. The appraisal was oddly asexual. She could almost see him performing calculations in his head, weighing her worth to him. "I don't think so."

Her mouth dropped open. "Why not? What's wrong with me?"

He leaned back, still eyeing her, although not as intently. "For one thing, you look about seventeen. I like my lady friends legal."

"I'm twenty-eight." It annoyed her that she had to persuade him to accept her offer. She wasn't homely, and most men would jump at the chance to have a woman serve them sexually for a predetermined amount of time.

"You aren't my type," he said bluntly. Roan braced his shoulder against the post of the bed.

"What's your type?"

"Submissive." He must have seen her surprise. "I like to dominate my partners. Vanilla sex doesn't satisfy me, and though it's kinky to buy your services for a time, it wouldn't keep me entertained."

Amy's heart pounded with a mix of anxiety and excitement. The idea of being this man's plaything aroused her in a way she had never expected. The thought of having him dominate her turned her on so much that she shifted to ease the sudden ache between her thighs. "I can do that."

He lunged forward with the agility of a leopard, his face inches from hers. "You want to be my sub? For how long?"

Amy shrugged, finding it difficult to speak with him so close. Her heart raced again, this time for a different reason. His proximity was affecting her. "I don't know."

He fell silent for a moment, obviously thinking deeply. Finally, he said, "Three months."

Automatically, she shook her head. "I can't be here that long. When the summer semester ends, I have to resume my teaching position at LV Tech."

"Hmm…" Roan stared at her a long time before nodding. "Six weeks, the duration of summer break. The weekend before Labor Day, you are free to leave, and the debt will be paid."

She angled up her chin. "How do I know you'll keep your word?"

With wide eyes, he countered, "Which of us has more reason to question the other's integrity? I should be asking you that, sweetheart."

"I'll stay until the debt is paid." An ominous echo seemed to accompany the words as she spoke them, as if she had just signed a pact with the devil.

"Don't worry, my little cheat. You'll enjoy this, more than you have any right to."

She wanted to deny his assertion but once again couldn't. What was the use in lying? As insane and inappropriate as the attraction was, she was drawn to Roan, and it was with more anticipation than fear that she faced the prospect of six weeks under his passionate domination.

She hadn't realized it would happen so soon. A surprised grunt escaped her when Roan grasped her wrists and stretched his body on top of hers, anchoring her to the mattress. "Let's seal it with a kiss."

Startled, Amy turned her head to evade his mouth, not wanting it to be like this. "Let me up."

"You aren't going anywhere, sweetheart." Roan slipped his leg between hers. "You don't want to, do you?"

She tossed her head in denial, desperate to escape as he settled between her thighs, cradling his cock against her pussy. Only a few layers of material prevented the intimate joining of their flesh. The thought enflamed her, and she couldn't help arching against him when he thrust against her. "Please?" It sounded like a question even to her ears.

"Please what?" He brushed his lips over hers. "Please let you go?" Roan's mouth molded to hers in a deep kiss, one she was powerless to fight. When he stroked his tongue over her lips, she parted them with a passionate moan of surrender. His tongue thrust inside her mouth as he pushed his cock deeper against her pussy. Abruptly, he broke the kiss, lifting his head to look down at her. "Or please fuck you until you don't know your own name?"

Amy grunted, incapable of answering verbally. Her body had betrayed her and given him a response already. Her beaded nipples pressed against the cotton sheet, and her wet slit seemed to be begging for his possession. He had to know. His gaze reflected he knew, and he was pleased.

"That could prove inconvenient. If you forget your name, neither of us will know it." Roan paused to kiss her again, this time his lips engaging in brief flirtation with hers. "So you'd better tell me first."

"Amy," she said in a small voice. It was a struggle to speak, because the only words she wanted to utter were ones demanding he finish what he had begun. All the reasons this was wrong were quickly fading from her mind. She had never experienced such overwhelming desire, and the heady feeling left her wanting more.

"Amy." Roan lifted her arms above her head, pinning her wrists with one hand. "Such a delicate, feminine name."

"You thought I was a boy." She was unable to hide her hurt.

Roan cupped her breast, thumbing the nipple to a harder peak. "I was wrong." His mouth took possession of hers again, as he continued to massage her breast. He seemed to be enjoying her moans of pleasure if his increased pace was any indication.

"It means beloved." Her breathless words cut across his harsh breathing.

He laid his palm flat on her small breast, squeezing the small globe gently through the cotton tank top. "Beloved." A brooding expression fell across his face. "Beloved little cheat." His gentle grasp turned rough.

Amy gasped with shock and pain. The shock came from the jolt of pleasure accompanying the pain. "That hurts."

He stared down at her. "Yes." Their gazes locked, a silent battle of wills playing out as he held her breast in the painful grasp. To her shame, her nipple beaded further, pressing against his palm like a dog seeking favor from its master.

As if he'd read her thoughts, he said, "Your body already knows who its new master is. Your mind just needs to learn that lesson, Amy."

She did her best to erase all traces of passion from her voice. "You can provoke a physical response, but you can't control my mind. That isn't part of the agreement."

He laughed, a sound of genuine amusement. "You really believe that, don't you?"

She glared at him, but surprise replaced her anger when he released her and stood up. Uncertainly, she crossed her arms over her torso, wanting to hide her arousal from his gaze.

Roan acted as if they hadn't spent the past few minutes in a sexual tussle. With a glance at his watch, he said, "You've been out for a while. I usually have dinner at this time. You'll join me."

She bit down the childish urge to refuse simply for the sake of being stubborn. Her stomach growled at his words, making it impossible to deny she was starving. Amy had been too nervous to eat before she and Kevin had set out for the casino earlier in the day. "All right."

"You'll need to change first."

She cast a look around the room. "Into what? These are my only clothes."

"I want you sitting at my dinner table in your natural state." His gaze dropped briefly to her breasts before returning to meet her eyes. "I want easy access to dessert."

"That's insane. I can't eat dinner naked." She made no effort to hide her ire with his idiotic request. Amy knew everything he had done in the past few minutes, and continued to do, was designed to test her resolve. While determined to live up to her side of the bargain, she wasn't going to bow to his every whim.

His lopsided grin revealed he was enjoying her anger. "I will provide garments when you require them. You will wear what I tell you when I tell you. Right now, you'll wear nothing."

She crossed her arms over her chest. "No. I…you can't expect me to…it's indecent."

Roan shrugged. "You haven't yet learned the rules, so I'll make it simple for you. You do what I say at all times, as you agreed to do." His voice softened marginally. "I know it's been a rough day. I'll cut you some slack tonight. You can choose not to eat dinner with me without clothing. I'm not going to drag you forcibly into the dining area."

She nodded, poised to say something inane.

"If you're hungry enough, you'll join me in the state I requested. If you aren't, you can stay here." He turned away from her, headed to the door.

"Wait." Amy growled with frustration when he ignored her, continuing to the door, hand on the knob. "You can't starve me."

He didn't even have the courtesy to turn to her to respond. "I can do whatever I want to you, Amy. Haven't you figured that out yet?" Roan chuckled, an unpleasant sound that sent a shiver down her spine. "You're the one who made it that way. You voluntarily put yourself at my mercy."

Anger overwhelmed good judgment, and she snatched a pillow from the pile behind her head, throwing it at him with all her might. It bounced harmlessly off the door as he closed it behind himself. "Go to hell," she shouted, hoping he heard her through the thick wood. She'd be damned before she went parading around naked in front of him. He could stuff himself silly, and she wouldn't care. She'd rather starve than give him the satisfaction of joining him on his terms.

♣ ♠ ♥ ♦ ♣ ♠ ♥ ♦ ♣ ♠ ♥ ♦

Chapter Three

Her determination lasted almost an hour before hunger got the better of her. Amy's anger faded, and rational thought returned. He couldn't really mean he wouldn't let her eat unless she was naked. She listened for sounds from the other room, but heard nothing. Indecision kept her in the bed for another five minutes, but finally, hunger and the need to pee drove her from her temporary refuge.

After using the facilities, she washed her hands and decided she was too hungry to play games with him, at least right now. Mouth set in a mutinous line, Amy marched from the bathroom and through the bedroom, opening the door defiantly. She made it several steps into the suite before pausing to look for Roan. He wasn't in the luxurious sitting area, dominated by a large television and oversized black sofas. Nor was he in the dining area she discovered a few feet away. A single step took her down to the room, and she walked over to the table, seeing two place settings. One hadn't been touched, and the other was neatly stacked with cleared dishes.

Casting a glance over her shoulder, Amy sat down in front of the covered plate. She grasped the handle to remove the cover. Rare prime rib, tender vegetables and baby potatoes awaited her, and she dug in. Occasionally, she remembered to look up to see if Roan had reappeared, but most of her attention remained on clearing the plate. When she had made short work of the dish, she lifted a smaller cover to find fresh strawberries and cream.

Amy dipped one of the strawberries into the cream and brought it to her mouth. She closed her eyes as she licked away some of the fresh cream, untainted by sugar. The fruit and cream were a delightful combination, and she moaned with pleasure at the first bite.

"That's the sound I want to hear."

Her eyes snapped open. Roan leaned against the wall, stripped of the suit jacket and tie, with his collar open. His eyes didn't waver from her mouth. Amy choked, dropping the strawberry and reaching for the linen napkin she had laid across her lap. While she coughed, he remained standing, watching her without expression. Her gaze fell to his crotch while she washed down the fruit with a gulp of water, and she gulped harder upon seeing how stiff his cock was.

He finally straightened, coming to join her at the table. Instead of taking the seat across from her, Roan came to stand behind her, putting his hands on her shoulders. "Did you enjoy your dinner?"

She nodded, finding herself incapable of speaking. It wasn't from choking, but from his presence. Her tongue stuck to the roof of her mouth.

"I know. I watched you eat every bite, that pleased smirk on your face. You were happy to have defied me and gotten away with it."

Amy's eyes widened, and she craned her head to look up at him.

Her confusion must have shown on her face. "This is a casino, Amy. I can watch you every minute of every day." His fingers tightened, digging lightly into her shoulders. "When you started in with the strawberries and cream, it was just too much. I knew it was time to join you."

She bowed her head, her heart racing. His touch was intoxicating, but fear more than arousal motivated the rapid thump. What would be his punishment for her not stripping off the tank top and jeans before coming to dinner?

"I hope you enjoyed your dinner and your defiance, my little cheat, because it is time to pay for both."

Amy's eyes widened, and her head snapped up. "What do you want from me?"

"Everything." With a jerk, Roan tore the thin shirt from her shoulders. It fell to her waist in a pool of fabric, trapping her arms. He dipped a hand into the tattered neckline to cup her breast. "I want your total surrender, Amy. I'm going to tear you down and rebuild you to please me in every way."

The words should have frightened her, and they did, but they also rocked an untapped core of desire that rushed through her, causing her to tip her neck to the side when he buried his face against it. His teeth grazed the sensitive spot at the bend of her shoulder, and she cried out, grasping handfuls of the linen napkin to steady herself.

"There is only one thing you need to learn to please me."

She licked dry lips. "What?"

"Obedience."

Amy closed her eyes as his mouth gentled, nibbling her

flesh and eliciting jolts of pleasure that transmitted throughout her body. Her pussy, still aching with dissatisfaction from earlier, convulsed with need as he turned her in the chair to face him. With efficient motions, he stripped the ruined tank top from her, and she didn't try to stop him. Roan knelt down, pulling her against him, taking her with him to the floor. He sank into the thick carpeting, and she sank into him. One of her arms had become free in the process, and she wrapped it around his neck, burying her fingers in his hair.

Roan took her mouth in a hungry kiss, demanding and gaining access. Shyly at first, but with confidence bolstered by passion, she met each thrust of his tongue with one of her own. Desire roared through Amy, scorching her. With a deep moan, she pulled him closer, pushing past his tongue to breach the barrier of his mouth. Roan's moans echoed hers when she explored his mouth the way he had hers.

He broke away, although she tried to hold his head still. Roan trailed his tongue down her chin and neck, pausing to bite her with more force than he had before. She shifted against him, pressing her neck into his mouth.

"You like that, don't you?" Roan bit her again before sucking some of her flesh into his mouth. The harder he sucked, the more she cried out. She arched her hips, rubbing her aching clit against the seam of her jeans.

"You're an expensive new toy, but I think worth the price," whispered Roan before sweeping his mouth lower, to her left breast. His words hurt more than his teeth when he grazed the sensitive nipple, but she didn't counter them or offer excuses. He wouldn't care about her reasons for cheating, just as she didn't care about the reasons she was in his arms. His mouth engulfed her nipple, and his tongue swept rapidly over the rigid peak, making her cry out again and again. Roan had her naked in less than a minute. While he buried his face between her breasts to nip the soft skin, she unbuttoned his shirt with surprising dexterity.

Amy flicked her nails across one of Roan's nipples when he moved to her right breast. His tongue stroked her nipple, and she arched her back, pressing closer. The light dusting of hair across his chest and belly rasped against her fingers as her hands roamed freely, moving lower. She wondered at her own bravery as one of her hands breached his waistband.

In one smooth motion, Roan flipped over, reversing their positions. He released her just long enough to pull off his dress shirt and toss it haphazardly behind him. Then his body covered hers, his mouth working a wet line down her stomach. Amy trembled with anticipation and buried her hands into his hair. When his hot breath caressed her clit, she arched her hips frantically, but he didn't lower his head. "Please, Roan."

Still, he hesitated, finally looking up. "You are beautiful here, Amy." He dipped his head to run his tongue lightly down her slit before looking up again. "I want to taste you."

"Please." The request was a sob of frustration.

He shook his head. "Not until you're smooth as silk."

She looked at him, mouth agape. "What?"

"I don't like hairiness, sweetheart." Roan stroked her lips with his hand. "But don't worry. I'll take care of the arrangements." Once again, he lowered his head to breathe on her clit as one of his fingers slipped into her opening. "I can't wait very long."

She moaned when his digit penetrated her, gasping at the stretching sensation as he eased it deeper inside her. Her hands fell away from his head, and she grasped handfuls of the carpet to steady herself as he finger-fucked her with increasing rapidity. She squeezed her eyes shut, lost in the sensations. Amy hovered on the edge of coming and pumped her hips, seeking release.

Roan withdrew his finger, and her eyes popped open. She shook her head. "I…"

He placed the same finger against her lips. "Shh. You'll come, but you're so wet. I want to be inside you."

He leaned away from her to undo his pants, and she felt a stirring of fear. Amy opened her mouth to speak, but he was with her again before she could gather her thoughts. He nestled between her thighs and put his arms around her back to lift her up to him. Roan's chest crushed her breasts, and the hair tickled her nipples, making her shift restlessly.

All the reasons they shouldn't do this flashed through her mind. He saw her as more of an object than a person, there for his sexual satisfaction in order to pay for her crimes. She knew she had to say something, that it should be words withdrawing her consent, but good intentions fled when the head of his cock breached her opening, resting snugly inside her. He sank in another inch, and she threw back her head. Roan sank to the hilt inside her, making her cry out with pleasure.

He thrust deeply into her again, burying his shaft into her core. He leaned back on his calves, and she wrapped her thighs around his hips. Once she was secure and could return his thrusts, he laid her back against the carpet.

"Oh, it feels…" She dug her hands into his shoulders and

lifted her ass to take him more deeply inside her. The new angle made his cock rub against her clit through her opening with every thrust, and she couldn't finish her sentence. A guttural growl escaped her when Roan cupped her buttocks and lifted her against him, forcing his cock as deeply as she could take it. A dart of pain accompanied the motion, and to her embarrassment, that sent her over the edge. Her sheath convulsed around his cock, and she screamed as release swept over her.

Roan uttered something incomprehensible as he came inside her. He bucked his hips a couple more times before stilling. They remained joined without moving for what might have been minutes or hours. Amy lost track of time as she rested her ear against his chest, listening to his heart rate slow from its pounding intensity to a more natural rhythm.

Eventually, he rolled onto his side and withdrew from her. Amy watched him slip on his shirt through half-closed eyes. Sated, she could feel sleep stealing over her and forced herself to stir. With languid movements, she reached for the remnants of the tank top, putting it around her shoulders. When he still didn't speak, she finally got to her feet. "I need a shower."

Without another word to him, she left the dining area to return to his bedroom. Bypassing the bed in favor of the bathroom, she locked the door behind her. It wasn't until Amy was in the shower, hot water sluicing away all traces of the experience, that she acknowledged her disappointment.

Physically, it had been everything she'd ever hoped for, and more. Emotionally, it had hurt her deeply. There was nothing between them except an intense attraction and Roan's egotistical certainty he could do whatever he wanted with her.

What stung her most was admitting he was probably right. Something about the man made her want to give in to his every demand, to please him any way she could. It was a new side of herself she hadn't expected to discover, and it both frightened and excited her to see where Roan would take her.

♣ ♠ ♥ ♦ ♣ ♠ ♥ ♦ ♣ ♠ ♥ ♦

Chapter Four

Amy slept deeply, to her surprise, and woke feeling refreshed. She had somehow found a tenuous peace with her situation, perhaps during her dreams. Whatever had caused it, she was more accepting of the task before her when she donned a robe that smelled too much like Roan not to remind her of last night and left the bedroom in search of coffee.

The shaky tranquility vanished when she entered the living area to find two women sitting on a sofa, sipping tea. Elegant and gorgeous, with similar dark hair and eyes, they both looked like they belonged there. Their presence rein-forced Amy's own plain Jane-ness, and she stood awkwardly before them, feeling as she had the one time the principal had summoned her to his office in junior high. "Hello?"

They eyed her up and down without speaking to her, although clearly they had a lot to say to each other in French. Amy withstood their rudeness for half a minute before deciding enough was enough. She walked past them, headed for the kitchen and the lure of hot coffee. One of them snapped their fingers, and she ignored it. If they were trying to get her attention, they could try manners. She wasn't a dog—although she was the master's newest pet, and obviously everyone knew that.

"Miss?"

She stopped walking and turned around to face the one who had deigned to speak to her. "Yes?"

"Monsieur Cavello has asked us to renovate you."

Amy's eyebrows shot up. "What?"

The other one laughed. "Cherise, the word is makeover." Her English was much clearer. She nodded to Amy. "We are to see to your beauty regimen, miss."

She rolled her eyes. "Thanks, but no. I'm fine."

The other woman arched a perfect eyebrow. "I see." Her expression revealed her disagreement with Amy's insistence she didn't need help. "We were told by Monsieur Cavello not to accept no, miss."

"Figures," she muttered under her breath. "Fine, but I have some things to do first." It gave her a small surge of satisfaction to see their lips curl with annoyance when she made them wait.

Amy went into the kitchen, fumbled through the cabinets and found a mug. As she poured a cup from the coffeepot that was still hot, her gaze fell on the landline hanging from the wall. She reached for the phone, but there was no one to call. She didn't dare ring Kevin at his hotel. She often offered the spare room of her condo to a select student, but the last girl had moved out at the end of the spring term, and she wouldn't have another student living with her until the semester resumed at Las Vegas Tech next month. Without close friends and with no summer job lined up, no one needed to know where she was because no one cared—

other than her aunt and uncle, and she couldn't call them. They had too many of their own troubles to add worrying about her to their burdens.

With a sigh of defeat, she drained the cup before placing it in the sink and leaving the room, determined to get the "renovation" over with as quickly as possible. The easiest way to do that was to let the two women have Roan's way.

Amy lost track of time as they subjected her to beauty treatments—cut a few inches from her hair, added amber highlights, showed her the correct way to apply makeup and waxed her eyebrows—all low-priority tasks for a professor of electronics at a regional college, but clearly essential to be the submissive mistress of a man like Roan.

She was in an undignified position on a table they had brought with them, simultaneously receiving a manicure and a bikini wax, when Roan sauntered in. She was annoyed with him for subjecting her to the morning of torture, but before she could say anything, the attendant ripped the hair from her bikini area with a quick yank. Amy howled in protest, and howled again when Suzette repeated the process on the other side of her labia.

Roan walked over, and without even a word of greeting, took up a position between her legs. Amy gasped when he ran his fingers across her hypersensitive flesh. The skin still tingled from the wax treatment, and now her clit came to life at the casual contact.

"Very nice, Suzette." He nodded approvingly.

Suzette smiled broadly. "It is my pleasure, monsieur, to do your bidding." The way she leaned closer to Roan left no doubt in anyone's mind exactly what she would do for him. "It was a challenge to realize your vision, but I believe we have done what we can with the raw material."

Amy glared up at Suzette. "I thought it was just a myth that the French are rude. Until today."

They both ignored her. Suzette was too busy fawning over Roan, and he was occupied with examining her from head to toe. After a long moment, he nodded. "It's amazing. She's beautiful."

"She's right *here*," Amy said through gritted teeth.

Cherise stood up from the stool where she had sat to perform the manicure. "I am finished, Suzette." She flashed a flirtatious smile to Roan. "Is there anything else you desire, monsieur?"

Roan met Amy's seething gaze, and a crooked smile flashed across his face. "Just privacy, ladies." His expression left no doubt about why he wanted privacy.

A shriek of shock left her when he dipped his head to lick her pussy with the other two women still in the room, watching every second. She tried to clamp her thighs closed, but Roan held them splayed effortlessly. When his tongue circled her clit with short, teasing strokes, pleasure overwhelmed her outrage, and she arched against him, bringing his tongue deeper inside her. He flicked his tongue against the sensitive skin, heightening her arousal even further.

A soft moan caught her attention, and she glanced briefly at Cherise and Suzette, pleased to see their naked envy. A thrill shot through her, and she parted her thighs wider, allowing them a better glimpse of Roan eating her out. Something wild inside her enjoyed having them watch her lover please her. She liked having them wanting to be her. Maybe if they hadn't acted as if she were beneath them, she wouldn't have enjoyed so thoroughly having something they wanted but didn't have. Or maybe putting on a show for anyone would have been exciting.

Roan lifted his head, looking over at Suzette and Cherise. "Ladies?"

With a start, they scurried to the door. It took a surprising amount of will for Amy to resist calling them back. Part of her wanted them to see Roan fuck her, to ache for his cock inside their pussies while he put it inside her.

Amy dismissed the women from her thoughts and turned her full attention to Roan. When he had first tasted her pussy, the others had distracted her, but now, she had him to herself. She held her breath while he dipped his head, soon losing herself in the sensations he provoked. He swirled his tongue around her clit slowly, again brushing against her newly bared flesh. He sucked her clit into his mouth in a random tempo that had her bucking her hips frantically against his face. Roan chuckled, sending a wash of hot air across the sensitive bud that caused shivers to race down to her spine. She tangled her hands into his hair, holding him against her, striving to bring him in as deeply as possible.

Her pussy convulsed as she hovered on the edge of orgasm. Roan lightly flicked his tongue across the tip of her clit, making her cry out. Her cry changed to one of outrage when he lifted his head instead of bringing her the rest of the way to completion. "I didn't—"

"I know." A wicked grin curved his mouth. "Come with me." Roan extended a hand.

Perplexed and annoyed, she disdained it and stood up on her own. The lips of her pussy rubbed together, and she started anew at the foreign sensation of having her hair missing. Her clit seemed bigger and more sensitive, although that could be from the hyper-aroused state in which Roan had callously left her.

He grasped her hand anyway, leading her down the hallway. She hadn't yet explored the suite, except for the common living areas and his bedroom, so she had no idea where he was taking her after they bypassed his room. The nondescript door he opened was a strange contrast to the contents of the room.

Amy's eyes widened as she looked around. Chains dangled from the wall, along with an assortment of whips and leather. A flat table, thickly padded and covered in leather, dominated the center of the small room. There could be no other word to describe it except *dungeon*. What the hell had she gotten herself into? She tried to tug herself free of his hold, but her resistance proved ineffectual.

Roan ignored her struggles, easily lifting her onto the table. He leaned forward to secure her with his weight while he fastened one of her wrists into a metal shackle. She pushed at him with her free hand, but he captured it, soon clicking it into the other handcuff attached to the table. "What are you doing?" Amy thrashed against the confines, kicking out at him with her feet until he moved out of range. She jerked against the cuffs, testing their strength and finding them steadfast.

Her hair had fallen over her face, and she tossed her head to clear her vision. She glared at him. "What's going on?"

Roan walked over to the wall, pausing to touch several implements hanging in precise order. With a soft sound of satisfaction, he took a leather paddle from the hook and came back to her. "You know what this is about. I want the name of your accomplice."

She shook her head. "I didn't agree to this."

He cocked an eyebrow. "You didn't?" Roan ran the edge of the paddle down her freshly waxed shin.

Amy shook her head more vigorously. "Definitely not. I agreed to submit, but I never agreed to this."

A hearty laugh escaped him. "You should have clarified what you would be submitting to when you agreed to be my sub, Amy. There's a wide streak of submissiveness inside you, and I'm going to tap into it. I told you what I was going to do to you, and you didn't run away."

"How could I?" She moved her leg away from the paddle, deciding the soft rasp of leather was disconcertingly pleasant. "You wouldn't let me."

"You could have chosen the police." Roan stepped closer, following her with the paddle. He trailed it from the inside of her arch up her leg, pausing at mid-thigh. "Instead, you chose this. In fact, you suggested it."

"I wouldn't have if I'd known exactly what you wanted me to do."

He moved the paddle higher, rubbing it softly against her pussy. "Yes, you would." She couldn't fight her physical response, and a moan escaped when he parted her lips with the implement to brush the leather against her swollen clit. "But don't worry, sweetheart. I'm not going to hurt you..." He swatted her outer labia with the paddle. "Much."

She winced at the contact, finding it both stimulating and stinging. "What do you want from me?"

"You're working off your debt, but you still owe me information." Roan swatted her again, making her draw in a sharp breath. "Give me what I want, and you'll get what you want."

"What's that?" she asked in a ragged voice when he returned to sliding the edge of the paddle into her slit.

"To come."

She closed her eyes. "I can live without that."

"We'll see, won't we?" He pressed the paddle deeper still, rubbing the edge against her clit. Amy tried to ignore the pleasure, but her body had a mind of its own. She bit her tongue to hold in a moan when Roan switched the rhythm to a firmer, deeper stroke. Her hips pumped in time with his thrusts, and she circled her pelvis. Release was only a breath away, and she hoped she could attain orgasm before he realized it, but he took away the paddle, removing the possibility.

Tears of frustration pressed against her eyes, but she refused to let them fall. Amy attempted to hide her ragged breathing as Roan loomed over her, not wanting to let him know he had gotten to her. "You bastard."

"Temper, temper." Roan smacked her hip with the paddle hard enough to make her catch her breath. When he slid the paddle under her buttocks to nudge her onto her side, she tried to kick him. He clicked his tongue at her. "It's going to be like that, is it?"

A dart of fear pierced Amy's chest, and she watched with trepidation as he set aside the paddle and walked around the table. When he reached for her left foot, she tried to evade his grasp, but he soon captured her. As she kicked against his hands, he pulled her foot to the table. She screamed in protest when he anchored her leg with his weight and snapped another shackle around her ankle, leaving her trussed, with only one leg free.

He patted her free foot. "It's easier for me if I don't have to bolt this one, too, but I will if I must. Now, be a good girl and roll onto your side."

Amy's gaze locked with his in a drawn-out contest of wills, but his determination glinted clearly in his eyes. With a small sigh of surrender, she turned onto her side. The process was awkward, and she had to contort her body unnaturally to do so. Once in the position, she waited with bated breath to see what he would do next.

The paddle smacked against her buttocks with a solid thump. The accompanying pain made her cry out, but his voice drowned it out. "Who was your partner?"

"Forget it." Her response earned another lash with the paddle, and a single tear leaked from her eye. Amy refused to acknowledge his question when he repeated it, leading him to spank her again. The only sounds punctuating the room for the next few minutes were the whap of the paddle, followed by her sniffling cries.

Finally, Roan backed off, wiping at his brow. "A new approach, I think."

Amy curled into herself, keeping her eyes on the wall in front of her. She couldn't see what Roan was doing and told herself she didn't care. Still, she jumped when he placed his hand on her hip, caressing her skin.

"Good girl. You didn't give in too easily." He leaned closer, and she shivered when he breathed against her lower back, before pressing a kiss to the spot above the dimple of her buttocks. "I'm really looking forward to this."

"Good for you." She didn't like the misery in her tone, but couldn't suppress it. He had hurt her, and even more than the physical pain, the emotional sense of treachery really inspired tears. She knew that was a stupid response, because he had done nothing to earn her trust, so he couldn't betray it. Still, after last night's experience, she had expected her sexual servitude to be wholly pleasurable. The trip to the dungeon had been unexpected and alarming.

"I'll be honest with you." As he spoke, Roan walked around the table to face her, tipping up her chin so she would meet his eyes. "You're going to like some of this, but it's also going to hurt. Are you sure you don't want to tell me his name and avoid this?"

She wrenched free of his hand, refusing to speak.

Roan patted her head like a recalcitrant child. "Good girl. I was hoping you'd do that."

Amy tried to push him away when he pushed her onto her back. Again, he expended little effort to subdue her, and she was too drained to put up much of a fight when he confined her other ankle. She was naked except for the expensive silk bra covering her breasts that she had donned earlier in the day when Suzette and Cherise had given her a moment to rest. It left her feeling even more vulnerable than she might have been if she was also wearing even just panties, shackled as she was in the spread-eagle position.

Roan trailed a finger down the edge of the cup, raking his fingernails across the lace to lightly scratch her flesh underneath. "Lovely bra."

"You're the one who picked it out." She had found it in

a well-stocked drawer in his bedroom, along with a closet-ful of clothes all in her size.

He smiled. "No, not me. I called down to the boutique in the foyer and asked Margerine to send up a selection of clothing in your size." He sighed heavily. "It's a shame to ruin it."

Her eyes widened. "What?"

With a quick jerk, he ripped the scrap of silk and lace from her. She whimpered when the elastic bit into her flesh. He rattled something, and in seconds, icy cold replaced the stinging. She gasped at the sudden change in sensations.

"It feels nice, doesn't it?" He ran an ice cube down her shoulder and across her breast. Amy held her breath when he hovered over her nipple, letting a cold droplet of water fall from the cube, but not touching the budding peak.

"Where?" She wasn't capable of forming a coherent sentence, especially when he rubbed another ice cube across her stomach, bringing it upward. She flinched when he ran it under her breasts to soothe the inflamed flesh where the band had cut into her skin. Seconds later, the icy cold replaced the lingering soreness, and she relaxed slightly.

"There's a small fridge and microwave in here." He brought the second ice cube up to her breast and circled one around each nipple.

Amy caught her breath in a ragged gasp when he pressed the ice cubes to both of her nipples simultaneously. The coldness seeped into the tender buds, and she tried to shift away. "Stop it."

"If only you really meant that." He continued to hold the ice in place. "Amy, you know you can halt this at any time. All it takes is a name."

"Bastard," she said in a choked voice.

Roan laughed. "Not that name."

She whimpered as icy droplets of water trailed down her breasts, while the numbing cold penetrated deeper into her skin. After what seemed like hours, the cubes finally melted, and he lifted his hands. Her nipples were insensate, and the ice had moved beyond painful before melting. She wondered if he would go for more ice and continue his torture.

Instead, Roan lifted something she couldn't see clearly from her angle, though it made a metallic jangle. He seemed to deliberately position his body so she couldn't see what he was doing. Amy tried to prepare herself for the worst as his hands brushed against her breast. Though she remained mostly numb, she felt it when he slipped something around one nipple, then the other.

When he stepped back, he wore a satisfied smirk. "It's not so bad now, but wait until the numb from the ice wears off. You'll really feel the clamps then."

She glared at him, refusing to speak, but watching intently as he reached under the table for a bolster. He lifted up her ass and slid it under her hips, so that she could see straight down the line of her body at her pussy, propped up like a sacrifice.

"It's all right, you know. You can keep quiet all you want, but this sweet pussy is talking to me right now." He traced a finger over her slick lips and engorged clit peeking out. He cupped his hand over her mound. "This is telling me you liked your little punishment. The restraints." He tapped his hand against her clit firmly. "The spanking." Tap. "The clamps." Tap.

His fingers were glistening from her, and he smeared her

juices across her belly. "For the time you are here working off your debt, I'm going to see just how much you can take."

He went over to a cabinet across the room and retrieved a box, which he brought back and set on the table next to her. She strained to see inside when he lifted the lid. He pulled out what looked like a short, stubby dildo, about four inches long. "This is an anal plug." Roan set it on her belly so she could stare at it.

She started shaking her head, her eyes wide. He tsk-tsked her. "You shouldn't refuse what I'm offering. One of these days, I am going to take this sweet ass of yours, and you're going to wish you'd let me prepare you for it."

He pulled out a tube of lubricant and squirted a liberal amount onto his fingers.

"Just relax. You'll like this part."

Fear, and a small bit of curiosity, kept her from protesting.

Roan stroked a tender finger across her clit. "I think you'll enjoy it, once you get past your fear." As he spoke, he slid his slick fingers over the bud of her anus and slowly dipped one inside her.

Oh, God.

Gently, he worked his finger in deeper and deeper, until it was buried to the webbing. He wiggled it briefly before pulling it out and repeating the process. He reached for the plug after a couple of more thrusts, painted a thick layer of gel over it, and pressed it to her opening. The plug was twice as wide as his finger had been, and she resisted. He pushed harder, gaining entrance one hard-fought inch at a time, as she did her best to make her body closed to the object. In the end, he lodged the toy deeply inside her despite her protests, and Amy was shocked to find it pleasurable, once she relaxed. She didn't want to like this. She didn't want him to have been right about her.

"Now then, let's find something to fill your tight little pussy." Her gaze looked over at his crotch, where his erection was tenting the front of his trousers. He chuckled. "No. Not me, not yet." He pulled another dildo from the box, dragged it once through her juices, and then steadily thrust it up into her to the hilt. Amy flinched when he flipped it on.

"Oh, God." She couldn't hold back the words when the dildo began vibrating. Her brain was overloading. She was stuffed, overfull. The stretch was just a hair too much and it hurt, just a little bit. Amy wiggled, not sure if she was trying to escape the sensations or lodge the toy even deeper inside her. The vibrations transmitted to her core, making her even wetter, and once again inflaming her clit with need.

"Tell me what you feel."

Amy just shook her head, not sure she could speak anyway.

"Tell me." His voice was insistent.

"No…it's too much." She squeezed the words past her constricted throat.

"Who is giving you all this pleasure?"

Amy said nothing, determined not to give in to his demands—any more than she had already.

Roan reached down to grasp the vibrator and thrust it in and out of her. "Who?"

The added stimulation of Roan's actions drove her right to the brink of orgasm. It skittered there, just beyond reach. Defeat crushed her, making her voice little more than a whisper. "You."

"Say my name. Tell me who is playing this sweet body like a violin. Who is showing you your dark desires?" He leaned down to whisper, "Who controls you?"

"Roan." His name was a long moan on her lips.

"Very good." As reward, he moved his hand a little faster. "And who is your accomplice?"

She didn't answer, and he stopped moving his hand, pulling her back slightly from the edge.

Writhing and bucking her hips, Amy tried to stimulate herself enough to come. Her pussy convulsed, and she moaned as the tide of her orgasm rose again.

With shocking intensity that distracted her from imminent release, feeling returned to her tortured nipples. She cried out as pain swept through her. Roan adjusted the clamps even tighter, and she completely lost the sense of being on the precipice of climax. Pleasure assaulted her lower body, while a burning sensation engulfed her nipples, making her want to sob and moan at the same time.

He leaned over her. "When I remove the clamps, your nipples will be so sensitive it will make you want to cry when I suck on them."

"Why are you telling me? I thought you liked your torture to be unexpected."

Roan brushed a kiss across her mouth. "I wanted you to know what's coming, to give you a chance to tell me his name."

Amy closed her eyes, both to prepare herself for the onslaught, and to keep her mouth shut. It was becoming hazier by the second why she had to protect Kevin. He had probably cleared out of Vegas last night, no doubt headed back to Washington.

Her nipples pulsed with fire when he removed the clamps with unhurried movements. She bit her tongue as feeling surged back into the sensitive buds, but couldn't keep from crying out when Roan lowered his head to suckle one. Fire radiated outward as he flicked his tongue over her nipple, while tweaking the other one with his thumb and forefinger.

Tears filled her eyes, but shame prompted them more than the pain. As he'd predicted, his ministrations hurt, but in such a good way. Once again, Amy hovered on the edge of coming, and when he grazed her nipple with his teeth, she came in an instant. Release swept through her, and she screamed her satisfaction, pumping her hips against the vibrating dildo, while arching her back to offer more of her breasts to Roan. She was vaguely aware of him withdrawing from her, but too consumed with pleasure to focus on him for several long seconds.

The waves of climax slowed and stilled, leaving her heavy-eyed. She turned her head to look at Roan. A flush suffused his face, and he was removing his clothes with shaking hands. She managed to lift her eyelids in order to have a better view. She started with surprise when he slid out the dildo and plug in one swift motion. A giggle threatened to escape as he unsnapped the manacles around her ankles with frantic movements and tossed the bolster to the floor. She might have lost control beyond all expectations, but she wasn't the only one. His need to possess her was evident in his rushed movements as he climbed on top of the table and levered over her.

He nestled between her thighs, and Amy locked her legs around his hips as he surged deep inside her with one thrust. Her pussy, still sensitive from the orgasm and vibrator, clenched around his erection as it abraded her flesh in a delicious way.

"Damn you." He buried his head into her hair as his hips pumped quickly. His cock reached as deeply inside her as he could get it, and she took it all, wanting more. It was just a little painful to have him fucking her so forcefully after everything he had done to her pussy since yesterday, but again, that heightened her pleasure. She buried her face against his chest, trying to hide from the thought.

Another orgasm swept through her, and his cock convulsed. The sensation of his cum spurting deep inside her pussy intensified her climax. To her surprise, Roan remained hard inside her. He stayed still for a short time before leisurely thrusting again. As he increased the tempo, she matched every thrust, shocked when she came yet again. He followed within seconds, and their harsh breathing filled the room.

As quickly as he had taken her, Roan slipped out, turning his back. Amy watched in silence as he struggled to calm his breathing. Her body ached, both with pain and satisfaction, and she didn't know quite what to do with that knowledge.

Roan finally turned back to look at her. Red stained his cheeks, but he appeared more composed. "I underestimated you, sweetheart."

It didn't sound like a compliment. She held her tongue, waiting for him to continue.

"You find pain much more tolerable and pleasurable than I thought you would. You're proving to be a lot more interesting than I anticipated." His lips lifted into a crooked smile, and he walked back to her. Roan took her chin in his hand, bringing his head lower. She closed her eyes when he kissed her, but opened them again when the kiss turned rough, with his tongue demanding access that she freely gave. He devoured her, seeming to want something but not getting it. Maybe he didn't even know what he wanted. The thought flickered through her dazed mind when he lifted his head with a growl for frustration.

"So we'll try something else."

The words hung in the air, and she waited with tense muscles to see what he would do. Her eyes widened with surprise when he removed the cuffs binding her wrists and pulled her up to stand next to him. "What?"

Roan shook his head. "No more warnings."

She stood uncertainly before him, wondering what would happen. When he didn't make a move, she dared to look at the closed door. "Are we finished?"

His smile didn't reach his eyes. "For now."

Amy didn't wait to see if he would change his mind. She brushed past him and fled the dungeon, intent on a shower. Hot water beckoned, and she hoped it could wash away the knowledge of what she'd just given away.

Roan watched Amy run from him but didn't try to stop her. He was out of ideas for the moment on how to coerce her to give up the information. Having discounted gentle persuasion as the way to convince her, he'd chosen this route. It had been fruitless because he hadn't understood her well enough. Who knew she would respond so enthusiastically to what should have made her surrender the name of her partner?

Or that he would react so violently to her response? That

she had come from the pain he'd administered had been surprising, but that Roan had lost control and taken her with a complete lack of grace shocked him. He was used to being in command of his emotions and actions. Women didn't shake him like that. Nothing surprised him because he wouldn't allow it. Years of sexual encounters, both vanilla and kinky, had left him confident in his self-control. But when she'd looked at him with shocked desire clouding her eyes, her pleading gaze filled with confusion as she'd silently begged him to give her more, he hadn't wanted to hold back. In that moment, all thoughts of retribution and coercion had fled. He had wanted to give her everything she'd never known she wanted. There was nothing more beautiful than a submissive in the first bloom of her dark desires.

Roan reveled in mastering a woman, in handling and manipulating her fears and desires. It had been years since anyone had made him act so eagerly and recklessly, not since Julia. The experience was unsettling but also liberating. It had been a long time since Roan had gotten more than he'd expected from sex.

Life held few surprises these days, but Amy was turning out to be a big one. It wouldn't do to let her gain the upper hand. She was there to do his bidding, to be sexual putty in his masterful hands. He wouldn't—no, couldn't—let her know she had gotten to him. In the future, Roan wouldn't let her excite him beyond all sense of reason. He simply wouldn't allow it.

♣ ♠ ♥ ♦ ♣ ♠ ♥ ♦ ♣ ♠ ♥ ♦

Chapter Five

After her shower, Amy had curled up in Roan's bed, finding it impossible to resist sleep. When she awoke some hours later, the afternoon sun had disappeared from the gaps in the blinds, and grayness shadowed the room. She turned her head to find Roan stretched out beside her, his face an unguarded mask as he slept. Slumber relaxed the lines of tension in his face, making him look younger and less intimidating. Vulnerable.

She was unable to overcome the compulsion to touch his countenance. Amy smoothed her fingers over his cheek, rubbing her thumb lightly against his lower lip. When he didn't wake, she grew bolder, tracing a finger up the bridge of his nose and lightly across his eyelid. She touched the lines forming under his eyes, wondering how old he was. A thousand questions filled her mind, from inane to important, and she marveled that she had shared so much with a man she barely knew.

His eyes snapped open, and she flinched. Amy tried to move her hand, but his was there to intercept it. To her surprise, he brought it to his mouth, turning her wrist so he could press his lips to the palm of her hand. The slow, gentle kiss was more erotic than anything he had done to her in the dungeon, and liquid heat filled her pussy as warmth surged through her chest, leaving her with a breathless feeling.

Roan's lips tickled when he asked, "How did you sleep?"

She shrugged, not certain how to respond to him. The afternoon of pain and pleasure had left her thrown off balance. She was still sorting through events, trying to reconcile her behavior with the person she had believed she was. If she didn't know what to think of herself, she could only imagine his opinion. Since he didn't know her, he could only interpret the behavior she had displayed thus far and make assumptions from that.

"What are you thinking about with such a pensive expression?"

She said, "How little I know about you, and vice versa. How can we be as...intimate as we are and still be total strangers?"

Roan blinked, and then laughed. "You're right. I don't even know your name."

She frowned. "Amy."

"Your *last* name."

"Oh." Amy tugged her hand free of his, surprised when he let go without a fight. She curled onto her side, facing him. "Gerard. Amethyst Gerard."

He made a face. "What were your parents thinking?"

Amy shrugged. "My mother was fifteen when I was born. I imagine she thought it was a cool name."

Roan quirked a brow. "Your father?"

Once more, she shrugged. "Gone. What about your father?"

Roan smiled, and his expression held just a trace of something other than amusement. "The legendary Robert Cavello, one of the founders of Las Vegas. At one time, he had six casinos but lost most of them when Vegas nearly went bankrupt. When he retired to Florida a few years ago, he had just the two left—The Liege, which he gave to me, and Luck of the Draw, now owned by my half brother, Rhys."

"What about your mother? I doubt she was a teenager who got tired of playing mommy when you were three and took off."

He lifted a shoulder. "Close. She was a showgirl, definitely not married to Dad, but wanting to be. She set out to trick him, and I was the result." His lips twisted. "I don't recall it, but Rhys tells me it was a stormy relationship. They had split by the time I was two, and when I was five, she left Vegas for fame in Hollywood."

Amy's eyes widened at the similarities in their backgrounds. "Do you ever see her?"

"Nah. She died in a car accident a few months after she got to Hollywood."

Instinctively, she reached out to touch his hand. "I'm sorry."

"Don't be. I don't even remember her." His clouded expression cleared, and he focused on her again. "Your mother ran off, too?"

She nodded. "She dropped me at my aunt and uncle's, and that was the last we saw of her."

"So they were your family?"

"Like my parents. My cousin Kevin is like my brother—" She closed her mouth with a snap, realizing she was venturing into dangerous territory. "But that's boring. Let's talk about something else."

Roan's eyes darkened, and he moved forward, rolling her onto her back to straddle her. He held her hands on either side of her head, and his cock pressed into her stomach. It was hard and ready. "Like what?"

"This." She stretched to give him a kiss, closing her eyes when he accepted her lips gently, giving her a slow kiss, punctuated by leisurely strokes of his tongue inside her mouth. Relief swept through her that she had diverted him, and she surrendered herself to the sensations his mouth invoked as it moved across her cheek to her ear.

She sighed when he nipped her lobe. A shiver raced down her spine when he blew into her ear, and she arched her hips, wishing he would scoot down just a few inches, so that his cock would nestle between her thighs instead of pressing into her stomach.

He kept her hands locked in a loose hold, frustrating her with the lack of ability to touch him. "Roan." His name was more of a sigh than a sound when he moved his knee between her legs, pressing it against her soft mound. She rocked against it, while his mouth evoked ripples of pleasure as he explored her neck.

She was so lost in the moment that it took her several seconds to realize he had released her hands and was cupping her breasts. His rough thumb across her hard nipple was a marked contrast to the gentle kiss he lavished on her, while rubbing his knee into her slit in unhurried circles.

Amy reached down between their bodies to find his cock. She had wanted to touch and taste it since the moment she'd first realized she would be having it inside her, and now was her chance. Although she couldn't see it, she knew from memory that his cock was thick and long, with a bulbous head that turned an angry shade of red when he was aroused. She cupped the head in her hand, imagining it was getting redder by the moment.

"Touch me," he said against her lips, continuing to massage her breasts.

Amy trailed her finger around the corona, applying pressure at the V. She smiled when he jerked in response before driving his hips forward, lodging his cock more solidly into the cradle of her hand. Her rhythm felt awkward, but she worked the length of him with strong, slow strokes, pleased when he bucked against her hand repeatedly, his cock twitching in time with his heartbeat.

She stretched her arm farther and cupped his balls in her hand, her eyes widening. He either waxed or shaved, because there wasn't a trace of hair on his genitals. She hadn't realized it until then, despite his having fucked her twice.

He lifted his head, grinning down at her. "You seem surprised."

She nodded. "I didn't know men…well, I guess I've heard of it, but I never knew a man who was hairless down there."

His expression darkened. "How many men have you known?"

She wasn't going to delve into her past. "Enough to know what I'm doing. That's all that matters."

"Okay." Roan put his hands flat on the mattress on either side of her head, leaning against her so that their chests touched. The change in position caused her to lose her grip on his cock and forced his knee away from her clit. She looked up at him, wide-eyed. "I thought you wanted me to…"

He shook his head. "No. I want to be inside you. Sometime later, I'll come in your hand." His lips curled into a thoughtful smile. "Or your mouth."

She licked her lips, surprised by how violently aroused the thought made her. She was dripping with need when Roan pushed the head of his cock into her opening. A flash of pain from her overused flesh accompanied his thrust of possession, but as he moved in and out of her, that faded.

Amy started to wrap her legs around his hips. "Don't. Try it this way. I think you'll like the friction." At his words, she kept her thighs together, enjoying having Roan ride her. He was right about the friction of his skin against hers, and the pressure of his pelvis pinning her to the mattress. Her clit ached with arousal, and she arched her hips frantically. Soon, she hovered on the edge of orgasm.

When Roan buried his face against her neck, she tipped her head, hoping he would bite her. Instead, he whispered in her ear, "Was it Kevin?"

"Huh?" Disoriented with passion, she couldn't switch gears quickly enough to keep up with the question.

"Your partner? Was it your cousin?"

"I…oh, God…" Satisfaction overwhelmed her, and Amy lost the ability to think logically. "Yes, it was Kevin," she said in a hoarse voice as her pussy convulsed around his cock, bringing them both simultaneous release. Her heartbeat roared in her ears, drowning out anything else he might have said, as she let the pleasure overwhelm her. She knew she had made a mistake but couldn't think clearly about the ramifications right then.

Roan thrust inside her once more before rolling to his

side, bringing her with him. Amy lay against him, her head against his chest, still dazed from the contrast in his lovemaking. Compared to the earlier experience in the dungeon, he had treated her as though she were made of glass. It was the difference between night and day.

And it had worked!

Her eyes snapped open when she realized what she had done. She lifted her head to glare at him, recriminations hovering on the tip of her tongue.

"Why?" he asked.

The question threw her, causing her to hesitate in launching a tirade. "What?"

Roan grabbed a handful of her hair, tugging it gently to encourage her to slide up to him. Amy went with the motion to avoid having him pull out the strands, and when he pressed a soft kiss to the bruise on her jaw, her mouth dropped open.

"Why did you steal from me?"

"I…" She trailed off when he licked the line of her jaw, moving toward her ear. Though she had just come, her core stirred to life again. It took all her focus to answer. "My aunt and uncle are about to lose their orchard."

He hesitated at her ear, not moving for a few seconds. Then he leaned forward to nibble her lobe, working his way up her ear, until he was back at her cheek, near her eye. His lips were soft explorers over the tender area, and Amy closed her eyelids when he brushed a kiss across one.

"Why me?" He tipped her head back to expose her lips, and she opened her eyes. His mouth hovered near hers, as his eyes drilled into hers. "Why my casino?"

The mix of anger and desire in his eyes excited her, although she wanted to resist. It infuriated her that he would use tenderness to coerce her to answer when pain hadn't worked. But was it his fault the pain had turned her on rather than compelled her to talk? "It was close to my apartment."

Roan blinked, and then a laugh escaped him. "Geography?" He shook his head before sitting up, ending all possibility of the hinted-at kiss. She took the hand he offered to rise into a sitting position, feeling the ache between her thighs from renewed desire that hadn't been satisfied. "Come on."

"What? Where?"

"To take a shower." He rose to his feet, pulling her up beside him. Amy tipped her neck, but he avoided her lips. "Just a shower, sweetheart. I want to buy you something pretty."

The something pretty wasn't quite what she had expected. It was a tattoo. A purple-and-gold butterfly, about the size of a quarter, right above her pussy. As she walked back through the hotel lobby with Roan an hour and a half later, she wondered what was happening to her. In a few short days, she had gone from a woman naive to her own deeply buried desires, to a sexually experienced submissive. With a tattoo! Aunt Mel would faint if she knew what Amy had done. Would still do—until Roan tired of playing with her.

The thought caused an uncomfortable pang in her chest. She told herself she should be anxious to get this over with, should be praying he would soon tire of the novelty of having his own living sex toy, but her heart still raced when he brushed his hand across her buttocks. She could try lying to herself, but what was the point? Regardless of the circumstances that had brought them to this, she was enjoying herself. Never in her life had she imagined she would someday have a lover like Roan, and she should enjoy having him for as long as possible. Since she'd revealed the name he wanted, a new calm seemed to have settled over him. She wanted to think he had lowered his guard a bit but was probably fooling herself. She knew it was just the sex making her feel so attached to him so quickly and forced her thoughts back to reality. This was not a romance.

"You're quiet," he said as they stepped into the deserted elevator.

She made a noncommittal sound as he inserted his key to open the panel that displayed the buttons not available to common guests. Roan pushed the P, removed his key and returned it to his pocket.

"Does it hurt?"

She shrugged. "A little."

He pulled her closer. "Are you still pouting because I made you get it?"

Amy curled her lip. "No. I'm just…thinking."

"About what?"

She sighed. "How disappointed my family would be if they knew what I've been doing with you."

Roan tipped up her chin. "Are you ashamed?"

It was impossible to hold his gaze. "Yeah."

"Why?"

"Because I'm a wanton." She winced at the volume of her voice, lowering it. "I'm not the person I thought I was."

"We seldom are, sweetheart." He lowered his head to touch his lips to hers before speaking again. "Would you rather go through life half-alive, unaware of what really turns you on?"

She buried her face against his polo shirt. "Yes." The linen muffled her voice, but he must have still heard her.

"Liar," he said with amusement. Roan's hands roamed down her dress, lifting the hem. "It's so much better to discover who you are now, at this age. I didn't know about my…proclivities for a long time."

She lifted her head. "Really?"

He nodded. "It wasn't until my early thirties that I met a woman who freed me." A hint of sadness marred his expression. "Unfortunately, she liked being free more than she liked me, so it was a brief affair."

"Do you still love her?" Why did the idea make her lungs ache and cause tears to burn her eyes?

He shook his head, and the sadness disappeared. "No. I stopped loving her long ago, although I'll always be grateful to her for showing me what I wanted." Roan shrugged. "It wouldn't have worked, anyway, because she was dominant. She helped me find that in myself, and once I was in control, I couldn't give it up."

His words made a lot of sense, and his honesty prompted her to say, "I don't have that urge. I couldn't imagine being in control."

Roan hugged her for a long moment before releasing her. "I know. You're submissive. There's nothing wrong with that. In fact, it's beautiful." He turned her in his arms, cupping her breasts as her back settled against his chest. "You do what you do, and I'll do what I do."

She let the tension flow from her body as he massaged her nipples. "Okay," she rasped.

She watched his hands move on her in the mirrors lining the elevator walls. His eyes caught hers in the reflection and glittered with intent. He hit the emergency stop button. By the time they arrived at the penthouse floor twenty minutes later, the faint twinges from her tattoo had faded to almost nothing.

♣ ♠ ♥ ♦ ♣ ♠ ♥ ♦ ♣ ♠ ♥ ♦

Chapter Six

They passed the next few days in a haze of passion. When Roan wasn't working, he was teaching her all about herself and her body. She reveled in being restrained. He had told her how freeing it was to relinquish that control willingly, and he'd been right. Despite the reasons they had come together she had given him her trust, to see to her pleasures, to understand her limits and not push her too far. All that she was learning about herself still appalled her at times, but being with Roan made her forget about the woman she'd been before.

What was more alarming was the realization that despite her best efforts to guard her heart, she was failing. Last night, they had watched a boxing match and had had wild sex in the locker room afterward while waiting to meet the fighters. All the while, she hadn't worried about being caught. Instead, she had fretted that there would be no more experiences like that with anyone else after she left Roan. No other man could ever be his equal. Knowing that instinctively had her fearing she would be forever alone once their interlude ended. Roan was out tonight—some boys' night thing he couldn't get out of. One night alone, and she was wallowing in self-pity, once again contemplating a bleak future. What would it be like for her when the six weeks ended? She didn't want to think about it, but couldn't seem to stop.

Roan tossed another fifty-dollar chip into the growing pile on the felt, although he couldn't remember what cards he held in his hand. Thoughts of pinning Amy against the wall as soon as he reentered the penthouse and taking her for a quick fuck crowded his mind. If it weren't for the fact that the men surrounding the table were regular customers of the casino, each dropping a million or more per visit, he would have begged off the prearranged game and spent the night taking Amy over and over again.

As if his thoughts had conjured the words, Steve Delminico raised his bet, saying as he did so, "Who was that gorgeous snatch you were with at the fights last night?"

His first reaction to the question was anger, but he swallowed it down. Steve was unrefined, at best, so it wasn't a deliberate insult to Roan that he would call his companion such a name. Attempting civility, he said, "She's a friend."

"I hear she's living with you, Roan," said Kahlil Ahmed, an oil company heir so embarrassingly wealthy that he seemed to feel the need to downplay it by dressing in ragged jeans and T-shirts with goofy slogans. Tonight's was I Got Rocked Hard At The Hard Rock.

He shrugged, ignoring their ribbing. With the exception of Steve Delminico, he genuinely enjoyed the others' company and knew they would leave him alone after getting it out of their systems. "Let's concentrate on the game."

"I wouldn't mind a *friend* like that, and I don't mind paying for it," said Steve. "How about a wager? My hand against yours, winner takes all."

It took every ounce of self-control not to jump across the table and smash his fist into the other man's face. It was only the shock of the reaction itself that kept Roan in his seat. He wasn't prone to violent impulses, and the thought left him blinking. "I already have it all."

"You're thinking about it, I can tell." Steve grinned. "I'll sweeten it. You know that plane you've been wanting? I'll have it made posthaste, personalized to your specifications and delivered right to your own airfield."

He wrinkled his nose. "That's what you're offering? A plane for a woman?"

Steve frowned. "For the game, of course. I wasn't suggesting an outright trade." After an uneasy silence, he laughed, although it held little amusement. "Aw, you know I'm just messing with you, Roan."

"Of course." He forced a smile, deciding to let it pass. After all, most things in Vegas were for sale, for the right price. For all he knew, maybe Amy would jump at the chance to sell herself to Steve. His crudeness didn't reflect in his Hollywood good looks. It might cost a lot less than a plane.

Not liking the thought of her with the jerk across the table, Roan tried to put it out of his mind. He groaned when Austin laid down a full house, tossing in the cards in his hand after looking at them again. A pair of eights. It wasn't his night. Maybe when he got back to the penthouse, his luck would change.

★ ★ ★

The following afternoon, Roan shuffled through the pile of purchase orders again, finding he had no more recollection of the figures than he'd had the last two times he had tried to absorb them. His head was fuzzy, but he knew it wasn't from the late night he and Amy had spent finishing off the better part of two magnums of champagne. A good portion of that had gotten *on* them rather than in them. No, it was Amy herself who was responsible for his lack of focus.

With a sigh, he turned the leather chair to the glass wall of his office. High in the casino, it afforded him a view of the main floor below. Business was brisk for three-thirty in the afternoon, but he paid little mind to the gamblers bustling about beneath him. Others in his employ were well-paid for that task. Instead, he looked through the people and the machines. He saw only Amy, her mouth open as she cried out in ecstasy. He had never seen anyone take so much delight in hot wax and cold champagne before her.

"Damn." He turned away from the casino and back to the paperwork. Why couldn't he stop thinking about her? Why did her smell linger in his nostrils, her hot cries in his ears? By flexing his fingers, he could recall the smooth feel of her hips, the arch of her foot and a thousand other places that made her alternately scream or cry when he touched them just so. She was with him even when they were apart.

He didn't like it. The pain of losing Julia had taught him not to surrender his emotions to any of the women who would come and go throughout his life. He had maintained that resolve until now. Roan preferred experience in his partners, not virgins to his lifestyle. A wry grin flashed across his lips. She certainly wasn't the typical new sub, shy and retiring. No, his Amy was more than happy to try anything he suggested. Anywhere. Anytime.

Roan frowned, not liking the possessive way he was thinking about her. Experience had shown him it was foolish to think love could last for a lifetime. Their arrangement was perfect, so he didn't want to muck it up by letting sentimentality get the better of him. Any day now, he was bound to grow tired of her, bored with her seemingly limitless enthusiasm for kink, and send her on her way. Right?

The intercom's buzzing caught his attention, and he depressed the button to speak with his assistant. "Yeah, Brad?"

"That fax just came through, sir."

"Bring it in." Roan gave a cursory thanks to the other man when he brought in a file and left with a quiet click of the door. He flipped open the file to read through the pages, growing angrier by the second. Nothing was as it seemed. *That little liar.*

Heart hammering in his ears, Roan slammed closed the file and lifted it. He ignored the pile of waiting paperwork and stormed out of the office, snarling at Brad, "Cancel my appointment," as he went by. He could imagine his assistant's shock, since it wasn't like Roan to cancel meetings with the Nevada Gaming Commission. He wasn't half as surprised as Roan by his behavior. He knew it was reckless and irresponsible to give in to the anger flowing through him, but he was beyond caring.

The elevator button bore a measure of his wrath, but didn't crack under the forceful stab. Roan looked through the papers once more while waiting for the elevator to take him to his suite, finding they fanned the flames, just as he intended. He wanted to be a raging, seething mass when he confronted her.

How could he have been so trusting? Her story about cheating to save her relatives was a common one, but he'd bought into it. Hell, he'd even felt sorry for her, had eased up on her after that. Roan squirmed, realizing he'd let down his guard with the lying little schemer. All along, she'd continued to play him for a fool.

He covered the distance to the front door of the penthouse in a blur of anger, not knowing or caring if anyone saw him. Roan opened the door with his key card, stepped inside and slammed the door with a satisfying thud. He couldn't help a cold smile when he saw the way Amy jumped. Curled up on the sofa, reading a book, she was the picture of innocence. In his business, he knew how to tell the fakes from the real masterpieces, so how had she fooled him?

"Roan?" She set aside the book, looking uncertain. "Is something wrong?"

He walked closer to her, the file clenched in his fist. "You could say that."

"Has there been a change of plans?" She flashed a look at the clock on the wall. "I thought I wasn't supposed to be ready for dinner until seven?"

"Things changed." When he reached the couch, he tossed the file at her. She caught it awkwardly. "*That* changed everything." She had no idea how much.

"What's this?"

"Open it."

She still eyed him with confusion as she opened the file. When her eyes dropped to the page, he saw her reading. Her brow furrowed. "What is this?"

"Financial records for your aunt and uncle." Roan stepped in front of her, looming over her. "I wanted to make sure you'd gotten enough out of your cheating to pay off their debts." He reached forward, grasping a handful of her hair in his hand, pulling her head backward. "You got more than enough, huh?" *You nearly got my heart.* He nipped that thought in the bud, refusing to allow it to bloom.

Amy shook her head. "I don't understand."

"Those papers show a healthy profit for their orchard. They've done well for the past eighteen years, never a hint of financial insolvency. Your family isn't on the verge of losing everything." He tightened his grip, pleased when she winced. "So, why did you really steal from me?"

Tears sparkled in her eyes. "I swear, Kevin told me they needed the money. Please, Roan, I wouldn't lie to you."

He sneered. "Of course not. You'd only cheat and steal but never lie."

"Not to you," she said again.

Roan shook his head. "You are good. Even now, knowing what a fraud you are, I almost believe the tears and sympathy act. Get up." He helped her to her feet by yanking on her hair, but not relinquishing his hold as he took her down the hallway. He wriggled away from the thought that he was reacting more from hurt than anger.

She trembled visibly as they neared the dungeon. "Please don't do this. I didn't lie to you." She was trying to dig in her heels, but he pulled her forward. "*He* lied to *me.*"

"Yeah." Roan shouldered open the door, dragging her inside. Her fear reflected in her eyes, forcing him to look away, lest he lose the edge of anger driving him. "Strip."

"But—"

He didn't wait for her protests. With more force than necessary, he tore the silk robe from her, leaving her naked. It pleased him to know she was following his instructions not to wear underwear in the suite, even when he wasn't there. "On your knees."

"You want a blow job *now?*"

He laughed at her shocked expression, although it did nothing to soothe his anger. "That's the least of what I want." With a firm hand on her shoulder, he pushed her to her knees. "Stay there." Roan watched from the corner of his eye as he fetched restraints.

"You can't do this. Not when you're angry."

"Watch me." He bent behind her, fastening her wrists into the cuffs, surprised by her lack of resistance. "Aren't you going to fight?"

"Why bother? You're going to do what you please, regardless."

Her response was unsatisfying, and he tightened the shackles around her ankles more roughly than necessary. Leaning back on his heels, he surveyed his work with a pleased nod. She was bound in a classic pose of submission, hands linked to her ankles by a bar. She was completely at his mercy, unable to stand up or get away. He could see the tension in her body as she braced herself—not in anticipation but apprehension.

"Do you still deny that you lied to me?"

Amy's head remained bent, and she didn't speak. Anger and confusion seethed in Roan, with ire winning. From a hook on the wall, he selected a whip with multiple leather lashes at the end of the mahogany rod. The handle had a smooth patina from years of use, and the wood had taken on slight grooves where his fingers most often gripped it. It was one of his favorite toys, normally reserved for passionate play.

As he walked back to her, the wood seemed warm in his hands, making them tingle. It seemed to be rejecting his intentions to use the whip strictly for punishment. In defiance of the wood, which was only a reflection of his own mixed feelings, Roan drew back the rod and brought the lashes across her back, leaving six red stripes on her pale skin. She flinched from the contact, but that and a whimper were her only reaction.

With a growl, Roan tossed aside the whip. He couldn't do this. As angry as he was, he had no entitlement to physically punish her. It was one thing to administer pain for the sake of pleasure, but a completely different matter to use it for retaliation.

He had no outlet suitable to vent his anger, and he was shaking with it. Rage thundered through his veins as he unfastened her cuffs. Whatever her sins, she was a budding submissive, and he had no right to cause her to develop an aversion to sexual discipline by tainting it this way. Once she was free, he cupped her bicep, helping her to her feet. The silence was thick, with an edge. Her expression reflected her knowledge that he wasn't finished yet.

Shaking his head, he turned from her to pace, pleased when she didn't try to leave the room. As he prowled around the room, his mind raced. The logical side of his brain tried to downplay what she had done. In light of stealing from him to start with, what difference did the lie make? Why was he so upset? Why the hell did he feel so betrayed by her?

Roan stopped cold in his tracks as a sick feeling came over him. His stomach churned, and he swallowed hard to force down the bile trying to rise in his throat. What a fool he'd been, to drop his guard so completely. He shook his head, shocked that he had let himself develop any feelings for Amy beyond the sexual. A casual lie from her had wounded him deeply. It shouldn't have if he'd been protecting his heart.

Roan turned to her, a cold smile on his face. He didn't speak, and neither did she, although he could see she was dying to ask what he had planned. Too bad he had no idea what her punishment should be. With a new purpose, he walked over to the phone. When Tim answered, he said, "Come to my apartment. Miss Gerard needs an escort."

She eyed him with obvious confusion when he hung up. "An escort to where?"

"Your own room. I am tired of you, and I require time to decide your punishment for lying." The truth was, he wanted her far away before he could give in to the urges consuming him. His brain told him to send her far away, even as his body warred with the need to both break her and hold her tenderly. Facing such a plethora of confusing emotions, he decided it was prudent to follow the dictates of his brain.

She shook her head, twisting free of his hold. "I won't do it. I won't leave it like this."

He arched an eyebrow. "I don't want you."

"Liar," she said with a disturbing amount of certainty.

He snorted. "Only one of us is the liar here, sweetheart, and we both know who that is." Roan gestured to the phone. "Shall I call the police and let them decide if you're telling the truth?"

Amy glared at him. "If you don't trust me, then dial away."

He laughed. "Trust you? Why in the world would I do that?" With a gentle tap of his finger on her cheek, he said, "Trust must be earned."

A tear fell from her eye, rolling with hypnotic grace down her smooth cheek. "I trusted you until tonight."

Roan's mouth twisted. "Then I guess we're both fools, aren't we, sweetheart?" At those words, she sagged forward, and he knew she had capitulated. So, why was he filled with a hollow ache in his solar plexus instead of the rush of victory he had expected?

♣ ♠ ♥ ♦ ♣ ♠ ♥ ♦ ♣ ♠ ♥ ♦

Chapter Seven

Amy lay curled up on the huge bed in the suite where Tim had taken her. Roan had been so quick to dispose of her that she'd had no time to dress in anything but a robe, and the security goon had taken full advantage of her lack of dress to ogle her.

When the door to the suite opened without so much as a knock, her heart skipped a beat. *Roan*. Instead, her visitor was a handsome man in a blue silk robe, with slicked-back, wavy blond hair, bright blue eyes and a gorgeous smile, complete with dimple.

Reflexively, Amy jerked the blanket over her thin robe. "Who are you? What are you doing in my room?"

"Steve Delminico. I'm a friend of Roan's." He sauntered toward the minibar, acting as though his words had explained everything. He lifted a bottle of amber liquid. "Drink, darlin'?"

She shook her head, too shocked by his presumptuousness to figure out how to respond. "What are you doing?"

"It seems as though Roan took me up on my offer after all. A plane, for you." He downed two fingers of the alcohol and poured another glassful before speaking again. "Why else would he put you so conveniently next to my room and make sure your door didn't lock?"

Amy gasped, still confused, but piecing together enough from his broken explanation to realize Roan had sent this man to her. He'd sold her in exchange for a plane? Tears pricked her eyes. "This can't be."

Steve shrugged. "You know how these things work. I'm one of The Liege's best customers, darlin'. Roan wants to keep me happy." He sipped his drink and smacked his lips. His eyes never strayed from her. "Right now, you're just about all I need to be the happiest man on earth."

As the truth sank in, she sagged under the blankets. Roan wanted her to do this, wanted to cheapen her, show her how insignificant she was to him as punishment for lying. She felt ill. All along, while she had been falling under his spell, Roan had viewed her as his toy. Neither she nor the passion they had shared had meant anything to him.

Steve came closer, pulling back the covers from her un-resisting fingers with a whistle. "You're even prettier than I remembered, darlin'."

His Texas drawl grated on her nerves, as did the saccha-rine endearment. Her heart had shrunk into a tight ball. She knew that the answer was going to hurt, but she had to know how this had come to happen. She needed to hear the brutal truth and force herself to comprehend what Roan had done to her. "When did you see me?"

"At the fights. You were a pretty little ornament on Roan's arm in that gold thing, but I think I like this better." He moved behind her, smoothing his hands down the shoul-ders of her silk robe. "Yes, indeedy. No bra." With an appreciative chuckle, he reached to squeeze one of her breasts. "Boy, Roan sure knows how to treat a guest."

Amy jerked away from him, coming out of her daze. She retreated to the other side of the hotel room to put some distance between them.

He made a whooping sound. "You are a bundle of fun, aren't you? Roan must have told you I like a little resistance." With a hasty motion, he discarded the robe he wore, coming at her in the nude. As he neared, Amy held her breath, realizing he hadn't needed the drink to intoxicate him. He'd already gotten a head start with whatever alcohol had been his companion before he'd helped himself to the bottle from the minibar.

His arms engulfed her like a prison she couldn't escape, and he stripped the robe from her with a clumsy yank that caused the silk to rip as she struggled to free herself. "I like how the package came wrapped." He paused to slobber on her neck, leaving a wet trail behind when he lifted his head. "You're brave, darlin', coming to your room in just a robe. This is a busy hotel."

She hadn't realized it then, but her state of undress must have all been part of the humiliation Roan had orchestrated for her. Fortunately, she had only run into two people when Tim brought her to the suite, and they hadn't batted an eye. "Get away from me, you bastard! Let me go!"

Steve nodded. "That's right, baby. I can tell you're going to be a real good girl."

He gripped her tighter as he slanted his lips over hers. His breath washed over her, making her gag at the combination of alcohol and garlic. "I'm going to pound your pussy so hard, you're going to bleed."

Fear spiked through her as he groaned his version of pillow talk in her ear. Her struggles grew more panicked as she fought against him with all her strength. Steve pushed her down on the bed with a complete lack of finesse. Amy's head spun from the sudden force of the movement. *She wasn't going to get away from him. This was really going to happen.*

His grip loosened for a moment as he followed her down on the mattress, and with a grunt, she shoved him off. Panting, Amy rolled away from him and raced to the door.

"What the fuck? You're leaving now?" Steve bellowed. The air crackled with his anger as he realized she wasn't playing.

"You like working a man up, teasing him and then backing out? Huh, bitch?"

He stalked across the room after her. "You started it, and now you're going to finish it."

Amy spun around and fumbled with the lock on the door, but Steve grabbed her before her shaking hands could get the door open. To her surprise, when he twirled her around, his anger had turned to amusement.

"I see how it is. Good acting, girl."

Amy tried to pull away when he tightened his arms around her. "What are you talking about?"

"The stripes on your back tell it all. You like it rough." He laughed, and it sounded full of joy. "Guess I've been a little too nice, so far."

"No—"

He twisted her nipple roughly. "You're an innocent little thing, right? I'm the big, bad wolf, set to eat you up." Steve pinned her arms with his hands and started sliding down her body. "I'll start with your bald little pussy, darlin'."

She twisted and bucked against his hold, kicking out with her feet, all to no avail. The harder she fought, the more he liked it. Finally, temporarily worn-out, she lay quietly as he circled his tongue on her navel, while tears leaked from her eyes.

When she saw Roan looming over her, Amy was convinced panic had seized her, sending her into a hallucination. It was only when he tossed Steve off her that she dared to believe he was there. As his arms fastened around her, lifting her into a protective embrace, she buried her head against his chest. All of her anger and confusion took a back burner to relief. Steve was cursing and shouting, but she didn't let his words penetrate the fog swirling in her brain. All she could hear was the low murmur of Roan's voice as he spoke in a level tone. Even when his muscles bunched, indicating his rising anger, his voice remained a reassuring calm. It seemed to take seconds for him to cross to the door of the suite and slam it behind them.

Amy was vaguely aware of his draping the robe around her nakedness as he strode down the hall, but she didn't look up. In the elevator, she thought she heard someone else's voice, but refused to focus on them. It wasn't until she was certain they were back in his penthouse suite that she raised her head to look at him. "I hate you," she said in a soft whisper, before sobs burst from her chest.

"I had nothing to do with him being in your room, if that's what you're thinking. I'm a bastard, but not that sadistic." Roan dropped onto a nearby sofa, rocking her in his arms. "Let it out, sweetheart."

Amy let the tears flow, releasing her anger at being victimized in a storm of words. Once, she hit him on the chest, and then buried her face against the same spot a second later, all while he stroked her back and smoothed her hair. How could she feel so grateful to him while still hating him so much at the same time? If he hadn't sent her away, she wouldn't have been at that man's mercy.

As he hugged her, his arms offering a reassuring support structure to which she could cling, she accepted she didn't hate him. Roan hadn't planned for Delminico to attack her. Sending her away was supposed to be punishment enough, she supposed. He had wounded her so deeply, had shattered any illusions she'd had that he might be falling in love with her, and had torn out her heart to stomp on it, but she couldn't blame him for the attempted rape any more than she could really hate him. She loved him too much to do that.

Roan held Amy as she raged at him, soothing and caressing her as the tension gradually left her body, and she fell silent. Her tears had soaked his shirt, but the soggy discomfort was the least he deserved.

When she was limp in his arms, he shifted her so that he could see her face. Exhaustion had caught up with her, and she slept deeply. Even in slumber, she sniffled occasionally, and purple bruises under her eyes revealed the depths of emotional ravage she had endured.

Anger aimed at Steve warred with concern for his lover. The anger nearly won, but he pushed it back long enough to settle Amy more comfortably on the sofa. Rage scalded the pit of his stomach like acid, but he forced it back to tend to Amy. She curled into a pitiful ball around the throw pillow, and he was compelled to sit behind her and rub her back as she settled into an even deeper sleep.

His touch must have soothed her into relaxation, because her body slowly unfurled, and she rolled onto her back. It did nothing to soothe him. He pacified himself with violent thoughts against Steve Delminico as he kept vigil over Amy. Only the knowledge that the man had already been physically removed from the casino kept him from beating Delminico to a pulp.

How could he have so completely misjudged the man? True, Roan had never liked Delminico, but he hadn't taken him for a rapist. Despite the man's insistence that he had assumed Amy was compliments of the house when he saw her settling into the suite next to his, Roan couldn't find an ounce of understanding to justify the man's actions. How had Steve interpreted Amy's locale and a malfunctioning lock as invitation to fuck her? He shook his head, still baffled.

Amy confused him, too. Why hadn't she screamed down the casino when the man had entered her room? It made no sense, unless she had wanted Delminico—but if so, why had she been fighting him when Roan had first seen them on the security camera?

In his search for answers, Roan went to the nearest computer. He punched in his code to access security cameras. With nausea churning in his gut, he watched Tim escort Amy into the suite and leave just a few seconds later. The door didn't appear to have closed all the way, but his security guard hadn't noticed the oversight as he walked down the hall to the elevator.

Roan pulled up a different camera to get a new angle

of the hallway. There was Delminico, lurking in the doorway of his suite. He seemed to be undecided but finally pocketed his key card and closed his suite door behind him. When he got to Amy's room, he seemed surprised to find the door hadn't locked. His posture suggested his confidence swelled at that moment, and he entered the room, closing the door behind him hard enough to ensure it locked.

Roan accessed the footage from the camera in Amy's room. He had missed the first few minutes of what had transpired as it happened because he had been fighting the impulse to spy on her. When he had finally turned on the camera, it had been to find Steve sexually assaulting her. Now, he watched the events leading up to it. As Steve laid out his interpretation of the situation, Roan winced. It was clear Amy believed every word Delminico spoke. Her expression revealed her pain more clearly than any words could have. She had believed Roan had betrayed her.

At the very beginning of their arrangement, Roan had told her he would break her and rebuild her to suit him. God help him, he had nearly succeeded. If Steve hadn't been so rough or repulsive, she might have let the other man do whatever he wanted to her. Self-preservation might not have overridden her budding submissive side if Delminico hadn't been such a bastard. What had Roan done to her?

It had to stop. Somehow, he had to find the strength to put an end to the affair before he destroyed them both. He had to find the will to withdraw from her, to send her back to the remnants of the life she'd lived before coming into his sphere of influence.

Even knowing he had to distance himself from Amy, he couldn't resist the impulse to return to the couch, gather her into his arms and hold her as she slept.

♣ ♠ ♥ ♦ ♣ ♠ ♥ ♦ ♣ ♠ ♥ ♦

Chapter Eight

Amy woke with a start, wincing at the pain in her neck. She lifted her head, her eyes widening with surprise when she realized she was in the living room, snuggled on Roan's lap. The sunlight through the blinds revealed it was sometime the following day. She remembered pouring out her heart but didn't recall their falling asleep, passing the night on the couch.

She turned her head to look at Roan, finding his eyes open, watching her with a closed expression. Amy waited for him to speak, feeling vulnerable, each nerve exposed. Her hands trembled as he maintained his silent scrutiny. When the quivering moved into her stomach, she looked away from him. Rising to her feet, she turned her back on Roan to head toward the bathroom. A shower would help to restore some of her confidence, she hoped.

Amy adjusted the water temperature to as hot as she could stand it before stepping into the spray. It lashed her body like a thousand punishing whips, but she welcomed the reviving sting. Along with a thick layer of soap, it made it possible for her to wash away all vestiges of Steve's touch, to feel almost clean again.

Once she had rinsed away the lather, Amy laid her head against the tile, letting tears flow. Her anguish came not from what had almost happened with Steve, but from Roan. He hadn't said a word this morning, and she didn't recall him speaking much last night as she'd cried, ranted and sobbed. An occasional murmur or stroke of her hair had been his contribution. She had no idea all the things that had spouted from her mouth last night, and she fervently hoped that she hadn't done something really stupid, like confess her feelings at some point during her crying jag.

The shower door opened behind her, interrupting her meltdown. Amy quickly ducked her head into the spray of water, letting the now-tepid water sluice away all evidence of crying.

When he put his arms on her shoulders, she didn't resist. Amy tipped her head back to allow his mouth to nuzzle the bend of her neck, as his cock pressed against her lower back, proof that he still wanted her. Did he still think she had lied to him? Was he still angry, despite his physical desire? Had she been punished enough? What did it matter if he continued punishing her? Last night when he had accused her of lying, it had been clear he would never care for her. She could have his body for the duration of their agreement, but she could never have his heart.

It wasn't enough, but it was all she would get from him. Amy clung to the knowledge, using it to buffer her tattered pride as she turned in his arms, wrapping hers around his neck. They shared a carnal kiss, one that she put all her heart into, though he wouldn't know that. Tears stung her eyes again as he explored her mouth, but she fought them. She knew her time with Roan was at an end. Love or no, she knew she couldn't stay. Question was, could she make herself go? Roan's hands roamed her body, finding all the spots he knew drove her crazy. Despite her turmoil, she lost herself in the sensations. When he tipped her back, lifting her so he could suckle her breasts, she wrapped her thighs around his hips. Her pussy was already wet and waiting for him. The water was growing colder by the minute, but she didn't want to take her hands from his body to adjust it. He must have felt the same way because he angled them away from the stream to sit on the bench.

Amy clung to the top of the shower door, her knuckles white from the intensity of her grip, as Roan parted her thighs to make room for his head. His tongue teased her lips before delving inside to circle her clit. He drew imaginary lines around the rigid bud with confident assurance. The picture he painted bloomed in Amy's mind with vibrant colors, as her hips pumped in rhythm with his mouth. When he sucked her clit into his mouth, she cried out as an orgasm approached. Her body hummed on the edge of release, and she held her breath, waiting for it to crash over her.

Roan denied her climax by withdrawing his mouth. He gripped her hips to lower her from her standing position on the bench. The glass squeaked as Amy's hands passed down the door until she could put them on his shoulders. She straddled his lap, her shins against the tile seat, her thighs parted on either side of Roan's. His cock pressed against her opening, and she lifted up slightly to align them properly. She caught her breath when he surged deep inside her, feeling larger than he ever had.

Amy dug her nails into his shoulders as she rode him. Roan let her set the pace, following with his hips. His hands cupped her buttocks, guiding her each time she pushed down on him, rotating her hips slightly so that her clit rubbed against his cock with each stroke.

Their gazes met and locked, but he didn't seem inclined to say anything. Amy let the silence grow. She had already said everything last night. It was up to Roan to break the silence. A ragged cry left Roan as his cock convulsed inside her. His orgasm triggered hers, and she shook with the force of release, even as an empty space inside her remained unfilled. Physically sated, but not satisfied, she laid her head on his shoulder to break away from his penetrating gaze. Tears burned her eyes, but she refused to let them fall.

He turned his head to kiss her cheek. "I'm sorry," he said in a rough whisper near her ear. "I'm so sorry that he hurt you, and that I helped him by sending you away. I wouldn't do anything like that to you deliberately. I hope you know that I care for you, Amy."

"I know." It wasn't all she wanted to hear, but for now, it was enough. Amy shied away from the voice in her mind clamoring for something else, something Roan was never going to offer. His love.

Roan seemed determined to act as though the incident with Steve hadn't occurred. That suited Amy, and she followed his cue, never mentioning the other man or what had transpired. He was distant, tacit, and she didn't know what more there was to say. In the end, it hadn't mattered how enthusiastically she responded to his kinky games, or how obedient she was to his sexual commands. They had enjoyed each other physically, but he couldn't give her what she needed. She tried not to resent him for it, because he hadn't promised her anything other than freedom from prosecution. Her stupid heart was the one that had filled in the blanks with fantasy endings of happy-ever-after. Knowing it wasn't Roan's fault she had fallen for him didn't make it any easier to accept that he would never love her.

Later that day, she found herself walking the shops of the main floor aimlessly, not quite sure what to do with herself. Not for the first time, she glanced over at the big bank of doors leading out to the Strip. If she loved herself at all, she'd walk right out those gilt-and-glass doors and never look back. It was the one way to retain some shred of herself.

She looked away and discovered that she'd wandered over to Divine Inspirations, the tattoo shop. As she started to cross the threshold, someone caught her arm. With a frown, Amy turned to see who had grabbed her. A gasp escaped her when she recognized Kevin. "You idiot, what are you doing here?" she asked as she threw herself against him for a long hug.

He didn't speak until she looked up at him. "I had to make sure you were okay."

"I'm fine," she said automatically, as she took in her cousin's haggard appearance. He was a few years her junior, but the new lines under his eyes and sallow skin added at least a decade, making him look like the older one. She touched the side of his mouth, noting the wrinkle there. "What about you? You look terrible." Amy had assumed she would be angry when she saw Kevin again, since he had lied to her and gotten her into this mess. Instead, she was concerned.

He looked around with wild eyes. "I'm okay now." Kevin grasped her elbow, trying to drag her toward the exit. "Let's get out of here, and I'll tell you what's going on."

Amy pulled away. "I can't leave." She bit her lip, wondering if she could actually walk out, or if Roan still had his goons watching her.

Kevin looked confused. "Why the hell not? I've been watching you for a few days, and I can't figure out why you're staying here."

"I have no choice." She straightened to her full height. "Roan Cavello caught me cheating."

Her cousin groaned. "I didn't mean—"

"I know." Amy winced at the impatience in her voice, lowering it an octave. "I've been working off the debt, so you'd better get out of here before he realizes who you are."

Kevin shook his head. "I can't let you take the heat alone." He looked horrified. "What's he making you do?"

Amy dodged the question by taking his arm, trying to force him to walk. "Get out of here." Movement over her shoulder caught her attention, and she recognized Tim Duffy. "They're coming. You have to go now."

"Wait." Kevin put up a hand. "I have to tell you something."

She sighed. "I know you lied to me about Aunt Mel and Uncle George being in trouble. Tell me why later."

"I—"

She wanted to stamp her foot with frustration as Tim and another goon she didn't recognize reached them. With one more nudge in Kevin's ribs, she turned to Tim. "Is Roan looking for me?"

He ignored her, reaching past Amy to grab Kevin's

shoulder. "Come with us. The owner of the casino wants to talk to you."

"Why?" Amy's voice emerged as a strident squeak, and she cleared her throat. "What does Roan want with this guy?"

Tim finally deigned to look at her, letting his gaze slide up and down her body in a way that made her skin crawl. "Probably not the same thing he wants from you."

Kevin didn't resist when the two men flanked him. She gnashed her teeth and fell in step behind them, unsurprised when they led Kevin to the same interrogation room where she had first faced Roan. She *was* surprised when they let her accompany them inside without a peep of protest.

Roan sat at the table, looking relaxed. He gave Tim and the other man a dismissive wave and indicated Kevin should sit down. Amy tried to look defiant as she took a seat beside her cousin, but it was wasted on Roan. He didn't even glance at her. It was like being at a trial as Roan surveyed her cousin expressionlessly, letting the silence stretch until she broke it. "You have to let him explain, Roan."

He finally looked at her, but his gaze gained no warmth. "I don't need him to."

She glared at him. "You're just going to punish him without letting him speak in his defense? That's so typical."

"Why should I believe he would tell me the truth when you didn't?" Roan continued speaking as she closed her mouth with an audible click. "I've already investigated the situation, Amy. I know exactly why you and your cousin cheated me."

"I wish someone would enlighten *me*." She sniffed at both of them before settling against the hard back of the uncomfortable plastic chair.

"Amy, I—"

Roan went on as though Kevin hadn't been speaking. "Your cousin got himself into trouble with another casino here in town." He tapped a page on the stack in front of him. "Odin St. Clair isn't a man you want to owe money to, is he, Kevin?"

"N-n-no, sir," said Kevin with a stutter.

He turned accusing eyes to Amy. "I guess that wasn't a good enough story, was it? Trying to sell the down-on-their-luck relatives was more heartrending." Roan shook his head. "The truth didn't even occur to you, did it?"

Amy swallowed her hurt, meeting his scornful gaze. "I never lied to you."

Kevin looked confused. "What's he talking about?"

She glared at her cousin. "Your lie."

Roan shuffled the papers, getting their attention again. "I do have some sympathy for your situation, young man." Kevin's eyes gleamed with a hint of hope. "St. Clair is a nasty piece of business. Still operates by the old rules. You're lucky he gave you time to cover your marker instead of just killing you."

Amy winced, compelled to reach out for her cousin's arm.

"I didn't mean to. It just sort of happened, you know? I was on a winning streak, and then it got bad…" Kevin stared at the table for a few seconds. "Before I knew it, I owed him three hundred grand." He looked up, first at Amy, then Roan. "I didn't know what else to do, so I went to Amy. She's the smart one, according to my parents." He looked at Amy again. "I'm sorry I dragged you into this mess."

"You could have told me the truth. I still would have helped you."

Her cousin looked skeptical. "Really? If I had come to you and asked you to help me cheat one casino to pay back credit to another, you would have done it?"

Amy couldn't hold his gaze. She looked at the wall, feeling guilt squirming in her stomach. Would she have helped him if she'd known he owed money for gambling? Wouldn't part of her have felt smug or condescending, like maybe he'd gotten what he deserved? Without knowing that St. Clair was the type to resort to murder, she probably would have sent her cousin on his way, accompanied by a sanctimonious lecture about the evils of gambling. She swallowed. "No, I guess not. I'm sorry."

Roan cleared his throat, his expression enigmatic. "Amy didn't know about St. Clair?"

Kevin shook his head, looking miserable. "I was too embarrassed…and I needed her help too much to tell her the real reason."

She met Roan's gaze with a flare of satisfaction in her eyes. "I've never lied to you," she said again.

He ignored her contribution, focusing his attention on Kevin. "I'm not calling the police."

Kevin slunk lower in his chair. "Amy said she's been working off the debt. I'll do whatever you have her doing."

Roan's eyebrow lifted slightly. "I have something else in mind for you. Call it my own gambling rehabilitation program."

He leaned forward, closer to Roan. "Whatever you want me to do, sir."

"You're going to work off your debt, and it's going to take you a long time." Roan waved a hand. "You aren't going to be in a position of trust. I'm talking the nastiest, most menial jobs in the casino. Do you have obligations elsewhere—a job, girlfriend, something like that? Is there someone who needs to know you will be working here?" When Kevin shook his head, Roan said, "Good. I'd like to have you where I can keep an eye on you. Do you have any objections to living in the casino?" What he left unspoken was the obvious—if Kevin objected to any facet of Roan's repayment proposal, he would be moving into jail instead.

Kevin swallowed audibly but looked determined. "That's fine. I'll do whatever I have to so this is made right. Amy shouldn't have to pay for my crimes."

Roan's mouth twitched. "She's not blameless." He leaned over, pushed a button on the panel embedded in the table, and the door opened within seconds, revealing the goons. "Kevin will be joining our staff. Show him where he's going to be bunking, and escort him to fetch anything he needs from his hotel room. After he's settled in, turn him over to Pierre in the kitchen."

Kevin looked nonplussed but followed Tim and the other man without protest, giving Amy a small wave as way of parting. She remained seated at the table, wondering what Roan would do next.

He got up from the chair and walked over to her, pausing only long enough to unplug the camera in the corner. Her heart raced with anticipation as he sat on the table in front of her, staring down at her with a look of contemplation.

"So, my little thief has a conscience."

She inclined her head slightly. "I wouldn't have helped Kevin without a good reason."

A cynical smile crossed his lips. "Good enough for you, anyway."

Amy lifted her shoulder in a half shrug. "As you say." She licked her lips. "Thank you."

He quirked an eyebrow. "For what?"

"For helping Kevin, for not sending him to jail."

"You're welcome." His lips twisted into a rueful grin. "I'm not a completely heartless bastard, you know."

"Really?"Amy couldn't help the hint of cynicism that crept into her tone. She had seen his gentler side a few times, and it was what had made her fall for him, but she hadn't seen much emotion of any kind from him in the past few days.

He looked wounded for a brief second before his expression hardened. Roan leaned forward, grasping a handful of her hair, tipping her head back. Amy didn't fight him. She tried to project a calm exterior, although every nerve in her body had awakened at his touch. She parted her lips when he leaned closer, their faces inches apart. "I may be ruthless, but you're still a little thief."

"And you're a man who basically bought a sex slave." Her cool reply surprised Amy. She was barely keeping her composure, but it didn't show in her words. "I guess we're both made of weaker moral fiber than we'd like to think we—"

His mouth slamming on hers silenced the rest of her retort, and she reveled in the barely controlled violence radiating from him. She had stirred his anger, and it perversely pleased her to see any sign of an emotional reaction. Amy met the fierce kiss equally, running her tongue over his lips and recoiling when he nipped her. A throaty laugh escaped her, and she tangled her hand in his hair to anchor him firmly against her.

He pulled away. "This will have to wait, sweetheart." Roan seemed unaffected by the passionate kiss.

She watched with hurt eyes as he turned away, leaving the room without even a word of parting. That was what was missing. He never expressed tender sentiments, but until the night he had saved her from Steve Delminico, he had usually held her during the aftermath of sex, curled up together as their heartbeats returned to normal. It was as close as he would come to letting her see any kind of emotion not related to sexual gratification. Since then, he had denied her even that. It seemed like he couldn't wait to get away from her once the sex was over—and now, he was rushing to escape even before the sex. She still hadn't reached him.

♣　♠　♥　♦　♣　♠　♥　♦　♣　♠　♥　♦

Chapter Nine

Three days after he had learned the truth, he still hadn't touched her. Frustration, both from lack of satisfaction and from his emotional distance, had her glaring balefully across the table at Roan. With a disgruntled sound, she laid the fork she'd been toying with on the plate of her untouched dinner. "Well?"

He looked up from the steak he'd been devouring with enthusiasm. "Well, what?"

She frowned. "Aren't we going to discuss it?"

Roan cocked an eyebrow. "Discuss what?"

His obtuseness had to be deliberate. She glared at him. "Us. Sex…and the fact we aren't having any."

He tilted his head, seeming to ponder the issue. "Are you feeling unfulfilled?"

It was her turn to quirk an eyebrow. "What do you think?"

He grinned. "I think you're an insatiable woman, just the kind I like." He gave her a wink and resumed eating, seeming to think the issue was closed.

Amy slowly counted to ten. She reminded herself she didn't care what kind of reaction she got, as long as she had proof that he felt something. She had hoped for some explanation for his distance or an epiphany that made him realize just how much he wanted her. "Why do you think I want you so frequently, Roan? Why am I so insatiable that I'm ready for you anytime, anywhere? It's because you've shown me something amazing, and I want to see even more."

Roan seemed to think for a moment, and then a bittersweet smile curved his mouth. "I get it."

She doubted it. "Get what?"

"You're ready to explore on your own. I've awakened you, and this is your way of telling me you want to be free of our arrangement." Her mouth dropped open with shock, and she shook her head, but he continued before she could speak. "I think you're right. We've gotten about all we're going to get out of this. Now that your cousin has taken his share of responsibility and is working off the debt, you've done your part." His smile changed to one that appeared pleased. "You're free to leave."

"Are you stupid?"

He frowned. "What? I didn't hear you."

Amy lunged to her feet, scooped up the crystal wineglass and tossed it against the wall. The shattering glass echoed like a shot through the stunned silence.

Roan tossed aside his napkin. "What the hell was that for?"

"Your idiocy." She stormed around the table, leaning over him to bring their faces level. "Yeah, you've freed some of my inhibitions and you've helped me discover a side to my sexuality I didn't expect, but that has nothing to do with why I stayed. And it wasn't because I didn't want to go to jail."

He jerked his head back. "Why then?"

"Dammit, Roan, I love you, despite everything you've

done, despite denying me the trust you demanded I freely give. How can you not see that? I've done everything I could to reach you. I didn't want it to come to this, with me groveling at your feet for a scrap of affection. You give great physical satisfaction but don't have an ounce of caring in you. I can't take it anymore." Tears streamed from her eyes, and she brushed them away with an impatient hand.

He touched her cheek. "You're hardly groveling, sweetheart."

His tender touch sparked hope, but his next words tore her heart asunder. "And you're not in love with me. It's natural to confuse lust with love, especially considering some of the games we've played. I might have encouraged too much dependence on me while cultivating your submissive side."

She recoiled from him. "I'm not a child. I know how I feel. I love you."

Roan heaved a deep sigh. "I'm sorry, but I don't feel that way." He reached out to touch her arm, but she avoided his hand. "You knew what this was about from the beginning."

"Restitution," she spat at him accusingly.

He shrugged. "I was going to say sex, but call it that if you want. It's accurate." Another sigh escaped him. "I never led you on, or made you think this was some fairy tale. I wanted you, and you wanted me. That's the end of it. You weren't supposed to fall in love."

"I couldn't help it." If she'd thought about it, she might have cringed with embarrassment to be so vulnerable with him, but she had let her emotions guide her. "I didn't mean to fall in love with you, but it happened."

"I'm sorry."

Amy shook her head. "No, I'm the one who's sorry—for you. You're so rigid, so worried about maintaining control over every aspect of your life, that you can't open your heart. You can't even show any real emotion. I'd rather feel the way I do, even with the pain, than be as closed as you. At least I know I can feel. When was the last time you really felt something for someone?"

Roan looked away. "Why don't you pack, and I'll arrange a ride for you? Take whatever you want."

"Except your heart," she said softly. "I don't want anything else."

He hesitated before shaking his head. "I can't give it to you."

A heavy weight settled on her chest, a combination of acceptance and defeat. "I know."

Roan got to his feet. "I'd better call to see who is free to take you home." He turned without another word, leaving the dining room without a backward glance.

"Goodbye," she said under her breath, knowing she wouldn't see him again. Roan could barely stand to be in the same room with her after her confession. There was no way he would put in another appearance before she left. He was too scared of her. She knew he felt something. He had been too tender and loving not to, but was too stubborn to accept it. Their affair was really over. She had gambled everything and lost it all.

Roan sat brooding in his office. A glance at the clock on his desk revealed Amy had no doubt left his suite by now. He could return there but didn't move from his chair.

He caught a glimpse of his reflection in the highly polished glass window but looked away, not wanting to meet his own eyes. He feared what he would find reflected in them. Amy's accusations were fresh in his mind, and he couldn't pretend they weren't true while looking himself in the face.

With a sigh, he leaned back in the chair, closing his eyes. Phantom impressions of her body remained on his hands, and her scent clung to him like static cling. His lips ached to taste hers.

"Dammit." He slammed his fist on the desk without opening his eyes, hoping to dispel some of the lovesick lunacy plaguing him. What kind of man was he to sit in his office and wish he could have the one thing he'd just rejected? It stung that Amy knew him so well, had pegged just what an emotional coward he had become.

He'd always taken his lovers as they came but never tried to keep them, or make them something they weren't. That philosophy had served him well. Until Julia. Until Amy.

His lust and emotions for Julia had blinded him to her faults. He'd fallen fast and hard. And she had not. It had hurt, both his pride and his heart, when she'd left, more so than he had ever admitted to anyone. He had dismissed his relationship with Julia as a fling when talking with Amy, but that had been a pale version of the truth.

She had hurt him but had also strengthened his resolve to forgo relationships in the future. After Julia, it had been easy to avoid emotional entanglements—until Amy had entered his life. Now, he was experiencing a familiar ache in his chest, but Roan resisted labeling it. He refused to allow his emotions to run unchecked and lead him where he didn't want to go.

Several calming breaths restored his composure, allowing him to open his eyes, get up from the chair and head for the penthouse. Yeah, it hurt to lose her, but at least it was on his terms. Better to deal with these unwelcome emotions now than someday in the future, when he might not be prepared. When he entered his apartment, the silence mocked him. The place felt empty without his lover. "Better off without her," he told himself as he met his gaze in the entryway mirror. His eyes belied the words, forcing him to look away. He still didn't believe it, but if he repeated the mantra often enough, he would see the truth of it. It was hollow comfort as he took a seat on the sofa alone, where she had sat just hours before.

♣ ♠ ♥ ♦ ♣ ♠ ♥ ♦ ♣ ♠ ♥ ♦

Chapter Ten

To Amy's disgust, Tim Duffy and one of the other goons were her escorts home. She maintained silence in the back of the black Cadillac, refusing to look at Duffy. His eyes remained on her throughout the short ride to her apartment; she could feel them.

It was a relief to see her apartment building. The unnamed goon driver hadn't even fully stopped the car when she opened the door to hop out of the backseat. Amy scooped up the small bag of cosmetics and personal items she had taken with her from the penthouse and slammed the door. She didn't speak to either of the men until she noticed Tim Duffy was opening his car door. "I don't need an escort. I know the way." Amy rushed into the building and up the stairs. Her battered door was a welcome sight. She dropped the bag on the table inside the threshold, cursing under her breath when it hit the edge and fell off. A mess of flyers and cosmetics scattered on the scratched hardwood floor, and she knelt down to gather them up.

A small shriek escaped her when Amy stood up to find Duffy standing in her doorway. Her stomach quivered, but her voice emerged forcefully, full of anger. "Get out of here."

"You left your sunglasses." He held them out, just out of range.

Amy jerked her head in the direction of the table near him. "Put them there and get out."

Tim stepped closer to her, still extending the sunglasses. "I want you to take them."

"And I want you to leave." She squared off with him, although her insides were quivering.

"Take them."

Amy didn't like the look in his eyes. "Fine." She extended her arm to snatch the glasses from his hand, but he withdrew them. She wasn't about to step closer. "You know what? Keep them."

Tim dropped them on the floor. "Oops," he said with an exaggeratedly apologetic expression. "I guess you'd better pick those up, princess."

"Get. Out." In her anger, she clipped the words.

He took a step back to close her door, giving them unwanted privacy. She was unable to maintain a brave front when confronted by his hungry gaze, only a few steps away. "What do you want?"

Duffy licked his thin lips. "Just a little bit of what you so freely gave Cavello…and Delminico."

Amy's eyes widened. "How do you know about that?"

"I was watching." His grin made her stomach churn. "Since you came along, I've been volunteering for a lot of video surveillance." He licked his lips again. "I particularly enjoyed watching you in the elevator."

She gasped, and heat blazed into her cheeks. He'd seen

them the night she'd gotten her tattoo. "I think you should go. Roan wouldn't like hearing about this."

He shrugged. "He won't care. The man passed you off to one of the high rollers."

Amy tried a different approach. "If you were watching, you'd know nothing happened. Roan stepped in before Steve could do anything."

"I didn't see that." He seemed to hesitate for a moment, and then shrugged. "So what if Cavello changed his mind? He's not going to change it now. He's not even here."

"He'll fire you." She managed to issue the words in a firm, confident manner, though her chest ached with doubt. "I only have to call him."

His hearty laugh overrode anything else she might have said. "He's finished with you. This is his routine—fuck and dump. Usually, the girls get some parting gift." A sly look contorted his features. "I guess yours was freedom from prosecution."

She stormed past him to open the apartment door. "Get out."

After a slight pause, he shrugged and turned around. At the doorway, he looked down at her. "Your loss."

Amy laughed. "I doubt it."

He kept going, and Amy made sure he was across the threshold before she slammed the door and engaged the dead bolt, knob lock and security chain. To be on the safe side, Amy looked through the peephole, watching her unwelcome visitor make his way toward the stairs.

When he disappeared from her view, Amy crossed the apartment to the window facing the street. She maintained her vigil there until she saw Duffy get back in the car and drive off. Only then did she relax and find herself capable of breathing normally again. *Shit*. She needed a beer. Or ten.

By morning, Roan had almost convinced himself he wasn't hurting over sending away Amy. With renewed determination, he tackled his day, clearing appointments and paperwork with gusto. But he couldn't summon an appetite for the excellent salmon the chef sent for his lunch and had to acknowledge his facade was crumbling.

He pushed away the plate and got to his feet, searching for a distraction. The bright afternoon sun drew his eye, and he decided a drive would clear his head. Roan pressed the intercom to summon his assistant. "Brad, have the garage ready my car. I'm going for a ride."

"What about your appointment with Greg Lynch?"

He sighed. "Reschedule. New machines can wait for another day."

"Yes, sir."

Roan slipped out of his office through the back entrance, bypassing reception and his disapproving assistant. He wanted to get to the garage as quickly as possible. The oblivion of the desert called to him.

As he entered the garage, the sound of voices reached him when he neared his parking space. Gordon and Tim leaned against the exit of the garage. They must have been on break because Gordon was smoking.

He spoke without removing the cigarette from his mouth. "Where's my ten bucks, man?"

"You'll get it." Tim appeared surly. "Quit hassling me."

"I'd better." Gordon snickered. "I told you she didn't want you."

Something in Tim's demeanor intrigued Roan, prompting him to remain quiet so they didn't detect his presence.

"Fuck you. I could have had her if I'd really wanted. You've seen the tapes. You know what a slut she was."

Gordon made an ambiguous sound. "I don't think it was like that. She and the boss had something special."

"Well, aren't you just Mr. Fucking Romantic?" Tim spat on the concrete. "There wasn't anything special about the thing. She cheated, and he made the slut pay him back."

"You're just pissed 'cause she turned you down."

The realization his employees were talking about his Amy, and that Duffy had hit on her, led him to act before thinking. He wasn't even certain of the steps that led to his pinning Tim to the hood of the nearest car. "What did you do?" He pressed his face into the other man's, his gaze daring Tim to lie or look away.

Tim licked his lips, looking around wildly. "Nothing, sir."

Roan shook him, slamming his back into the car again. "Answer me. What happened? What did you do to her?"

"Nothing happened."

"Did you hurt her?" Fear clawed at Roan's insides like a rat trying to dig its way out. He shook him again. "Tell me."

"I just tried to get some of what she's been giving away to everyone else." He sounded like a sulking child. "The bitch turned me down."

Roan released his hold on the security guard, taking a step back. Several deep breaths did little to restore his calm, though his heart rate had slowed a tad upon hearing Amy wasn't hurt. "You're fired."

With his lips bowed into a pout, Duffy looked like a two-hundred-pound spoiled child. "Why the fuck do you care? I've worked here twelve years, and you're going to fire me over this? You gave that bitch to Delminico, but I'm not good enough to have some?"

Roan balled his hands into fists. "Don't speak about her like that. She's a special person, and you had no right to treat her that way. You've betrayed my trust. You're lucky firing you is all I'm doing."

Duffy shook his head. "You're a hypocrite, man. Acting like you care about her or some shit…well, where the fuck is she if you care so much for her? Why isn't she with you, Cavello? You don't care about her, so why do you care if I fuck her? Hell, everyone in the casino could line up to pound that tight little cunt, and you wouldn't care. So what's this really about?"

He surrendered to the impulse, releasing the reins of his control. Roan's fist made a satisfying thud when it connected with the other man's nose. The warm spray of blood across his hand made him grin with savage pleasure. He liked seeing blood flowing from the other man's face, easily imagining beating him to a pulp.

His own reaction sickened him, restoring Roan's control. He turned to Gordon. "Get this piece of crap out of the casino." Without waiting for the other man's response, Roan went to the box of keys, entered his code and grabbed the first set of keys he saw. He was compelled to find Amy, to ensure that she was really okay. To…

Roan drew a blank, not certain what would happen after that. All he knew was his brain refuted Duffy's accusations that he didn't care for Amy. He'd known for days that he cared for her. Too much for his comfort. It had been imperative to send her away, but his reasons for doing so no longer seemed as clear and logical. For the life of him, he couldn't remember why he had been so afraid of accepting her love, of keeping her by his side. It irked him that Duffy's behavior had been the catalyst to show him just what a self-deluding fool he'd been.

♣ ♠ ♥ ♦ ♣ ♠ ♥ ♦ ♣ ♠ ♥ ♦

Chapter Eleven

Amy ignored the first knock. After yesterday's experience with Tim Duffy, she didn't want to open to anyone, just in case he was on the other side. A man like Duffy seemed likely to try to get revenge for her rejection. Cognizance of that had been one of her motivating factors to clear out of Vegas as quickly as possible.

She kept packing the box she was filling as the knocks escalated, becoming progressively louder, until the door vibrated under the force of each slam. Finally, with a sigh, she set aside the box and went to the door, fearing one of her neighbors would phone the police if she didn't answer.

She gasped when a look through the peephole revealed a disheveled Roan on the other side. Amy's hands shook, making it difficult to work the locks. She finally fumbled them open, letting the door swing inward. He didn't wait for an invitation. She gasped again when he shoved the door out of his way with a slam and pulled her into his arms, not giving her a chance to speak.

"I'm so sorry," he said against the top of her head. His embrace was almost painfully tight, but it felt too good to break away. "I had no idea Duffy would try anything. Are you okay?" Roan ran his hands over her body, seeming to be assessing her physical state.

She pulled away enough to look up at him. "I'm fine. He didn't touch me."

Roan hugged her again. "I'm such an idiot. If I hadn't sent you away…"

Amy's heart swelled with hope, although she cautioned herself not to get too excited. Once Roan was certain she was all right, he might withdraw all the heartfelt words falling from his lips. "I'm fine," she said again. "Really." She cupped his face in her hands to hold his gaze.

He seemed beyond hearing. "I messed up. You probably won't forgive me, and I don't blame you if you don't believe me, but I am sorry. I shouldn't have sent you away like that."

Her heart clutched, torn between hope and despair. "How should you have sent me away, then?"

Roan groaned. "I shouldn't have let you leave. You belong to me…with me…and I want you to come home. I don't care if you leave in a week or a month, or if it lasts a year. I'll take whatever amount of time I can get."

Amy's eyes misted at his unintentionally revealed vulnerability. It wasn't that he didn't love her. He just didn't want to lose her, so he'd sent her away. The logic was flawed, but she understood him, anyway. Leaning forward on her tiptoes, she brought her mouth close to his, lips almost touching. "What if I don't ever want to leave?"

His eyes widened. "You don't have to do this, Amy. We're both adults. Let's be realistic. Relationships never last—"

"Shush. We're going to be together, and we're going to

be disgustingly happy. If you can't live with that, then you'd better go so I can resume packing. I'm leaving this place today—either with you, or headed back to Washington."

He looked poleaxed, and his mouth opened and closed a couple of times before he managed to speak. "I…guess I can meet those terms. But I have a confession."

She lifted an eyebrow. "Yes?"

"I wanted to put distance between us so I wouldn't get attached. It didn't work." Roan held her against him for a long moment without speaking. "I thought I would lose you in the end, and I'm the one who drove you away. I'm a damned fool."

"Yeah," she said in a hoarse whisper.

The air was pregnant with tension before he finally spoke. "I'm crazy in love with you. I don't want to let you out of my sight. Is that okay with you?"

Amy couldn't suppress the single tear that rolled down her cheek. "I can live with that," she said in a choked voice. "Now, take me home."

★ ★ ★ ★ ★

THE DEAL
Anya Bast

This one's for Laura Bradford, the best agent in the world. Thanks for helping me make my dreams a reality.

And a big thank-you to Susan Swinwood for allowing me to tell this story that burned in my brain until I could get it out onto paper.

Chapter One

"Kiss it for luck?" The brown-haired businessman beside Cassidy at the roulette wheel held up a chip. He gave her a smarmy grin and a slow head-to-toe perusal.

Cassidy knew that look. She got it often. He was trying to figure out if she was blond…all the way down. This guy would never find out. She might be going through a sexual dry patch since her fiancé had stood her up at the altar, but she wasn't *that* desperate.

She glanced at Darcy, the croupier, but Darcy only grinned. No help there.

Oh, hell, fine. It was kind of her job, after all. Cassidy was a shill. She acted like one of The Liege Casino's patrons, gambling with house money and attracting customers to the tables. Only sometimes she attracted unwanted male attention, too.

She smiled and leaned in to give the chip a peck. The man lingeringly kissed where she had and gave the chip a lick before placing his bet on the layout.

Ye-e-ech. Cassidy fought to keep a polite smile on her

face and not dig in her purse for sanitary wipes. She'd never touch a chip the same way again.

The roulette wheel spun. The ball bounced. The man lost. So did Cassidy. It was a familiar song and dance. Cassidy knew all the steps. Little strategy existed with roulette. It was mostly just blind luck.

While Darcy collected chips and made payouts, Cassidy turned and walked away. "Aw, too bad," she called to the man over her shoulder. "Better luck next time."

"Hey, wait," the man called. "Buy you a drink?"

She shook her head and kept walking. No way on earth.

It was past time to cleanse her palette with a bit of eye candy.

Spotting James Carter at his blackjack table across the room, she made her way through the early-evening crowd, surrounded by the familiar dinging and whirring from the bank of slot machines surrounding the blackjack pit.

Near James's table a gaggle of young women loitered. They looked like they wanted to play, but were too intimidated to step up to the table. Cassidy saw it a lot, out-of-towners visiting Vegas for a gambling adventure but too chicken to really go for it once they were there.

Cassidy lingered in front of the table, giving James a secret smile.

"Wanna play?" he drawled with a touch of Texan accent and a lift of his dark gold eyebrows.

Oh, yeah, *that* was the candy.

The man had a voice that could drop a woman's panties in about two second flat—deep, a little husky, with a natural purr to it. The ultimate male bedroom voice. She felt goose bumps rise on her arms.

"I don't really know how," she answered, falling into the steps of their nearly daily routine.

James gave her a slow, confident smile, complete with dimples. It was a little, she imagined, like the devil's. "Oh, now, honey, I'll teach you," he drawled out in that warm honey voice. "Come play with me." He winked.

Gah.

Teach her, huh? She had a few things she'd love to teach him. Sweaty skin-on-skin type things. Between-the-sheets type things.

Every time she had such thoughts she felt guilty. James was her friend, after all. Not only that, he was one of her closest and dearest friends. Hell, he was probably her *best* friend. It was against some natural law of friendship that she should think so often about fucking him. Maybe it was true what they said—maybe men and women could never truly be friends. Maybe sex always got in the way of that.

Of course, if forced to choose between sex and friendship, she'd choose friendship. But, damn, if sex was ever offered she wasn't sure she'd be able to resist.

When her ex-fiancé, Damian, had stood her up at the altar about a year ago, James, who had been no less than Damian's best man, had stepped in and helped her through it. She'd quit her job at Gold Diggers Casino because Damian had worked there, and James had set her up at The Liege as a shill with the possibility of advancement to dealer. Because she was helping to support her mother financially, she'd really needed the gig.

Yeah, James was a good, good friend.

She glanced at the group of loitering college girls again.

They didn't seem like huge risk takers, but they looked like they had daddy's cash on them. Why were they just standing there? What self-respecting woman could resist a dealer like James? Tall, broad shouldered and possessing a nice muscular build that a woman could see hints of through his white button-down shirt.

Everything about James Carter was pretty nice. He possessed a unique masculine beauty with his dusky skin, longish, perpetually tousled, tawny-colored hair and cara-mel-colored eyes. She loved his wide cheekbones and full, sexual-fantasy-inducing mouth.

Damn, that mouth just slayed her.

What was wrong with them? Here was this gorgeous blackjack dealer willing to give them gambling lessons and they just stood there being stupid. She rolled her eyes. Too many all-night keggers and bottles of self-tanning lotion had clearly rotted their brains.

"You'll teach me?" she answered James, loud enough so the girls could hear her. "Oh, you're so sweet." She sat down at the table and pretended to concentrate as James explained the rules to her.

"So the king, queen and jack are all worth ten?" she asked.

"You got it."

"And the ace is worth one or eleven, whichever I want?"

"You catch on quick. Let's play a game."

"Okay!" Cassidy tilted her head to the side, gave him a ditzy smile and blinked a couple times.

He grinned. "Saw you get hit on over at roulette," he said in a soft voice.

Cassidy rolled her eyes. "All in a day's work."

"All in a day's work for a gorgeous blonde, that is."

"Whatever. That guy probably hits on women with warts and post-nasal drip."

James gave a low, silken laugh that made her shiver.

She made her bet and James dealt her cards. The game went slower than usual because Cassidy had to act like she didn't know what to do. In the end, she won and made a big, noisy deal out of it.

"Did you say that you're giving out instructions?" came a feminine voice to her right.

"I am," James replied. "If you care to sit down."

Cassidy turned and gave the young redhead a dazzling smile and patted the seat next to her. "Oh, please, come play with me. I've never done this before." She wondered if she should giggle, but then decided that would be over the top.

The college girl and two of her friends were brave enough to approach the table and play some blackjack. James explained the game to them with just a little bit of the flirt he always used on the ladies, the same bit of flirt he used on her every day.

Cassidy wished she knew what that flirt meant when it came to her. Was it just harmless, slightly sexual banter, or something more? Not that she was looking for a relationship or anything. She wouldn't mind a sexual friendship with James, though.

Many times over the past six months, after her heart had healed enough for her to notice other men, she'd thought about initiating something with him. But, despite the flirting, she didn't know how James felt about her and she was a bit afraid of making a move, of being rejected and ruining their friendship. His friendship meant a lot to her.

And, wow, had she had enough rejection to last her a lifetime. Being stood up at the altar in front of seventy-five of your closest friends and relatives tended to do that to a girl.

James called for wagers, then dealt each player two cards faceup out of the shoe and dealt himself two cards—one up, one down. The girls looked stiff and pensive, deciding how to play. When she left the table, Cassidy would send a few free drinks their way and loosen them—and their wallets—up a bit. It was mostly for James's benefit. She bet these ladies would tip well.

Cassidy lost, lost, and then hit a winning streak. She played her hands and laughed with the college girls, but her mind wasn't really on the game. She watched James's fingers slide the cards across the felt from the shoe. He had nice hands, nice forearms.

Cassidy wondered what those hands would feel like on her body. Sometimes, late at night with her vibrator, she wondered a whole lot more.

When some of the other coeds drifted over to the table, Cassidy collected her winnings and left to make room for them. Her work here was done and her spot could be occupied by a body who'd bet with his or her own cash. That was better for the casino and better for James.

Before she left, she tipped the dealer big to set a good example and gave James a slow wink. He grabbed her hand, taking her chips. His gaze held hers as his fingers grazed her palm, sending shivers up her spine.

She could feel herself get wet just from that much contact.

♣ ♠ ♥ ♦ ♣ ♠ ♥ ♦ ♣ ♠ ♥ ♦

Chapter Two

James sat waiting for Cassidy in a lounge chair outside the employees' door leading from the back to the casino floor. Finally, Cassidy walked out and headed toward the front, done with her shift.

She hadn't noticed him sitting there, and he watched her for a moment. Damn, she was hot. Her long, pale blond hair was caught up in a ponytail that hung halfway down her back today. The style revealed her high cheekbones, dark blue eyes and a full mouth he'd love to kiss. Of course, he'd fantasized about that luscious mouth doing a whole lot more than giving innocent kisses, too. The thought of it gave him a hard-on even as he sat there.

Tonight she wore a blue button-down shirt that set off her eyes. Her black skirt hit her just above her knees, revealing shapely legs he wanted around his waist in a bad, bad way.

He'd lusted after Cassidy from the moment he'd moved to Las Vegas three years ago, met Damian and laid eyes on his new friend's girlfriend. Maybe it had been wrong to desire his friend's girl, but James hadn't been able to help himself. She was attractive in so many ways, intelligent, strong, sexy as hell, with a good sense of humor. He loved spending time with her and was proud to name her a good friend.

He never would've guessed Cassidy was vulnerable, but when Damian had chickened out of marrying her last year, James had seen a side of Cassidy he hadn't known was there. She'd been hurt badly. She'd really loved Damian. Damian had not deserved her regard. He'd never appreciated her enough in James's estimation.

James didn't know how Cassidy felt about him. For him the flirting had all been foreplay, but for her?

He thought it was about time he found out.

He'd given her the time and space to heal from her breakup. They'd flirted their way through the entire year. He'd been patient with her up until now, but that patience had come to an end. Today had been a work day like any other, but things were going to change this evening. One way or another.

James wanted Cassidy in his bed with a need that drove all other considerations away. It was way past time he got her there.

Cassidy stopped on the multicolored rug and dug into the depths of her shoulder bag for something. Behind her some old lady pulled the bar on a slot machine like a rat in a cage trying for a sugar pellet. James was a dealer, but not much of a gambler, never had been. Maybe that's why making the play he intended to make for Cassidy tonight scared him a little. Her friendship was the stake and he didn't want to lose.

But he just couldn't go on like this.

From a distance, James caught sight of the man who'd hit on Cassidy at the roulette table. The man glimpsed her, started walking over, a confident swagger in his step.

No way. Cassidy was his tonight…not that Roulette Man had a chance in hell, anyway.

James stood and walked to her, staring the other man down as he staked his claim on the pretty blond woman rooting through her bag. The other man got the hint and veered off in another direction. That was smart of him.

"Come out for a drink with me," James said once he reached her.

She pulled some tube from her bag and looked up at him. "I don't know. It's late. Gotta work tomorrow." She uncapped the lip balm and he watched while she spread some on her lips. His mouth went dry at the sight.

"What do you mean? What are you planning to do tonight, anyway? Eat a TV dinner and watch a little *CSI?* Come on, I'll buy you a Jack on the rocks." No froufrou drinks for Cassidy. He knew that well enough.

She grinned and fell into step beside him. "Well, you do make a hell of a lot more money than I do, bastard. How'd those college girls work out, anyway?"

There was a slight emotional twist in her voice when she said *college girls.* James knew she had a little complex about the fact she'd never been able to attend college after high school. Cassidy had been forced to work right after graduation in order to financially take care of her nearly blind diabetic mother. Cassidy never complained about the sacrifices she'd made, but James knew she wished she'd been able to continue her education. It was a pity she hadn't since she had such a sharp mind, one better put to use by doing something more than shilling for The Liege.

He shrugged. "They lost a ton of cash, but they were laughing about it. They tipped well."

"Good. I thought they might, since you're such a good-looking guy and all."

"You think I'm good-looking, huh? Cool. Think I'll get laid tonight?"

Cassidy snorted and rolled her eyes. "You wish, stud," she said, easing into the cadence of their normal, friendly banter.

Oh, yeah. He wished all right.

She glanced at him, giving him an easy smile. "I never see you with women, you know. Makes a girl wonder. Do you have something you want to tell me, James? A closet you want to come out of?"

He didn't even think before he acted. He grabbed her wrist and stopped her dead in her tracks. A couple steps backward had her up against the side of a slot machine. He bracketed her in with arms on each side of her and stared down at her. He gave her long, luscious body a leisurely perusal and groaned. "If you want proof I like women, baby, I'd be more than happy to provide it."

She stared up into his face for a long moment with very feminine interest in her eyes. In that space of time they momentarily slipped beyond the line of flirty friendship into unknown territory.

And, damn, that look in her eyes made his cock hungry.

She leaned forward, onto her tiptoes, put one hand to his waist and her mouth to his ear. "You better buy me that drink first, cowboy," she breathed.

Oh, fuck.

He slipped his hand around her waist and their gazes

found each other's slowly. He could feel her breath on his face. Her eyes were heavy-lidded and she had the look of a woman who wanted to be kissed. He leaned in.

Somewhere near them, the pit boss, Gerald, bellowed. Cassidy jumped, startled, and backed away from him.

"You take that elsewhere," Gerald said. "Not on our property, you hear?"

James nodded. "Got it, sir. We were just leaving."

Gerald nodded at them and stalked off, muttering to himself and shaking his head.

Yeah. That had definitely broken the mood.

He took her to the Yellow Parrot, down the Strip from The Liege. It was one of their regular hangouts. After the shift, when they wanted to have a drink before heading home, they split their time between the Yellow Parrot and one of the many lounges in The Liege.

They sat at the end of the bar, the patrons a mess of bodies and noise around them. They had their own private corner in the friendly chaos. It was almost intimate. Even better, he was close to her. Close enough to smell her shampoo, the light, musky perfume that he'd become addicted to. Close enough to feel the heat of her body and aid his fantasies.

What had just happened in the casino hung between them, unspoken but tangible. It made the air between them different tonight, a bit heavier, rife with a possibility that hadn't existed before. If it hadn't been for Gerald's interrupting them, James thought she would've kissed him.

It had been rash of him to make a move like that on her,

but it had been completely involuntary. It was the result of one too many nights lying in bed and imagining himself with his cock sunk deep inside her slick sex. Too many nights fantasizing about how her lush lips would feel on him and, in turn, how she'd taste.

Cassidy was a friend, yes. And, damn, he wanted to fuck his friend. He wanted it so badly he was ready to potentially ruin their relationship over it. He didn't want that, but he was a man obsessed.

He ordered drinks and mulled his next move. After seeing the look in her eyes back at the casino, the look that had said she'd wanted him to rip off her clothes right then and there, he felt a little more confident. Maybe the attraction was mutual after all.

She swirled the whiskey in her glass, making the ice cubes gently clink. "Talk to Damian lately?"

Crash.

He let out a puff of air. Damian. Hell, he really didn't want to talk about him right now. "Yeah, but I don't hang with him very often these days."

"Really?" She glanced up at him and a smile flickered over her mouth. "Why? Is he pissed because you took my side after the thing?"

The thing. That's what she always called that day she'd stood in the White Wishes Chapel on Hamilton Street and Damian had just never bothered to show. It had been an awkward day. Even the Justice of the Peace slash Elvis impersonator they'd hired to do the ceremony had gotten emotional for Cassidy.

She'd been standing there in her gorgeous wedding dress,

her bouquet hanging limply at her side, looking miserable and alone while she explained that Damian had called and said he didn't want to marry her after all. Her mom had wept openly, which hadn't helped Cassidy deal with the situation. Damian had proclaimed his rejection of her in front of all her family and friends. The asshole.

He shrugged. "I guess." Truth was, he thought Damian was an idiot for not marrying her. His opinion of him had dropped a lot that day. So much that he just didn't enjoy his company anymore.

She downed the last of her whiskey and pushed the empty glass away. "I've forgiven him."

James's hand tightened a little on his bottle of beer. "Yeah?"

A sheepish smile flashed across her mouth. "Well, mostly."

"What do you mean?"

Cassidy shrugged and turned on the bar stool to face him. "He wasn't sure he wanted to commit to me for the rest of his life. Maybe he was right to not show that day. I mean, what if he had married me? We might be at each other's throats these days. Maybe I'd be fucking miserable."

James held her gaze. "I think that's a wise view to take."

Pain flashed through her eyes for a moment before she glanced away. "Maybe."

The harsh reality was that Cassidy had loved Damian, but Damian hadn't loved her back. Not enough, anyway, to commit to all time for her. Damian had done the right thing, but James still thought he was an idiot. Cassidy deserved a man who really loved her, every aspect of her.

"Want another drink?" he asked.

"No, thanks."

He took a long drink of his beer.

"The worst thing," she said, "is that I'm sex-starved. I need to get laid in the worst way."

James choked. She patted him on the back and he swallowed hard and coughed. "Sex-starved?" he echoed in a raspy, choked voice.

"I haven't had sex since it happened. It's been a whole year."

"A year?" he echoed.

She ran a finger around the edge of her empty glass. "Yep, it's just been me and my vibrator."

Images of Cassidy getting herself off with her vibrator filled his mind, made his cock stiff. "Wouldn't mind seeing that sometime," he murmured.

She grinned. "Pervert."

He turned toward her. "I don't get it, Cass. You have men slobbering over you every day in the casino. Just pick one."

She laughed. "It's so easy for you guys. You just pick any woman and you're guaranteed a good time. Men always come. Doesn't matter if their partner is female, their own hand or a freaking goat. For a woman it's different. What if I end up picking some goober who doesn't know his ass from his dick in the sack? Then I wasted a whole night on bad sex and I feel like a cheap whore in the process." She sighed. "I need to trust a guy to relax in bed. So one-night stands with strangers are kind of out for me."

"Point taken. You need a man you're familiar with to help you out with this problem." James grinned. She'd given the perfect opening gambit. "So pick a guy you know, someone you can trust, one who isn't bad in bed."

She looked at him. "And that would be…?"

He paused, then grinned and said, "Me, Cassidy. That would be me."

Her face went slack with shock for a second and then she laughed. "God, you are such a flirt."

He reached out, grabbed her bar stool and yanked her close to him. She let out a little squeal of surprise. "I'm not flirting," he said in a deep, serious voice. "I wasn't flirting just now at the casino, either." He gave her a slow smile. "Understand? I want you. I want you to come home with me tonight. I want you to spend the night with me, in my bed. I've wanted you for a long, long time, Cassidy. You wouldn't believe the things I want to do to you."

Shit. His heart pounded, even though outwardly he exuded an air of total confidence. Guess he'd shown his hand.

The smile faded from her lips. "But we're friends."

"We could be more than friends."

She glanced away. He glimpsed shadows in her eyes before she turned her head. Bad. Shadows were very, very bad. She licked her lips nervously.

"We could be friends with benefits," he amended, back-pedaling. Judging by her body language, he needed to take this slow. He was losing her fast. James had always suspected another relationship might scare her, even something as casual as the one he was proposing. Guess he'd been right.

All he knew was that he wanted *her,* in whatever capacity she would allow. James would always want more of her, whatever amount she was willing to give. For the time being, friendship with benefits sounded damn good to him.

"Cassidy?" he murmured, sliding his hand to her waist. She felt so warm, so perfect. "Listen to me."

She looked back at him and her breath hitched in her throat. Her eyes were dark, heavily lidded, and her lips were parted a little. She looked interested…and turned on.

Good. That was very, very good.

"I've been attracted to you since you were with Damian," he continued. "I've wanted you in a bad way for a long time, Cassidy girl. I don't want to be just friends with you. I want you in my bed." He paused. "I want to have a very skin-on-skin kind of relationship with you."

Cassidy looked stunned. His heart pounding, fearing he was about to crash and burn and lose a friend in the process, he let his face drift closer to hers. She didn't move away.

"I've been attracted to you, too, James. I always thought it was against the rules, you know?" she murmured practically against his lips. "Since we're friends."

"Let's make new rules."

Their breath mingled, lips brushed, and then he kissed her.

Her lips felt wooden beneath his for a moment, and then she melted and kissed him back. Every nerve in his body shot to life with hunger.

She twisted, leaning into him so he could feel her breasts against his chest, and eased her hands slowly up his arms and over his shoulders.

James let his hands find her waist, then slanted his mouth over hers and flicked his tongue against her lips. Damn it. He wanted to pull her over onto his lap. He wanted to undress her, set her up on this bar and fuck her senseless.

She opened for him and he slipped his tongue inside. He could taste whiskey in the hot, soft interior of her mouth, but that wasn't what made him feel drunk.

They broke the kiss, both breathing heavily. "Cassidy, come home with me," he murmured against her lips.

"But…" She bit her lower lip for a moment. "How do I know you're any good in bed?" she asked with a little teasing grin playing around her lips.

He groaned and eased a hand between her knees. "What, you want a demonstration?" he murmured. He didn't wait for her answer; he just eased his hand up her inner thigh, beneath the hem of her skirt, grateful for the dim light of the bar.

His fingers found the edge of her thigh-high stockings. Oh, hell. His brain was going to melt. Thigh-high stockings. This was the outer limits of heaven itself.

His cock was rock-hard then. James raised an eyebrow in question as he rubbed his index finger over the bare skin at the top of her stocking.

"They're more comfortable than the other kind," she answered breathlessly in explanation, a blush faintly tingeing her cheeks.

"Lucky for me you think so," he purred into her ear. He hooked her hair behind her ear with his free hand and whispered, "Spread your legs for me, baby. I need to touch you."

She shifted on the stool, giving him room to move. His hands traveled up farther and soon felt the heat of her pussy against his fingers. Yes, he'd reached the gates of heaven. She'd spread her thighs as much as her skirt would allow. It was enough. He eased his fingers over her sweet, plump little clit through the cotton of her panties.

Cassidy inhaled sharply as he stroked her, teasing her clit into a swollen, needy thing. He brushed his lips against hers, then kissed her again, sliding his tongue between her lips while he pulled her panties to the side and stroked her bare pussy.

Around them people talked and laughed, and ignored them. That was good because he had every intention of making Cassidy orgasm right there and then.

Cassidy gasped into his mouth as he worked a finger inside her. She felt like pulsing, hot, wet velvet. James stroked her clit with his thumb as he thrust gently, minutely, in and out of her sweet little pussy, rocking her back and forth on her stool with the short pumps. God, he wanted her on his bed, stripped bare. He wanted her thighs spread wide for his tongue.

He twined his other hand around the nape of her neck and whispered into her ear. "You're tight, tight and hot. I want my cock in here, Cassidy. Do you want that, too?"

She nodded, panting.

"Does this feel good? You like my fingers inside you like this? All these people around us? Do you think they know I'm going to make you come right here at the bar?"

She shuddered against him and kissed him deeply instead of answering his question. Her tongue tangled with his as he stroked his fingers deep into her.

He broke the kiss, nipped her bottom lip and murmured, "I can't wait to get you home. I want to feel your orgasm when my cock is inside you."

She sank her white teeth into her lower lip. He increased the pressure on her clit, circling and pressing on it with his thumb until he felt the first stirrings of climax tightening through her.

She gasped against his lips. "I'm coming," she whispered. "Oh, God, don't stop."

Sweeter words had never been spoken. He pressed his mouth over hers as the orgasm hit her full force. He felt the sweet rush of her juices over his hand and the pulse and tremor of her innermost muscles around his thrusting fingers. James caught all her little moans and pants in his mouth. They tasted damn good and gave him an appetite for more.

When her climax had eased, he took his hand from her skirt and let her sag a little against him. She covered his cock, hard and straining against the zipper of his pants, with her palm and stroked him through the material.

"Come home with me," he whispered roughly in her ear. "I want to fuck you till you can't think anymore."

♣ ♠ ♥ ♦ ♣ ♠ ♥ ♦ ♣ ♠ ♥ ♦

Chapter Three

It was strange that she was about to sleep with James. Sure, she'd lusted after him for a long time, but he was also a *friend*. That gave this whole encounter a depth that was both pleasant and a little uncomfortable.

At the moment, falling through his doorway and into his darkened apartment, that notion only skittered around at the very edges of her awareness. Her senses were filled with him, with the promise of mind-blowing sex, and with her own pounding, starving libido.

In the half-light of his apartment, James guided her to stand by the couch and yanked the hem of her skirt up to her waist so it was more a belt than anything else. Breathing heavily, they both knocked hands in an effort to get her panties down and off. Then Cassidy went for the button and zipper of his jeans. Just the sound of it being undone made her pussy cream. God, she wanted him inside her *now*.

She pushed her hand down inside the front of his jeans and gripped his hard cock. He tipped his head back and groaned as she stroked him. He was long, wide and gorgeous.

He fisted his fingers through the hair at her nape and used

his grip for leverage as he kissed her hard and long, his tongue stabbing into her mouth and his teeth nipping occasionally at her lower lip. He pushed his hand under her shirt and cupped her breasts, petting her hard nipples through her bra until her pussy felt hot, aching and unbelievably needy. She needed him inside her soon.

Cassidy gripped the edge of his shirt and forced it up, kissing her way over his washboard abs and muscled chest as she went. Oh, God, he was more gorgeous than she'd ever imagined. James was male-model beautiful, and the best part was he didn't even know it—attractive, with no irritating ego about it.

He gripped his shirt, pulled it over his head and tossed it to the floor. Then he dragged her up against his chest and devoured her mouth. His hand found her aching pussy and stroked upward, deep into her. She broke the kiss and whimpered into his mouth.

"Down on the couch," James ordered softly. "Sit down and spread your legs."

She sank down onto the couch slowly and spread her thighs. In the half-light, James stared down at her, shirtless and with the top button and zipper of his jeans undone. Moonlight caught across his chest, revealed the jut of his hip and the top of his boxers where his pants rode low. "Well, now," he drawled. "That's a pretty sight. You look good enough to eat."

She'd just been thinking the same about him.

He went to his knees, placed his hand under her ass and yanked her forward so her butt practically hung off the edge of the couch. His hands clamped down on her inner thighs, holding her spread and open.

"What are you doing?" she asked, a little alarmed.

"I don't want you to get away from me," he murmured, staring down at her pussy. "Not now that I finally have you." A rumble of interest rolled out of him a moment before his hot mouth closed over her.

Cassidy's back arched and she gasped at the sensation of his tongue exploring her. It flicked over her clit and slid through her labia, leaving a trail of fire wherever it explored. Sensations flowed over her, drawing a deep groan from her throat.

He eased his tongue deep inside her and she tried to move instinctively away from the incredible intimacy of his mouth on her. His hands braced her down, not allowing her to move, and he made a low hum of disapproval.

"Not until I feel you come against my tongue, Cassidy girl." He groaned. "Damn, you taste good. So hot and sweet. I could eat you up for hours."

He stared at her through the dim light and freed one of her thighs. He eased his finger through her labia, watching her face as he rubbed over it, then slid up inside her and pumped.

She bit her lower lip, her breath coming heavy and fast. Her gaze rested on his intent expression as he thrust his fingers into her slowly. "Feels like heaven in here," he murmured, rocking her body a little back and forth on the couch with every inward stroke. "Unbutton your shirt."

With trembling fingers, she reached up and undid the buttons of her shirt one by one, revealing her black lace demi bra.

"Touch them," he whispered.

She passed her fingers over her nipples through the fabric, and then pulled each of her breasts free from the cups. Shuddering with pleasure, she teased her long, pink nipples until they were hard as diamonds.

James leaned forward and licked over one of them, then sucked it into his mouth. Cassidy cried out. Still thrusting his wickedly skillful fingers into her, he rasped his teeth gently over the tip. She felt her pussy spasm and he rumbled with approval. God, she was going to climax hard.

He left her breast and trailed his tongue back down to her clit, where he licked, nibbled and sucked. Intense pleasure filled her, overwhelming her until an orgasm exploded and stole her breath and her ability to think.

She gasped and ground her pussy against his face as the orgasm washed over her for the second time that night. He kept licking and finger-fucking her through the whole thing, making noises like she was the best thing he'd ever tasted.

While she still quivered from the end of her climax, he slid her from the couch so she lay facedown on the floor. She lay there feeling boneless and relaxed, her body still humming.

He pulled her skirt up around her waist, exposing her bare bottom, and yanked his pants down just low enough to get his cock out. Then knelt between her spread legs, grasped her hips and drew her up a little, so her rear fit against the curve of his hips.

Cassidy gasped as she felt the broad, slick head of his hard cock bump against the entrance of her pussy. *Oh, God*…those were the only two words filling her mind as the wide crown breached her entrance and slid inside. Cassidy braced her palms on the carpet and lifted her ass into him, spreading her thighs to allow him to penetrate her, one mind-blowing inch at a time.

"Damn, you're tight," he groaned. "You taste like honey and wine, and feel like velvet and fire. You're just about perfect in every way, Cassidy."

"James!" she gasped.

He stopped instantly. "Are you all right?"

She gave a crazed-sounding little laugh. "Yes! Don't stop. Please, don't stop. Just fuck me."

"You want more of me?" With one smooth inward stroke made easy by her wetness, he hilted.

Cassidy's breath rushed out of her and she made fists on the floor. James stayed that way, motionless, allowing her muscles to adjust to his length and width. He filled every tiny little part of her. She felt completely possessed, spread wide and vulnerable.

Just when she thought there couldn't be any more pleasure, he pulled out…and thrust back in.

"Oh, James," she panted. "It's so good." She tried to rise up on all fours, but he came down over her back, pinning her to the carpet with his big body and thrust deeply into her, tearing a cry of pleasure from her lips.

Her slick interior muscles gripped his cock as he fucked her hard and fast, barely giving her time to breathe. Rational thought was long gone. Her whole world was about James's body on hers, his cock tunneling in and out of her sex, his hips slapping against her bottom on every pump.

His hips rocked back and forth, the head of his shaft rubbing her G-spot on every inward thrust. Their groans, pants and the sweet, sweet music of their bodies coupling filled the air.

Pleasure built, spiraling up and up until she felt the brilliant edge of a climax and rode it. "Don't stop," she whispered. Then yelled, "Oh, don't stop!"

He didn't. He kept up the hard and fast thrusts until the pleasure enveloped her in an intensity that bordered on pain. She cried out, scrabbled at the carpet in front of her as the muscles of her pussy pulsed and convulsed around his still pistoning cock. He held her down and rode her through it, intensifying the ecstasy.

As her muscles still trembled with the end of her climax, he thrust deep into her and groaned her name low. "I'm coming," he pushed out in a rough voice. She felt his cock jump within her.

He collapsed on top of her and rolled to the side. She lay there, facedown on the carpet, her skirt around her hips, her breasts freed and bared to the floor, her pussy humming with pleasure.

"Oh. My. God," she whispered.

"Yeah," he breathed. With one hand gripping the base of the condom, James kissed her shoulder. "You and me? We've got chemistry."

He could say that again.

James got up, went into the bathroom and came back to find her still lying on the floor, caught in web of sexual satisfaction. He laughed, a silky, rough sound that rippled over her flesh. Then he got down onto the floor with her and dragged her into his lap. He'd pulled his pants back up and buttoned them.

She glanced down and saw her shoes were still on. "We didn't even get undressed."

"Come to bed and I'll undress you. Stay the night and

I'll make eggs and bacon for you in the morning." He angled her face to his and kissed her deeply, his tongue spearing past her lips.

She broke the kiss and covered her face with both her hands. "James…" She struggled to sit up and push away from him. "What the hell did we just do?"

He smiled in that disarming way he had. "Had fucking incredible sex, Cassidy." He reached for her, but she pulled away, shaking her head.

They'd both just slept with their best friend—that's what they'd done. She stared at him, his familiar smile, the face she'd seen every day for the past year. This was the man to whom she'd confided nearly all her secrets. The man who'd helped her through one of the most challenging years of her life.

Cassidy sighed, feeling sorrow well up within her. It was all different now, changed forever. "This is too weird, James. This was a mistake. A colossal, friendship-breaking mistake."

His smile faded. "Cassidy, it's all right. I'm still your friend. This doesn't change that essential fact."

"No." She stood. "You're something else to me now. Our relationship is not the same. God, I can't believe we did this. I can't believe I let you seduce me. I—I can't believe how weak I was. I've got to go." She struggled to her feet and went for her panties, pulling them on hastily.

James remained quiet for a moment, then stood and walked to her. He put a hand to her shoulder, but she shrugged him away. "Why do you think that rushing out of here right now is going to erase what happened between us? It will still be there when you leave. It'll still be there in the morning. You can't make it go away by running off on me. What's done is done and I don't regret it."

"I…" She glanced at him and sighed. "I know, but we did this in the spur of the moment, in the heat of passion. Maybe we can forget about it and things can go back to normal."

"Cassidy…" He cupped her chin and forced her to look at him. "We just had mind-blowing sex, you and I. It's done with, no going back. Our relationship *has* changed, but that doesn't mean it has changed for the worse."

She only stared up at him, not able to find the words to reply.

"Cassidy, I don't want to forget what just happened. Are you telling me you do?"

"James, I don't know…no." She smiled. "It was *really* good."

"Thank you. Do you regret it?"

She chewed her lower lip and reflected on her answer. She regretted changing their relationship, not the sex. "No. So now what?"

He grinned. "Come to bed with me. Let me take these damned offensive clothes off you. Stay over. I'll make you breakfast in the morning."

Something went cold inside her. This was too much, too fast. She shook her head. "I've got to get home. My mom—"

"Is fine on her own." He cupped her chin and forced her gaze to his. "Cassidy, spend the night with me."

She held his hooded gaze. It was tempting, so very tempting. She wanted to feel his skin on hers. For a moment, she even wanted to wake up beside him. She closed her eyes.

God, no…she wasn't doing this again. Not again. Not for a long, long time. Maybe not ever.

She shook her head. "I've got to get home. My mom might need me."

He sighed. "Cassidy…"

"Another night," she replied firmly. She bit her lower lip until it hurt. God, she was weak. "Maybe."

James stared down at her for a long moment.

"But, James?"

"Yes?"

She pushed a hand through her loose hair, long pulled free of its ponytail holder. "This…what just happened…it changes our relationship drastically. I want to stay friends with you. I value you. But I don't want anything more than friendship with you. Understand? I want this to be clear as possible. No misunderstandings."

"You want friendship with sexual benefits, like we discussed in the bar."

She nodded. "Yes. It would be a good deal for you. You'd still be able to see other women. I just want to keep this…informal. And I want to stay your friend."

She didn't know if they could do it. This might be the end of their friendship completely. Fuck, it probably was. Tears stung her eyes for a second. It was too late to go back now. The damage had been done. Anyway, she wanted a physical relationship with him. Hell, she just wanted *more* of him, period, but that more had to come without emotional commitment.

James looked out his living room window for a moment, at the busy street near the Vegas Strip. "That's what I want, too, Cassidy. Friendship with benefits." He turned to her and smiled. "The ground rules are clear."

"Okay." If they were both clear on the fact neither of them wanted anything more than sex from this, well, maybe it would be all right…maybe. Only time would tell.

"Want something to drink?" he asked.

"Water would be good."

"You got it."

She watched him walk into the kitchen, and then followed him. Cassidy leaned against the wall separating the kitchen from the living room and watched him pull a pitcher from the fridge and pour two glasses of water.

He gave one to Cassidy and took a drink from the other.

She closed her eyes, enjoying the cool water slipping down her overheated throat. Her body felt inflamed. She still tingled everywhere and her pussy felt well loved, satisfied. "That's good," she groaned. She meant more than just the drink. It had been too long since she'd had sex.

James set his glass down on the counter and walked to her. He backed her up against a counter and took the glass from her hands, setting it down.

"Um, James?"

He tipped her chin up so her eyes met his and traced her jawline with his thumb. "It was great between us, wasn't it?"

His voice was an intimate purr in the dark kitchen. It gave her goose bumps, made her pussy respond instantly. The man had the most erotic voice she'd ever heard.

"It was incredible," she said softly. "You made me come three times."

"You trust me, Cassidy, right?"

She nodded.

He raised an eyebrow. "Wanna play a game?"

"What?"

"I want to make a deal with you. Five nights. Five black-jack games. Five sexual acts decided by the winner. No holds barred."

"What do you mean?"

He rubbed his thumb under her earlobe and put his other hand to her waist. "I mean, we gamble for sex. The winner of each game gets to choose what we do, or something done to him or her. Anything, within reason, goes. What do you say?"

"Five nights," she answered.

"Five kinky sex acts." He shot her that devil's grin, dimples and all. "Hell, honey, I'm just trying to get into your pants as much as I can."

She smiled. It could be fun. "Okay."

He leaned forward, grabbed her lower lip between his teeth and dragged across it slowly. She was panting by the time he'd freed it. "Tomorrow we play our first game at The Liege," he murmured against her mouth.

Excitement made her voice come out breathy. "All right."

"We'll play—" he paused and gave her his best wicked grin "—and then we'll *play*."

Chapter Four

James watched Cassidy approach his table while he dealt for one of their regular patrons, an old grizzled man named Harvey. Harvey glanced at her as she slid into a chair. As a professional gambler, he probably knew she was a shill. They weren't hard to spot for the real players.

He liked Harvey, liked to see him win because he tipped him a dollar for every winning deal. He'd lay a buck on the top of his bet and let James ride his coattails. Every time Harvey won, he got a buck. Not bad.

Cassidy was wearing a pink top that dipped in the front, showed off the swell of her breasts. He knew those breasts intimately now, knew the way her pretty nipples looked and how they tasted, too. The memory alone made his cock twitch.

A delicate gold chain roped her neck and a small diamond sat in the hollow of her throat. Like yesterday, she wore a skirt and heels. Was she wearing thigh-highs again? Panties? *Fuck.* The thought she might not be wearing panties made his mouth go dry.

The night before, after they'd made the deal, they'd discussed the ground rules. They'd each set boundaries they'd agreed wouldn't be crossed.

"Hello, there, gorgeous," James greeted her. "Here to play me head-to-head?"

A flush crept up her neck to her face. She had such fair skin. It wasn't hard to make her blush. She gave him a grin. "Something like that."

"Goddamn it!" Harvey yelled, throwing his cards to the table. While he'd been talking to Cassidy, James had beaten him.

"Sorry, hoss," James answered genuinely.

"Eh. I need a drink." Harvey toked him with a couple chips and left the table.

"Hoss?" questioned Cassidy with a smile playing around her lips.

He grinned. "You can take the man out of Texas. Can't take Texas out of the man."

"You came up here for a woman, didn't you?"

He grinned. "I did, but she wasn't for me. City was, though." He paused. "Then I found another woman."

Her face shuttered and she looked away. Fuck, fuck, fuck. He had to take this slow. Cassidy was like a skittish mustang. Push her too far, scare her, and she'd bolt. Damian would never understand how he'd destroyed Cassidy, made her fear relationships—even casual ones like he and she now had. In that moment, if Damian had been anywhere in his vicinity, James would've punched him.

James cared about Cassidy deeply. If he could be the one to ease her back onto the relationship horse, to help her get over Damian so that she could go off and meet her Prince Charming, he'd be satisfied with that. James didn't mind being the transitional man for her. There were many fringe benefits that came with that gig.

James leaned forward and made his voice a low purr. "So you want to make your bet, baby, or are you too frightened of me and what I might decide I want to do to your sweet body?"

Her gaze snapped to his. "What if I win? Then I'm calling the shots. Then maybe it's me doing something to your body."

He let a smile spread over his mouth. "Honey, I win either way. Can't think of a thing you'd want to do that I wouldn't want, too."

Her gaze smoldered. "That's only a reason to think something up."

James chuckled. "You gonna place your bet anytime in the next century?"

Holding his gaze, she slid her chips forward. "Here you go, my bet…along with the other thing."

"Mmm, can't wait for the *other thing.*" He dealt.

The game went fast. Cassidy was a sharp player when she didn't have to play dumb for the crowd. Initially she drew an eleven and doubled down. She won with a total of twenty.

James made her payout with a smile on his lips. "So, what was the other thing?"

"You'll find out later."

When she reached out to take her chips, he asked, "What are you wearing under your skirt today, Cassidy?"

She looked up at him. "Almost nothing."

Oh, hell. "Are you trying to kill me, woman?"

Cassidy only smiled at him.

A group of tourists wandered over to the table and Cassidy

took her chips, then herself, from the table. As she walked away she gave him a look that promised his debt would be something he enjoyed.

She glanced at the table. "There. That table in this room."

"Here? This is the employee locker room, Cassidy."

She smiled. "I'm aware of that."

Across from the table was a big mirror. Employee lockers stood on either side. It was late on a week night and this was only one of many employee areas, but it was still public. Cassidy knew what James was thinking. Anyone would be able to walk in on them. They could lose their jobs.

"You like it a little risky, don't you, baby?" He glanced at the mirror. "You like to watch, too. You want to watch me fuck you?"

She shook her head. "Not quite, cowboy. I want to watch you go down on me. I want to see your head between my thighs. I want you to make me come and then I want you to go home with the taste of me still on your tongue."

He tipped his head to the side. "Whoa. You're cruel."

"It was my bet." She shrugged. "My win."

He leaned in toward her, slid a hand over her breast and teased her nipple. It responded instantly to his caress. "I'll be jacking off tonight thinking about you."

She felt a gush between her legs thinking about James getting himself off. Wow, she'd like to see that sometime, the slide of his strong hand and the flex of his forearm as he stroked his big cock. She swallowed hard and almost asked him to fuck her.

"One of these days I really want your clothes off...*all* the way off," James said. "This halfway stuff is killing me. I want to feel your skin on mine."

She backed up against the wall, letting a coy smile play around her mouth. "One day you *will* get my clothes all the way off. But for now…" She reached down and pulled her skirt up, showing him the lacey thigh-highs and the matching pink thong she wore. "I dressed for easy access tonight."

"Oh, Cassidy," he groaned.

She turned toward the wall and showed him her ass, bare but for the thong. The night before she'd worn regular cotton panties and ordinary nude thigh-highs because she always dressed that way for work. Tonight she'd dressed for James.

He placed his hand to her ass, rubbed her cheek and then gave her a hard slap. Cassidy let out a squeak of surprise. It had hurt just a little, but the tingle had turned to pleasure fast, warming her pussy.

James eased a hand to her stomach, slipped it down to her mound. He rubbed her clit slowly, in a circular motion that drove her crazy. He brought his hand back and spanked her again. She let out another surprised cry that ended up a moan. The vibrations rocked through her core and the first painful rush of pain quickly turned to pleasure. Her sex felt hot and wet.

He groaned and kissed her head as he delved between her cheeks. His fingers sought and stroked up inside her. He thrust and pushed her forward into the wall. She placed her hands flat against it, biting her lower lip.

"Mmm…I think little Miss Cassidy here has more than a couple kinks." There was a trembling note of awe in his voice. "How…lovely. Now, before I drop my pants and fuck you up against this wall," he continued in a strained voice, "I suggest you shimmy this fine ass up onto that table so I can make good on our bet."

He released her and backed away.

She turned, her skirt in disarray. Her cheeks were flushed—both sets—and she was panting. He glanced meaningfully at the table and she climbed onto it, pulled her skirt up and spread her legs.

James let his gaze slide up her body to her face. He kept his eyes on her as he approached her wearing a hungry expression on his face that made her cream. "You look good enough to eat."

Holding her gaze, he reached up and eased her thong down and off. Then he slipped it into his shirt pocket, so it peeked out a little from the top. "I keep this, Cassidy girl."

They were so far from mere friendship now that it both excited her and made her a little sad. Where were they headed, she and James? Right now she had no idea how their relationship would end up. Then he knelt, put his mouth on her and she stopped wondering, stopped thinking, stopped doing anything but *feeling*.

James was good at going down on a woman and the mere thought of his full, luscious lips working over her delicate flesh nearly undid her. She watched his head between her thighs, glanced at the mirror and saw the reflection of it—her spread legs, his mouth on her as he licked and nibbled her clit, his muscled arms and shoulders flexing as he held her waist.

Pleasure skittered up her spine, warmed through her body. He made a low sound in his throat and glanced at her. "I can feel you're close already. So fast. Do you like when I do this to you, Cassidy?"

She nodded. "Very much." There was a breathless edge to her voice. She sounded that way often lately.

"I like it, too." He licked her clit, teasing it with the tip of his tongue, then laving over it. Her body jerked a little as the leading edge of a climax stirred through her.

He stood up, pressed down on her thighs and spread her legs apart as far as they would go.

A flash of excitement went through her, edged with a little alarm at the position he'd put her in, completely spread and held down. Her breath came out in a rush.

"I think you like to be restrained. It's arousing to you, isn't it, baby? I think you like it when I hold you down and do whatever I want. Am I right?" He held her thighs in strong hands and dropped his head to lick her slit.

She arched her back and moaned. "Yes, you're right."

"Something for another bet," he purred predatorily.

At this point he could do anything to her he desired. She was putty in his hands and against his wickedly skillful tongue.

He stroked her clit with the pad of his finger, and then replaced it with his mouth. Holding her down, he sucked the bit of excited flesh between his lips and massaged it.

"James," she whispered as her orgasm skittered through her. Then she cried out, "James!" not caring that anyone out in the corridor could hear.

Her climax crashed through her body in mind-numbing waves. When it eased, James pulled her up into his arms, threaded his fingers through her hair and kissed her hard.

His tongue slid between her lips and she tasted herself faintly on his tongue.

"Damn it. I want you, Cassidy. Come home with me," he murmured. "I'll get these fucking clothes off you, put you in my bed and treat you right."

She hesitated, her mouth opening and closing. Finally, she shook her head. "I need to get home." She pulled away from him and eased down off the table.

He made an agonized sound, reaching out and yanking her back into his arms. "This is torture. No fair."

She laughed. "It's within the guidelines we set for the game, James."

"It's still cruel." He cupped her face in his hands, angled her head to his forcefully and kissed her breathless again. James set his forehead to hers. "Fuck, Cassidy, please. Come home with me."

She bit her bottom lip. "Maybe you'll win tomorrow. You can call the shots, then."

"Damn, woman, you're a tease. If I win tomorrow you'll pay for sending me home alone all hot and bothered like this."

The next day she lost.

He made her pay.

Chapter Five

"I can't do this!" Cassidy pulled at his arm in front of the Kitty Kat Klub and laughed. "James, I'm serious."

He turned to her and pulled her into his arms. "You lost the bet, baby. I get to choose what happens after that. That was the deal, remember?"

She'd been so pretty losing, too. Cassidy had come to his apartment after shift and they'd had dinner. Then they'd enjoyed a couple nice glasses of brandy and cigars. She'd coughed at first, but had settled into the new experience of the rich brandy and the fine cigar with pleasure.

He'd had both stuck in the back of his cabinet and she'd come across them looking for glasses. She'd insisted they try both after their meal, when they played their game of blackjack. She'd looked so damn sexy that James had been hard-pressed not to order her to strip and wrap her luscious lips around something other than the cigar that very minute. He had different plans for this evening.

Cassidy enjoyed discovering new things and she was about to discover something really new tonight.

She tipped her head back and laughed again, a blush

coloring her pretty cheeks. Yes, little Miss Cassidy had a few kinks. He wondered how far they went.

"Fine," she murmured. "I'm a woman of my word. Let's go into…" she squinted up at the neon sign "…the Kitty Kat Klub. Oh, God."

They entered the dimly lit club. It was one of the more high-class strip clubs, a place where the high rollers came for entertainment of the female variety. The club was packed this evening and the music could barely be heard over the conversation of the patrons. The bartenders were doing a bang-up business behind the bar, slinging bottles of beer and hard liquor. A slim brunette pranced and shimmied on the stage, drawing the eye of every red-blooded male in the place. Other strippers milled the room in scanty clothing, cajoling men to buy lap dances.

He guided Cassidy to the bar and bought them both drinks. "Stay here," he instructed her with a quick kiss to her temple.

He found a brunette stripper, one of the only ones in the room who appealed to him since she looked like she still had her natural breasts, and negotiated a lap dance for Cassidy. He pointed to Cassidy across the bar and the stripper, Melody, arched a perfect eyebrow. "Definitely," she purred in acceptance. "That one's pretty."

Oh, yes, Cassidy was pretty. Pretty and so much more. If he started with flattering descriptors for her, he'd never stop.

Melody jerked her head toward a staircase beside the stage. "Bring her up upstairs and we're in business."

James gave her the thirty dollars for the lap dance, then walked back and guided Cassidy up the stairs to a series of small rooms on the second floor.

"What's going on?" Cassidy asked with a nervous laugh as they mounted the stairs.

He rubbed her shoulder. "You'll see soon."

"In here, honey," Melody called.

Cassidy's eyes widened as they entered the room and saw the nearly nude stripper. Music from below filtered up into the small, dimly lit space. He had to hold Cassidy's arm to make sure she didn't bolt from the room. "A lap dance?" she asked in a shaky voice. "From a woman?"

He pulled her against him, kissed her temple and whispered in her ear. "If you're really uncomfortable with this, Cassidy, we can leave."

She leaned up and kissed him. "Hey, a bet's a bet. I don't welch." Then she pulled away from him and sat down in the high-backed, armless burgundy velvet chair in the center of the room.

Well, okay then.

The woman swayed in front of Cassidy, dressed in a red bra, matching red thong and high heels. James thought Cassidy was sexier dressed in her frayed jeans and blue knit top, but it was highly arousing to see Cassidy staring up at Melody with a look of open sexual interest on her face.

Intriguing. Just how adventurous was Cassidy?

"Normally, touching isn't allowed, but I'll let you touch me, honey," the woman purred.

James's mouth went dry.

Cassidy blushed a little and didn't answer. The woman began to move, her swaying to the music becoming more pronounced. She turned and bent over, slipping a thumb underneath the thong and giving Cassidy little flashes of her bare pussy.

Then Melody turned around and straddled the chair, and Cassidy, and began to move erotically and provocatively, her hips rotating and her small breasts swaying in her bra in time to the pulsing rhythm filtering up from the floor show below.

James's eyes were all for Cassidy. The stripper—although physically attractive—couldn't hold a candle to her. Cassidy sat still, though her posture gradually softened, her lips parted a little and a blush colored her cheeks. Cassidy shifted in her seat, but James couldn't tell if it was because she was uncomfortable or if it was for some other, far sexier, reason.

He had a very male moment of imagining Cassidy with a woman and clenched his fists, pushing the thought away. That would get him into trouble. His cock couldn't get any harder than it was already.

Melody finished the lap dance by slipping her bra off and leaning forward to not quite kiss Cassidy. Their lips may have brushed, but he wasn't sure. James groaned at the sight. This was going to kill him.

The stripper stood and winked at James. "You can bring her back anytime," she purred in her low contralto and sauntered away.

Cassidy stood on visibly shaky legs. James caught her up and kissed her right there and then. His body ached for hers. She twined her arms around his neck and kissed him back with a ferociousness that revealed how the lap dance had affected her. Her body felt hot against his.

He broke the kiss and put his mouth to her ear. "Let's get out of here."

She nodded. They hooked hands and he led her from the club. He intended to lead her straight back to his place and take every bit of her clothing off her.

He had her shirt over her head before he even had his apartment door open. The feel of her skin, so soft on his, was better than anything he could imagine. It was something he thought he could get used to fast.

She toed off her sandals in the entryway while James slammed his door shut. He gripped the waist of her jeans and yanked her flush against him.

"Did you like it?" he asked.

She glanced away and bit her lower lip. "A little." She sighed. "Okay. I liked it a little more than a little."

He chuckled. "I wondered."

She leaned up and touched her lips to his. Her bra-clad breasts rubbed his chest as they exchanged a deep open-mouthed kiss. His fingers deftly worked the button and zipper and got both her jeans and her panties off her in record time.

She pushed his shirt over his chest and ran her tongue down his chest in the darkened hallway. Hell, they hadn't even made it to a bed yet and, at this rate, they wouldn't. He got his shoes off and she knelt to unbutton and unzip his jeans. She pushed them down and off.

Cassidy remained kneeling in front of him. Flashing a mischievous grin up at him, she gripped the base of his cock and licked him.

The sensation of her sweet tongue along the length of his cock ripped a ragged groan of ecstasy from his throat. His fingers found her hair and threaded through the long, silky lengths as she swallowed the head. His cock was suddenly engulfed in hot, soft, wet heat.

In the dim light of the entranceway, he watched the glide of her full, red lips over his length. He had to brace a hand against the wall to keep from falling over. James didn't know how long he'd fantasized about exactly this situation. Maybe just a little less long than he'd fantasized about spreading her legs and going down on her.

Gripping his hips, she slid him in and out of her sweet mouth until he had to fight not to come. When he went, he wanted to do it inside her body, feeling the ripple and pulse of her answering climax.

He pulled away from her before he spilled in her mouth. She looked confused until he helped her to her feet, pressed her against the wall and kissed her deeply, sucking her skillful tongue deep into his mouth.

"Bed?" she murmured after he'd broken the kiss.

He didn't answer; he only glided a hand down her waist and thigh, hooked her leg over his hip and slid his cock inside her. Her breath left her in a rush that became a moan. He answered with his own, feeling the silken clasp her pussy close around him.

"Way too late for a bed," he finally answered, staring deep into her eyes.

He held her gaze as he withdrew and thrust back inside her body. She rested her head against the wall behind her and bit her lip.

The first time they'd fucked, he'd been behind her and hadn't been able to see her face, look into her eyes, gauge what she was thinking and feeling by her facial expression. This position was far more intimate. James liked it, enjoyed being able to stare into Cassidy's eyes as he thrust in and out of her sweet pussy.

Cassidy tilted her face to his and kissed him as he took her there up against the wall. He could feel the tremors in her sex as her body responded to him. Her breathing hitched when he caught her bottom lip and dragged it slowly through his teeth.

He rotated his hips a little, making sure he hit her clit, giving her the friction she would need to climax, and was rewarded by an intensification of the tremors, signaling she was about to orgasm.

Cassidy whispered, "I'm coming." She closed her eyes, tipped back her head, but he forced her gaze to his.

"I want to watch you," he murmured back.

Her eyes widened as the climax hit her full force. She held his gaze clearly for a moment longer before her eyes unfocused and she moaned long and low.

He felt the muscles of her sex ripple and squeeze around his cock. The sensation of it, coupled with the sweet sounds she made and the sweeter look on her face, made James lose it.

"I'm coming, too, Cassidy," he murmured brokenly a second before it rose up and engulfed him in total pleasure. James kissed her deeply, letting his tongue stab into her mouth, until the waves of it eased and passed. Then he set his forehead against hers. "That was amazing."

Her hands smoothed over his shoulders. "Mmm-hmm," she agreed in a husky voice.

He cupped her face and stared into her eyes. A satisfied

smile played over her lips. There was something intimate and special about staring into her eyes while still buried deep inside her.

He cared very much about Cassidy. There was no doubt about that. For him, it went past sex. Hell, it went past friendship. Maybe he was just now starting to realize that. He smiled at the welcome realization. Maybe they had what they needed to go beyond mere friendship with benefits. Maybe they had what it took to have a real relationship. Weren't the best relationships rooted in friendship?

But how did Cassidy feel?

He tenderly brushed the hair away from her face and smoothed his thumb down her perfect cheek while he stared into her eyes. The moment felt heavy between them, charged with some deep possibility of *more*. "Cassidy..."

The smile faded from her lips. "I have to go."

"What? Cassidy, stay here with me. Stay the night."

She shook her head and pushed past him, started to gather her clothes. He watched her dress, oddly saddened that he wouldn't be able to curl up with her under the covers of his bed, wake up beside her in the morning and look at her over a cup of fresh coffee.

She turned to him after she pulled her shirt over her head. "Hey," she whispered. She leaned up to kiss him. "This is casual, remember? We bet, we have sex, I go home. Come on, it's every man's dream."

Casual, right. He remembered the arrangement. The thing was, he was beginning to suspect he might want more than just casual from Cassidy. Maybe every man's dream wasn't his dream.

"I'll see you tomorrow." She flashed him a smile, breezed past him and left the apartment. The door closed behind her with a final-sounding click.

James stood for a moment in his darkened entranceway, feeling the emptiness of his residence far more acutely than he had in some time.

♣ ♠ ♥ ♦ ♣ ♠ ♥ ♦ ♣ ♠ ♥ ♦

Chapter Six

Cassidy watched the last card slide across the green felt of James's table. It flipped over—an ace. It went perfectly with her ten, five, three and two, making twenty-one.

"Aw, man," James exclaimed.

She beamed at him. "My win."

He made her payout and lifted an eyebrow. "Your win, all right. Though it's my win, too, Miss Cassidy. It always is. So what's the bet?"

Two middle-aged women sat down at the table, curtailing further discussion.

"Like I'd tell you, anyway," she answered. "Thanks, James," she said, rising from her seat. She flashed a smile at the female tourists and winked. "He gives good game, this one. Hope you win big." They tittered at her in response.

She walked away from his table with a smile of satisfaction on her face and letting her hips sway just a little because she knew he was watching. James gave a whole lot more than good game. James was great in bed, magnificent everywhere else.

The rest of her shift was difficult to get through, knowing

what she had in store for James that night. Somehow she made it through her shift without spontaneously combusting.

"So," James said as he closed his front door. "You haven't said anything all day. What was your bet?"

She said nothing. She only flipped the light on in the living room and set her bag of goodies down on an end table.

"And what," he continued with a raised eyebrow, "is in that bag?"

Cassidy sauntered across the room, went up on her tiptoes and kissed him. He dragged her against his chest with a groan and deepened the kiss.

"Well," she answered in a husky voice, "I'll give you a hint. We'll finally make it to your bedroom."

He took her hand and pulled her toward the hallway. "Then what are we waiting for?"

She laughed and grabbed her bag off the end table as they passed by.

James's bedroom was sparsely decorated. A king-size bed with a blue-and-green-hued comforter dominated the room, flanked on either side by matching dark wood night tables. The hardwood floor was covered with multicolored throw rugs. A chair and a dresser completed the furniture in the room. James was a bachelor and it showed in his decorating choices. No unnecessary clutter, no frivolous pieces of furniture for aesthetics.

He looked as impatient as she felt, so she quit her teasing, set her bag on the bed and rummaged through it. James came up behind her and put his strong arms around her as she pulled out her long, thick green vibrator and a small tube of lubricant.

"Mmm, what's that for?" James's voice rumbled through her back.

She set the objects on the mattress and turned in his arms. "You're going to watch me masturbate," she murmured. Her mouth curved into a grin.

"Oh, God, you're evil."

She smiled. "You said you wanted to watch. Remember? Back at the Yellow Parrot?"

"Mmm…hell, yes, baby. I want to watch." He kissed her savagely until she could barely draw a breath. If he kept that up, she'd never carry out her plan. She'd just drop her pants right now and let him fuck her.

She pushed at his chest and he broke the kiss.

"You just better let me *touch,* at some point," he growled.

"We'll see." Reaching behind her, she snagged the bag and breezed past him, breathing heavily. Her body was already humming from the feel of his. It was like she had an addiction to him. Like her skin craved the touch of his and went into withdrawal without it. "I'll be back in a second," she told him, casting a playful look over her shoulder before disappearing into the bathroom.

A few minutes later, she walked out completely nude, wearing only a thin silver belly chain that hooked into her belly button ring. She stopped coyly in the doorway and looked at James. He lounged on the bed, with an expression of appreciation on his face. He'd lubed the vibe and set it on the night table. Such a helpful man.

Cassidy walked toward him slowly across the room, letting

him drink his fill of her nude body. This was the first time he'd ever seen her this way. The night before in the hallway, it had been dark. It was always dark when they had sex, always rushed because of passion. This was the first time he'd probably ever seen the small silver belly button ring she always wore.

He reached for her when she came close, but she clucked her tongue. "No touching. Tonight you watch and nothing more."

"At least let me give you a massage before you drive me crazy."

Massage? Hmmm. Well, in that case… "Okay, I can't turn those down."

"Lie down on the bed, beautiful."

She lay facedown on the bed and James whistled low, his hand smoothing over her ass and delving between her cheeks. She wriggled on the bed, sighing. Her pussy creamed at the mere brush of his fingertips. "You could give a dead man a hard-on, Cassidy, and I am not a dead man so imagine what you do to me."

She laughed. "You know how to flatter a girl." She heard him root around in a drawer and then heard the pop of the top of a bottle. He scooted onto the bed near her, and she heard the squirt of liquid into his palm. He rubbed his hands together to warm it up.

"Do you have any idea how much I want you, baby?" he whispered as he put his oiled-up hands to her shoulders and began to massage. "You make me completely crazy."

Cassidy let out a soul-deep groan of satisfaction as he began to knead her muscles, working out the tension. "Probably as much as I want you. Probably as crazy as you make me."

"Then why do you torment me this way? Let me make love to you, Cassidy. I promise I'll make this gorgeous body very happy."

Make love. That was the first time he'd used those words. They sounded strange to her ears. Uncomfortable.

She cared a great deal about James. He was her best friend, in fact. But she just wasn't sure she could go anywhere deeper with him, any further than where they were now. After being so emotionally injured by Damian, she wasn't sure she could have a relationship with anyone ever again.

She turned over on her back and heard James's breath catch in his throat. "You want to fuck me?" she asked, deliberately using the word *fuck*. It gave her a certain amount of distance, made her feel safer.

He oiled his hands again and set them to her breasts. He cupped and rubbed, teasing her nipples until she squirmed on the mattress, feeling her pussy react by creaming warmly.

"Always," he answered.

He trailed his fingers down her abdomen, catching on the chain, pulling gently at her belly button ring. He brushed through the hair of her mound and delved between her thighs, drawing a sigh from her. He rubbed her clit with his warm, oiled finger until Cassidy moved restlessly on the bed, growing more and more aroused. If he kept touching her this way, she'd disregard her plan altogether and beg for his cock. He was a dangerous man with dangerous hands.

She closed her eyes and breathed, "James."

"Yes?" He sounded hopeful.

She opened her eyes. "Let me sit up."

With regret on his face, he removed his hand and allowed her to move so that she had access to the things on the night table and she was propped up by the pillows.

The candlelight spilled over the comforter, and made James's skin look like velvet and burnished gold. She eased back against the pillows, feeling the weight of his gaze on her. Cassidy could almost feel his arousal like a palpable force in the room.

She picked up her vibe from the table beside the bed. Slowly, her gaze on James, she parted her legs and slipped the head of the vibrator between her labia.

James groaned. "I don't know if I can take this, Cassidy."

"You wanted to see," she answered in a breathless voice. Already, she was growing powerfully aroused. The thought of James watching her while she did this was very exciting.

She parted her legs a little to give herself more room to move. With one hand, she played with her breasts, teasing her long pink nipples into hard little peaks. Her body was oiled from his massage and glistening in the candlelight. She knew how she looked to him, knew how badly she teased him...and loved it.

Her pussy was hot and wet from James's hands on her body and the vibe slid deep within her. He watched avidly as she thrust it in and out of her body, his own body obviously tense as though he tried to hold himself back from taking control of the toy himself.

She became caught up in the rhythm and closed her eyes, feeling the pleasure of the vibe sliding in and out of her pussy, pulsing through her body. The fact that James was watching, that his cock was hard and straining against his jeans, only made the situation more intoxicating.

Her eyes flickered open. "Undress," she murmured.

James didn't need to be told twice. As she pushed herself closer and closer to climax, he shed his clothing and came to lie beside her.

She felt his hand on her stomach. He moved down and she didn't stop him, she was too close now. When she worked the toy in and out of her pussy, he stroked her clit over and over, sending skitters of ecstasy through her body.

James leaned down and murmured into her, "Come, baby. I want to see you come."

She arched her back and moaned loudly. The waves of the orgasm slammed through her body and James bent to take one of her upthrust nipples into his mouth, laving over it and gently nipping at it, while the muscles of her sex contracted and worked around the toy.

When the waves passed, she withdrew the vibrator and lay panting, sated. James's cock was hard and he wore a look of hunger on his face.

In that moment, she wanted him inside her with an undeniable need. Even though she'd just climaxed, she wanted to know the taste of his groans and sighs on her tongue, wanted to feel his body as he came deep inside her.

She rose to her knees and yanked him toward her. She forced him to lie down and then mounted him without a word. Cassidy angled her hips to feel the jut of the head of his cock against the opening of her pussy, and then slid down.

They both groaned. He filled her so well. In this position she could take him incredibly deep.

He put his hands to her waist, but she grabbed his wrists and pressed them down on either side of his body.

"Hey," he objected with a smile playing around his lips.

"Yeah…*hey.*" She leaned down and kissed him, delving her tongue into his hot mouth. "I'm in charge," she whispered against his lips.

"Maybe one day I'll have to tie you up, take control away from you."

A shiver of excitement at the thought of being at James's sexual mercy ran up her spine. She raised an eyebrow. "If you ever win a bet again."

He flipped her faster than a blink of an eye. She let out a squeal of surprise as she landed on her back and then laughed. "Yeah, you're right," he said, settling between her thighs. "Maybe I'll just take it now."

Cassidy opened her mouth to answer him, but then he began to thrust and all her words left her, all her thought, too. He dug his fingers into her hips, driving his cock fast and hard into her wet, suctioning flesh. Every stroke reverberated through her body, sending ripples through her and driving her closer and closer to climax. She pushed back at him, forcing him farther into her body with every stroke. As he took her so hard and fast, he held her gaze. It was oddly penetrating and emotional.

When she came, she did it staring up into his eyes, her body convulsing with pleasure under his. He came only but a moment later, groaning her name.

They lay tangled together, still joined at the pelvis. Perspiration sheened their skin and their breathing sounded harsh in the suddenly quiet room.

After several moments, James rolled to his side and pulled her up against him. She went stiff at the feel of his body cupping hers like a lover's…which, of course, was what they were, after all. Lovers. Of course. Did lovers *fuck* or did they *make love?*

Maybe they did both.

"Relax," James breathed behind her. "You just tensed up."

She took a deep breath and did just that, letting go of her worries of the future and her evolving relationship with James. She let the deep sexual satisfaction she felt leak through her body like warm honey, and she closed her eyes.

"I want you to be here when I wake up, Cassidy. Let me make you breakfast in the morning." He paused. "Please."

Cassidy opened her eyes, her relaxation fading with those softly spoken words. She cared so very deeply for James. It was a feeling that came close to love. They were fond of the same books, the same music, could talk for hours about many things. They enjoyed each other's company. All the reasons why they were such good friends.

But she wasn't ready for this to become anything more than what it was now. Cassidy felt the possibility of *more* acutely while she lay there in James's arms, wrapped in his warm, strong embrace like a lover…like a girlfriend. She hadn't felt this way since she'd been with Damian.

More. A relationship with emotion, with risk.

Their relationship had already slipped from friends to friends with benefits. How easily could it slip from friends with benefits to a real, full-blown romantic relationship?

They walked a thin line and it seemed to get thinner with every encounter they had. With every card she laid on the table, the stakes grew higher.

Once she heard the deep, easy rhythm of James's slumber, Cassidy slipped from his grasp, dressed and went home.

♣ ♠ ♥ ♦ ♣ ♠ ♥ ♦ ♣ ♠ ♥ ♦

Chapter Seven

James knew as soon as he woke that she was gone. He couldn't feel her in the room any longer and the scent of her perfume had faded. He opened his eyes and stared out the window into the morning sunlight before turning over and verifying that his bed was empty.

"Damn it, Cass," he murmured.

He sat up, tangling the sheets around his legs, and pushed a hand through his hair. James knew he was developing deeper feelings for Cassidy, but catching her after the number that Damian had done on her would be like trying to tame a wild stallion.

Of course, that didn't mean he wasn't up to the challenge.

The phone rang near him and he reached over to pick it up. It was his sister, Anne.

"Hey, James. Thought I'd call you this morning instead of the other way around."

He stretched, groaning. "Damn, is it Sunday already? Where'd the week go?" He knew. It had gone quickly while he'd been buried between Cassidy's sweet thighs.

"Big brother, I knew you were going to forget to call me," Anne shot back, playacting at being mad.

"I would have figured out it was Sunday eventually." He could hear his accent had thickened. It tended to do that whenever he talked with someone from home. "It's been a great week, sis, so good most everything else has slipped my notice."

"Really? What's going on up there in Sin City that's so distracting?"

"A pretty woman and whole lot of sinning."

"Another one? James, you run through them like Great-Uncle Bob goes through bottles of whiskey." She laughed.

"This one's different." The words were out of his mouth before he knew it. He was so used to telling his little sister everything that he hadn't thought twice about it.

Inwardly he groaned as Anne took his careless comment up and ran with it. Anne and his mother had been wanting him to "find a nice a woman to marry and have kids with" for a long time now. "Different? James, do you have yourself a steady girlfriend? Are you finally settling down a bit?"

"Didn't say that." Shouldn't have said *anything*. Dumb, dumb him.

"What's she like? What's her name?"

"Her name's Cassidy and she's not my girlfriend." Not yet, anyway. "She's gorgeous, caring and intelligent and you all would love her even though she's not a Texan. I think Mom would especially like her." He leaned his head back against the headboard and laughed. "And Cassidy's got a powerful will on her. Only the women in my family could appreciate it."

"Any woman willing to put up with you has to be a champ."

"Well now, that's the truth." Before Anne could start asking too many more questions, he changed the subject. "Speaking of Mom, how's she doing?"

Sufficiently diverted, Anne talked about their mother's various volunteering activities and how she was driving their father batty with her new hobby—learning the guitar. They talked for about a half an hour and when James hung up the phone, he felt better but his mind was still on Cassidy.

When he'd left Texas to come to Las Vegas, he'd left a big, tight-knit family behind him. The pressure to stay a part of that family, to settle down and marry after college, have kids and stick close to home had been so great that it had repelled him. He'd left to get away from all that suffocation, but it appeared maybe settling down was in his blood.

Looking back on the past year, he could see clearly how he'd had his sights set on Cassidy in more than just a sexual way. After he'd met her and befriended her, he'd stopped chasing every bit of skirt that had come his way. No other woman he'd met seemed to be able to measure up to Cassidy. He'd thought that by seducing her, sleeping with her, that strange compulsion he'd felt toward her would fade. It hadn't, though. Since he'd drawn her into his bed, he only wanted her more.

Still, he had to be sure that what he was feeling for her was real before he attempted to draw her into something more permanent than their current arrangement. He didn't want do any more damage to her heart than had already been done.

Although he was fast beginning to suspect that it was Cassidy who was going to do the damage to *his* heart.

Cassidy looked up in surprise as the last card landed on the table between them with the flick of a professional dealer's wrist.

Shit. She'd lost.

James had insisted on taking her to dinner at an expensive restaurant on the Strip. She'd brought the card deck and they'd played their fourth game over crème brûlée and cups of exquisite dark coffee.

"Your sweet ass is mine tonight." He leaned over the table and smiled, his dimples prominent. "And I don't mean that in anything but a *literal* way."

Shock jolted through her, mixed with curious excitement. "You can't be serious."

"As a heart attack, baby. It's my win and you remember the rules of the game. There were boundaries set. This is well within them."

"I've never done it before."

"I'll be gentle." He lifted an eyebrow. "Aren't you curious? Just a little?"

She shrugged and glanced away. She was, but she didn't want to say it out loud. Slight heat rose to her cheeks.

He smiled in that confident, masculine way of his that half pissed her off and half aroused her. "I'll take that as a yes." He paused and the smile faded. "But, Cassidy, if you really don't want to do it you just say the word, all right? This is supposed to be an enjoyable game for both of us."

She took a bite of her dessert, letting the creamy sweetness fill her mouth. Slowly, she drew the spoon between her lips, seeing his gaze center on her mouth. "I want to do it," she answered evenly.

James reached under the table and fingered the hem of the flowered skirt she wore. "Good. I'm glad to hear that because I really want to do it to you." His eyes had gone dark and his voice a shade darker.

A rush of pleasure made her shiver. Her gaze dropped to his hand, where he idly played with his spoon. The mere sight of his hands, wrists and forearms turned her on. His smile did it for her. His voice. The way he held his body, the way he moved. Hell, everything about him lit a fire in her.

He'd said nothing about her sneaking out like a thief the night before. A part of her regretted it. She wondered what it would be like to wake up in his arms, have him make her breakfast. Of course, it wouldn't have been the first time she'd awoken lazily to the face of a man she cared about, and that memory, with its unpleasant eventualities, made her mostly *not* regret it.

"By the way, I talked to Gerald and he told me The Liege is instituting a new tuition reimbursement program," James said causally.

She looked up from her crème brûlée with a start. "Really?"

He took a sip of his coffee. "You were interested in taking some business classes, right? They'd reimburse you for that if you wanted to start going to the University of Nevada."

She looked back down at her dish. Cassidy had wanted to attend college for a long time, but she was helping to support her mother financially. "I don't think I can."

James leaned forward. "Why not? I think now is the

perfect time. Your mom has adjusted to her limited sight just fine and is able to spend more time on her own. You wouldn't have to quit your job to attend, so there'd be no loss of compensation and The Liege would pay for all of it." He shrugged. "I'm not seeing the downside."

"I see you've really thought about this."

"I know you want it and I want you to be happy."

She looked up and smiled at him. "Thank you. I'll look into taking some classes. Maybe I can find a way to work it out."

"Good. You know I'll help you any way I can, Cassidy. If you need me to look in on your mom or anything." He grinned. "Or, you know, *help* you with your homework."

She laughed. "I can only guess where that would lead."

He waggled his eyebrows. "Kinky sex acts among the stacks at UNLV?"

They finished up their coffee and dessert and went back to James's apartment. He followed her into the entrance-way, eyeing her like a bit of candy he couldn't resist. She loved the way his gaze traveled from her heels, up her body and over the swell of her bosom in the fitted blue top she wore. James didn't look at her just for her body, although she greatly enjoyed the fact that he loved it. He seemed to look at her for the whole package, her personality along with her looks.

Pinning her with his gaze, he turned from locking the door and walked toward her. He cupped her cheek and stared down into her eyes. "If I was given a choice of anyone in the world to spend time with, I'd choose you, Cassidy."

Her mouth went dry. "Ditto," she whispered hoarsely. It was an honest answer. James was her best friend.

"Are you sure about this? I'm giving you the opportunity to back out now."

She tipped her chin up and smiled at him. "Anything you can dish out, I can take, James."

He grinned. "Oh, baby, that's what I like to hear." He jerked his head toward his bedroom. "In there."

A shiver ran down her spine at the command, issued from an aroused James. Cassidy had to admit that in the bedroom, she liked it a lot when he took control.

She walked into the bedroom and crawled onto the bed, kicking off her shoes and watching James with a heated expression on her face, her body already tightening at the prospect of his hands on her. She watched him take a bottle out of a drawer, then he crawled after her on the mattress and lowered himself down on top of her.

Their mouths met in a hot tangle of lips and questing tongues while their fingers sought to free the other of their clothing. Finally they were both deliciously nude, their skin sliding together like hot satin.

"Damn, you're the prettiest thing I have ever seen," James growled right before his mouth closed over her nipple, suckling the hardened tip with an intensity that made her cry out from the pleasure. Her back arched and her fingers closed around his cock, pumping him with long, sure strokes where she'd slipped her hand down between their bodies.

The lights were on, blazing bright. Normally that would bother her, but in James's arms she felt perfect trust. It was a comfortable place to be. In his embrace, she felt able to let go of all her inhibitions, all her fears. For the time he made love to her, she felt free of everything.

James groaned and pulled from her grasp. "You're pushing me too fast, wicked woman. I want to make this last." He eased down between her thighs and pushed her knees apart, sealing his mouth over her sex with no warning or hesitation.

"James," she breathed, closing her eyes and threading her fingers through his hair. He tongued her clit and then sucked the bit of flesh between his lips, working it back and forth until the edge of an orgasm fluttered through her body, making her moan. He tongued her again and it exploded out of her, racking her body with waves of pleasure. "James!"

While she still hummed from the climax and her clit pulsed and tingled, ready for more, he crawled up her body and growled, "On your stomach."

She rolled over and instantly felt his impatient hands grasp her hips and pull her upward to fit into the cradle of his pelvis. The hard ridge of his cock slid between the cheeks of her ass to rub along her swollen, aching sex. Her breath hissed out of her as she grabbed fistfuls of comforter.

Cassidy lowered her head to the mattress and thrust her rear up at him, in a gesture of pure submissiveness. How she wanted to feel that thick cock tunneling in and out her.

James took what she offered him and rolled his hips, angling the smooth head of his cock past her labia and into the entrance of her pussy. A groan rumbled out of him. "You're hot and creaming, Cassidy."

In answer she pressed her hands flat on the bed and pushed up, impaling herself on the length of him. He pushed into her at the same time, filling her full with him. Her head resting on the mattress, Cassidy bit her lower lip and closed her eyes at the exquisite sensation of being so possessed.

He dug his fingers into her hips, and began driving his cock fast and hard into her. Every deep, penetrating stroke reverberated through her body as another orgasm flirted with her body, nearly stealing her ability to breathe.

For a few moments, while James took her that way, she thought maybe he'd forgotten about their bet, but then he dipped his fingers down between her thighs from the front and stroked her sex. She bucked against the feeling of his questing hand as he coated his fingers with her slippery juices, and then rubbed them over the taut entrance of her ass.

A jolt of uncertainty went through her, tensing her muscles. His gentle teasing of all those nerves felt so unbelievably good, but what would come afterward? James stroked and petted until she relaxed a little and then gently inserted his finger past the ring of muscles.

She instantly stiffened.

He shushed her. "I'm not going to hurt you, baby. Just relax and let it happen. Trust me." He pushed his finger in and pulled it back out, thrusting slowly.

Oh! It felt so good that Cassidy forgot what she'd been so concerned about. His finger speared in and out of her, making her moan. Cassidy was soon consumed by the foreign sensations assaulting her body. Her body wasn't hers anymore, now it was James's to command. He'd gained total mastery over her and she hardly minded giving up control.

James reached over and took the bottle of lube from the

top of the bedside table. He flipped the top open and squirted some of the thick liquid onto her. Using a gentle touch, he coated her rear entrance with it, then added a second finger to his play.

Cassidy's breath hissed out of her at the sensation of her muscles stretching and the exquisite pleasure of all those nerves firing to glorious life. She'd never realized that the stimulation of this part of her body could be so exciting. While he worked to widen her enough to take his cock, he still fucked her slowly, thrusting his hips back and forth in an easy rhythm.

Having both her orifices so thoroughly stimulated was a pleasure she could not put into words. The sensations played counterpoint to each other, swamping her body in such pleasure that she hardly knew which way was up. All Cassidy knew was that she definitely didn't want it to stop.

The intense pleasure had her eyes rolling back in her head. What James did to her coupled ecstasy with just the slightest bit of pain until she couldn't tell the difference between the two. Soon the two were one and she couldn't get enough of the troubling, exciting sensation.

"Baby, you're so damned sexy like this," James rasped in a low voice. "All spread out for me this way, letting me do whatever I want to your sweet body." He slipped his free hand from her hip to her clit and played with the swollen and sensitized bit of flesh.

She whimpered deep in her throat, unable to form any words for a response. Pleasure had tapered her world down to only James and the way he played her body. She wanted to sob she was so aroused.

His cock remained thrust up within her, motionless while

he worked her clit and rear. "Do you like it when I finger-fuck you this way?"

His coarse words sent shivers of pleasure though her. "Y-yes," she managed to push out.

"I can't wait to take you back here," he groaned. "You're not afraid, are you?"

"No." She paused, and then whispered, "I trust you." The words that had rushed out of her so easily made her jerk. James even stopped moving for a moment.

"I'm glad to hear that," he murmured.

Oddly, so was she. She allowed herself to relax again, letting herself trust him not to hurt her.

"You're loosening for me, Cassidy, getting nice and relaxed. Your body is just begging me to take your sweet little ass." He put his free hand back on her hip and began to shaft her again with those long, mind-numbing strokes. At the same time, he continued to thrust his long, thick digits in and out of her ass. "You're so filled up with me right now, baby." He increased the pace of his thrusts. "Every inch of you back here has me in it. Do you like that?" he growled, withdrawing and plunging his fingers in tandem with his pounding cock.

"Yes," she cried out, pumping her hips back against him, driving him deeper.

"You ready for the rest of me?"

"Yes!" she sobbed.

He shuddered against her, his cock jumping deep inside her. James's slick, hot skin pressed against her back as he leaned over and brushed his lips across the nape of her neck, then gently bit her. The feeling of his teeth nipping her heated flesh made gooseflesh erupt over her body. The act accentuated the animalistic component to having him behind her in this position, ready to enter her rear.

He pumped into her hard a few times, making them both groan in response to the delicious friction. Then he pulled free of her body. Cassidy went stiff, anticipating his next move.

James smeared more of the lube over her and then down his cock. She twisted around and watched as his strong fingers stroked his length, his head thrown back on a groan. He was so big—so wide and long. Wouldn't this hurt?

James grabbed her hips, holding her in place. He must've seen the look on her face and felt the sudden stiffness of her body because he murmured, "Easy, darlin'. It will hurt a little, but it will be just play counterpoint, making the pleasure all the more intense. Are you ready?"

Cassidy bit down on her lip and nodded. "Yes."

An aroused groan rumbled out of him as he brushed the head of his cock across her anus. All the nerves reacted, crying out for more stimulation, and she felt her muscles relax. "That's right, Cassidy. Perfect."

"Now, James, please," she whispered.

He placed his hands on her hips and thrust gently. The head of his cock breached the tight ring of muscles of her anus. A mixture of pleasure and pain filled her, sharp and overwhelming. It was a delicious, irresistible pleasure-pain combination from having those muscles stretched that far by the thick, silky head of his cock.

He pushed in a fraction more, slipping in easily with the amount of lube he'd used. She gasped at the sensation of it. For a moment she wasn't sure if she wanted him to back out or push farther in. Then he withdrew a little and thrust again, giving her another inch of his cock, and her muscles relaxed some more, letting the pleasure override the pain.

"James," she cried out, feeling her clit pulse, heavy and sensitive, between her thighs. "More! Give me more!"

He groaned and slapped both hands to her hips, easing her back against him and slowly thrusting the shaft of him deeper into her. The thick width of his cock pressed into her slowly until he was seated to the root.

Cassidy fisted her hand and thumped it against the mattress. "James, oh, that's good."

He gave a low, silken laugh then started to thrust.

She gave a groan that seemed to come from the center of her bones. James set up an easy rhythm, pulling almost all the way out of her and thrusting back in with long, deep thrusts that snapped the little control she'd maintained up until that point.

The pain was all gone now, replaced with a pleasure that was different than vaginal sex, not better, although it was more intense. Every stroke into her body seemed easier as she learned to accept the length and width of him.

She dug her fingers into the blankets and hung on under his thrusts, feeling an orgasm tease her body. She liked it when James took control in the bedroom, and she had to admit that *this* was ultimate control. Never had she felt so penetrated, dominated, possessed, than she did in this moment. The act was animalistic, base and oh-so-exciting.

"Cassidy, baby, I can't hold back," he groaned as he pushed her harder and harder with his piston-like movements. "I'm going to come, but I'm taking you with me."

He slid his hand around her waist, dragging his fingers

over her mound to thrust two fingers deep into her slick, creaming pussy. He pressed against her clit as he worked her between her thighs, still thrusting into her ass.

Cassidy cried out, overwhelmed by all the sensations. They blended together until she couldn't tell up from down anymore.

"More, Cassidy. Give me more," he demanded into her ear. "I want to hear you scream when you come. I want to know you're mine."

"James," she cried out brokenly, riding the crest of a swiftly approaching climax.

He withdrew his fingers from her pussy and he worked her clit between two fingers relentlessly. His cock tunneled in and out of her ass, exerting that odd, powerfully alien pleasure over her body.

Her orgasm crashed over her ferociously, and she cried out his name again in a hoarse voice as she drowned in it. Her vision grew dim for a moment under the force of it.

"Yes, Cassidy. That's what I wanted. Oh, baby, I'm coming!" He gave out a hoarse shout to match hers and she felt his cock jump deep inside her.

They collapsed together in a tangle of arms and legs. Both of them were coated with perspiration. They were a mess, sticky and wet, but it didn't matter. Nothing mattered in the aftermath of that amazing experience. Cassidy let him pull her against him and she buried her head against his chest, feeling the accelerated thump of his heart and enjoying the sound of his exerted breathing.

Once their heart rates had begun to return to normal, James tipped up her chin and kissed her all over—her forehead, her cheeks and her lips. "Are you all right?" he murmured.

She smiled. "That was…indescribable."

"In a good way, I hope."

She nodded, feeling the prick of tears come to her eyes. She lowered her head to his chest again to hide her expression. Cassidy had opened herself up, trusted James, and he hadn't let her down.

Trust.

Yes, she trusted James deeply. Doing this with him had clearly demonstrated that. In fact, her whole body swelled with emotion for James right now. She wished she could push away the feelings she had for him, but at the moment they were overwhelming, something she just couldn't ignore.

The question remained—would he hurt her? God, she couldn't take it again, she just couldn't. Especially not from James because he was her best friend. Damian had never been that. She and Damian had been lovers from the beginning. What she had with James felt deeper because they'd been good friends first.

I want to know you're mine…. That's what he'd said at the height of their lovemaking.

"Hey," James murmured into her hair. "Are you really all right?" He pulled her closer to him. "You feel tense."

She sighed, enjoying the clasp of his arms around her. She was too tired to think about anything right now, let alone contemplate her confused emotions for James. "I'm fine," she whispered, lying.

I want to know you're mine….

About two hours later she'd left a sleeping James tucked in his bed and had gone home. She closed the front door of her apartment, hearing the soft sounds of the TV coming from the living room. Her mother was still awake.

Her mother lay sleeping on the couch, bathed in the flickering blue glow of the screen in the otherwise darkened room. Her mother couldn't see the TV very well, but that didn't stop her from trying to watch. Cassidy tiptoed past to get to her bedroom.

"Cass?" her mother said drowsily from the couch.

Damn. Busted like a teenager past curfew. She detoured and sank into an easy chair near her mother. "Hey, Mom, I thought you were sleeping."

In the pale flickering light, her mother smiled. "Out with James again, were you?"

She felt herself flush. "Yes, we just had dinner after our shift tonight."

"Not *just* anything," her mother replied in a knowing voice. "You two are romantically involved."

"It's nothing, Mom, only a little flirtation."

Her mother leaned forward and squeezed her hand. "I hope not! I think James is a wonderful man. It would do my heart good to see you with him."

Cassidy remained silent, holding in all her emotions. A part of her wanted to confide in her mother, tell her how she thought she was falling for James but was afraid he'd hurt her like Damian had. She wanted to tell her that she'd invested all her emotions in Damian, trusted him, and he'd plowed right over her soul. Damian had left her standing at the altar in her stupid wedding gown with all her family and friends there to watch her endure the ultimate rejection, with looks of pity on their faces and words of it dripping from their tongues. God, her stomach hurt just from the memory.

Her mother sighed. "Cassidy, honey, sometimes in life you have to take a gamble, even after you've lost everything."

Well, apparently she didn't even need to tell her mother. She already knew her daughter's heart. A tear slipped down her cheek and she wiped it away. "I don't know how James feels about me, Mom."

She leaned back against the couch. "I can't see very well anymore, Cassidy, but I have ears. When I hear him talking to you, his voice is so tender and caring. He doesn't talk to anyone else in the same tone he uses with you. It's all there in his voice. I can hear it all. I *know* he has feelings for you."

Cassidy buried her face in her hands. That's exactly what she was afraid of because she didn't know what to do about it. "I might take some classes at UNLV, Mom." It was a nice change of subject. "The Liege is going to be offering tuition reimbursement for its employees soon."

Her mother's expression brightened. "Oh, I think you should, hon! That's wonderful news! What kind of classes are you thinking of taking?"

Cassidy fell into a discussion about college with her mother, although her mind wasn't really on it. Despite the emotional whirl in her head and her excitement over the prospect of finally furthering her education, her thoughts were still back in bed with an intoxicating, whiskey-eyed man.

Chapter Eight

James sat near Cassidy in one of The Liege's many bars. She wore a bruised and wary look in her eyes that James didn't like. He wanted to chase it away, but he wasn't sure how.

She glanced at him and smiled. "I checked out UNLV's curriculum yesterday and had a chat with Gerald. Looks like I'll be taking some classes in the fall."

"That's great, Cass. I'm really happy to hear that."

"Thought I'd go for a business degree. Maybe I can get into management here at The Liege eventually."

He lifted his bottle and chinked it against her glass. "To going back to school."

She smiled and, for a moment, the shadows were gone. "To school."

He tipped his head to the side and looked at her speculatively.

"What? You're staring at me."

"Did I hurt you the other night?" he asked her over his beer before he took a drink.

"No," she answered, not meeting his gaze. "Not at all." She raised an eyebrow. "On the contrary."

He let out a relieved rush of air and moved a little closer to her. "Then what's the matter?"

She shrugged a shoulder and ran the pad of her finger down the side of her glass to catch the condensation. "I'm just a little tired."

He turned her toward him and, tipping her chin up, he forced her gaze to meet his. "If you want to skip tonight's game, that's fine with me."

Her pupils dilated, darkening her eyes for a moment. "Hell, no. I want you, James." She caught his hand and kissed it. "I watched you all day at work. Watched and wanted you. I kept watching your hands while you dealt cards. I want those hands on my body."

Oh, fuck. He was getting a hard-on.

He leaned forward and pressed his lips to hers. She responded hungrily, forcing her tongue between his lips for a deeper contact. Someone near them whistled low and he remembered they were still in the casino, although far from their work area. Even so, there could still be some of their coworkers around.

James broke the kiss. "Come to my apartment, then," he murmured, limning the line of her jaw with his thumb. "We'll play the hand there."

She nodded. James settled the bill and they left. She followed him in her car. He'd tried to talk her into leaving her car at the casino—a sneaky way to get her to spend the entire night with him—but she wasn't having any of it. James didn't want to push her too hard, so he'd dropped the issue.

Soon they were at his place. Cassidy sat down on his couch while he pulled out a deck of cards from the drawer in his coffee table. After shuffling, he knelt in front of the small table and dealt two cards faceup to Cassidy and one card up, one down to himself. Cassidy ended up with a total of sixteen, a stiff hand, and chose to stand. He beat her in the end with a perfect twenty-one.

"That was fast," Cassidy groused. "I beat you at least ten times today at The Liege."

James grinned and gathered the cards. "That's the way it goes, Cassidy girl. Now stand up and c'mere so I can take off all those clothes. They've been offending me all damn day."

Instead of standing, she slid to the carpet and crawled toward him, her gaze dark and fixed on him. Rising onto her knees, she twined her arms around his neck and kissed him.

His cock stiffened at the touch of her lips on his and the sweet brush of her breasts against his chest. Aggressively, he speared his tongue between her lips and sank it deep into her hot mouth. Ravenous for the feel of her silky skin, he found the waistband of her pants and undid the button and zipper. He pushed down, sliding his hands into her underwear to cup her curved ass in his palms and using it to drag her up against his chest. He couldn't wait to feel all the tight silken muscles of her sex rippling around his cock. God, how he loved to make love to this woman. He would make it into a lifelong hobby if she'd let him.

He broke the kiss and murmured, "On the bed, naked. Now."

Her breath hitched and she gave a little laugh. "Impatient, aren't we? You never told me what you've got planned for tonight."

James slid his hand between the cheeks of her rear and

rubbed her labia until she moaned. "I'm tying you up tonight, Cassidy girl. You're going to be spread-eagle on the bed for me in a matter of minutes, and you'll be all mine. Every luscious inch of you."

Cassidy lay nude on James's bed, watching him stalk around her, still fully clothed, wearing a feral expression on his face. One small light burned in the corner, spilling golden luminosity onto the blankets and pillows she lay on. The fact that she was nude and he was clothed excited her. Oddly, it seemed to shift the power into his hands even before he touched her with the rope.

In one strong hand, James gripped a length of hemp rope. Just the sight of it made her hot between her thighs, made a trickle of cream run down her leg. She shifted uneasily, her nipples hardening into little peaks.

"Slide down onto your back and spread your thighs," he commanded in a low voice. "Spread them wide for me."

Cassidy shifted on the bed and did as he asked, bringing her heels closer to her rear and allowing her legs to fall open.

James crawled onto the bed and drew the coiled rope from her knee, up her inner thigh to her pussy. The rope, while it looked rough, was actually fairly smooth and pleasant to the touch. He rubbed the rope against her clit until she moaned.

"Put your hands above your head," he rasped, "wrists together."

Oh, God.

She did it while he kept up the slow, steady stroke of the rope between her thighs. When she squirmed against the torment of it, closing her thighs, he pushed them back open.

"That earned you a tying," he said, moving to one ankle. He looped the rope around one ankle and tied the other end to the far rung of the footboard. He made a loop around her knee and did the same. He copied his actions on the other side. Now she had very little give in the rope. She couldn't close her legs even if she wanted to.

James stood and stripped, admiring his handiwork even as she admired his solidly muscled chest, narrow hips and long, hard cock, revealed with every article of clothing he dropped to the floor.

"You do this often?" she asked in a shaky voice while he picked up yet another length of rope. "Tie up your bedmates?" She couldn't bring herself to say the word *lover.*

He straddled her, looped the rope around her wrists and tied the other end to the headboard. The position brought the hard jut of his cock near her lips. Her mouth watered to taste it.

"I like control in the bedroom, Cassidy. Test the knot." She pulled on the rope and found herself caught tight. "So, yeah, I like to tie my women up sometimes, if they're the type who like to be bound." He paused. "Like you do. You like this, don't you, Cassidy? You enjoy giving it up to me in the bedroom."

She nodded. "But anything involving you and a bedroom excites me, James."

He grinned. "Well, now, that's good to hear." He gripped the headboard and pushed the smooth head of his cock against her lips. "Suck it."

Eagerly, she flicked out her tongue and licked it. He thrust it past her lips gently and she engulfed it, tonguing her way along the shaft.

He tipped his head back, making his Adam's apple prominent, and groaned deeply. "Aw, fuck, Cass. As much as I'd like this to last…*I* won't." He pulled from her mouth. "Seeing you tied up like this already has me too much on edge."

James came down over her and kissed his way across her breasts, laving and pulling each nipple in turn between his skillful lips, before continuing down her stomach to her pussy, where he happily buried his mouth.

"James!" she jolted in surprise, but the rope kept her from moving.

He didn't answer her, he only swirled his tongue around her clit until all the nerves fired white-hot bursts of pleasure through her body.

Her hips bucked. "Oh, God, that's good."

James let out a low rumble of amusement that vibrated through her sex and reached up to palm her breast. As he laved and sucked her clit and labia, he rolled her nipple between his fingers. The pleasure points being concurrently stimulated made Cassidy's eyes roll back into her head.

"You're killing me, James," she rasped.

"Mmm," he answered, lifting his head. "I haven't even gotten started yet. Don't be dying on me yet." He looked down at her pussy and rubbed a skillful finger through the folds of her labia. "You're all nice and creamy down here for me, Cass."

She bit her lower lip. "Fuck me, James."

He chuckled. "I think you're forgetting who's tied up and who did the tying."

"Please!"

"Do you still trust me? The other night you said you did."

Once again, it struck her how much she truly did trust

James. She'd allowed him to put her into this situation where he could do anything, absolutely *anything* he wanted to her and she didn't feel an ounce of unease.

No, it wasn't unease that she felt at all....

"I trust you, James," she whispered.

"Good, because this might be all kinky with the rope, Cass, but I'm not fucking you." He paused. "Whenever I touch you, it's *making love.*"

She squeezed her eyes shut. "James..."

"Hush, baby. I just want to be clear on that point." He pinched the nipple he still rolled back and forth and her breath hissed out of her at the sensation of it. At the same time, he speared a finger deep inside her and rubbed it over her G-spot. Her body responded with a new rush of honey. "You want to feel my cock in here?"

"Yes!"

"Well, I want you to climax first. Are you going to come for me, Cassidy?"

"God, a couple of times, I'm sure," she gasped.

He pinched her nipple again and added a second finger to his thrusting, making sure he stimulated her G-spot thoroughly on every outward stroke. "Come on then, baby. I want to taste it when you come. I want to feel your muscles pulsing around my fingers. I want to hear you, taste you *and* feel you when you go."

Cassidy strained against the rope, wanting to move but unable. "James, please—"

He latched his mouth over her clit and sucked. Cassidy's orgasm exploded through her body, making her cry out and pull savagely at the rope binding her wrists and legs as she bucked and moaned under his tongue and thrusting fingers.

When the ripples had eased and she lay breathing heavily, James began to undo the ropes binding her legs. "I love it when you come."

She gave out a drunken-sounding laugh. Her muscles felt so weak. "I kind of like it, too," she slurred.

He pushed her knees up and slid the head of his cock into her. She dug her fingernails into her palms as he kept her legs clamped between his strong hands and burrowed deeper into her slick, tight sex.

She grasped the rope and allowed her body to adjust to the length and breadth of him. It didn't take long for her sex to pulse pleasurably around the massive invasion.

He pushed her knees up higher and adjusted himself so that he thrust almost straight down into her pussy. Because of the way her head was propped up on the pillow, she could see his cock as it tunneled in and out of her.

"I want you to watch, Cassidy. Watch me make love to you. See where our bodies become one." His gorgeous face was tight with desire, his eyes dark. He gritted his teeth as he fought for control. It was apparent he wanted to take her fast and hard.

She glanced up at him. "Do it," she murmured. "Fast, hard."

He did it. He thrust faster and faster, delving piston-like between her slick walls. Each stroke felt devastating, driving her hard toward another shattering climax. She kept her gaze on his cock penetrating her so mercilessly, until she couldn't focus her eyes anymore because of the edge of the orgasm that teased her body.

"Cassidy," James groaned. "Oh, baby, I'm coming."

So was she. She grabbed on to the rope and let her climax take her over, steal her thoughts, her breath, everything. At the same time, James groaned and she felt his cock jump deep inside her. Their cries mingled in the air as their bodies danced in shared ecstasy.

"Oh, Cassidy," James groaned, gripping the headboard above her head. "You're going to kill me, woman." He dropped his hands to either side of her head and lowered his face to hers. His gaze, strangely emotional, held hers for a moment before kissing her tenderly.

His lips skated over hers like silk before pressing intimately against her mouth. The kiss was so slow, so passionate, it made her body flare to life once more even though it had been very well satisfied…twice. His tongue slid between her lips and brushed lazily against hers, making her sigh into his open mouth.

He raised his head and stared down at her with half-lidded eyes. His cock was still buried deep within her body, giving this situation an intimate air that made her a bit uncomfortable. "I have half a mind to keep you tied up here. Make you spend the whole night with me."

She felt her eyes grow a little wide. Almost unconsciously, she twisted her wrists in the rope.

James sighed and reached to untie the knots. "But you know what they say about letting something go free."

Yes, she knew. *If you* love *something set it free….*

The rope dropped to the pillow, but James didn't let her go. He rubbed her wrists and pinned her there on the bed, her legs spread and his cock, now going flaccid, still inside her, and kissed her again. Finally, he rolled to the side.

Cassidy tried to scoot to the edge of the bed and roll off but quickly found herself grasped and pulled back into brawny arms. "Where do you think you're going?"

"To get dressed."

He nipped her shoulder and sent goose bumps over her skin. "No way, baby. Some men might not like to cuddle after sex. I am not one of them."

"Maybe for a few minutes." She settled back against his chest, giving in. He did feel awfully nice and warm and she was tired. "My mom needs me at home, though."

His arms tightened around her. "She does not. I talked to Carol this morning and she made sure to tell me she was fine and didn't need you fussing over her night and day anymore."

Cassidy turned over in his arms to face him. "You talked to my mom this morning?"

"I called to see if you wanted a ride to work, but you'd already left."

She snuggled down and laid her head against his chest, hearing the pleasant thump-thump of his heart. God, he felt good. She sighed and closed her eyes. "She likes you. I think she likes you better than she ever liked Damian."

Shit! She stiffened and her eyes popped open. Had she really just said that? Had she really just made any kind of a comparison between James and Damian in romantic terms?

But James just gave a low, masculine laugh that rumbled through her. "Your mom is definitely a good judge of character."

He rubbed her back with long, strong fingers until she relaxed again and closed her eyes once more. "Mmm, that's nice."

James kissed the top of her head. "You sound sleepy."

"I am." Her muscles were beginning to feel like warm honey from his steady touch. He rubbed a wrist, where she had a faint line from where she'd tugged at the rope.

"You wounded me." She sighed into his chest with a smile. Hardly, of course, the rope hadn't hurt one bit. She wasn't in pain now or when she'd been tied. The man was good with a knot, that was for certain. Good with more than a knot, too.

"I hope not. The last thing I'd ever want to do is hurt you, Cass."

"Mmm...that's sweet," she answered sleepily.

"But I have to admit I like the fact I marked you a little," he murmured, bussing the top of her head with his lips. "Does that make me an asshole?"

"It makes you a dog. Just don't pee on me, okay?"

He chuckled. "I promise." Then he went back to rubbing her back, his fingers working the muscles with a deftness that drew a deep groan of pleasure from her. Soon sleep beckoned with heavy hands.

"Cassidy?"

"Hmm?"

"Stay the night with me. Be here when I wake up."

She remained silent for a moment and finally said, "Yes."

His body relaxed against hers.

When James awoke the next morning, he could feel Cassidy still in bed with him. He smiled and opened his eyes, feeling his chest swell with contentment. Her presence was sweet and substantial in his bed.

She'd stayed of her own accord, all night long.

Damned if he didn't want to wake up every morning like this.

He turned over to see her lying nude, with her back to him. She'd pushed the sheet and blankets down past her hips, revealing the tapered arch of her back with its pale, creamy skin.

Unable to resist, he reached out and traced her spine with his index finger. She rolled over drowsily, smiled at him and stretched like a cat.

"Morning," he murmured, unable to take his gaze off her eyes.

"Morning," she answered, while taking his hand and settling it over her breast. He felt the nipple harden against his palm. His cock responded instantly.

She said nothing, only wrapped her arms around his neck and kissed him. Deep in her throat, she made a purring sound and threw one long leg over his hip in invitation.

It was one he could not ignore.

With a groan, he rolled her over onto her back and felt the head of his cock slip between her labia. He shifted his hips into position and pushed inside her wet, silken heat.

Oh, fuck, she felt good around him. He closed his eyes and let his breath hiss out of him as he sank into her to his root.

Cassidy sighed and arched her back, spreading her thighs to allow him to withdraw and thrust back inside her. "That's good, James," she murmured, biting her lower lip.

Morning sex with Cassidy? Hell, yes, it was beyond good; it was magic.

He set up an easy, slow rhythm, sliding in and out between

her slick, hot walls, while she rolled her hips up to meet his every thrust. He took her slow, then even slower, drawing out their pleasure for as long as possible.

Their breathing became heavier and their kissing became more frenzied. James noted the changes in her body as she grew closer and closer to her climax. Her inner muscles gripped and rippled around his cock and her little pants and moans became more centered in her throat.

James rotated his hips and thrust deeply within her, increasing the pace of his thrusts in order to rub the head of his cock over her G-spot.

She whispered his name as she tossed her head back and forth on the pillow, her eyes closed. "I'm going to come."

He pinned her wrists to the bed on either side of her. "Look at me," he murmured.

Her eyes fluttered open and locked on his just as she came. James felt the pulse and pull of her pussy around his length, the sound of her sexy cries and the look of ecstasy on her face, and he lost it.

Throwing his head back, he roared out his climax. It bubbled up like an explosion from his balls to envelope him in pure pleasure.

Once the tremors had eased, he lowered his mouth to hers and kissed her long and deeply. When he raised his head, she was smiling.

"You know you really like someone when you don't care about morning breath," she said.

He laughed and rolled to the side, pulling her against his chest. "Trust me. That was the furthest thing from my mind."

She grasped his still half-erect cock. "You mean this mind?"

He smoothed her hair behind her ear. "Yeah, well, what's a guy supposed to do with a woman like you in his bed?"

Cassidy grinned and snuggled against his chest while he rubbed her back. He was wonderful for a woman's ego. "Last night was our last bet," she whispered. There was a note of regret in her voice that she couldn't quite get rid of.

His massage faltered. "Yeah. Hope it won't be the last time we make love, though."

Make love. She said nothing in reply, but she felt her body go stiff.

"Cassidy? Cassidy, look at me."

She raised her head and saw the look in his eyes. She knew what he was going to say. It had been coming for a long time now. "Don't say it," she whispered, moving away from him.

His expression, so full of love and caring, transformed to one of confusion. "What's wrong? Don't say what?"

She backed to the edge of the bed and pulled a sheet up to cover herself. Suddenly she felt well and *truly* naked. "Don't tell me you've fallen in love with me. Don't tell me this should be more than what it is. Don't make any commitments to me, James. Just don't do it."

He reached for her, but she hopped off the bed before he could touch her. If he touched her, her resolve might melt away and she had to stay strong now. "I don't want to hear it. I can't do it again. I don't have enough left in me to spend all that emotion a second time."

"Cassidy…"

She ignored him. She only scooped up her clothes and dressed. Her breathing came fast and shallow, almost like she was having a panic attack. Hell, maybe she was having a panic attack.

"Cassidy!"

She shook her head and sat in the chair to pull her shoes on.

He was there then, right in front of her. He took her by the shoulders and forced her to look into his face. "Calm down! It's not like I was about to ask you to marry me."

She shook her head. "I can see it in your eyes, hear it in your voice. You think you have feelings for me and I—I *know* I have feelings for you, James. But what if your feelings aren't as strong as mine? What if I love you more than you love me and one day you—you—" Tears obscured her vision.

He grabbed her and pulled her against him, dragging her up against his chest and off the chair. "Damn it, I didn't even get to tell you what I wanted to tell you. *I love you, Cassidy!* I wouldn't say that if I wasn't absolutely sure."

She sat in his lap, trying not to sob, and shook her head back and forth.

He took her by the shoulders. "I am totally and incurably head-over-heels crazy in love with you. Do you hear me? I love you more than Damian ever did."

"You broke the rules! This was just supposed to be a game. Friends—"

"Friends with benefits, I know. Damn it if I don't want you to be my *friend* with a whole lot more than *benefits*. I want all of you, Cassidy, every neurotic, self-deprecating, wonderful, sexy inch of you. I want you every day and every night. I want your smile, your companionship, your body, your breath—"

"James…"

"I'm not asking you to marry me...yet. I'm just asking you to take one final gamble, take a gamble on me and try it. You've admitted you have feelings for me, so what's the problem?"

She squeezed her eyes shut. The problem?

She stood at the front of the chapel with all her family and friends in the pews behind her, waiting for the man who'd told her the previous night how much he'd been looking forward to their wedding day.

Waiting…

Until James's cell phone had gone off. She'd known just by the glance James had given her after a second on the phone that the man to whom she stood ready to pledge her life had rejected her. In front of everyone she cared about, Damian had declared his lack of love for her.

Her breathing hitched in her throat and suddenly it felt like she was suffocating. "I have to go." She struggled up, out of James's grip, grabbed her other shoe and her purse and ran out of his apartment.

Fifteen minutes later Cassidy pulled into the parking lot of the White Wishes Chapel. She sat in front of the building and hastily dragged her fingers through her hair, wondering why she'd needed to come here.

She'd spent a year avoiding this place, taking the long way around when driving past would've cut her travel time. Maybe she hadn't been ready to face Damian's rejection of her before, but now she knew she needed closure. She needed to snap this chapter of her life closed so that she could move on.

It was past time.

She walked up to the double doors and found them open. "Hello?" she called into the interior. No one answered.

Cassidy entered the small chapel. Rows of pews lined each side of the main aisle. They were decorated with daisies, oddly reminiscent of her own wedding day. The white paper that lined the aisle showed recent wear. Apparently there had just been a wedding there. Perhaps that's why the doors had been unlocked.

Cassidy shivered. She just hoped the groom had showed.

She made her way down the aisle, something she'd not been able to do a year ago. She could still remember the excited murmur of her friends and family, the laughter and the happiness they'd shared with her.

All that had so swiftly changed.

She reached the altar at the front of the church, memories assaulting her. She herself had made the announcement that the wedding was canceled. She'd insisted on it, although she barely remembered that part. She did remember that afterward the smiles and laughter had turned to whispers and looks of pity. She could also remember that her heart had literally felt like it was breaking. There had been a heavy weight in her chest and throat, sorrow choking her.

James had been by her side the entire time. She smiled. She remembered that now. He had held her hand, put his arm around her—there had never been a point when he hadn't physically and emotionally supported her.

The most interesting part of this trek down memory lane was the realization that she'd never really loved Damian. She'd only *thought* she'd loved Damian.

No, the man she really loved was James.

With all her heart and soul.

God, she'd been so blind. What had she been thinking? What had she been so afraid of?

She closed her eyes and let the memories of that day wash over her and through her…then she let them go. She let Damian go for once and for all. He'd moved on and so should she.

And she so wanted to move on…with James.

She took out her cell phone and punched in a number she still knew by heart. "Damian?" Her voice echoed in the small chapel.

Silence. "Cassidy?" Pause. "Oh, God, how have you been?"

"I've been fine, but I didn't call to make small talk." It was so strange hearing his voice. It didn't affect her at all the way she'd supposed it would. She'd thought it would hurt more than this little pinch she felt. That pinch was mostly to her pride, not because she'd lost Damian.

"Then what did you call for?"

"I just wanted to tell you that I forgive you."

"What?"

"I forgive you for standing me up at the altar."

He remained silent for a long moment. "Thank you." He sounded so relieved. The thread of tension between them lessened palpably. Perhaps, he'd been feeling some guilt for what he'd done. "I'm so sorry. I should've talked to you before that day. We should've called everything off long before our wedding day."

"Yeah." She sighed, sitting down in a pew. "That's for sure, but woulda, coulda, shoulda. It's done now. I guess I just needed to tell you that I forgive you, that…I thank you for it."

"Thank me for it?"

"Yeah, I mean, if you'd gone through with it out of a sense of duty or something we'd both probably be miserable right now, you know?"

"Yes, I know." He paused. "So, does that mean you're happy, then? I really want you to be happy, Cass."

She smiled, thinking of James. "Yes, I am. I think I'm finally, *truly* in love." They were honest words, not meant to wound him. All the same, they had to hurt a little.

He hesitated only for a moment. "You're with someone?"

"James."

"Aw, fuck." Damian laughed. "I always knew he had it bad for you. I guess he finally made his move."

She grinned. "In spades." *Literally.* "Hey, I gotta go, Damian. I have it bad for James, too, and I think talking to you finally brought just how much I care about him into perspective."

"Cassidy?"

"Yes?"

"I'm glad you called." He paused, drawing a deep breath. It sounded full of relief. "And I'm glad you're happy."

She smiled into the mouthpiece. "I hope you're happy, too. Goodbye, Damian." She closed the phone with a snap, stood and walked out of the chapel, closing the doors behind her.

She had a better place to be.

♣ ♠ ♥ ◆ ♣ ♠ ♥ ◆ ♣ ♠ ♥ ◆

Chapter Nine

She stopped short in the parking lot. James was there, leaning against his car with his arms folded over his brawny chest and looking sexy. The man always looked sexy.

He uncrossed his arms and stepped toward her. "You aren't getting away from me that easy, Cassidy." He shook his head. "Not since I've had this little sip of you. I want more."

"How'd you know I would come here?"

"I know you better than you think I do." He came to stand in front her. "Better than Damian ever did."

She looked up into his face, shielding her eyes from the sun. "I was headed back to your place, James. I made a mistake. I let fear distance myself from you, but I'm through with that now."

He cupped her cheek. "Are you sure? Because I fell for you hard, but I've still got a long way to fall if you're going to reject me." He paused. "And it's going to hurt. See? I'm taking a gamble, too."

Cassidy spoke four little words she knew were true without a doubt. She spoke them loudly and clearly. "I love you,

James." Then she smiled. A light, warm feeling fluttered through her chest. Love, that had to be it. She smiled broader.

He dipped his head and kissed her. "I love you back," he whispered against her lips. "Now do you want to get some breakfast?"

"Let's take your car."

Together they turned and walked hand in hand to his car and got in.

"Before you start school this fall, I want you to meet my family," James commented as he started the engine.

"What? You mean go to Texas?"

He nodded. "We can bring your mom along. I think she'd enjoy the trip."

She nodded. "I think so, too." Spying a box of cards on the gear shift, she picked it up. "Hey, what's this?"

"Oh, I don't know," he drawled as he turned out of the parking lot. "Thought we might play another game." He winked. "For sexual stakes, of course."

"Of course." She laughed, reached over and squeezed his hand. "I'd take a gamble on you anytime."

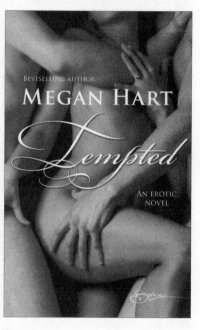

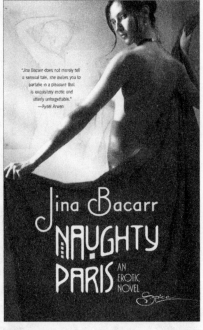

WHEN YOU WANT

JUST A TASTE

OF SPICE...

...because size doesn't matter.

Highly erotic short stories
sure to emblazon
the mind and body...
E-books have never been
this delicious.

Spice

www.Spice-Books.com   SB2007TR